Praise for *New York Times* bestselling author Tawny Weber

"A sexy, hot SEAL undercover in more ways than one…. Tawny Weber nails this steamy suspense."
—*New York Times* bestselling author Cristin Harber

"This hot and sexy adventure takes readers on a thrilling ride of romance, secrets and SEALs."
—*RT Book Reviews*

"Wow…a fantastic series by Ms. Weber. This amazing story line manages to make you cry, make you smile and make your heart turn inside out…. Get it, read it, love it."
—*Harlequin Junkie*

"Tawny Weber…has created the perfect hero for our time and a sizzling page-turner! What an awesome start to her Team Poseidon series."
—*New York Times* bestselling author Vicki Lewis Thompson

"I love a good SEAL romance and Tawny Weber knocked this one out of the park. Don't miss it!"
—*USA TODAY* bestselling author Karen Fenech

"Reminiscent of Suzanne Brockmann's Troubleshooters series, Weber's latest will appeal to her fans as well as other military-romance readers…a good read with an engaging heroine and child."
—*Booklist*

"*Call to Honor* is a tightly plotted story with a few startling turns of events, the characters are all credible and…the pace never falters."
—*Fresh Fiction*

TAWNY WEBER

CALL TO REDEMPTION

HQN™

HQN™

ISBN-13: 978-0-373-80366-8

Recycling programs for this product may not exist in your area.

Call to Redemption

This edition published by arrangement with Harlequin Books S.A.

For questions and comments about the quality of this book, please contact us at CustomerService@Harlequin.com.

® and TM are trademarks of Harlequin Enterprises Limited or its corporate affiliates. Trademarks indicated with ® are registered in the United States Patent and Trademark Office, the Canadian Intellectual Property Office and in other countries.

www.HQNBooks.com

Printed in U.S.A.

To Birgit, with thanks.

CALL TO
REDEMPTION

PROLOGUE

"Lieutenant Commander Dominic Savino, you stand accused of conduct unbecoming of an officer, disobeying orders and conspiracy to commit treason."

The voice boomed like a cannon, its roar a vivid contrast to the courtroom's silence. As he stood at attention on the stand, the sound ricocheted down Nic's spine like a piece of shrapnel, ripping and tearing.

"Commander, do you understand these charges?"

Understand? Nic had a solid understanding of the fact that he'd been framed, that he was the fall guy for some treasonous son of a bitch. Someone in power with a network of Navy personnel was focused on lining their bank account at the expense of their country.

Yeah.

He understood that.

That, and everything that came with the charges leveled against him. Court-martial. Prison time. The end of his career. The loss of his freedom. The destruction of his team. Fury rose, rolling like waves that crested higher with each heartbeat.

But none of that was evident on his face. Neither awareness nor fury was allowed to show.

"Affirmative."

"How do you plead?"

Nic's gaze didn't shift left, didn't move right. His dead-eye stare was aimed straight ahead, focused on the rippling glory of the American flag hanging over the courtroom's double doors.

He replayed the accusation. He thought back over the previous year's events.

An operation gone horribly wrong that'd resulted in life-threatening injuries to one team member and the supposed death of another.

The realization that a SEAL, a man sworn to serve his country, would steal classified information to sell to the highest bidder, put his teammates lives in peril and fake his own death—all for money. That shocking acceptance that the same man would target a young child and a defenseless woman, and kill a fellow SEAL.

And now the emotional train wreck of watching his team targeted by an asshole with an agenda who was determined to ignore the fact that Poseidon was being framed by a traitorous sociopath with psychotic tendencies.

It'd all been coming down to this.

The moment of truth.

After fourteen years of service protecting the safety and freedom of his country, it wasn't Nic's life on the line this time. This time, it was his team. His career. His reputation. His own freedom.

Ignoring the tight knot in his gut, he shifted his gaze infinitesimally to the right. He gave Lieutenant Thomas a look cold enough to freeze the man's innards and, in a clear voice, stated, "Not guilty."

Thomas's eyes narrowed, his lips tightened. Why the man would flash frustration was baffling. Any first-year JAG would have expected that exact plea. Nic filed away the expression to decipher later.

For now, he simply let his stare intimidate until the Lieutenant turned away. But not before Nic caught the line between his brows twitching.

For the first time since he'd walked into the court-room that morning, the tension tying his intestines in knots loosened.

He was innocent.

Poseidon was clean.

No matter what information the Lieutenant and his team thought they'd bring to the table over the course of this trial, Nic knew that neither he, nor any of his men, had done anything illegal, against orders or in any way traitorous.

But knowing that didn't ensure he'd walk away from this trial. Not with his freedom. Quite possibly not with his career and reputation intact. The odds of keeping his command, of holding together an elite Special Ops team after being brought up on such charges, were slim.

But now?

Nic watched as Thomas exchanged frowns with the Lieutenant Commander seated at the prosecutors' table.

Now? He had hope. More, he had faith that he'd not only be vindicated, but that he'd also keep his command, his team and, dammit, that they'd nail the real traitor before this was over.

It was then and only then that he allowed his gaze to shift. For a millisecond, he glanced toward the gallery.

His team spanned the first row. Ten men in uniform, each one wearing a look of implacable determination. Each one radiating strength and dedication. And yes, each one looking equally pissed at the insult they knew they'd been served.

Nic's gaze shifted to the right, toward the woman sitting just behind the prosecution.

Beneath an edgy fringe of bangs, a pair of huge gold eyes stared back at him. In those molten depths he saw two things. Strength and challenge.

How had he gotten this far in life without her?

And what the hell was he going to do now that he'd found her?

Nic had spent his adult life training, leading, fighting for his country. Without hesitation, he'd put his life, his guts and his reputation on the line time and time again. But today, his innocence wasn't the only thing at stake.

Nor was this a simple matter of justice.

He was a Lieutenant Commander in the United States Navy.

He was a multidecorated Navy SEAL.

He was a SEAL team platoon leader, he commanded over a hundred military and civilian personnel.

He'd fought in wars. He'd led missions. He'd orchestrated clandestine operations. He'd conceptualized, created, evaluated and nurtured the elite force of Team Poseidon. He'd honed his skills in leadership, combat and procedure.

In the last six months, he'd lost a man. He'd killed another. He'd had a building explode around him. He'd been betrayed and brought to trial to face the accusation of the very crimes he'd fought to end.

And for the first time in thirty-three years, Nic risked something that many people—including himself—had come to believe didn't exist.

His heart.

Lost it to the woman who could easily destroy his life.

CHAPTER ONE

Two Months Earlier

OH, MY.

She'd been told the views in Hanalei were impressive, but she'd had no idea just *how* impressive.

Darby Raye ran her tongue over her bottom lip, planted her elbows on the balcony railing and leaned out farther to get a clearer view. Not of the beach, although the pristine surf churning over the sand of Hanalei was unquestionably worth a second—and third—look. And she wasn't sighing over the indigo-streaked cerulean sky, although there was no denying that it deserved a few deep breaths of appreciation.

Nope, what had snagged her attention on her first night of the first vacation she'd taken in years was the unbelievably gorgeous man seated at the beach-side bar below.

There was something familiar about him, but whether it was the double Scotch she'd already knocked back or the glare of the sun off the ocean, she couldn't quite figure it out. Eyes narrowed, she leaned out just a little farther.

Dark hair was cut short enough to frame a face made more powerful by the contrast of angles and curves. Sharp cheekbones were emphasized by a goatee that ran along his chiseled jaw while full lips and lush lashes hinted at softness. She couldn't tell the color of his eyes from here, but they looked dark. A worn blue T-shirt was draped over broad shoulders, cupped biceps impressive enough to bench-press a Harley and lay flat against abs that didn't appear to even have a concept of the meaning of the word *flab*.

But how was his ass? Great abs were all well and good, but the true measure of a man was how fine of an ass he had.

She craned her neck to the side, squinting a little behind the amber lenses of her shades. But the angle was wrong. She shifted a couple of steps to the right and tilted her head a little, brushing at the swath of hair skimming her chin. Still nothing.

"Can I get you anything, Ms. Raye?"

Darby gave brief consideration to embarrassment, but this was a vacation. A time to let loose and have fun. Besides, embarrassment simply wasn't one of her key personality traits.

"Hey, Tito," she greeted, giving the waiter a friendly smile. "Just checking out the view and debating whether to head to the downstairs lanai for dinner instead of staying here."

"The band will be setting up on the lower lanai soon. Much better choice for a lovely single woman to meet a dance partner." Dark eyes dancing, the cocoa-skinned waiter waved one husky arm toward the circular stairs leading down the side of the hotel. "Please, go downstairs. I will bring your pupu platter beachside to enjoy."

That sounded crowded.

Like embarrassment, spending her first night of

relaxation around a bunch of people wasn't high on Darby's list of things to do.

"I think I'll stay here."

"No, no, you should go. Enjoy the music and have some fun. To start you on your way, here is a *haupia*." He offered the tray with a half bow, delivering the frothy snowfall in a martini glass. A glistening raspberry nestled against a delicate pink orchid while a hint of pink sugar dusted the edge of the glass. "Ms. Nulty called and ordered it for you. Please, enjoy."

Uh-huh.

Wondering if she'd ever seen anything more girlie, Darby eyed the drink. She was tempted to refuse.

But her secretary, Grace, would undoubtedly do a follow-up.

And, hey, vacation.

Darby was under strict orders to do it up right, and those orders had come from the Deputy Director of the US Attorney's office. He was the man who, being the soul of trust, had assigned Grace as a guard dog to make sure she complied.

So Darby took the drink.

Then, just in case her boss had enlisted spies in addition to the guard dog—federal prosecutors really did have major trust issues—she took a cautious sip.

"Mmm."

"Most delicious, isn't it?"

"Mmm," she repeated, sucking down another taste of the creamy rum and coconut. It actually wasn't bad, but it wasn't Scotch.

"Now go, down to the lanai. Enjoy the *haupia* and the beach while making new friends."

Did she have to?

Darby didn't consider herself an introvert—she didn't have a shy bone in her body—yet she definitely wasn't a people person. But she'd come on this vacation to someplace she'd never been, telling herself to try things she'd never done. Vacation was time to shake up life, to step outside the box.

"The lanai sounds great," she agreed. Adding a smile to her thanks, Darby headed for the stairs, sipping more of the frothy drink.

She'd only made a few steps when her cell phone chimed.

"AUSA Darby Rayc," she answered automatically.

"I thought you said this was going to be a totally relaxed, one-hundred-percent-committed-to-only-having-fun vacation. Shouldn't that include leaving your phone in your room, partying too loudly to hear a ringtone or relaxing enough to forget your job title." The accusation came with just enough laughter to make Darby roll her eyes.

"Hey, I'm in Hawaii wearing a flower in my hair and drinking pink froth at sunset. That says real vacation to me. Besides, it's my first night. I've been here a total of two hours and am wearing flat sandals. Flat. Sandals. What's that if not relaxed?"

Darby glanced down at one of the sandals, angling her left foot this way and that. Flats definitely weren't as flattering as heels. But maybe the copper beadwork rescued the look.

Maybe.

"Holy crap! You, Darby Raye, Assistant United States Attorney, ferocious federal prosecutor and general all-around hard-ass? Instead of mile-high sexy stilettos, you're wearing flats?" The sound of

Grace's finger snap came through loud and clear over the robust sound of her laugh. "Send a photo. This I have to see."

"Nope. It's your fault that me and my sandal-clad feet are even on vacation. Well, yours and the HR department. No photos. Not unless you want to trade places."

"I'd laugh, except I know you're not kidding. You'd actually rather be here, slogging through another eighty-hour week instead of hanging ten on a surfboard or being pampered in a spa." Grace's sigh came through loud and clear.

Of course she'd rather be working. She loved her career. Her job was her life, and she was damn good at it. Good enough that she was fast-tracking it to be one of the top attorneys in the Southern California office. Or she was, until Grace had mentioned to her lunch buddy in HR that Darby hadn't taken a single vacation since she'd started with the US Attorney's office in Virginia two years ago. She'd learned from the best that work was life and life was work. Since the tender age of twelve, she'd lived by that oft-quoted motto of her father's. They were the last words he'd spoken to her on one of the rare times he'd availed himself of his custody visits.

Darby puffed out a breath with enough force to flutter her bangs, but refrained from reminding her friend of that. Not because she wanted to avoid the argument. She was an attorney. She loved to argue. But the key to a good argument was knowing when a loss was inevitable. So Darby had easily recognized the uselessness of arguing with Grace when she'd pointed out that this vacation was Darby's best shot at the upcoming slot on the National Security Division that was rumored to be opening in a few months.

Darby wanted that spot. It'd be a big shiny feather in her cap, to say nothing of a smooth jump over a few rungs on the success ladder.

She was good enough. She had a solid rep, an impressive case-closure rate in cybercrimes and human trafficking. And she had the support of a number of influential higher-ups. But her age, her lack of experience arguing terrorism cases and the new head of Human Resources' fixation on a healthy work-life balance were working against her.

She couldn't do anything about her age, but thought her work on the Antiterrorism Advisory Council helped offset her lack of trial experience in matters of national security. Which left that work-life-balance crap. Darby grimaced.

Hence, Grace's answer… Vacation.

As if reading her mind, Grace said, "Office pool puts you at three days, fourteen hours before you give up and hop a flight home."

"Any idea if Jenkins is in on that pool?" she asked, referring to the new head of Human Resources.

"You know the bets are confidential," Grace chided.

"So?"

"He puts you at two days."

Darby smiled—leave it to Grace. That ability to ferret out the tiniest of details was one of the woman's best traits. Between that, enough tenacity to do a bulldog proud and a personality that blended like butter with anyone anywhere, the woman made a stellar legal secretary.

A fact for which Darby was forever grateful.

She'd gone through four secretaries in her first two weeks at the Southern California office and had been well on her way to cementing her reputation as a hard-ass with an attitude. That part she hadn't minded, but the changeover and lack of decent help had put a serious crimp in her plans toward career stardom. That, and having to remember the names of the parade of secretaries had worn on her last nerve. When Grace Nulty had walked in the door looking like someone's favorite aunt, she hadn't bothered adding the redhead's name to her cheat sheet.

Within five weeks, the cheat sheet was trashed and Darby was satisfactorily tracking her way toward career stardom again. Not only did Grace keep up with Darby's breakneck pace, but she also anticipated, intuited and, when necessary, argued.

All awesome things.

Until she'd turned them on Darby herself.

First it'd been her relentless pursuit of friendship. Darby was perfectly content—happy, even—to be friendless in the workplace. As far as she was concerned, office-based friendships only led to trouble. Especially in a job as competitive and cutthroat as hers.

She still wasn't sure how the other woman had outflanked her, but somehow, they'd become friends. But not even Darby, a woman who argued for a living, had been strong enough to win against Grace's relentless cheer and focused determination.

She'd used that same cheer and determination to convince Darby that a week of luaus and lying on the beach would help her career.

Damn the woman.

It wasn't that Darby had moral or religious objections to vacations...

She just didn't see the point.

Oh, sure, maybe she should have taken a big celebratory vacation last year when she'd become a federal prosecutor. A lot of people had said making Assistant US Attorney by the time she was twenty-seven was an amazing accomplishment. Others had muttered about nepotism, citing Darby's late father's reputation with the federal prosecutor's office for her foot up onto the fast track.

But Darby had learned young to ignore what people said. As always, she'd aimed her focus on work. On finding the quickest climb up the ladder her father had chosen for her when she was ten. And nowhere on that ladder was there room for vacations. Work, education, networking. That was her focus. Her only focus.

She'd have happily continued her vacationless lifestyle if Grace hadn't ferreted out that the HR exec was reluctant to recommend Darby for the new position. The woman was a stickler for that wimpy work-life balance she was always lecturing Darby on.

"I'll make the entire eight days," Darby vowed in answer to Grace's comment about the office pool. Not just for the shot at the promotion, but because she was hardwired to prove that she could do whatever anyone said she couldn't.

"I have every faith that you will. But do it right, okay? Treat it like a vacation, not a point of pride. Prove that you can have a life outside of work."

"My career is my life," she said with a sassy smile.

But her sass turned into a sigh as soon as the words were out.

That catchphrase had been her personal mantra since graduating law school. A mantra she loved epitomizing because it made her feel powerful, and dammit, kept her on the fast track to success.

A mantra that had, quite recently, been thrown in her face along with a whole lot of other accusations that were probably just as true.

"Don't start doubting yourself," Grace responded, obviously reading her mind. The mothering tone came over the line like a finger shake with a hug on the side.

"Why would I doubt myself?"

Just because the guy she'd dated for eight months had accused her of caring about nothing except her career, to say nothing of being coldhearted, narrow-minded and obsessive.

"Exactly. Why would you?" Grace responded. "You're a powerhouse. Darby Raye, Assistant US Attorney. Powerhouse federal prosecutor. Ballbuster, crime fighter, law wielder. You take no crap from anyone on your fast flight up the ladder of success. If a guy can't handle that, too bad."

"Exactly," Darby agreed with a laugh. And she did agree. She'd never made a secret of her ambitions or her priorities.

But maybe Paul had had a few points. It'd been her obsessive focus on her career that had kept her from noticing the telltale warning signs that he saw their relationship as something much more serious than she did.

Darby had dated the man for almost four months

while she was still living in Virginia. The JAG attorney had thought it was romantic to transfer from Little Creek to the San Diego naval base. She, on the other hand, thought it was creepy.

But knowing the value of well-placed bridges, influential circles and tiptoeing around fragile male egos, it'd taken her three months of letting him down gently to break it off.

And another one to convince him that it was actually over.

She should have skipped worrying about bridges and circles and tramped his damn ego as soon as he'd shown up on her doorstep in San Diego, Darby thought with a grimace.

Still, she had considered Paul Thomas a convenience. The guy had looked good on her arm, could handle the schmoozing through the social events she saw as a necessary component of a successful climb up the career ladder. His own commitments as a lawyer in the Navy Judge Advocate General's office meant he was as busy as her, meaning he wasn't around much. He was an entertaining dinner date, an undemanding sex partner and an interesting conversationalist.

And that relationship had given Darby the comforting, if false, belief that her life was well-rounded enough to not worry about eighty-hour work weeks and no interests outside of her career.

Now look what happened, she thought as she maneuvered the twisting, shell-encrusted steps.

The guy got emotionally grabby and demanding, she dumped him and here she was, stuck on a gorgeous island paradise, forced to prove she was well-rounded and obsession-free.

"This sucks," Darby muttered, unconsciously pausing halfway down the stairs to stare out at the bleeding colors of the sun as it dripped into the ocean.

"This vacation is vital for your well-being," Grace insisted with a sniff. "Weren't you listening during that safety lecture last month on the necessity of a good work-life balance to avoid health issues and burnout?"

"I must have been in court that day."

"You're always in court on lecture days."

"Funny how that works out," Darby observed with a laugh as she continued down. "Have I mentioned how much I appreciate you putting those safety lectures on my calendar?"

"Things like that are the reason why you need this break."

"What the hell am I supposed to do with myself on this break?" Darby blurted out. Even as the words escaped, she wanted them back. She hated admitting that she didn't know what to do, no matter what the situation. But since the confession was out there, she might as well score some advice. "Work relaxes me, Grace. Reading case law makes me happy. Climbing the ladder of success is my idea of staying healthy. Now I'm stuck here on a spit of sand, surrounded by water and strangers. No cases to argue, no work to do, not even a single law book to read."

"Read the resort's brochure. Avail yourself of all of those inclusive amenities. Do all the things you don't normally do. Sleep late, indulge, sightsee.

Lie on the beach, read a steamy romance novel, be friendly with strangers."

Grace sighed at Darby's grunt.

"You're at an exclusive resort on one of the prettiest islands in the world," the woman decreed, her frown coming over the phone line loud and clear. "If those brochures Jenkins shared are anything to go by, there's a lot to do there. And keep in mind that since you took her recommendation on where to vacation, she's very likely to ask you questions about your trip when you get back."

"Like a pop quiz," Darby muttered.

"The quiz is coming no matter what you do. So why not have a little fun. Let loose. Get wild." Grace's voice lowered, her words husky with laughter. "Have a vacation fling."

"A man is what got me into this situation," Darby pointed out as she continued her descent to the lanai. A man who'd accused her of being so uptight and controlling that she was incapable of handling a relationship of any kind.

"One of the reasons you're on vacation is to forget about that loser, Paul. So start forgetting and start relaxing. Otherwise I'll be forced to take steps," Grace warned.

"Are you threatening an officer of the court?" Darby asked with a laugh.

"If that's what it takes, sure."

"Fine. I promise. By the time I get back in the office, I'll be so relaxed you won't recognize me."

"Will it include a hot guy and orgasm options?"

"You think about sex too much," Darby said dismissively.

"You never think about it because it doesn't exist in your world. How long has it been?"

Since she'd had sex? Nine months, nineteen days and—Darby glanced at her watch and calculated the time difference—eight hours.

Since she'd had good sex? Tack on another three years to that tally.

Not that she was counting.

"A man isn't necessary for happiness or success," she pointed out instead of answering.

"You're young, gorgeous and single," Grace argued. "If you don't get some soon, people are going to start giving weight to Paul Thomas's whining."

"Okay. That's a valid counterargument."

Darby pursed her lips as she reached the lower lanai and found a seat. Despite the cliché touches of bamboo and palm fronds, it managed to be elegant and welcoming at the same time. A dozen cozy tables with shells under the glass were scattered over the glossy wood floor. Two sides were flanked by unlit torches, with the ocean claiming the third and a well-appointed bar the last.

Heat fluttered in her belly when she noticed the man she'd seen earlier was still seated at that bar.

Gorgeous. He looked even better from here than he had from a distance. Tall, a few inches over six feet she gauged, noting the length of toned legs in khaki cargo shorts. His dark hair was fashionably short and a sculpted goatee emphasized sharp cheekbones and a chiseled jaw. And sexy in a take-charge, man-of-power kind of way that made her tingle.

Talk about a change. She was definitely thinking about sex now.

"Call coming in," Grace warned, her tone shifting to all business. "I'll touch base later and expect a progress report."

"I'll spend my time availing myself of every possible option for fun and relaxation in order to prepare for my pending quiz," she promised with a laugh.

Not a bad closing statement, she decided as she watched the man toss a handful of macadamia nuts in his mouth. Solid hand-to-mouth coordination could be a good thing, she noted with a smile.

Suddenly, Grace's plan held a certain appeal.

Darby missed sex. At least, she missed good sex, which was something she hadn't had in at least three years. Since focusing on her career wasn't going to cut it as an excuse for the next eight days, she might as well explore her options.

Maybe. Darby leaned back in the cushioned chair, the soft evening air dancing over her skin. The setting sun glinted gold off the man's profile as he checked his cell phone.

She skimmed her fingers over the rim of her glass as she watched the man tip back his beer. Who knew swallowing could look so damn sexy?

He turned on the stool to take a quick scan of the lanai.

Wow. The full-on face view was even hotter. His impatient frown didn't put her off. She was practically made of impatience. But the hint of vulnerability in his eyes? Caution signs triggered in her mind. Then he blinked and power replaced pain.

Enough power to make her breath lock in her throat.

The tingles in her stomach turned to heat, flaming hot and high. High enough to burn caution to cinders. Darby shifted in her chair, arched her back and breathed in the warm ocean air.

Oh, yeah. She'd found the perfect way to get through this vacation. The only question was, where did a hot guy like that land on the quiz? Because as she looked him over, she had to admit that relaxation didn't seen to be the word that popped into her mind.

"ANOTHER BEER, MR. SAVINO?"

It took Nic a moment to realize the waiter was talking to him. He was so used to being addressed by his rank that the civilian term threw him.

"Yeah. Another one, please." Normally, he'd stop at two. As a Lieutenant Commander in the US Navy, he could be called to duty at a moment's notice. As the leader of Team Poseidon, a select Special Ops group within the Navy SEALs, he had a reputation for always maintaining control. And as a man who valued the ability to clearly see his way through whatever was thrown his way, he rarely let anything fog that vision.

But as soon as it was set in front of him, Nic tilted the bottle, letting the icy beer wash away the dregs of bitterness coating his throat.

Because Mr. Savino was on mandatory leave. So Mr. Savino didn't have to worry about being called to duty, holding true to his reputation or clear insights.

Mr. Savino didn't have a team of men depending on him, trusting his judgment. He didn't have to face those men when his judgment failed. When, for the first time in his career, he wondered if their trust was misplaced.

His knuckles whitened as his fist clenched tight around the beer bottle.

Mr. Savino didn't have a damn thing to do but relax and enjoy the forced vacation his Admiral decided he needed. But it was hard to relax when tension was spiking down his spine like a harpoon gun.

He hitched up one hip and snagged his cell out of his back pocket.

"Yo, Lansky here," greeted the voice on the other end.

"It's Savino," Nic said, since even on vacation, his cell transmission was scrambled and wouldn't show a name or location. "Status report."

"Aren't you on leave?" A heartbeat later, he added, "Sir?"

"When was the last time I was on leave?"

Nic took a couple swallows of his beer while he waited for his Lieutenant to figure that out. When he'd downed half of it, he put the guy out of his misery.

"Four years," he said, answering his own question. "That'd be four years ago, when you and I, Torres, Danby and Powers went to Spain to take those bulls for a jog."

"We ran with bulls. Danby missed out because he was holed up with that pretty Spanish dancer," Lansky reminisced with a laugh. "Time before that was when six of us did the Everest climb. Before that was Brazil for Carnival."

The tension in Nic's spine slowly disappeared as he listened to Lansky recite their various trips over the last decade. Each trip was accompanied by the memory of one of the team's adventures with the opposite sex. By the time the man got to the Vegas trip the twelve of them had taken to celebrate earning their tridents, Nic had found his place in the zone again.

"Now that we've had that little trip down memory lane, how about that status report," Nic said with a laugh. His tone was light. But the command was clear.

"Reporting, sir. Ward, Torres and Danby are due back from Yemen in two days. Word on base is that their training mission went well. They had three platoons doing night maneuvers to the tune of Maroon 5's 'Don't Wanna Know' and adding ketchup to their field rations."

"Nice," Nic replied with a laugh.

"Prescott and his lady are still debating whether to do the wedding thing the second time around or just hit up a justice of the peace. Ava's trying to be practical with the no-fuss angle, but you know Rembrandt. He's all about the romance. He'll have her decked out in a fancy dress, carting pretty posies while they say their second 'I do.'"

Lansky paused to crunch into what sounded like an apple before continuing. "On your orders, Louden, Rengel and Kane are retracing Ramsey's contacts, talking to everyone in the Navy they can find who knew him. They've tracked down some interesting stories. You want the deets?"

"I'll debrief them when I get back. Anything else?"

Nic finished his beer while Lansky filled him in on the rest of the team, base gossip and the status of his own relationship. Damn if the man didn't scope gossip better than a granny at a church social. That, combined with the man's way of charming information out of men and women alike and his sick tech skills, made him a force to be reckoned with when it came to intel. Which was why Nic had called him instead of one of his commanding officers. The Admiral? The Captain? They supported Nic's team, but their first loyalty was to command. Lansky, like the rest of Nic's handpicked team, had one purpose. To serve Poseidon.

So when Lansky ran out of gossip, Nic didn't hesitate to ask the question that had followed him to Hawaii. "What's the status of the investigation?"

"According to Captain Jarrett, it's currently lollygagging in red tape. They're holding Ramsey in the brig but he's got a hotshot rep who, while not denying the assault charges, insists his scumbag of a client isn't guilty of murder or treason."

No more than Nic had expected.

"Jarrett said they're still digging, but so far his men haven't discovered any leads on Ramsey's partner or, more likely, partners. Jarrett doesn't deny there are others," Lansky added quickly when Nic gave a low growl. "He simply doesn't have a clue who they are."

Nic exchanged his empty beer for a full one, rubbing the cold bottle against his forehead. He respected Jarrett's skills, and had faith the guy had Poseidon's best interest in mind. Hell, the Captain had almost been one of the team. If they hadn't decided to stick with BUD/S graduates only, they'd quite likely have brought their first-phase instructor in with them. He'd been damn awesome at motivating and pulling them together as a team. But while Nic had been all for it, the others had elected him leader and mandated they close the team at the twelve of them.

But the guy should have more intel by now. Hell, he should have shut down Navel Intelligence's investigation of Team Poseidon from the get-go. That he hadn't was giving Nic a serious knot in his gut.

"I shouldn't be on leave," he muttered. His scowl faded a little as he watched a sexy brunette sashay across the patio, her little sundress highlighting one hell of a figure. But all it took was a blink to put her out of his mind. Because nothing interfered with his focus when it came to doing his job.

"You couldn't ignore a direct order," Lansky pointed out. "Word is Admiral Cree wanted you out of the way until the… How did he put it? Oh, yeah, the shit storm died down."

Shit storm. The murder of one of his men in a mission to clear their name and take down a traitor, leaving Team Poseidon framed to take the blame for the entire treasonous network.

Yeah. Shit storm was a good description.

"I'm back in six days. Storm or no."

"Good. I'll have something for you then."

And just like that, the knot in Nic's belly loosened.

"You're close?"

"Damn close," Lansky promised. "I hacked deeper into Ramsey's computer history. I just need to dig through some layers, pull out a few more bytes. I'll have it cleaned up by the time you get back."

"Good. I'm ready to end this."

With that and a few instructions, Nic ended the call with his Lieutenant.

And wished like hell he was still on duty, doing his damn job. Leave was all well and good when he could roll it into a team-building excursion, or even the occasional family obligation. But this vacation while his men were under fire?

It was a fuckup.

He'd have argued against it—the timing was wrong, his team needed him, instincts told him to stay alert and ready for the next hit to strike. But none of his arguments could counter the simple fact that he'd taken a hit. A hard one. It'd left him vulnerable. And his men knew Nic Savino for many things, but vulnerability wasn't one of them.

Orders were orders, and Nic prided himself in making the best of any order.

You're on leave, Savino. Take a break. Get away. Clear your head, shed the baggage and relax, for God's sake. The Admiral's order echoed like a bell through his mind, a loud reminder of why he was here. Or rather, why he wasn't in Coronado, where he belonged.

Nic pressed his fingers to his eyes, trying to relieve some of the pressure beating behind them like steel drums. He could have pushed against the Admiral's suggestion. But he couldn't ignore the lack of sleep, the headaches or the feeling that he was losing hold of the fraying thread of the control he so prized.

So he'd finally had to admit it. He needed the break. He needed to get away, before he put them at any further risk.

So here he was.

On Kauai, where he'd always come as a child to renew. At his uncle's resort, where he could kill two birds with one stone. Family obligation and relaxation, all rolled into one.

He angled his jaw left, then right, and turned in his seat to scan the patio. Tiki-style right down to the totem-pole bar and palm-frond overhang, the area boasted a dozen small bamboo tables set up to provide cozy beachside relaxation.

To his right was a seashell-shaped dais sporting yet more palm fronds. Since it was too early in the evening for the band, music drifted down from cleverly hidden speakers.

To his left was his life's blood. His one true love. The ocean.

The Pacific, to be exact. Oh, he loved the Atlantic, the Indian and the Arctic just as truly. But he'd first lost his heart to the Pacific here. Right here on Hanalei, actually, twenty-five years ago when his uncle had opened his first resort. He'd sat in the soft sand, pail in one hand, shovel in the other, and stared in fascination at the endless waves of blue.

In the years since, Keola Hanalei had become one of the premier luxury destinations in Hawaii and Nic had continued his love affair with the sea. He managed to make it back here every few years for a little downtime.

Not just downtime, he admitted as he absently took another swallow of beer. Renewal. There was something about this particular view that always reminded him of where he'd come from—and why he'd ended up where he was.

He didn't mind that the reminder came with

400-count sheets, island entertainment and gourmet food. It made for a pretty sweet setup.

His gaze, always watchful, shifted again.

Because the sexy powerhouse at the third table was pretty sweet, too. The woman he'd watched sweep down the circular staircase ten minutes before.

Vivacious was the word she brought to mind.

Not in a bubbly, sparkling way. She looked like the type to kick a guy in the head before she'd giggle.

No. She looked alive. Powerful, intense and intriguing.

He didn't know if it was his body's reaction to the woman—hot, intense interest that reached deep into his gut and demanded attention—or if it was simply the idea of having something to focus on other than the emotionally exhausting thoughts that kept circling his mind like a vulture waiting to pick his soul clean.

Whatever it was, he was grateful.

Because like Lansky said, if he was going to be forced to take leave, he might as well enjoy himself.

And he'd just found a way to do exactly that.

All he had to do was convince the pixie to join him.

CHAPTER TWO

As DISTRACTIONS WENT, Nic had to admit this one was pretty damn compelling.

Short black hair framed her face with sharp lines and spiked edges, the glossy style reminding him of a jagged piece of obsidian. The late-afternoon sun glinted gold off a face worthy of a second, third and even fourth look. Slashing cheekbones aimed toward her lush mouth and strong brows arched over her wide-framed sunglasses.

There was nothing overtly sexy about her simple green sundress. Wide straps and a squared-off neckline didn't show a lot of skin. The loose fabric fluttered and settled, but didn't hug tight enough to show the curves beneath. And while the skirt hit her knees, he'd gotten a good enough look at those legs on her trip down the stairs to know they were prime.

She looked like a sexy anime figure or a sassy fairy. Not the sugary sweet kind, though. The kind that could kick serious ass and stir up all manner of mischief. It was an interesting contrast to the back-off vibe she exuded.

He probably could have ignored her sultry intensity, or the hint of wildness. But all of that *and* the challenge of breaking through her shield of indifference? That was almost impossible to resist.

Nic tipped back his beer and watched her scan her cell phone. After a quick check, she set it face-down on the table. Tapped her fingers on the case while staring out at the ocean. Lifted the phone and checked again. This time when she set it down, she slid it behind her drink.

He started the countdown in his head.

Ten seconds.

He could practically see her vibrating her way through them before she reached for the phone again.

Not used to relaxing, he deduced.

He could relate.

It'd taken him years to learn to shut it off and be in the moment. Especially if the moment demanded relaxation.

His gaze roamed her face again, with its impression of sharp energy contrasting with her sensual beauty.

Maybe he could give her a few tips.

Nic leaned against the bar and considered.

Not since his college days had Nic had to pick up a woman. Since he'd joined the Navy, especially since becoming a SEAL, the women usually made the initial move. From a time-management standpoint, he appreciated that. It meant he simply accepted or deflected, depending on the circumstances.

Not that he was a dog about it. But like Flipper always said, there was something about being a SEAL that turned any man into a total chick magnet.

A rock-hard knot of pain hit him in the gut at the thought of Flipper, as the team had dubbed Chief Warrant Officer Mason Powers over a decade ago. Nic swallowed against the misery in his throat, trying to shrug off the heavy weight of what he knew a Navy shrink would term depression.

Another reason he'd agreed to take leave—to avoid the threatened psych eval the Admiral's assistant kept muttering about.

So instead of delving into his reasonable grief in search of underlying issues, or parsing the text of his remorse over the lack of power in an untenable situation, he'd opted for the beach.

Now he had the choice to sit and brood in his beer over things that couldn't be changed. Or to make the most of the moment.

A man trained to respect that moment rarely lasted long, Nic didn't have to debate that choice. Instead, he stood and, beer in hand, headed across the patio.

"Hello," Nic greeted, and sat down opposite the sexy pixie.

She was even better looking up close, he noted, his gaze skimming the fullness of her lower lip and the tiny sprinkle of freckles scattered over her shoulders.

"Hello," she returned in a voice just as sexy as her appearance. The sound was low and hinting at husky—the underlying strength spoke of confident assurance.

She didn't act surprised or attempt coyness. She simply gave the slightest tilt of her chin and waited.

"Are you here alone?"

"Why? Are you looking for a threesome?"

Whoa. Nic blinked. He didn't know if it was the image flashing through his mind—both women looking exactly like the one in front of him—or the bold declaration. But damn, he got hot.

It'd been a long time since his squid days if a comment like that could make him blank on a response. But shore leave was like riding a bicycle. Hop back on, take a second to balance, then ride it for all it was worth.

"I'll be honest. I've never had to go looking," he admitted with a rueful smile. "How about you? If I stay in this seat, is it going to be an issue for someone joining you?"

She seemed to consider that question for a long moment before her smile widened. Reaching up, she slipped those oversize glasses off so the dark lenses no longer shielded her eyes.

Nic could only stare.

Damn.

He'd taken a hit to the head once when blocks of an exploding building bounced off his helmet. It'd left him stunned, staring and stupid.

Kind of like now.

The woman was hot, no question about it. But those eyes? Those eyes were amazing.

Huge, so big they almost overwhelmed her face. Round, with just the slightest tilt at the corners, her molten-gold gaze was lushly lashed and oddly erotic.

Before he could say anything stupid—before he could even think of anything stupid to say—a movement caught the corner of his eye.

Shit.

Nothing put the skids on a successful pickup than a gregarious relative with a million stories to tell and family pride oozing from his veins.

Before he could signal his uncle to stay back, the older man strode over with a wide smile and slapped Nic on the back.

"Dominic, there you are. And with such a lovely companion. Welcome to Keola Hanalei, madam," the large man greeted, lifting the brunette's hand to his lips. Nic watched her face, noting her surprise at the move, but he was glad to see there was no insult or disdain on her face.

"Your resort is lovely, Mr. Keola."

"Michael. Any friend of Dominic's must call me Michael."

Nic sat back, silently watching as his uncle deployed his legendary charm and asked the brunette if she'd ever visited Hawaii before, then suggested sights to see, things to do. More, he watched her reaction. Respect, a hint of flattery and sincere interest as Michael covered topics ranging from his favorite meals to try to the best places to buy souvenirs.

"It's not often that my nephew is here to visit, but he knows the island and its delights as well as anyone. You're in good hands. But if there is anything you need, you've only to ask."

With that and another of those old-world hand kisses that Nic figured only his uncle could pull off, the man left them to greet more guests.

And the woman simply stared, those anime eyes assessing for a long moment before she smiled.

"So, Dominic? What do you recommend?"

He started to correct her. He was only Dominic to a few stubborn holdouts in his family. Everyone else had called him Nic since he was ten. But there was something about the way she said his name, the syllables rolling off her tongue, that stayed his words.

"Are you a fan of fluffy drinks?" he asked instead.

"Only inasmuch as I can now say I've had one," she responded with a laugh.

"Then I recommend we get to know each other better over a real drink."

"Define real."

Nic's smile widened. He leaned back in the chair and prepared to enjoy himself. As he did, he noted that the band was setting up. Within twenty minutes of tuning up, the lanai would be crowded with bodies boogying to the island beat.

"Real, as in not decorated with flowers. If you're hungry, the food down here is good. Simple, upscale from the usual bar choices." He tapped the menu she'd yet to check out. "I can recommend the taco platter. The chef has a way with pork and pineapple."

"Mmm." She drew one long finger over the menu but didn't pull it closer or try to open it. "Any other recommendations?"

A few came to mind, but it seemed a little early in the evening to suggest naked dancing. Yeah. His gaze swept over her curves. He'd bet she'd look damn good at it.

But he had no clue if she could dance.

He should find that out, first.

That, and her name.

"The band is solid and you've got a good seat for the show. But if you were more interested in a quiet dinner watching the sun set over the ocean, you might want to try the third-floor restaurant." He indicated the spiral staircase she'd descended earlier. "The view is worth the climb."

"Is that a fact?"

"Yes, ma'am, it is. Call it my public service announcement for the evening."

That teased a hint of a smile out of her. One she quickly hid by sipping her drink.

"Do you do that often? Serve the public and help them avoid overly loud dinners?"

"You could say I've made a career of it."

"Do tell." Her body language was subtly flirtatious, but even with those huge eyes locked on his face, he couldn't read her well enough to know if that was a green light or a cautious yellow.

Nic didn't brag about what he did, but he didn't hide it, either. Simply put, there was nothing relaxing about talking about his work. Not right now. Not when just thinking about it felt like a blow to the chest, leaving him breathless and empty.

So he sidestepped.

"Let's just say I'm gifted at seeing my way around any variety of obstacles while engineering the successful outcome that serves people of all walks of life."

Check him, he thought, grinning. He could have a future in politics. Or with the Navy brass, which was sometimes the same thing.

"Well, that's intriguingly vague," she said with a laugh.

"Intriguing enough to tempt you to have dinner with me?"

Narrowing those eyes in a cautious way that made him want to know all of her secrets, she gave him a considering look before offering the smallest of shrugs.

"I'd hate to let your public service announcement

go to waste. And this will give you time to tell me all about how you serve people with engineered outcomes."

Instead of answering, he held out his hand to help her to her feet. As soon as her slender fingers were tucked in his, he changed the subject. Walking up the stairs to the restaurant, he shared the family story of how his uncle and father had collected every single shell that was embedded in the airy spiral staircase.

He wasn't going to talk about his career.

He was on leave, and for the first time in his life, he was focusing on his wants. His needs. And right now, he needed to simply be a man.

One evening wouldn't hurt, he told himself, ignoring the stabbing sense of disloyalty.

Not if that one evening brought him even an iota of solace against the pain.

So...

This was romance.

Darby released a long, surreptitious breath as she stared across the table, crystal shimmering in the moonlight, silver gleaming in the glow of three fat candles flaming in their abalone bowls. The ocean hummed a gentle symphony in the background, the waves cresting white while rich purple blossoms scented the air with sweet seduction.

Even as she settled into the plush chair cushion, she could feel her muscle fibers twitching against the need to get up and run.

She shouldn't be here.

She wasn't cut out for romance.

Hell, she didn't even believe in the concept.

But as Dominic slid into his chair, all those thoughts faded in a haze of lust.

God, the man was gorgeous.

Her muscles twitched again, this time with the need to slide her hands over the breadth of those shoulders. Just to see if they were as rock-solid as they looked.

But she was pretty sure once she had her hands on that body, she'd be hard-pressed to keep her exploration to just his shoulders.

Desire tingled over her skin. Tingled, for Christ's sake. She, the woman who'd laugh if anyone else said that, was tingling.

"Before we order, there are two things I need to tell you," he said, his tone as serious as his eyes were hypnotic.

She could lose herself in those dark depths, she thought before playing his words back.

Darby's smile faded. Tell her things? Well, that was never good.

"First, I think you're one of the most beautiful women I've ever seen. You remind me of a sexy pixie."

"I knew I should have worn heels," Darby murmured, trying not to be too charmed by the image his words invoked. But dammit, she'd taken a lot of hits about her stature over the years—this was the first that made her want to embrace it.

"It's more about your look than your height. You've got that sharp, edgy, too-gorgeous-to-be-real thing going on." His smile quirked, one brow arching in amusement. "Add in a hint of sass and a look that says you have a way with wicked, and there you go. Sexy pixie."

"Mmm, I can do wicked," Darby agreed, relaxing enough to reach across the table and slide her fingers over the back of his hand. "Or is that naughty? I have trouble telling the difference between the two."

Ahh, there it was. Heat. Her pulse picked up a beat as she watched it flare in his eyes.

She might owe Grace a thank-you gift for putting sex in her head.

"You said two things," she reminded him.

"Damn. Looking at you made me lose my train of thought."

He shook his head as if trying to clear the fog. She liked that. Appreciated that he didn't try to play cool or pretend he wasn't affected. Who knew how sexy honesty could be?

"Okay, second thing." He took a quick drink of his ice water before continuing. "I'm here for vacation. But when I'm not on, um, vacation, my career is intense. It demands all of my time, every ounce of my attention. I'm the kind of guy who makes workaholics look like slackers."

"Your career is your life," she murmured.

His arched brow said, "Exactly."

Oh. Darby felt the tingle all the way down to her toes. See, she thought. Her mantra was sexy.

"You sound proud," she said, appreciating every word. She'd heard plenty of people claim their career was priority. She'd come across quite a few workaholics, especially in her line of work.

But this was the first time she'd seen the same passion, the same at-the-cost-of-anything zeal in someone's eyes that also drove her.

Oh, yeah. So sexy.

"I am proud," he admitted. "Dedication is vital in my world. Because of mine, I'm damn good at what I do."

His smile faded, something that looked like pain flashing in his eyes for a moment before his expression cleared. "Yeah. Damn good. But that doesn't leave room in my life for anything else."

And there it was, she realized as she felt a tiny ping in her heart. It was as if he knew the exact words to dissolve every single smidgen of her resistance.

Now, resistance-free, she felt a little giddy. And ready to dive into her first romantic vacation fling. With that in mind, Darby flashed a sassy smile then pursed her lips.

"Oh, no." She heaved a deep sigh. "Does this mean you're not planning to ask me to run off after dessert to get married so we can open a cute little bed-and-breakfast on the beach, where you'll cook, and homeschool our eight children?"

"What are you doing while I'm slaving over stove and chalkboard?"

"Eight children," she reminded him, her smile masking her bafflement at the idea of how much work that must be. Eight. Did anyone have that much love? Her mother hadn't even had enough for two. But this was a game, she reminded herself. "Which means that I, of course, will be splitting my time between mommy duties and making sure I look hot and sexy in order to lure you into bed to work on number nine."

"Does that lure include hot-oil body rubs, see-through nighties and the occasional role-playing game?"

"Of course."

"Sounds tempting," he decided with a long, slow smile so sexy that Darby felt its impact deep in her belly.

"Only one problem," he confessed. "I'm a lousy cook."

"Me, too." She shrugged. "I guess there goes that dream."

"It's a good thing we found out now, before we got in too deep."

Mmm, deep. God, a part of her wanted to give herself a good forehead smack to shake those sexy thoughts out of her mind. It wasn't as if she was frigid—no matter what Paul said—but still, she'd never been one of those sex-obsessed women focused on the varied and satisfying ways to get off.

Yes, sitting here with Dominic, thoughts of sex were filling her mind. Sexual innuendos. Sexual positions, sexual pleasure. Oh, yeah. Pleasure.

"So now that we know we're not destined for happy-ever-after?" she ventured, wanting to get herself back on track along with the conversation.

"Now I do the gentlemanly thing and tell you that as attracted as I am to you, all I can offer is this week."

Darby's pulse leaped with delight.

Talk about perfect. If she had ever thought there was anything to magic or intuition, Dominic's words would have cemented her belief. But she was a pragmatist through and through.

So she took it as a sign, instead.

Paul thought she was too much of a control freak to ever let go, to ever just enjoy the moment without having to know every single detail. Well, look at her now. Here she was, proving exactly how wrong he was.

"Just this week? As in, no commitment, no expectation of more than a little vacation fun?" She leaned forward with narrowed eyes, angled her chin and arched one brow. "So basically, all you want is sex? A little vacation fling? Some naughty nooky with nothing on the side?"

"Is that a bad thing?" he asked, tipping back a chug of Scotch.

Both brows rose now. She'd made seasoned defense attorneys cry with that tone, but Dominic didn't even blink.

"Actually, it's an excellent thing," Darby decided, sipping her own drink and wishing the froth was something stronger. "My life, my real life, gets intense. My career demands a lot of my attention, most of my focus. And there's nothing wrong with that."

She bit her lip, wishing that last sentence hadn't sounded so defensive. Another reason to dive into this vacation fling, she decided. She would rock the hell out of work-life balance.

"You won't hear any argument from me. I'm a big believer in giving one hundred ten, even one hundred twenty percent, to your career. As long as you're happy and fulfilled, it's all good." His smile slipped a bit. "Barring anything that breaks the national, state or city laws, of course."

"Well, that's specific," Darby said with a laugh. Not just the law, but all shades of the law.

"I believe in covering all contingencies."

"I like that in a man."

"Excellent." He gestured for the waiter to pour the wine, waiting until the man left before lifting his glass. "Here's to vacation mysteries and pleasurable fantasies."

"I think I can drink to that," she agreed, a little thrilled to realize that she could not only drink to it, but she also actually welcomed it.

"So what do you do when you're not sipping frothy pink drinks in Hanalei?" he asked after they'd clicked and sipped.

"You had your two things, here are mine." Mind made up, she leaned forward with a smile hopefully tempting enough to lure him into agreement. "First off, you're a gorgeous man who is filling my head with thoughts and fantasies so detailed and erotic that I'm surprised I'm not blushing."

"Is that a fact?" When he turned his wrist so their hands were palm-to-palm and gently rubbed his thumb over her pulse, even those thoughts blurred. Darby had to take a couple of deep breaths to pull them back into focus.

"Mmm, yes. That is a fact. So thing one is to assure you that despite bursting my beachside B-and-B bubble, the attraction is very mutual."

"That's good to know." His smile shifted, his dark eyes narrowing with desire. "Since I plan on finding out a lot more about those fantasies of yours so we can play them out in exquisite detail."

Oh, boy. She wanted a sip of ice water to cool her

throat—or a gulp of wine to steady her nerves. But she forced herself to continue without either.

"Which brings me to the second thing."

Talk about wicked. His smile shifted, sparking a curl of hot desire deep in her belly. The kind that made Darby want to press her thighs tight together to intensify, to build until the pleasure exploded.

"The second thing is that we agree that whether our time together is limited to dinner, to the night, or the entire week, that it's only about here and now." Afraid she was sounding like some goofy romantic in a sappy movie, Darby cleared her throat and continued. "Whatever time we spend together will be focused on the matter at hand with no sharing of personal details. Topics such as careers, job demands, educational specifics or anything work-related is off-limits."

"Interesting." He arched one brow. "Are you involved in anything illegal?"

Tempted to laugh, Darby shook her head.

"Immoral? Illicit?"

Immoral? Thinking of the thousands of lawyer jokes she'd heard over the years, Darby's lips twitched again.

"There is nothing about my vocation that the United States government would frown on," she said primly.

"So that's it? No sharing home addresses or phone numbers, and no job talk?"

"Not even a hint."

Considering, he leaned back in his seat while the waiter set salads lush with leafy greens, spears of fruit and a dusting of fried plantains in front of them.

"Any other personal details off-limits?" he asked as soon as the man was out of earshot.

"Last names," she added, just for fun. She knew all it'd take was a visit to the front desk—probably even less for him—to get that information. But it added to that the mystery. "We stick with Darby and Dominic. Which would have been a great name for that B and B, by the way."

"I can see the carved driftwood sign hanging over the door," he agreed. "But since you've put the kibosh on that particular fantasy, I guess we'll settle for the other one. A week of vacation pleasure. We'll live in the moment, with no pressures and no expectations on either side. Except for pleasure. I have a lot of expectations when it comes to pleasure with you, Darby of no last name."

His expression was easy, the look in his eyes promising that the pleasure he offered was more than anything she'd ever imagined. But there was something else there, Darby realized. She'd seen hints of it already, an intensity and guarded pain, that made her realize that while this little escape into fantasy was something she wanted, it was actually something Dominic *needed*.

A tickle in her belly joined the sexual tingles teasing her skin. Darby wasn't sure what it meant. She recognized the attraction—the guy was gorgeous, after all. But there was something deeper pulling at her, tugging her heartstrings. Making her want to cuddle the man close and smooth away any pain. To give him a safe haven against the miseries she saw in his eyes.

Whoa.

Freak-out alert. Darby could feel her brain scrambling back from the concept of emotional anything.

Emotions led to feelings. Feelings led to pain. Pain led to debilitation. The kind that slayed hearts, destroyed families, ruined lives.

No can do.

No way.

No thanks.

Darby drew in a slow, deep breath, feeling as if she'd just backed away from a mental cliff on a windy day.

Emotions didn't come into this, she assured herself. This thing, this week, it was all about the physical. Or, better yet, the fantasy.

"That's exactly what I want," she told Dominic, leaning forward take his hands in hers. "I want the fantasy. I want to lose myself in the pleasure of this gorgeous resort, this beautiful island and each other. I'd like to see what life is like outside of the world I usually live in."

Dominic lifted both her hands to his lips, brushing a warm kiss over the knuckles of one, then the other. He smiled, his mouth still warming her skin.

"If it's a fantasy you want, darling, it's a fantasy I'll give you. One you'll never forget."

Uh-oh.

Darby knew trouble when it was kissing her hand.

But this was vacation.

Her chance to prove that she had a life outside of work. A way to relax that she could actually enjoy.

So what if the guy was trouble?

Nobody was going to be hurt by this. They were

both single, both free to enjoy themselves. And both interested, with a solid finish line already spelled out.

It was perfect.

For the first time in her life, she was ready to simply live in the moment. To grab on with both hands and ride it like a wild stallion, wringing every drop of pleasure there was to be had from it.

Talk about work-life balance.

Who knew it could feel so delicious.

CHAPTER THREE

BY THE END of dinner, Nic was mentally writing a thank-you note to whatever universal being had sent Darby his way. Fate, his guardian angel—and no way a man saw what he did and lived through it all without believing there was an angel watching over his ass—or, in his case, the god Poseidon, whom he'd pledged service to when he'd earned his trident.

Whoever, whatever, there was no question that they were looking out for him. Darby wasn't just stunning, she was intriguing. There was an edgy sophistication in her demeanor that pricked at his curiosity and engaged his mind. As easy to talk to as she was to look at, she had a husky laugh, a wicked sense of humor and an easy sexuality that spelled interesting things for this week of living a fantasy.

Nic watched her lick the last smear of caramel from her spoon, liking the way she seemed to give her entire focus to enjoying experiences. Food. Drink. Flirting. So far, the woman seemed to embrace every sensual moment of them.

"The band is good," she observed as the music drifted up from the lanai.

"They've got a solid reputation," he agreed. Then, after a long moment, he asked, "Would you like to dance?"

His hesitance didn't stem from reluctance to hit the dance floor. It was simply a matter of not bursting the fantasy bubble before they'd even got naked. The lead singer of the band currently rocking out an island version of "Welcome to the Jungle" was his cousin. If they went downstairs, there was no way his identity—or rather, his career, which was one and the same—would stay secret.

"Do you not like to dance?" Darby asked, resting her elbows on the table and leaning toward him with a teasing smile. "Are you self-conscious about your moves? Oh, I know. Maybe you're one of those awkward, flailing dancers? Or do you give Frankenstein a run for his money?"

She added a jerky, stiff-armed shimmy that made him laugh.

"My moves are solid," he assured her as he mimicked her stance to watch the candlelight dance highlights over her face. "And I promise, there's nothing awkward about my body when I use it."

Her mouth rounded in an O, even as her eyes narrowed as if she was imagining just how that'd feel.

Then, her hypnotic eyes locked on his, she arched one brow, pursed her lips and said, "Prove it."

For all the fantasy talk, he'd figured it'd take them a few days to build to a climax…so to speak. He hadn't thought he'd be proving anything tonight. He'd left his rack-'em-and-stack-'em days behind a decade ago. But, dammit, he'd never been able to resist a dare.

So, planning it out with the same quick thinking and detailed focus as he would any operation, Nic stood, holding out his hand to her.

"Shall we?"

"You're going to show me your moves?"

"They'll leave you begging for more," he promised.

"I've got to warn you, I don't usually dance with a partner."

"You have something against moving against a partner?"

She gave a tut-tutting sigh even as she slipped her hand into his.

"Sadly, I've yet to find a partner who has the right rhythm to match my moves."

Nic shot her a doubtful look and asked, "Are your moves really *that* awkward?"

Appreciation and humor danced in those big whiskey eyes for a moment before challenge took their place. With her head tilted to the side, she locked her eyes on his and, taking a minute step forward, rose.

Just close enough to hint at their bodies brushing against each other. His body tightened, heat kindling. The look in her eyes said she knew she had his interest, and she was deciding just exactly what she wanted to do about it.

Nic liked that.

He liked that a lot.

It wasn't just the appeal of a woman who could laugh at herself that turned him on—although that was sexy as hell.

For a man whose entire life was built on overcoming challenges, was there any sexier allure than a woman whose expression promised that she was up to meeting any challenge he tossed her way with absolute assurance and confidence?

As he drew her toward the railing, where they could better hear the music, the distraction he'd been searching for took on a whole new light.

"Here?" Looking self-conscious for the first time, she glanced at the other diners. There were only four tables on the balcony, but they'd be the only ones dancing.

"Here. Under the moonlight, away from the crowd. It's all about the fantasy," he assured her.

Then, because it was, he drew her into his arms. Nic had never narrowed his interest to only one type of woman, but he realized as he pulled Darby close, that he'd never gone for petite. If he'd ever thought about it, he'd have figured the foot difference in their height would make dancing awkward.

He'd have been wrong.

As his hands skimmed down her back, sliding over the gentle curves of her butt, he realized just how wrong.

She was the perfect fit.

OH, YEAH.

Darby's heart stuttered a little, almost tripping over itself in the shock of feeling Dominic's body wrapped around hers.

Music drifted up from the beach, the band's rendition of "Iris" wrapping around them like a soft breeze off the moonlit ocean. A lesser woman might have called it romantic, especially with the heady scent of plumeria and candle wax filling the air.

But Darby Raye was a hard-ass. Everyone said so. So she knew this wasn't about romance.

Nope, like Dominic had said, it was all about the fantasy.

And the fantasy was sex.

Sex, and, she could admit only to herself, a chance to simply let go. To enjoy herself without worrying about stepping on a man's ego. To make her own demands.

It was a heady feeling, she thought as she let her body ease against Dominic's and, eyes closed, rested her head on his shoulder and let herself enjoy it.

From the breadth of his rock-hard chest to the strength of his thighs to the gentle power of the arms wrapped around her waist, the man felt amazing.

Mmm, it'd feel so good to snuggle in, to tuck her head beneath that firm jaw and sigh her pleasure.

Even as the thought crossed her mind, Darby slapped it right back out again. Snuggling was romantic, like cuddling. It was soft and trusting and sweet.

She was so *not* the snuggling type.

But as her dress pressed between her thighs, the fabric rustling as it brushed his legs with every easy step, she had to admit that she just might be the sex-at-first-sight type.

She'd never met a guy before who'd made her want to strip him naked and lick caramel sauce off his body. Maybe it was time to give it a try.

"You've got some sweet moves."

Lifting her head to stare into his dark eyes, she debated pointing out that Dominic was the one with the moves. She was only following along.

Before she could, he lowered his head, just those few inches, and rubbed his lips over hers.

Soft, a mere whisper.

Her knees went to water, her body flashing hot and needy in response to the instant inferno that touch set off.

God, was all she could think.

Then, still swaying to the beat of the music, he did it again.

Like grabbing for a lifeline, Darby's hands linked behind his neck, her fingers delving into the short, thick strands of silky hair.

She tried to swallow her soft breathy moan of pleasure. No point making him think that all it took was a simple kiss and she was his for the taking. Why fool the man into thinking anything about her was that easy?

But, oh, baby. Darby melted. She actually felt herself melting into a puddle of lust.

She knew she should take a step back and think this through. Consider the consequences, weigh her options and devise the most logical scenario to work this situation in her favor.

Then his tongue swept over her lower lip, and she was done. She simply couldn't think. And she didn't care that her brain wouldn't function. Not while she was reveling in her lusty puddle.

When he lifted his head to stare into her eyes with that midnight gaze of his, she was ready. The agreement was poised on the tip of her tongue, just waiting for the question.

"Would you like to take a walk?"

Not her hotel room? Darby's tongue almost tripped over itself adjusting.

"A what?"

"Walk." He tilted his head toward the spiral staircase. "On the beach."

Was his bed on the beach? Because hers was only two floors up. Before she could point that out, he shifted away. Stepped back. Gave her space, she realized. Space and plenty of time to decide what she wanted. Something Paul had never liked, probably because what she wanted rarely coincided with what he wanted.

But Dominic seemed perfectly content to let her decide.

So she considered the options.

Upstairs, where they could immediately quench the heat stirring and blowing through her. Or a walk on the beach, letting the heat build, hotter and stronger.

She wanted him. Wanted to see if the feelings he stirred were just a tease, a fluke, or the simple result of celibacy.

But he wanted to walk on the beach.

Before the bitter taste of insult could overwhelm the delicious flavor of his kiss, she looked into his eyes again. And realized this wasn't disinterest. Oh, he was plenty interested and not hesitant to let it show.

He was simply being a gentleman.

God, that was sweet.

But she wanted sex, not sweetness. And the sooner they found privacy, aka her hotel room, the sooner she figured she'd get him naked.

Then he smiled. A flash of white against dusky cheeks.

And her heart yearned.

"I'd like to walk," she heard herself say.

"Perfect." Still holding her hand, he lifted it to his mouth, brushing a soft kiss over her knuckles before leading her toward the spiral staircase. She saw him signal to the waiter, settling the dinner bill with a simple head tilt and nod.

Why that should be almost as sexy as kissing her hand, she couldn't say. But it got her even hotter.

They silently walked hand in hand down the shell-encrusted path bisecting the sand. To the left was a row of bungalows, each one set farther away from each other than the last. To the right was the ocean, the waves dancing in time to the beat of the band's cover of Poison's "Something to Believe In."

He bypassed the as-advertised crowded lanai filled with celebratory sounds and gyrating dancers. The path he chose was well lit, with tall tiki torches spearing from the ground every ten feet and strings of twinkling fairy lights strung between. The juxtaposition of the primitive and the whimsical only added to the fantasy feel.

About halfway down the beach, far enough that the resort crowd was shadowed specks, he stopped.

Stepping off the path, he pulled her into his arms. His gaze held hers as he lowered his mouth, the kiss a soft whisper that filled her with a heady need even as it asked, and waited.

Still the gentleman, she realized.

She bit his lower lip, sucking the flesh between her teeth to lave it with her tongue.

He gave a low growl of approval and, obviously reading her answer correctly, took the kiss from sweet to incendiary. Tongues thrusted, teeth scraped, lips melded in a hot dance of intense pleasure.

She skimmed her hand under the hem of his T-shirt, her palm smoothing the hot planes of his abs. The rock-hard muscles were a vivid contrast against the soft fabric of his shirt as her fingers climbed higher, smoothing and circling their way up to his chest.

God.

There had to be another exclamation that would do justice to his awesomeness. But she couldn't think of it. Bottom line, the man had the body of a god.

"I have to say, this fantasy is even better than I'd expected."

"Darling, you haven't seen anything yet," Dominic promised.

That cocky assurance was almost as much a turn-on as the feel of his bare chest beneath her fingers. She shivered a little as desire grabbed hard and strong.

He untied the straps of her dress, stepping back so the fabric fell, unimpeded, to her waist. Darby stood in the moonlight, shoulders, back and chest bare, as turned on by the look on his face as she'd ever been by anything else in her life.

His eyes caressed, his expression admired.

Then he touched.

And she damn near came.

His fingers swirled, skimmed, teased her nipples into new heights of aching pleasure. She dug her hands into his shoulders, wanting more, needing everything.

"Privacy?"

"That's my bungalow," he murmured. His mouth slid soft kisses over the aching curve of her breast.

"Inside?"

"I will be."

Darby's laugh was a breathless puff of air.

The logical, analytical, cautious voice in her head that was usually in charge of her every choice screamed at her to stop. This was insane. She didn't even know the guy's last name, had met him less than four hours ago, and was getting naked on the beach when there were perfectly private walls to get naked behind only a few feet away.

She needed to stop.

She gasped when his fingers skimmed inside the elastic band of her thong, sliding over the throbbing wet heat between her legs.

Or at least slow down. Yeah, slow down long enough to eliminate one of those issues from the list. The last name. Or knowing each other longer. Or even walls.

Walls were good.

"Here?"

"Now."

Her breath coming in pants, Darby knew very little oxygen was making it to her brain. But there was enough—just barely enough—to spur her to ask…

"Sand?"

A little rough stuff could be fun. Exciting, even. But she didn't think sex and exfoliation should go hand in hand. Or, in this case, thigh-to-thigh.

"Leave it to me," he promised, the words hot and moist against her flesh as he slid nibbling kisses over her throat.

He lowered them both to the sand, shifting so she was sitting on his lap. His hands moved faster now, racing over her bare flesh, teasing and tempting. As she tugged off his T-shirt, he sent her dress flying.

Clothes disappeared, bodies heated. His hands were everywhere, his mouth hot and wet as he lifted her high over his body. His fingers delved deep into her wet heat, stirring her hotter and higher as she poised above him.

He took care of protection in a swift, easy move before pulling her back into his arms, then positioned her over the impressive power of his erection.

"Give yourself to me," he demanded, his husky words melding with the sound of the surf.

Watching his face, reveling in the appreciative pleasure she saw there, Darby slowly took him inside her. Her breath shuddered out, body quaking with the first orgasm as he filled her.

He let her set the pace, watched her like a hawk to gauge her pleasure, taking his own as he intensified the moves that she liked best.

Need tightened, coiling hot and hard.

He reached between their bodies, his fingers sliding over her wet, throbbing folds.

She exploded.

The roar of pleasure surged through her, ripping her to pieces. The feel of his climax, the grip of his hands on her hips, only sent her flying higher.

Holy freaking hell, was all she could think as she tried to reconnect her mind and her body.

Darby didn't know how long it was before she melted into his arms, the sound of the ocean's waves playing a soft backdrop to the feel of her body slowly floating down from passion's crest.

Damn, she thought as she tucked her head under Dominic's chin.

This fantasy thing was amazing.

NIC WAS GOOD. Damn good.

He'd never had to think much about it. He considered that a simple reality. And given the amount of verification he'd had over the years, he'd never had reason to doubt that reality.

But with Darby, damn…

He'd met his match.

He'd figured she was hot. He wouldn't have introduced himself to her otherwise. He'd felt a connection—he wouldn't have hit on her otherwise. He'd figured they'd rock the sex. But he hadn't expected her to make him pant with need, then blow his mind. For a man known for his skill in seeing probable outcomes, it was one hell of a nice surprise.

They'd hit it on the beach, then they'd followed up with round two on his bungalow floor. He was pretty sure she'd have slipped out the minute they found their clothes again, so he'd snagged her underwear and carried her into his bed.

He called that strategy.

He called their third round of hot sex incredible.

Now, his body hummed with bone-deep satisfaction, the kind that could only be had from mind-blowingly intense sex. He counted the beats of his heart, waiting for it to return to normal. But even as Darby's breath warmed his chest, his body stirred for another round. She burrowed closer as the night air drifted over their entangled bodies, her thigh sliding over his already hardening erection. Desire shot through him like an electric current, energizing even as it demanded satisfaction.

Figuring she needed sleep—or at least a little time to recover from that last sweaty bout of passion, Nic carefully slid out of her arms. Snagging the comforter from where they'd kicked it to the floor, he carefully draped it over her, tucking the ends to keep in the warmth.

For a second, a long delicious second, he watched her sleep. She didn't look any less wicked with her eyes closed, and now that he knew what her body was capable of? He'd never think of her as cute again. Nope, this woman was all heat. All power. All temptation.

Nic turned away before he could give in to the lure.

He crossed the bedroom, his steps silent on the sisal rug. Pushing aside one section of the wall's sheer panels, he pulled open the glass door and stepped onto the patio. The wooden slats ran the length of the bungalow, a low railing open at one end for easy access to the beach.

Nic ignored the deeply cushioned chairs, instead hooking one knee over the rail as he breathed in the damp, salty air.

He stared out over the black waves, letting the power of the ocean fill him, wishing it would soothe the unrelenting pain lodged in his heart.

But now that the sex was done, the memories that haunted him every night flooded back in.

His team was under attack.

He was one man down.

And he couldn't even see the enemy. He'd tried. He'd put his best man—himself—on it, but while he'd identified the frontline attack, whoever was masterminding the operation was still off his radar.

Team Poseidon was good. Damn good.

That's why they'd formed. Because they were the best.

Although Nic had known a few of them since his petty officer days, the twelve men had become a team in BUD/S training. It'd been over a decade, but all he had to do was close his eyes and he was right back there in the Grinder. They'd bonded over the challenge, over the pain, over the intense demands on their bodies. One minute they were competing for the best time in the thousand-meter swim, the next they were working together to cart a 150-pound log down the beach. The records they'd set still hadn't been surpassed. They'd worked together as a team, each one pushing the other to be the best, then better than the best.

So impressed with the way the twelve of them had come together, had teamed up and had balanced each other in those six months, Admiral Cree had wondered just how good they could be.

Under his auspices, Poseidon was born. In return for their promise to pursue his mandate, he'd guaranteed they'd deploy and serve together.

In the decade since Team Poseidon was created, they had become the best. Their reputation was on par with SEAL Team Six. Except unlike SEAL Team Six, whose members switched out regularly, Team Poseidon was exclusive. Each man on the team trained in multiple ratings, each man served under a variety of officers and each one was sent on the most dangerous missions. Together and apart, they upheld the reputation of Poseidon, the god of the sea.

Nic dropped his head back against the wall of his bungalow and stared at the sky. The stars had guided sailors for centuries. He wished like hell they'd guide him now.

Because his team was under attack. His team, and his reputation.

Maybe it hadn't started as an attack against Poseidon. They'd simply become a convenient scapegoat after Operation: Hammerhead, when an attempt to sell the formula for a stolen chemical formula had gone bad. In the process of clearing his men of the fallout from that foiled operation, Nic had discovered the crime went a lot deeper. And had been going on for a lot longer than just one mission.

If there was ever an enemy Poseidon had to beat, it was this one. But they couldn't win until they determined the exact identity of that enemy, established his position and assessed his power.

Nic just had to figure out how. But so far, he was failing.

He sighed as he watched a star streak across the sky, its light a blur against the inky black backdrop.

Maybe it was time to revisit the reason why they'd formed the team, what drove them. To do that, he had to start with himself.

The last couple of years, he'd spent more time riding a desk than seeing any action. Sure, he still showed for daily PT, he still trained with the SEAL team. He participated in all of the training maneuvers. But he spent more time administrating than fighting.

He frowned, realizing that it'd been over fourteen months since he'd last had boots on the ground on a mission. And that was way too long. It was time to get back to basics.

That'd help him reconnect to his roots, and help shore up any flagging morale among the team. They'd up their training, too. Time to intensify a few things, including their skills in cryptology.

Lansky was his best tech guy, but the rest of the team needed to up their expertise. Poseidon operated under the belief that every man should be able to do every job, no matter what his rating. So they'd all bone up on their computer skills.

Torres, Rengel and Powers had the most training in intelligence. Given the investigation, it was unlikely that anyone in the intelligence community would offer the rest of the team training. But Nic could tap those three to give the rest of them a refresher.

Except he didn't have three, he reminded himself as his heart gave a heavy thud in chest. He was down to two. Just as the team was down to eleven.

Because they'd lost Powers.

Rubbing his hand over his suddenly aching eyes, Nic tried to push aside the emotion. The minute he returned to duty, the team was embarking on the biggest mission of their careers. The one to save their reputations and take down a covert enemy. He couldn't lead that mission if he was wallowing in grief.

And maybe a few of them should take some additional law courses. Louden, for sure, maybe Danby and Prescott, too. They had the analytical skill set to see the nuances that could help if this all went south.

Trouble was coming.

Trouble that could take down the team. That could destroy a decade of hard work. It'd damage the reputations of good men who'd devoted their lives to their country. If they failed, a treasonous mastermind would continue undeterred in their destruction of everything men like Nic and his team fought to protect.

Which meant they couldn't lose.

He never lost.

With one last glance at the moon riding over the sea, Nic rubbed his hand over his vacation goatee and headed back inside.

Damn.

Looked like he had the beginning of a solid battle plan.

As usual, Cree was right. All Nic needed was a little time, a little distance, and he'd get his head together. He'd use the rest of this week to map out his strategy, to think through the steps and to consider every obstacle and counterstrategy.

As Nic crossed to the bed, he noted the woman sprawled over his sheets. Her dark hair spiked around her face, the sharp angles softened in sleep. The sapphire comforter covered but didn't disguise her petite curves, her lush breasts rising temptingly over the crisp linen. Even as his body stirred, he wondered how much credit she deserved for his mental breakthrough.

A gorgeous woman, intriguing conversation and

the hottest sex he'd ever had in his life. Yeah, that might be the perfect combination for a sweet break-through.

Which meant he'd need to put all of his energies this week into ensuring it happened again and again. And again.

Nic grinned, wondering if someday he'd look back and credit sex with Darby as a key turning point in saving his career. He slid back between the sheets, wrapping himself around her soft warmth. As she curled into him, her scent surrounding him like a sensual fog, he finally felt sleep beckon.

Before he drifted off, he thought of what was at stake. Of the years of work, of focus and, dammit, yes, of brilliance that'd made Poseidon the best. The god of the sea.

He'd be damned if anything was going to tear that down. As long as one man was still devoted to Team Poseidon, Nic knew he'd be right there, lead-ing the charge.

CHAPTER FOUR

DARBY FELT AS if she'd dropped into some sort of alternate universe. The kind where mornings started with alcohol-infused frozen drinks, fresh fruit and *malasadas*.

Where breakfast was served on the patio of a cozy bungalow overlooking the ocean, with the sun already warming her skin, which was bare but for a vivid purple bikini and a wrap in the bleeding colors of sunset.

Where her body still buzzed from a night of amazing sex, aching in places she hadn't realized could ache. Her thighs still quivered whenever she moved her legs, inciting a tingling sort of heat.

"You okay?"

"Of course," Darby said, her smile fluttering. "Just enjoying breakfast."

And the view.

Although she didn't mean the white sands and blue water, although they were stunning in the morning light. Nope, what fascinated her was the gorgeous man sitting across the table.

His hypnotic eyes were shielded by dark sunglasses, and the sun glinted off the inky black of his hair, casting a gilded glow over the sharp angles of his cheekbones. Like her, he was dressed for swimming in navy trunks and a matching T-shirt that molded itself over tempting muscles.

Muscles she'd explored, enjoyed, embraced over and over last night. Biceps almost as thick as her thigh and ripped shoulders broad enough to hold on to no matter how wild the ride. And his skin. Hot silk over rigid strength.

Grabbing her frozen breakfast cocktail, Darby sucked up a long drink of juice to wet her suddenly dry mouth. But the icy drink did nothing to cool the fire in her belly. Her body still tingled from the remnants of their shower sex-induced orgasms, and all she wanted was to go again.

How could she be this obsessed?

She'd only known the man for twelve hours.

It was just sex, she assured herself. Desire.

That wasn't anything to worry about.

"Another *malasada*?"

"I should say no," Darby said even as she reached for another sugar-coated ball of fried dough. "But I can't. These are delicious. Better than any donut holes I've had before."

"They're my favorites," Dominic admitted, studying one before popping it into his mouth. "When I was a kid, Avo Celia used to make *malasadas* whenever I'd visit because she knew I loved them. Just like this, covered in cinnamon sugar. My uncle gave the chef his mom's recipe, so it's always a little bit of nostalgia when I'm here."

"It must be great to have that sort of family tradition," she said, liking how his face softened as he talked about them.

What was that like, having a treat-making grandmother? Darby's mom's parents had died before she was born, and her dad's hadn't had much interest in their son, let alone his progeny. Both were only children, which meant there hadn't been any aunts or uncles to fill that family role. No family, no family treats. Something Darby had never regretted until just now. Because, damn, it would have been amazing to grow up with a family tradition of delicious fried dough balls.

"Did you have a favorite meal growing up? You know, like a birthday dinner or holiday brunch?" Dominic asked, looking like he actually cared.

The idea sent a thrill of delight through her, making Darby wish she could say yes.

"I forgot about my last birthday until it was two days passed," Darby admitted with a self-deprecating sort of laugh. "But when I remembered, I hit Starbucks for an iced smoked butterscotch latte. It wasn't a tradition but it was damn good."

"You forgot about your birthday? As in, you were so deep in work that you didn't realize what day it was and skipped right by it?" Dominic popped a slice of mango into his mouth and shook his head. "I've been away, on…on jobs, traveling, that kind of thing, on my birthday, but I always make damn sure I at least knock back a Scotch to toast another year."

"Every year?" Not sure why that impressed her, Darby ran her fingers through her still-damp-from-the-shower hair, widening her eyes as it fell in spikes around her face. "Do you do that blowing-out-the-candle thing, too?"

"You're telling me you don't even blow out candles?"

"So?" The look on his face made Darby want to

squirm. "My family was never big on the whole party or candles thing. I think the last time was maybe my seventeenth birthday when my brother got me a cupcake."

"A single cupcake?"

"The frosting had a flower on it," Darby said, wondering why she felt the need to apologize.

"And the rest of your family?"

"I don't have much of a family. No aunts or uncles, my grandparents died before I was born." She rolled the remaining *malasada* around on her plate. No delicious family recipes handed down, no real traditions. She dusted the sugar from her fingers and shrugged. "My parents divorced when I was five, then my dad died. So mostly it was just my mom, brother and I."

"Were you close?"

"No."

Sure, her mom and brother had been close. So close that her mom hadn't had much room—or need—for her. But with five years between her and Danny, he'd had his own life. His own interests. Still, he'd cared enough to make a fuss about her birthday once. But he'd left her. He'd joined the Navy, decided he had something stupid to prove. And died.

Her mouth trembled as she tried to keep her smile in place. Not because she was upset or hurting. Hell, no. She'd spent almost a decade teaching herself not to wallow in grief. But she'd forgotten how nice it'd always been when Danny fussed about her birthday.

"Seriously." Darby shrugged off the dragging sadness and returned to their earlier topic. "Don't you think candles are on par with kids beating on piñatas or scary clowns making balloon dogs?"

"I think every year we mark off should be noted in a special way. You think we should stop celebrating life when we hit a certain age?"

"You make it sound as if you like getting older."

"Don't you think it beats the hell out of the alternative?" Dominic considered another *malasada*, rolling it between his fingers a few times before tossing it into his mouth. "I like to think that someday, I'll be blowing out eighty or ninety candles on a big ol' cake covered in chocolate frosting."

"Chocolate?"

"I do love me some chocolate."

"Mmm, chocolate," she murmured. Darby didn't know if it was the way he said it or if it was her oversexed imagination, but she had the sudden image of Dominic laid out on the bed covered in frosting so she could nibble and lick her way up his body, then back down again. "I have a sudden craving for a taste."

"Maybe I'll ask the chef to whip up a bowl of my favorite," he suggested in a husky tone.

Darby knew what he was asking.

This was supposed to be a friendly morning-after breakfast. A friendly, mature way to end a very intense night of hot sex so it didn't seem like a cheap one-night stand.

The way it was now, Darby could get up, grab the bag she'd brought back after a quick trip to her hotel room between bouts five and six and, with a friendly kiss on the cheek, end her vacation fling.

The door was wide-open, a neon sign flashing overhead a guarantee of no regrets or recriminations on either side. But only if she walked through that door in the next half hour.

If she stayed, if she agreed to chocolate frosting, she was making a commitment. The kind that said, yes, she'd be spending more of her vacation with this man. That instead of enjoying her next seven days at the resort alone, wallowing in doing anything and everything she wanted by herself, she'd spend at least some of that time with him.

The only commitment Darby was willing to make in life was to her career. That was the only thing she had control of, the only place she had any guarantee that her hard work, devotion and emotional investment would give any sort of return.

Unlike relationships, her career didn't make unreasonable demands. Unlike friendships, her career didn't let her down. Unlike family, her career didn't break her heart.

Yet, as she stared at his compelling face across the breakfast table, she was tempted. And, hey, this was vacation. In normal life, she didn't have random sex. She wasn't a one-night-stand kind of gal.

Yet, here she was, having a vacation fling.

Sitting across the table from the man she'd had random sex with, contemplating the wisdom of extending one wild night into a weeklong frosting fest.

All she could do was shake her head.

"Well, I have to say this sure beats my normal morning routine." She scooped up a spoonful of fruit, reveling in the burst of flavor from the fresh pineapple. "Why not see if we can beat my usual evening routine by enjoying a little chocolate frosting. Maybe you could pull some strings and get cupcakes to go with that frosting."

"You want cupcakes, I'm your man. What's your favorite flavor?" His smile flashed, and was so damn sexy that Darby almost squirmed in her seat. "We'll combine mine and yours."

Oh, how many images that brought to mind. Darby pressed her hand against the butterflies doing the tango in her belly. When had she become totally obsessed with sex?

She wanted to think all she felt for him was a physical attraction. Sure, maybe there was an energy between them, and she liked the way he talked. And yes, she liked the way he seemed to appreciate her strength, how he seemed to admire individuality. And there was something powerful about the intensity that seemed as much a part of him as his sexy smile.

Her gaze scanned the man across from her, noting the way the sun glinted of his muscles, how his smile seemed to reflect that light.

And suddenly she didn't care. It didn't matter why. She wasn't worried about where it was going or what she was feeling.

She was on vacation.

She was simply going to enjoy it. Every delicious second of it.

"Chocolate," Darby admitted. "Chocolate goes great with chocolate."

"Chocolate-chocolate, hmm? That sounds delicious."

Intrigued, Nic watched the play of emotions chasing each other across Darby's face. The woman was a study of conflicting emotions. Sweet one second, edgy the next. She spoke of that birthday cupcake with a hint of joy, then dismissed it with a voice that spoke of heartbreak. She enjoyed the meal with gusto, from fried dough to champagne-laced fruit juice, yet seemed satisfied to celebrate her belated birthday with a generic latte.

"Tell me more about these birthdays of yours."

"What's to tell? A year passes, age increases. Sometimes increase brings privileges, sometimes it brings wrinkles. And every once in a while, it includes candles, wishes and presents."

From her tone, it was just that matter-of-fact. Nic wondered what had happened to make her that way. Was it simply a lack of sentiment or was it something more?

"What about holidays? Do you have a favorite?"

"Holidays?" Her eyes widened behind the big round lenses of her sunglasses. "You want to know my favorite holiday?"

"Sure. C'mon. We've put jobs, careers and personal-life details off-limits, right? So let's talk generics. What's your favorite holiday?"

"President's Day."

"Seriously?" Nic grinned.

"Seriously. It's the one time of year that everyone in the country is equally enthusiastic about anything to do with political figures."

Now that was a great point. Well argued, clever and devoid of any partisan inflection. Nic's brows arched as he tucked away that fact.

"Favorite vacation spot?"

Darby waved her hand to indicate the beach.

Hanalei was his favorite, too, so Nic couldn't fault her taste.

"Favorite pastime?"

"Work."

"Work is your favorite pastime?"

"What can I say? I love my job." She shrugged, the move making her breasts shift temptingly in that snug purple swimsuit. Yeah, beachside vacations in Hanalei were definitely his favorite.

"Me, too," he admitted, totally feeling her. What he did, his career as a SEAL, as a team leader, a Navy Lieutenant Commander? That's who he was. "I suppose it's important to love what you do, to do what you love."

"Even if it takes over your life to the point that you forget your birthday until two days later?" she teased.

Sure. But as involved as Nic was in his career, he'd never missed a birthday. Or rather, his friends—his team, his family—had never missed it. One year on a mission deep in the mountains of Afghanistan, he'd hunkered down in a cave, blowing out a match stuck in a MRE while the men of Poseidon sang an X-rated birthday ditty.

Did that speak to his ties to his team being too tight? Nic pondered that for the brief second it deserved, then dismissed it as ridiculous. Which left Darby's ties being, well, nonexistent? Didn't she have family? Friends who remembered? Who celebrated with her? For her?

A part of him—a part he barely recognized—was tempted to reach over and pull her into his arms for a hug. A hug?

What the hell? Nic mentally cringed.

Time to lighten things up, he decided.

"Favorite song?"

"'All Summer Long.'"

"Kid Rock's mash-up of Warren Zevon and Lynyrd Skynyrd." He nodded when Darby inclined her head. "Nice."

"How about you?" she asked, sipping the last of her drink with a slurp. "What's your favorite movie?"

The Hurt Locker.

"Hmm, intense military flick starring hottie Jeremy Renner. Nice," she returned with a smile, pushing her cleaned breakfast dish aside and leaning her elbows on the table to lean toward him. "Favorite color?"

"Purple."

Obviously picking up the humor in his tone, Darby arched her brows. But to her credit, she didn't ask. Instead, she kept the game going. "How about your favorite treat?"

You.

But just in case his taste for her was a fluke, he went with his second favorite since he'd enjoyed it a lot more often.

"Snickers."

"Mmm, nuts, nougat and caramel. Great choice." Darby flashed a wicked smile. "Favorite position?"

"Now that's a tough question." His smile was slow and appreciative. "I was pretty into the ones we tried out last night. The standing in the shower this morning was pretty sweet, too."

"But?"

Tempting, but Nic refrained from going smart-ass and went with honesty instead.

"But I think in some things, I simply don't have a favorite. I'm willing to give it some time, to experiment with a variety of positions and compare notes. You know, see if we can find a mutual favorite."

"I like that," she said, sounding delighted. "It shows an open mind and a willingness to experiment."

"Babe, when it comes to experimentation, I'm all for doing it until I've got it right."

Darby's laugh danced over the sound of the surf, filling Nic with an easy pleasure. Damn if he wasn't actually looking forward to the next few days of leave now, with her here to enjoy it with.

"So. Last question," she promised as she stood. Her fingers made quick work of the fabric knotted at her waist. The watercolor hues slid off the temptation of her hips, leaving her standing in a bikini the color of crushed grapes. As bikinis went, it wasn't exactly skimpy. The bottom rose high in the sides and came nearly to her belly button, while the halter-style top showed a delicious view of her cleavage, but mostly covered those lush breasts.

Damn.

His brain went blank as the blood drained south.

"So." Nic cleared his threat. "What's your question?"

"I'm just wondering what are your plans for the rest of the morning?"

"I'm supposed to meet my cousin, catch a few waves," Nic said absently, watching as she looked up the beach one way, then down the other. "But I can blow that off."

"Are you sure?" she asked as she reached behind

her neck with one hand, behind her back with the other. The move made her breasts thrust out, and put his body on full alert.

He tried to clear his head when Darby tilted her head to one side as if waiting for his answer. Really wanting to see what she'd do next, he hurried to give it to her.

"Yep. Sure. Definitely." He sat up a little straighter. "I'm positive."

With that and a flick of her fingers, the top of her bikini dropped away. Leaving her standing there, the sun glinting off those cherry-tipped breasts and making his mouth water.

"Why don't we try a few of those positions and see if we can make up your mind."

Mmm, yeah. Darby stretched her body out on the padded beach recliner, her flesh tingling as her toes dug into the warm sand and the sun drenched her supersensitized body with soothing rays. Her skin slathered with SPF 40 and her sunglasses shielding half her face, she stared out at the ocean in fascination.

Hours ago, she'd ridden Dominic's body the way he was riding those ocean waves. With the same enthusiasm, the same verve and—she tilted her head to the side—hopefully with the same skill.

She was going to go with a yes to that last part since he'd seemed to enjoy himself.

Almost as much as she had. And why not. The man's body was like sculpted gold glittered with diamond-like sparkles of the ocean's spray. Darby spent a good five minutes watching Nic surf, wondering how the guy's muscles were impressive even from this distance. Not quite as impressive as they were up close and personal, but it was still enough to make her mouth a little dry.

Was it that body, though? Or was it his personality that had her so hooked? She'd never met a guy who challenged her brain, made her laugh and turned her on all at the same time.

It was a little scary how much she'd liked it.

Desperate for distraction, she grabbed her ever-present cell phone and auto-dialed. It only took five minutes for her to wish she'd found a different distraction.

"Let me get this straight," Grace said, dragging the words out in her surprise. "You, Darby Raye, ballbuster extraordinaire, woman who no man can con into anything, a chick with a deep mistrust of anything even approaching the emotional level, is having an affair with a stranger."

Cringing, Darby pressed the phone closer to her ear, then realized it was stupid to worry about the people around her on the beach overhearing that she was doing the naked mambo on vacation. Smarter would be to wonder what she was doing making such a huge confession by phone with her secretary. She was so not the touchy-feely sharesy type.

But she couldn't seem to stop herself.

"He's not a stranger."

"You met the guy last night," Grace argued.

"Have you ever met someone and felt an instant connection. Not some soul-mate romantic drivel connection," Darby quipped before Grace could finish the *aww* sound she'd started. "Just a connection.

Like, you understood them. Even without all those random details, you feel as if you know them well enough to relax and be yourself."

Leaning back in the lounge chair, Darby slurped up a deep sip of her smoothie to the sound of silence.

"Go ahead," she finally said, figuring Grace would grind the enamel off her teeth trying to bite back her opinion. "Say it."

"First, I want to know that you're really Darby Raye and that you're not responding under duress. So answer these questions three. First, what color is your desk chair? Second, what was the last thing we ate together? And third, who irritates you the most in the office?"

This time it was Darby who went *aww*, although she kept the comment in her mind. There was something seriously sweet about having someone care enough to ask silly questions that most stalkers wouldn't have a clue the answers to, just to be sure that Darby wasn't being forced into multiple beachside vacation orgasms against her will. Especially since Darby knew that if she answered any one of them with anything but Grace's expected response, the other woman would be on the phone to the authorities, pulling every legal string and connection she could to ensure Darby's safety.

It was the first time that Darby could remember anyone caring that much about her, and it was kind of touching.

"My desk chair is aubergine, and don't try to say that it's purple because we both know I won that argument when I showed you the receipt. The last meal we had together was some weird tofu stir-fry thing you insisted I try, but you know perfectly well I threw my portion in the trash as soon as you left the room." Darby waited for Grace's relieved laughter to fade before answering the last part. "And third, I'd say that giggly brunette with the huge teeth in research irritates me the most, but I think this is a trick question."

"Since you nailed the first two, I'll give you a pass on the trick question," Grace replied. "Just tell me you're being careful."

"Are you asking if I'm having safe sex?"

"Darby!" Grace's gasp was half giggles.

"C'mon, remember to whom you're talking," Darby reminded her with a laugh. "You said it yourself. I'm made of mistrust. Added to that, I'm trained to read people. To understand body language, and to take care of myself. There's nothing to worry about."

"Nothing? You don't know his last name. You don't know where he works or what he does for a living. You don't even know if he lives in the United States. None of that merits a little worry?"

Darby grimaced. She was already regretting mentioning Dominic in any way, let alone confessing her trip into sexual nirvana. Since she hadn't kept her mouth shut, she shifted to damage control.

"I know his first name. The owner of the resort, an upstanding citizen who, according to the framed photos in the lobby, is on a first-name basis with numerous elected officials, as well as three Navy Admirals, is his uncle. I know that whatever he does for a living involves using his body—and given the quality of said body, he's damn good at what he does."

She waited while Grace made a low humming noise, then asked, "So when you get back, are you going to fill me in on the details of what he does with that body?"

"Isn't that a little tacky?" Darby said as she leaned her head back on the thick lounge cushion and tried to keep from laughing. "I'll plead the Fifth on that."

"Appropriate."

This time Darby didn't try to hide her laugh. But she did try to reassure her friend.

"Grace, I'm good at taking care of myself. I promise, I'm not in danger."

"Okay, but please check in every once in a while, just so I don't worry."

Darby wanted to roll her eyes. She was a grown woman. She couldn't remember a single time any of her family had asked her to check in, let alone shown any worry for her. She wanted to tell Grace to quit being such a worrywart and chill out.

"I promise," she said instead. Then, because feeling all gooey inside made her uncomfortable, she changed the subject. "So how's everything in the office? Any exciting new cases?"

"Um, yeah. About that. I don't want to put a pall on your wild vacation fling or anything, but you should probably know that a certain ex has been in and out of the offices more than once this week."

Darby's smile fell away as she pictured Paul Thomas. She didn't shift from her lounging position, but her body tensed all the same. She tried to ignore the guilt trickling down the back of her throat.

"Did you tell him I was away?" Darby resisted the urge to look over her shoulder. She wouldn't put it past Paul to follow her on vacation.

"Please," Grace sniffed. "You know perfectly well

that I wouldn't tell him anything. But I never got a chance to show off my discretion because he never actually stopped by your office. Word is he did stop by Carson's office, though."

Why was Paul chatting up the Deputy Director of the US Attorney's office?

Her unseeing gaze locked on the waves, Darby's mind raced. He was up to something. But what? He couldn't get her fired for dumping him, and besides, that wasn't his style. She could easily imagine him romancing another woman in the office to make her jealous. But she couldn't see him risking his own reputation by involving her boss in some scheme to get her attention.

She adjusted her sunglasses and blew out a long breath.

Odds were, he was simply playing it up to get her to call. He was playing her. It was totally his style.

She squirmed a little in her chair, shifting her weight from the right to the left and back again. Curiosity was so damn hard to ignore.

"Is he actually spending time with Carson? It could be completely legit. Maybe he's there to talk about a case for the Judge Advocate General's office."

Her fingers tapping a rhythm on her bare knee, Darby considered that possibility. She wouldn't put it past Paul to make it look as if he had some big case to try to get her attention. She wouldn't put anything past him, actually. The man had followed her across the country, for God's sake.

On the other hand, working with the JAG office would not only be the perfect feather in her cap, but it was also quite likely the type of case that would snag her that spot in the National Security Division.

She wanted that spot. But how tangled were the strings going to be if she paired up with Paul to get it?

"I've only caught a couple of his visits, and they were short. Like, ten-minutes-or-less short. But I heard he's been in other times." Before worry could dig its teeth too deep in Darby's gut, Grace continued, "I'm going to lunch with Carson's secretary tomorrow, though. She won't gossip, but Susan likes me. I'll find out as much as I can."

And that, Darby realized, was just one more reason why Grace was the perfect secretary. The woman had her back whether she was in the office or not.

"You'll keep me in the loop?"

"Guaranteed. Oops, there's the other line. Gotta go." With that, and a quick goodbye, Grace hung up.

And Darby was left trying to shake off the feeling that she needed to get her ass back to San Diego. But she was under orders to take her vacation time. Going back—going into the office—would ruin the whole facade that she cared about work-life balance, and likely jeopardize her shot at a promotion. She was better off toeing the line, sticking with the vacation plan and letting Grace do her stealthy thing.

She knew that was smart thinking. She knew it was the right choice. But she still wondered how much was justification. Because an equal truth was that she was having a great time enjoying this little fantasy she and Dominic had going.

For the first time in as far back as she could remember, she'd found something more intriguing, more inspiring, more demanding than her career.

Call it passion.

Call it lust.

Call it fascination.

Hell, call it work-life balance.

Darby pressed a hand against her belly to try to quiet the dancing butterflies.

Whatever she called it, she knew it wasn't for her career that she was staying in Hawaii for the rest of the week.

No.

It was for Dominic, pure and simple.

CHAPTER FIVE

EVEN AS SHE tried to tell herself her fascination with Dominic was purely physical, a million questions ran through her mind about him.

She knew he was single, but did that mean he never did relationships? Or that he simply hadn't found the right woman yet?

She knew he was dedicated to his career, that he loved his family and that he threw himself whole-heartedly into everything he did. But what drove him? Was he simply an all-out kind of guy? Or, like her, was there someone in his past who'd inspired his drive?

So many questions ran through her mind, questions she knew she couldn't ask. At least, she couldn't ask Dominic.

Her attention sharpening in the warm sun, Darby straightened in her chair just a little.

And there he was. The perfect man to satisfy her curiosity.

Darby watched Dominic's uncle cross the sand looking every inch the wealthy, respectable hotelier, despite the fact that there were eye-searing pink flowers dancing over his short-sleeved turquoise shirt. Paired with slacks so white they reflected light, Darby was glad she was wearing her sunglasses.

"Good afternoon, Ms. Raye. I hope you're enjoying your stay."

At Michael Keola's friendly greeting, Darby lifted one hand to shade her eyes and, even as she returned his smile, did a quick scan of the ocean to make sure Dominic was still surfing.

It wasn't as if her last name was a state secret, but she was having fun playing this fantasy game to the hilt. Maybe not quite as much fun as it had been playing the ice-cube game in bed last night, but still fun.

"Hello, Mr. Keola," she returned, gesturing to the empty seat next to her. "Please, join me."

"Call me Michael and I'd be delighted to." He sat like a king on his throne, his avuncular gaze surveying the beach, where it wrapped like a frilly skirt around the haven that was his resort. "Today is a good day to relax, yes?"

"I can't imagine a more beautiful place to relax," she agreed. "Everyone seems to be enjoying it, too. I don't think I've ever seen so many happy people as I do here."

"As it should be." His nod held a hint of the same arrogant power she'd seen so often in his nephew. "And speaking of, can I offer you anything? Another drink? Would you like to reserve a rooftop table for dinner? Or perhaps a seat at tonight's luau?"

Darby was momentarily tempted by the idea of traditional island entertainment. But a luau meant people, and right now she had a feeling she'd rather keep her evening private. Except for Dominic, of course.

"I'm fine, thank you, Michael." She bit her lip to keep the words from jumping out, but couldn't hold them all back. "It must be nice having your nephew here to visit."

"Family is a pleasure, yes?" His dark eyes danced beneath the wide brim of his white hat. "Especially when one's family is small, the time together is all the more welcome."

Uh-huh. Sure it was.

Thankfully, he continued before the cynicism made the trip from her head to her lips.

"I have only one sister, and she only one son. Sadly, we've both lost our life mates. So we value each other's children all the more."

"I'm so sorry," Darby said, briefly laying her hand over the back of his in sympathy. "I know how difficult it is to lose a loved one."

"A heart that's known love is never empty." He gave her hand a pat in return, then shrugged fatalistically. "My time with my wife was short but we lived a wonderful lifetime in the dozen years we had together. And I see her always in our son, Luc. He travels from time to time to share his music, but he always come back. He and his band play here and draw a great crowd. Perhaps you noticed?"

A light wind danced over them, a gentle contrast to the warming sun dancing over Darby, and lifted the edges of the sarong she wore over her swimsuit.

"The band we heard last night?" She blinked in surprise, absently tucking the filmy fabric back under her thigh. "They were fabulous. It's not too many bands that can cover everything from Clapton to Guns n' Roses to Alison Krauss. I was impressed."

Especially since the band had provided a great soundtrack for her first night of vacation fantasy.

"Luc, he has talent. Like his cousin, he's found his path in life." Michael's eyes scanned the water, his face creasing into a smile when he pinpointed his nephew. "Ahh, the surf is good today, yes? Look at Dominic. He takes to the water like a seal."

A seal? Not a fish? Raising her brows at the interesting twist on an old saying, Darby glanced out at the water in question. Shades of sapphire melted into turquoise and were tipped with white—it was unquestionably gorgeous.

"There is a dive scheduled tomorrow. You could go out, try your hand. Dominic is quite good, he'd be an excellent guide to teach you."

"No, thanks." Darby didn't dive. No way, no how. Flashes of the nightmares that'd haunted her for years danced into her head to do a quick boogie before she shoved them right back out again. Looking at the water might give her a nice feeling of inspired peace—much as looking at a work of art would—but the idea of being in it any deeper than her toes? That sent a nasty shiver right down her spine.

"You don't dive? Instead, you are lounging and relaxing." He nodded his thanks to one of the white-shirted waiters as the man set two drinks on the small table, each garnished with a pineapple spear. Not one for alcohol in the afternoon, even on vacation, Darby ignored hers. As soon as Michael had taken a long sip through his straw, he gave her an assessing look. Not the pervy older-man kind, but more a sizing up.

"You seem athletic. Fit, yes?"

"Not fit enough for diving," she said, heading off that idea.

"No, no diving. You don't want to spend time with

certification to dive when you could be relaxing instead. Hiking, though. You could hike, yes? If nothing else, you should visit the Hanalei Valley Lookout. The view? Exquisite." Just as Darby's shoulders started to relax, he waved his hand toward the half-dozen bodies riding the waves. "Or perhaps surfing? Surfing is an adventure. One every person should experience and you do look like an adventurous soul."

"Not that adventurous," she said, putting on her best lying-in-court face. The one that convinced judges and juries that she spoke the absolute truth. "You had it right with relaxation. That's my entire focus this vacation. To lie on the beach and soak up sunshine."

Then, because she didn't want to hurt his feelings and it actually had sounded good, she added, "But I do want to visit the Lookout. And the waterfalls."

"Excellent. I'll arrange a car for later today." Before she could protest, he got to his feet. "And soon, you try parasailing. It can be your adventure."

Parasailing?

Like, on a surfboard with a sail on the ocean?

Even as Darby gave Michael a noncommittal smile, she thought, no. No, no, a million times no. Dominic might have seduced her into any number of wild sexual delights, but there was no way in hell he'd convince her to straddle a stick of wood attached to a flap of fabric and ride the waves like some kind of water-skimming daredevil.

"Perhaps you'll try tandem parasailing. Dominic is skilled, he can teach you," Michael said, giving her one last smile before moving off to greet another guest.

Dominic certainly was skilled. Lips pursed, her gaze shifted to the ocean again.

Tandem?

Hmm…

IT TURNED OUT that Darby loved parasailing.

Who knew?

Two days later, she realized that she apparently also enjoyed moonlit sails, beach volleyball and hiking through Namolokama Falls.

Of course, the common denominator in all of that was Dominic. The sexy, intriguing, entertaining Dominic.

Darby grinned as she juggled her overstuffed beach bag to use her key card to open the hotel room door.

Dominic, who challenged her to try new things. To revel in new experiences. Every minute with him was alive. Enticing, exciting, invigorating.

Darby stared out the floor-to-ceiling window for a long second, basking in the view of the ocean.

Who knew?

There was life outside of work.

And she was enjoying every second of it.

As if mocking her thoughts, her cell phone rang out, loud and demanding.

For three long, glorious seconds she debated ignoring the call. She was on vacation. She had a date to get ready for. She could call back later.

But duty, as ingrained as her ambition, won out.

"Hello," she answered with the swipe of her thumb.

"Darby?"

"Mother," she greeted as she dumped her beach bag on the overstuffed chair just inside the door. She automatically ran her fingers through her windblown hair, trying to push it into place, then fluffing the ends. "How are you doing?"

"Not well, actually. Dr. Sternberg said it's nothing, but he's running tests for an ulcer. Which says it all, doesn't it?"

It said that Laura Raye and her ongoing affair with hypochondria was a force to be reckoned with. Sometimes when Darby was feeling generous, she thought her mom needed a hobby. Something to distract her from swimming in the deep well of worry she'd gotten so used to. In her less generous moments, she figured the woman had dived so deep into grief in the years after Danny died that she was addicted to the misery. And like any addict, after she'd sucked the sympathy dry over the loss of her son, she'd had to go looking elsewhere for her fix.

Darby wasn't sure what it said about her that her generous moments were few and far between. So maybe it was guilt over her lack of sympathy—or she was simply riding the feel-good wave of her vacation—that had her digging deep for compassion.

"Tests are smart. It's always good to know what's going on," she said, trying to sound encouraging. "You'll feel better once you know what you're dealing with."

Or she'd decide the doctor was conspiring to hide her actual test results for some reason or another.

There was always one reason or another.

Before she'd even finished the thought, her mother was off and running with her litany of reasons why the doctor hadn't taken her seriously enough to offer a true diagnosis. He should have done more tests, his nurse had taken an unfair dislike to her, her insurance wasn't good enough to demand better testing…

Darby tossed her purse on the bed and kicked off her shoes. She might as well get comfortable. This would go on for a while.

God. Why couldn't her mother just be happy? It'd been better when Danny was alive. He'd been her world, even before the divorce and definitely after. In her bitter moments, Darby figured her mother had been so obsessed with Danny that she'd barely noticed her workaholic husband's absence. And his death seven years later? She'd missed the child-support payments, but it'd seemed like a fair trade for an end to visitation visits.

Bare toes digging into the plush carpet, she crossed to the minibar and, after her fingers hovered over the tiny bottle of tequila for a moment, grabbed a bottle of water.

She carried it to the bed before curling up, with her back against the pillows and forehead resting on her upraised knees.

And she listened.

Three minutes turned into five, then into ten. She knew her role. She was a sounding board. Input and opinions were as unnecessary as they were unwanted.

"Don't you have any pull, Darby? You work for the government. Isn't there anything you can do?"

Ahh, there it was. Darby's role. To do *something*.

"Why don't we wait for the test results before worrying."

"But they won't be in for days, maybe longer. Can't you call the hospital? Use your credentials and put a rush on it?"

Rush the doctor's test results.

Dig into the Navy's cover-up.

Track down the men responsible for filling Danny's head with crazy visions of being a SEAL.

Prosecute the maker of the equipment Danny had used in his dive since there had to be a defect to blame. Not user error.

Prove, once and for all, that the death of Ensign Daniel Raye had been someone else's—anyone else's—fault, rather than his own.

"Mom, I work for the US Attorney's office. I don't have any jurisdiction in the medical field or any power to demand that your doctor bypass his usual channels to speed up test results." The swift inhalation of breath came over the phone line with enough power that Darby was surprised it didn't ruffle her hair. Before she could get hit with the fury that she knew accompanied it, she added, "But I'll call your doctor's office. I'll see what I can do."

She didn't bother to add that given patient confidentiality, that call wouldn't net any actual information. She was sure, in some part of her mother's mind, the woman knew that. But facts barely flittered over Laura Raye's reality.

"It'd make a stronger statement if you went into the office and demanded those results in person. I know, I know—you can't because you moved all the way across the country and can't be bothered to come back and deal with my problems."

And people thought she'd moved to California for

the great weather and career advancement, not necessarily in that order.

"It's almost Friday. You must have time coming, Darby. Make it a three-day weekend and fly back. I don't know why you didn't put your law degree to better use working somewhere you'd be paid well. And I suppose since it's a ridiculous amount to live in that decadent state, I'll pay your way. I don't mind."

Subtext—being a federal prosecutor was only convenient when Laura wanted her daughter pulling imaginary government strings. Further, since Darby was clearly frittering away her substandard income on living it up in decadence, Laura would tap into the funds she should be saving for old age to fly her daughter home.

Darby lifted her head and pressed the water bottle against her cheek, trying to cool the heat pulsing beneath her skin. But it ran too deep. So she unscrewed the cap and gulped down a few swallows, mentally reciting various examples of tort law until she knew both her thoughts and her tone were clear of emotion.

"I appreciate the offer, but I can't fly to Virginia this weekend." Since any mention of the fact that she was living it up in Hawaii was akin to a confession of guilt on par with matricide, Darby skipped right over that fact. "Text me your doctor's information and I'll call tomorrow and see what I can do."

"I really think it'd be better if you came in person."

"Mother…"

"Fine, fine. If they do find that I have some horrible, debilitating disease, will you come home then?

Or will you stay away, selfishly wrapped up in your own life while the last member of your family dies?"

Wrapped up in her own world? Darby knew better than to defend that she'd been away at her first year at Columbia studying prelaw, busting her ass to make scholarship grades when Danny died. Was that selfishness when she, a raw, grieving nineteen-year-old, had flown from New York to Little Creek alone and on her own time to claim her brother's body?

For the next three years, Darby had juggled college and the responsibility of trying to help her heartbroken mother through the shock, misery and pain of losing her favorite child. A responsibility that even she had to admit she'd failed.

Was it any wonder she'd followed her father's path instead and put every iota of her focus on her career?

"I'll call you after I talk to the doctor," she finally promised. She deliberately didn't mention she wasn't in her office putting in her second round of forty hours for the week. Why admit that she was wasting a decadent amount of money to lounge poolside in a lush Hawaiian resort, having an affair with a stranger, wasting time that was better spent furthering her career.

By the time she'd finished her call, the last thing Darby was in the mood for was meeting Dominic for a romantic, moonlight picnic on the beach. She debated leaving him a message, but whatever excuse she offered, she figured he was stubborn enough, gentleman enough, to come to her room to check on her.

So she changed out of her pleated shorts and silk tank top into a slip dress the color of morning. She tucked her feet into the gunmetal pumps she'd worn over on the plane, finding comfort in the stilettos' extra five inches. Vanity demanded she at least swipe a coat of mascara on her lashes and a slick of gloss on her lips.

She cast a look of regret at the pillow-strewn bed, tossed her phone and room key in a tiny beaded cross-body purse and, with a deep breath, forced herself to leave the room.

She'd said she'd meet him at the bar, and the bar was where she'd be.

NIC WAS HALFWAY out the door when his cell phone buzzed.

"Savino," he answered, one hand on the doorknob while he waited to see if it was a private call.

"Jarrett, here, Commander. Just checking in to make sure you're having a good time and not wasting your vacation worrying."

"What would I have to worry about?"

"Nothing. Absolutely nothing," Jarrett said with that gruff walrus laugh of his. "But in the interest of bringing you up-to-date, Ramsey has brought in a new attorney. They're calling for a tribunal."

"And?" Nic asked, not sure why that was a surprise, or why it would concern Jarrett enough for the man to be calling.

"And, they are making noises about a deal. Offering up names in exchange for special consideration." At Nic's continued silence, the Captain added, "In the absence of Admiral Cree, it falls to me to respond."

Ah. So that's what the call was about. He stepped back into his room and shut the door.

"You want my input?"

"Well, it is your team at stake," Jarrett countered. Then he huffed out a breath and in a more conciliatory tone, said, "The decision falls under my jurisdiction, but it's your team, your reputations on the line. I have too much respect for you and Poseidon to make this call without hearing your thoughts."

In other words, he wanted Nic to tell him what he wanted him to do.

"No special consideration," Nic told him. "No breaks, no deals. Ramsey is going down. All we need is a little more time and we'll have a line on everyone involved. Every element, every treasonous act, every traitor."

Nic said the words with the same fervor he'd used when he'd taken his vow as a SEAL. Because they were the same. Exactly the damn same.

"You have new intel?" Jarrett prompted, his voice on edge. Nic pictured the guy in his office, ready to leap up and run after any lead Nic offered.

"We're close" was all he said. Because as much as he trusted Jarrett, he wasn't outing anyone on his team or their progress until the details were solid.

"Close?" Jarrett repeated expectantly. But when no information was forthcoming, he huffed again, cleared his throat and said, "Who is taking point while you're gone? I'll liaise with them before moving forward."

"My team. My call."

"Fine," Jarrett said after a long pause. "I'll delay this new attorney with a few layers of red tape. You'll fill me in soon, right?"

"When I get back."

He knew Jarrett wanted to argue, just as he knew he wouldn't. To make it easier on the guy, he ended the conversation.

But he didn't leave the room yet.

Instead, he considered the ramifications of Jarrett's call. He wanted to believe the Captain would stand firm against Ramsey's attorneys. But he knew that while Jarrett was a clever tactician, a solid instructor and a damn good desk jockey, the man wasn't known for his fortitude. Cree was the backbone, the heart and the force behind Poseidon. Jarrett was faultless at carrying out Cree's orders, but on his own, the guy was lacking.

Nic glanced at the clock on the nightstand. He was supposed to meet Darby in a few minutes. He'd been looking forward to seeing her, and had some damn hot plans for the night.

But priorities were priorities, so Nic did what came naturally.

He dialed the phone and put duty first.

DOMINIC WAS LATE.

Darby blew out a sigh as she glanced at the clock for the third time in as many minutes.

She should leave. If he couldn't bother to be here on time, why should she bother to wait? She'd only come out of courtesy. She'd planned to cut the evening short. Why not cut it completely and go curl up in her jammies?

Even as she mulled a dozen excuses to leave, she shifted on the cozy, low-backed stool at the far end of the bamboo bar and let her gaze wander. Wreathed with flowers in watercolor hues of orange and pink, the bar hit the high end of upscale with its glinting bottles before a mirrored wall and servers dressed in crisp white shirts while bustling to hustle drinks.

Music played loud enough to be heard over the crowd that was two deep around the bar. Partying, celebrating, vacationing. She scowled.

They were all so damn happy.

Well, almost all, Darby noted, watching a statuesque redhead throw her arms in the air.

"This is ridiculous. A ten-minute wait for a table? I told you to make reservations."

Ready to be distracted from her brooding thoughts, she turned to watch the disgruntled diner and her companions. Twentysomethings, well-dressed and already sporting an alcohol-induced glow, the two couples jostled for a spot at one of the tall tables overlooking the pool.

"I asked about reservations but the front desk said we didn't need them. Besides, ten minutes isn't long," the man next to her defended.

"I'll bet everyone's in here trying to get more information about the incident," said a buxom blonde, her eyes dancing with glee over her martini glass.

"What incident?"

"I heard some guy almost drowned," she exclaimed, sounding almost as excited at the prospect as she might over finding a half-off sale on Valentino. "He had, like, a heart attack underwater and everything."

"That's not what happened, Marla. I heard it from the bell captain. The guy partied too hard last night, then went diving this morning with a hangover." It was hard to tell if the man's look of disgust was over the guy's drinking, his hangover or over his girl-friend's glee at someone else's misfortune.

"The man was dehydrated, overheated from the sun and sick on top of it. He was lucky that one of the other divers was even better than the instructor. Like, a dive master or something. As soon he realized what was happening, that guy hauled the hungover dude to the surface. Saved his life, maybe."

"Saved the resort is more like it," the girlfriend muttered, casting an envious eye around the bar. "They're lucky someone on that trip knew what they were doing. Obviously whoever was running it didn't have a clue. Their screwup could have killed that guy. Probably would have, if some random stranger hadn't played hero. And they'll never pay for it, ei-ther. Big shots like this resort, they have the local law in their pockets, plenty of people on the payroll to make them look clean."

Seriously? Darby's fingers tightened on her glass.

"Talk about jumping to conclusions," the second woman said, rolling her eyes. "I checked into the dives before we booked this trip. They're profession-ally led, and everyone who participates has to show their diving credentials and they went through a cer-tification yesterday. So now it's the resort's job to make sure nobody does anything stupid after veri-fying they can dive? How fair is that?"

The first woman bit her lip, frustration shimmer-ing around her at their united front in the face of her accusations. The waiter chose that moment to step over and invite them to their table, so Darby didn't get to find out if the woman kept arguing or gave up. It wouldn't matter what her friends said. Once someone had their teeth into an idea like that, no amount of logic or reason could change it.

Darby knew the type. She'd grown up with a woman who worshipped at the altar of her unsubstantiated beliefs like some worshipped the cross.

She rubbed two fingers against her temple, wishing she could massage away the pain there before it took hold. She should go, she decided. She'd leave Dominic a message, put the do-not-disturb sign on her door and hope he was gentleman enough to take the hint.

Before she could slide off her perch, though, he strode into the bar. Darby blinked but the image didn't change. Which left her to wonder how one man could look more and more gorgeous every time she saw him.

Long and lean, he wore jeans with the same air of power that some men wore three-thousand-dollar suits. His button-up shirt was the color of the moon, a smooth silvery blue with sleeves that barely covered his rippling biceps. She could tell his hair was damp from the way the overhead lights gleamed off the soft curls.

But it was his smile, that sexy smile, flashing white against his dark goatee, that made her sigh. The man could rule the world with that smile.

"Darby," he greeted when he reached her, sliding one finger over the curve of her cheek. "Sorry if I kept you waiting."

She'd been ready to leave. Hell, she'd been ready to call this whole night off long before it started. But now all she wanted was to lean in and taste that mouth. To lose herself in his voice as they talked about anything and everything.

How did he do that?

And more importantly, why did she let him?

Maybe it was the fact that just the brush of his index finger made her entire body tingle. Darby shifted a little on the stool, warming even more as she thought about what a distraction those tingles could be if he used all ten fingers.

"I don't mind waiting if you make it worth my while," she said.

"I can do that," he promised.

"How?" she challenged.

"How about I start with this," he said, his smile flashing toward wicked just before he leaned down and took her mouth with his. A quick sweep of that delicious tongue of his over her bottom lip and every drop of tension drained from her shoulders. His teeth nipped gently, hands warming her waist as he drew her closer.

And just like that, passion burned away all of her worries and Darby felt as if all was right in the world.

CHAPTER SIX

NIC FELT GOOD. Damn good.

All because of the sloe-eyed hottie staring up at him like he'd blown her mind with a simple kiss.

More like she'd set his mind straight, he realized, rubbing his thumb over the full lips he'd just enjoyed.

He'd had four nights of great sex with a smoking-hot woman whose conversation was almost as fascinating as her body.

No reason to let Jarrett interrupt that.

Focus, he reminded himself. One of his greatest skills was focus, and tonight his focus was totally on Darby. A few laughs, a good time, some steamy sex. Because damn if he hadn't found what might be the only possible distraction from his career troubles. So with that in mind, he put treason, the Navy and even his teammates out of his mind, and focused on his date.

"You look fabulous," Nic told Darby, slipping his finger from her cheek to her arm, then sliding it along the silken warmth. Between the amount of bare skin and the sexy pout of her mouth, she was pure temptation. Her hair was a little spikier, her makeup a little smokier than he'd seen before. It gave her a little bit of a badass edge.

Badass was damn sexy.

Then he got a load of the expression in her eyes. A little tense, with something under the surface. Something he couldn't quite read.

"You okay?"

"Sure. Fine."

Uh-huh.

"I'm sorry I'm late."

"I wasn't waiting long," Darby said with a shrug, looking as if she was debating whether to give in to the brood in her eyes, or to let him distract her.

"There was an incident on the dive that kept us out on the water longer than expected."

Her expression tightened for a second, then she forced a smile.

"Ahh, the dive." She turned on the stool to give him an arch look. "Don't tell me. You're the hero."

"The what?"

"Everyone's talking about it. Some idiot with a hangover almost drowns, one of the divers saved him." She gestured with her glass before taking a drink. "I'm betting that was you. You have *hero* written all over you."

Nic narrowed his eyes, wondering why she said that like it was a bad thing.

"Do you have something against heroes?"

"Don't you think that's an overused phrase? A guy runs into a burning building to save a cat, he's a hero. A dude flies through the sky wearing tights and kicking villain ass, he's a hero. Some guy hits a home run, he's a hero. A kid does his homework, he's a hero." She shrugged. "It's one of those words that is either impossible to live up to, or is so overused that it loses all meaning."

Huh. Nic jerked his chin a little, surprised she'd skipped right over any military mention in her list. It wasn't like he did what he did for the glory, but c'mon, dammit. Didn't they count on the hero list?

"So you're not a fan of the word *hero*, or of people being heroes?" he asked, not sure why he needed the clarification. "Or is it the overuse of the term that bugs you?"

"Look, I don't believe in participation trophies. It's like everyone on the team gets credit, even if they sit on the bench," she said defensively. "But neither do I like impossibly high standards. The kind that, once set, are practically an in-your-face dare, challenging people to try and keep up."

How the hell was he supposed to respond to that? Nic wondered with a frown. Challenges were what pushed people to be the best. And while he didn't believe anyone deserved credit just for showing up, good teams were a sum of their parts.

"Hey, I don't mean to sound like I don't appreciate excellence. That man was lucky you decided to go diving today," she said, giving him an apologetic smile before reaching out to give his chest a quick rub. "This is one of those times that the label fits. Because from the sound of it, you were definitely a hero."

"Right time, right place. Nothing heroic about doing the right thing." Nic shrugged, still watching her expression carefully as he took the stool next to her. She might have put on a sexy smile, but there was still something painful lurking in her eyes. "And that's enough about my day. Why don't you tell me about yours? You're upset."

"I'm not usually so easy to read," she said, clearing her throat, then trying a laugh. "Either you're really observant, or I'm really obvious. And I've never been obvious."

As if toasting his powers of observation, Darby lifted her lowball glass and gave the remaining liquid a little shake.

"Nothing another one of these won't fix."

"Scotch?"

She leaned back, resting one elbow on the bar with her brow arched as if daring him to object. Instead, he lifted a finger, pointed it at her drink, then doubled it in the air.

"I'll join you."

And just like that, the resentment that'd been lurking in Darby's eyes faded.

"You look like you could use a double," she observed quietly, giving him a searching look as intense as the one he'd nailed her with. "Are you okay?"

Nic frowned into his glass, not liking this flip of the tables. He was all for supporting Darby and helping her work through any emotional crap she was carrying. But that was a one-way street.

"Of course I'm okay," he said with a shrug. "I spent the day on the water, got some good diving in and now I'm having drinks with the most beautiful woman on the island."

"Aren't you a charmer," Darby said with a laugh. Still smiling, she leaned over to give him a quick kiss. Just the brush of her lips over his. Soft, sweet and brief.

All too brief.

Nic corrected that, taking her mouth with his. His

tongue thrust, sliding along the welcoming heat of her to lead her in a wild dance of pleasure. Hot, intense pleasure.

Damn, she tasted good. Too good to enjoy in public, he decided as he slowly lifted his head to stare into those big whiskey eyes.

Darby pursed those delicious lips and let out a long, slow breath.

"And to think, I was going to call off dinner," she admitted.

"I knew you were upset," he said. He leaned back enough to search her face. "Do you want to talk about it?"

Well. Nic knocked back the rest of his Scotch, wondering when he'd lost his mind. He wasn't the dog some of the guys in his team were, but even he knew better than to ask a woman to share her emotions. Emotions led to expectations. Expectations led to demands. And the only demands Nic had room for in his life came from his career.

But he couldn't yank back the words, so he slapped on his best fake interested look.

Meanwhile, Darby sipped her drink and gave his expression a good, long study. Her smile turned wicked.

"Do I want to talk about what's bothering me?" she asked rhetorically, "How about you talk about what's bothering you first?"

Why the hell would she think there was something the matter with him? He'd started his day with hot sex, then spent lunchtime saving some hungover diving guy's life from eighty feet deep.

"Nothing's bothering me," he scoffed.

"Okay. Nothing's bothering me, either," Darby said with a smile, wrapping her hands around her glass

"Touché," he countered.

He glanced down when she laid her hand over the back of his. That simple touch was like flipping a switch, that flare of desire that burned whenever he saw her flashed hot and high.

"Let's walk."

"Walk?" Nic grinned. "Is that a euphemism?"

Darby rubbed her thumb over his bottom lip and gave him a naughty wink before sliding off her stool. She tilted her head toward the exit.

"Why don't we find out?"

Who was this woman?

Darby barely recognized herself.

Walking under the moonlight with the sand shifting under her bare feet, she breathed the salty warmth of the night air, her new silk tank dress drifting over her skin and the surf tickling her toes.

With Dominic's body warming her side and his arm wrapped around her waist, their steps were oddly in tandem as they strolled along.

Her shoes dangled in her free hand and Dominic had a blanket tossed over his shoulder. A gentle wind kept the night air moving and the ocean scent wrapped around them. There were a few people here and there, but the farther they walked from the resort, the more deserted the beach.

Darby sighed.

Despite her mother's call, she felt happy.

How was that possible?

She'd had a crap afternoon, a guilt-tripping phone call and a stress-fest of a start to her evening.

She should be miserable.

Upset, irritated and, at the very least, pissed.

Instead, she was relaxed and adventurous and at peace.

None of which were go-to emotions in her world. Unless climbing the ladder of success or convicting federal lawbreakers counted as adventures.

She blamed Dominic.

"I feel good," she confessed, her words low enough to float away on the cool ocean air. "With you, here, I feel really good."

"Yeah? Me, too."

It wasn't that she didn't believe him. Even as enigmatic as Dominic could be, she did believe he enjoyed her. Her company, her conversations. Her body.

But something was bothering him.

Darby didn't consider herself a nurturing sort of woman. She wasn't touchy-feely and she'd experienced enough emotional drama with her family that the idea of trying to poke into someone's feelings was firmly on her hell-no list.

So instead of poking at a sore spot, she tried to distract him from it.

"It's a beautiful night to walk on the beach," she said, leaning closer in case the warmth—or the feel of her body—brought him comfort. "I was surprised you didn't want to stick around the resort and listen to your cousin play, though. Everyone was talking about how great his band is. They just got back from touring, right?"

"Hmm? Oh, yeah. They're called Reception. They're

actually pretty good," he agreed, his hand running up and down the side of her waist in a way that made Darby's insides tingle.

Focus, she told herself.

Conversation.

"So, Luc's band. Reception. Tonight's their last night, isn't it? Didn't you want to check them out?"

Dominic stopped, shifting so they were face-to-face. His hands warmed her hips, fingers grazing the upper curve of her butt as he smiled down at her.

She sighed. The man had the face of an angel. Gorgeous, elegant and regal all at the same time.

"I'm doing you a favor," he explained, his fingers sliding up her back to tease the slender crisscrossed straps holding her dress closed. "The last thing you want to do is listen to my cousin rave about how awesome I am. He's fiercely devoted to family and likes to brag. A few minutes of listening to him expound on my many virtues and you'd probably never want to talk to me again."

"You have enough virtues to fill a few minutes?"

"I have enough virtues to fill a few hours."

"I'll bet you do," Darby said in her sexiest tone. As she'd hoped, it was enough to get Nic to focus on her body instead of whatever was still dragging him down.

"Gorgeous," he murmured, looking down at her in a way that made Darby's insides melt into needy little puddles of desire.

"Fascinating," she agreed, staring right back. And he was. Moonlight glinted off the sharp angle of his cheekbones, leaving his eyes cloaked in mystery. Her fingers smoothed over the hard breadth of his chest—

she appreciated the rigid muscles even through the cotton of his shirt.

"Want to sit and watch the moon?"

"Is that code for something else?" she teased.

"What would I know about code?" he asked with a weird laugh. But as he pulled away, Darby noticed that whatever had stressed him out earlier was back.

And just like before, he was ignoring it.

"This could be your spot," he pointed out as he flicked the blanket with a sharp snap to lay it flat on the sand.

"My spot?"

"Private beach with an unobstructed view of the ocean. Remote enough to be romantic, accessible enough for tourists to find if they have a map." Dominic gave the view a considering look before nodding. "Yep, this could be your fabled B and B."

"The one where we raise our brood of home-schooled kids?"

"All eight of them."

"I have no idea why that keeps coming up," Darby laughed, a little embarrassed that she couldn't shake the image.

"No lifelong dream of being a mom to a huge brood?"

"No lifelong dream to be a mom," she admitted, watching his expression in the moonlight. There were worse confessions she could make, but this was one that often bit her in the ass. "I'm not the mom type. At least, not the good-mom type."

"I guess that blows our plan for eight kids, then."

That was it? No argument that every woman

should want to be a mom? No lecture on the joyful parenting being the natural purpose of womanhood?

"So what do you think is the good-mom type?" he asked as he pulled her onto the blanket.

Her mom.

At least, Danny had always said so.

Maybe because he'd been the good kid. The one who did everything right. Something Darby never managed, not even now. Nine years after his death.

No big deal, she reminded herself as she shoved down the pain and curled up on the blanket, the soft sand shifting and settling beneath the thin cotton to cup her seat. Not letting herself look at Dominic now, she breathed in the moist air, hoping the faint saltiness she tasted was ocean spray and not tears.

"There all types of good moms," she finally answered, pulling out her best attorney-in-crisis voice. Clear, concise and clipped, the words were factual without a hint of emotion. "But good moms are consistently devoted. Dedicated. Committed to doing anything and everything to be there for their child."

"Child? Not children?"

Why was he so damn perceptive?

"Why don't you think you could do all that?" he asked after a few long moments of silence.

"I suppose because I didn't have it," she confessed. Even as part of her gave a horrified gasp, Darby couldn't stop herself from elaborating. "I had a brother. He was the world to my mom. Smart, athletic, responsible. He was her favorite. Firstborn, boy, all that."

"Did that bother you?"

"Not really. I mean, he was pretty great. And it's

not like I was ignored or treated badly. But there was a clear favorite in our house and I always knew I wasn't it."

Alive or dead, her mother had never had enough room in her heart for both of her children. Her love for her firstborn was too encompassing. Darby liked to think that if her father had lived, they'd have had a good relationship. Not the love and devotion Laura had showered on Danny. Darby knew her father's career would have always come first. But she liked to tell herself that he'd at least have been proud of her. That because she'd followed in his career footsteps, they'd have had plenty of common ground to build on.

"What happened?" At her look, he shrugged. "You said you had a brother. Past tense."

"He died in, well, I suppose it was an accident," she said, not able to put the horrible, wrenching agony of Danny's death into words. "Losing him, it broke my mother's heart."

"Death is hardest on those left behind," Dominic murmured, his hand rubbing soothing circles over her back. "Each stage of grief is its own circle of hell."

Darby let her head fall back, her gaze blurred by hot tears as she stared into the star-strewn sky.

"It's easy to get stuck in those circles," she said, thinking of her mother.

"Anger, denial, they're sticky," he mused quietly, staring out at the black waves. "Blame is easier, I suppose. At least with blame, there's a focus. A drive to right a wrong."

Was there?

Her mother blamed the Navy. She blamed Danny's commanding officers, his fellow sailors and even the existence of the SEALs because Danny had wanted to join that elite group.

As far as Darby could tell, none of that blame had done her mother any good. Grief had destroyed her family and she'd vowed to stay away from all of those stages as much as possible.

Like the pain of losing her father to a heart attack, Darby locked her grief for her brother away deep in her heart, hiding it there in hopes of dulling the pain.

She'd never talked to anyone about it. But there was something about Dominic that made it easy. Natural. Maybe it was because he seemed to understand so well.

"Have you ever lost anyone? Not to age or disease, I mean, but to life?"

She watched his face, seeing the pain chase itself over his features before his expression cleared to a look of easy sympathy.

"Yeah. I have. It's rough."

It was only because she was leaning against him that Darby knew he let out a deep, shaky breath with those words. In the moon's soft light she could see his gaze locked on the ocean, but she wondered what he really saw out there.

"Your brother was killed on the job. Did he like what he did? His career? Was he good at it?"

Being a SEAL, that's all Danny had ever wanted. He'd plastered his preteen walls with posters of frogmen, had played sailor when the other kids played cops. He'd wanted it so much—and that ambition had been enough to overcome his disadvantages.

He'd learned to compensate for being smaller than most of the rest of the guys. He'd found ways around his shortcomings, hiding some, overcoming others. It'd taken three attempts but he'd finally graduated BUD/S SEAL training.

And one attempt at extreme diving, at believing he was a strong enough swimmer to make up for letting his air tanks run low, had gotten him killed.

"He was as good as he could be," she finally admitted. "And he was doing what he loved. He'd finally reached what he called the top of Mount Hell Yeah. At least he had that."

"It's the lucky ones who find their calling in life. Who find that something that sparks fire within them, calls to them to excel, to do their best," he said, his words all the more comforting for their matter-of-fact tone. "It sounds as if he found his. You could take comfort in that."

She could.

She knew she should.

But Darby was seriously lousy at comfort.

"I know there really isn't any way that I could have stopped it from happening. There's no way I could have saved my brother from dying. But still, I have to wonder." Darby bit her lip, then, impatient with her unusual hesitance, blurted out, "You said you knew what it was like to lose someone. Do you ever ask yourself if there's anything you could have done? If there was something you could have said? Like, if you'd just paid more attention you could have stopped it?"

For a long moment there was only the sound of the wind rustling through the palms and the ocean's muted roar. Darby wondered if she'd gone too far, poked at a pain too raw. Then she felt his sigh.

"Yeah. Except I know I could have stopped it. I know exactly what I could have said to keep my friend alive. I know precisely where my attention should have been."

When he finally looked at her, Darby wished he'd kept his gaze on the water. Because the pain drenching those midnight eyes was vicious in its intensity. Misery and blame, they went so deep she wondered how he didn't drown from the agony.

Wow, she thought as she let out a shaky breath.

She'd sure districted him from all that talk of kids and life and happy-ever-after.

Now, instead of romance and laughter, she'd filled the man with pain and regret.

She really did suck at this relationship thing.

Nic wondered at the emotions playing over Darby's face. He understood the flash of sadness given the topic, but the frustration and anger? What did she have going on in there that'd caused those?

Her brother? Nic frowned. What had she called her brother's career pinnacle? Mount Hell Yeah.

A term a lot of squids used when they reached the peak and earned their trident as a SEAL.

He wanted to ask.

But he didn't.

They'd agreed. No questions about their real lives off this island. No discussion, direct or oblique, of their respective careers.

And as odd as it was for a man who lived and

breathed his career, these last five days had been pretty sweet. No tactics, no training, no strategy.

Just enjoyment.

One of the first tenets of being a SEAL was silence. A good SEAL was smoke, whisking through cracks, seeping into the night, never seen, never heard. Never taking credit.

And he believed that. He lived it.

And that, he knew, was part of the reason behind his almost mythic reputation. A reputation he simply let speak for itself. He didn't seek acclaim, he didn't chase prestige.

But Nic was damn proud of what he did. Of what he'd built. And especially of the team he led.

Damn proud.

But just now, when his emotions were raw and the memories too vivid for comfort?

Just now, he was glad he and Darby had agreed to keep their careers confidential.

Just now, he wasn't proud of who he was. Wasn't satisfied with what he'd done.

"Are you okay?"

Put it away, he told himself, a little surprised that he even had to think about it twice. He'd lived most of his life in a classified bubble of silence. He was used to that. He was comfortable with it.

So why did he want to share with Darby?

Before he could find the answer, before he could think through the multiple ways that silence was golden, he did the unthinkable.

He opened his heart.

And, somehow, his mouth opened right along with it.

"No. I'm not okay. The loss, my friend's death, it's still pretty raw. But unlike you, I know I was responsible."

He'd commanded the mission that'd resulted in Powers's death. The man had been his teammate. His responsibility. His friend. And because Nic had misjudged the severity of the operation, had underestimated their enemy, Powers was dead.

"Responsible, like a work thing?" Darby asked quietly.

"Work is my life," Nic said with a sad attempt at a smile. He didn't know if her wide-eyed stare was because of his sappy saying or because the smile failed on all levels, so he dropped it and said, instead, "Yeah. You could say it was work-related. You could say I was his boss."

"That doesn't make you responsible."

"All jobs have a chain of command, a step-by-step process in place to ensure the precise implementation of any assignment," he explained. "In what I'd thought was the best interest of the, um, assignment, I sidestepped a couple of those chains, circumvented a few steps. That makes me responsible. I was in charge, it was my choice."

As the words swirled in the night air, Nic snapped his mouth shut, even as his mind screamed *What the fuck?* It didn't matter that they knew nothing about each other's jobs, had no plans to connect in the future. He never talked about mission details, choices or policies. Not even obliquely.

"Do you have a boss?" Darby asked when the silence grew painful.

Thinking of that chain of command and the many, many ranking officers over him, Nic snorted.

"A number of them."

"Were you held responsible by your higher-ups? Did your boss deem your performance unacceptable?"

"Let's just say that while what I did wasn't determined as out of line, my decision still cost a life." And that was something he'd have to live with for the rest of his.

While Darby sat next to him, shifting sand from hand to hand, Nic brooded.

"So your bosses, who probably know their job, decided you weren't to blame. And your friend?" she finally asked after a long moment. Even as she asked, she brushed the sand from her hands in a clear message to ditch the self-pity. "Did he like his job? Was he good at it?"

"Nice job tossing my words back at me." This time the smile came easier.

"How about tossing an answer back to me?" she suggested, shifting closer. Her hand skimmed, as gentle as air, over his leg.

Soothing.

Comforting.

God, he wanted to close his eyes and lose himself in the solace of her touch.

"Yeah," he finally admitted when she shot him an arch look. Nic almost smiled at that look. Who knew being both pushy and sympathetic could go hand and hand? Or that it could be so sexy.

"He was damn good at his job. One of the best. He

was so damn devoted to excelling that he used to joke about getting the word tattooed just to mess with us."

"You have a moral objection to tattoos?"

Morals had nothing to do with it. Identifying marks of any kind weren't smart when a man operated in enemy territory. Nic had made it clear that his men, his team, were branded by the duty they carried, the excellence they served. Any physical markings would be superfluous.

"Ahh, so it's where he wanted it that was an issue?" Her tone shifted to teasing. So did her hands, now that her fingers had climbed a little higher on his thigh.

He liked the way she lightened the mood.

"Deciding the where is what kept him from getting it. No clue why he didn't like our suggestion."

"You told him to put it where the sun wouldn't shine?"

"That's what friends are for. Ribbing, razzing and raising hell." Leaning back on his hands, he stretched his legs out in the sand and grinned at the memory of Mason's usual response. "He always gave as good as he got. Always."

Until he hadn't.

Nic's smile faded, his mind flashing to the image of Mason Powers, Chief Warrant Officer, Poseidon member and one of his best fucking friends, lying dead on the ground.

In his fourteen years in the Navy, Nic had seen death. Caused it. Escaped it.

But even now, three months later, he had trouble accepting that image as real. Maybe because instead of a uniform or the battle gear, Powers had bought it in a Denver Broncos T-shirt and jeans, his dog tags the only nod to the duty he served so honorably.

The duty Nic had assigned him.

The one that'd netted him a bullet to the brain.

"We should head back," Nic said as he started to push himself to his feet. Darby grabbed his arm before he could. He wanted to pull away. From her, from the topic, from his memories. But manners, honed by years of his mother's nagging and the Navy's protocols, had him staying seated.

"Your friend, you knew him pretty well, right?"

Ten years they'd served as SEALs together. Eleven if you added BUD/S. They'd served together, fought together, trained together.

They'd been more than teammates.

They'd been brothers.

"Yeah. I knew him damn well."

"What do you think he'd say if he was here now? If that whole life-after-death thing was real and he could drop down here on the sand and have one last chat with you?" She wrapped her arms around her knees and gave Nic an intense look, one that demanded that he take her seriously. "Would he be pissed? Upset? Would he blame you?"

That tore a reluctant laugh from him.

Powers? Blame anyone?

"No. This is a guy who was almost as cocky as he was decisive. He used to joke that whether things went right or things went wrong, he deserved all the credit." His eyes focused on the foaming waves as they danced over the sand, and Nic shook his head. "But it isn't a question of blame. It's a question of responsibility. And that's mine."

They both lapsed into silence. Nic took comfort from that, appreciating the way Darby simply let him be with his thoughts. Even as he lost himself in them, he was still aware of her next to him, warm and comforting.

"We should go back," she finally said, her soft words almost lost on the whisk of the wind.

Nic knew she was right.

This wasn't playful or fun.

There was no romance, no vacation sass going on here. This was pure sorrow for both of them. Not much of a prelude to seduction.

But he didn't want to go back.

One of the basic requirements to thriving in a military career was self-sufficiency.

But right now? Right now he needed more.

He'd needed to lose himself in her. To escape his own thoughts, to hide from the memories.

He needed Darby.

His hands tunneled through her hair, gripping the delicate curve of her scalp and tilting her head toward his. He took her mouth in a kiss hot enough, desperate enough, to catch fire.

"Dominic—"

"Now," he murmured, grabbing both of her hands in his to yank her arms overhead. He pinned her there, arms high, back arched. And, oh, yeah, baby, chest high. Nic leaned down to nuzzle her full breasts, his teeth nipping through the fabric.

Darby gasped and wrapped one leg around his hips, grinding against his burgeoning erection.

More. Nic wanted—no, he needed—more.

He stripped them both in record time, hands and

mouth never leaving hers as he delighted in her silken flesh laid out in the moonlight. Her golden eyes were a sultry invitation as Nic positioned himself between her legs.

He shifted her hips higher, grabbing her legs and draping them over his shoulders so he could lose himself in her welcoming heat. He plunged hard and drove deep.

Darby's gasps filled the air, her pants as enticing as the sound of the ocean beyond. She arched, her fingers digging into the blanket as an orgasm ripped through her.

The feel of it clenching him tight, the sight of her body trembling with pleasure, sent him over the edge.

The world exploded.

He heard it detonate over the ocean's gentle symphony.

He collapsed against her, dimly grateful to feel her hands soothing gentle circles over the small of his back instead of slapping him away.

He wasn't sure how long he lay there, his body drawing comfort from hers.

He knew it was too long, though, when he had to force himself to move away instead of wrapping himself around her and holding tight.

But as soon as they shifted away from each other, he wanted to grab her back. To hold her again. He wanted to wrap himself around her and never let go.

Insane.

Nic rubbed his hands over his face, reminding himself that he'd long ago vowed that until he made Captain, his career was his one and only priority. There was no room for wanting to hold on to a woman forever.

But when he glanced at Darby, watching as she pulled that silky bit of a dress over her head, he knew forever with her was damn tempting.

Too damn tempting.

What the fuck was wrong with him?

CHAPTER SEVEN

As USUAL, NIC woke with the sun.

What wasn't usual was not jumping right out of bed, pushing his body to its limits, then reporting for duty. Maybe it was the sexy woman wrapped around him like seaweed. Or rather, the fact that he didn't want to slide out of her arms and get on with his life.

Which was reason enough to go, he realized. He was in no position to care about a woman. His emotions were raw at the loss of his friend. His career—his sole purpose for over a dozen years—was a mess. Turmoil might be good for overtaking a country, but it was a lousy time to start thinking about a relationship.

Muffling his sigh of regret, he slowly peeled his body away from the addicting warmth of Darby and slid from the bed. He gave himself a moment to appreciate the tempting display of golden skin. His fingers itched to slide over that silky flesh. To warm himself one more time.

Instead, he pulled up the sheet and tucked it around her to keep the morning chill away.

Used to dressing fast, it only took him about a minute to be ready to walk out the door. But he still hesitated.

He watched Darby breathe, then—despite feeling

like an idiot but unable to resist—he leaned down to brush a whisper-soft kiss over her cheek.

Damn, he was getting sappy.

But he didn't care.

She made him feel good.

But more, she gave him a feeling of peace. Something that, in all his years of fighting for peace, he'd rarely felt within himself.

Something to think about, he decided, looking back one last time before slipping out of the room.

After a sweaty trip to the gym, an invigorating ocean swim and a quick shower, Nic made his way down to breakfast. As soon as he stepped onto the lanai, he saw his uncle at the far table with his coffee and his tablet. So far he'd managed to avoid the prolonged one-on-one with its inevitable life lecture, but family was family.

So he strode across the porch to do his duty.

"Uncle Michael," Nic greeted when he reached the older man. "Can I join you?"

"I was hoping you would." His Panama hat low on his brow to shield his eyes from the morning sun, Michael set aside the tablet, with its morning news story, and gestured to the empty seat next to him. "Are you alone, Dominic? Where is your lovely companion?"

"Sleeping, then shopping." Dominic gave his uncle a grin as he slid into the chair and snagged one of the muffins from the basket. "Not that the resort doesn't have great stores, but if you don't want people spending their money somewhere else, you shouldn't provide a bus tour to all the best local shops."

"More variety makes our guests happy," Michael said, shrugging off the possible loss of sales. "And you, my nephew, look like a happy guest. This has been a good visit, yes?"

"Yes." Nic left it at that. He knew perfectly well that Michael was making regular reports to his mother. There was no point giving his uncle any reason to get the woman's hopes up.

"She's a lovely woman," Michael said, rich scent wrapping around them as he poured Nic coffee. "Not your usual type."

"I have a usual type?"

"Beautiful, interesting career women who are not interested in more than the here and now."

"Huh." Nic nodded his thanks to the waiter who set the family-style platter of eggs, pancakes, bacon and ham on the table. "If that's my type, then it sounds like Darby fits."

"No, no. She's more." Michael waited until they'd filled their plates, poured sugarcane syrup over their stacks of pancakes and had a few bites before he pointed his fork at his nephew. "She intrigues you."

Hell, yeah. She was sexy, clever and damn creative in bed.

"She's an intriguing woman," he agreed, forking up another stack of pancakes.

"This is good. You're reaching an age that you need more balance in your life."

Nic paused in the act of eating his second piece of bacon to arch a brow. "I've got great balance."

"No. If you're not careful now, you'll tip too far to one side. Your world will become one-dimensional. You are so committed to duty that you don't allow anyone into your life that will distract. Even family is kept at a safe distance." Michael lifted one hand before Nic could say anything. "Yes, yes, you put that wall around the family for our own good. And more importantly, for yours."

"I'm not one of those guys who thinks a SEAL can't handle a relationship," Nic protested. "Two of my guys are married, another is hitting the aisle in the next couple of months. If a guy has a handle on his career and falls hard for the right woman, I think he should give it his all."

"Ahh, but what defines the right woman?"

"First, she has to hook a guy—body, mind and soul." Nic mulled over his words as he drank the coffee. "Second, she has to understand what it means to be involved with someone on active duty in the military. And third, she'd have to accept that being involved with a SEAL multiplies the risks, the stresses and the demands."

"So you believe all the understanding and compromise are on the lady's side?"

"Of course not. It requires equal work and commitment from both sides." Nic refilled his cup, gestured with the pot before setting it back on the warmer at his uncle's refusal. "But it takes an amazing woman to handle a relationship with a SEAL."

"Which invites the question, do you consider Darby to be an amazing woman?"

"Uhh." Speechless in the face of his uncle's grin, Nic could only shake his head as his breakfast turned to lead in his stomach at that question.

Thankfully, his phone buzzed, saving him from having to answer a question he wasn't ready to consider.

"Speaking of Navy business." Nic dug his phone

out of his pocket and lifted it in apology as he got to his feet. "Excuse me."

He waited until he'd reached the water's edge before answering.

"Savino."

"Louden here. How's Hawaii? Having fun? Enough small talk. You need to return to base."

No longer enchanted by the ocean's dance, Nic's easy mood evaporated like the sun hiding behind a cloud. Any thoughts he'd had about something—someone—taking precedence over his career disappeared as all his senses came to attention.

"Report," he ordered his second-in-command. Lieutenant Commander Ty Louden was known as a hard-ass, a man with a special instinct for men and situations that was legendary among his team. If he said Nic needed to return to base, he had a damn good reason.

"Things are heating up and it's all going to blow to hell if you're not here to contain it."

"New intel?" With three men digging further into Ramsey's past and Lansky on tech, he'd been expecting a breakthrough. But not one that'd get Louden twisted with concern.

"Not yet. We're gathering a lot of details, but no solid breaks. Lansky's close. You know how he gets. He's muttering and swigging Mountain Dew like it's water. Guy's gonna glow in the dark soon, but he hasn't broken through all the firewalls yet."

Nic allowed himself a single second to feel the surge of impatience and frustration, then he set it aside.

"And look, I know Jarrett said it was no big, but

that's bullshit. No way a three-hour meeting with Naval Criminal Investigation doesn't carry weight. He was sweating, too. Guy is like a minnow when it comes to any sort of confrontation."

It was common knowledge that Louden didn't think much of Jarrett. But Nic knew the man's personal opinion never factored into performing his duty. Just as he knew Jarrett's inability to live up to the SEAL's high standard didn't make him a bad officer. Still, the disgust in Louden's voice needed to be curbed before it got out of hand.

"On Cree's orders, Jarrett is building the case against Ramsey. He'd likely meet with NCI to do so."

"He was sweating when the NCI weasel left his office. He was still sweating when he ordered me to give him every piece of intel we've gathered so far. Every piece, verified or not."

"Procedure—"

"Our investigation is unofficial, sir," Louden reminded him. "You requested that our men be assigned to the official investigation but Jarrett claimed we'd hurt the case. Some stupid crap about tainting evidence or something."

His eyes on the waves, Nic watched each one pour over the other in a froth of white until the fury at that reminder faded. He'd understood his men's insult at the time, he understood it now. But he understood Jarrett's point, too. It wasn't just Poseidon's reputation at stake. It was the team itself. If they weren't cleared, they'd be ordered to disband. Instead of all serving together on SEAL Team Seven, they'd be scattered. Instead of being the elite, they'd be outcasts.

"Stall," Nic ordered. "I'll deal with Jarrett's request when I get back."

"Thanks," Louden muttered, dropping his military tone for one of frustrated gratitude. "This is crap, Nic. We're clear. Ramsey tried to pin his crimes on Torres, we cleared him. He tried to lure in Prescott, we nailed his ass and threw him in the brig. Why the hell is Poseidon being targeted, and what's it going to take to clear our names for good?"

Excellent question. Since he was technically on vacation, Nic gave in to the need to pace along the sand—something he'd never do in front of his men.

"We pin down the mastermind, find whoever is behind this treason ring, and we'll take down the entire operation. We do that, our names are clear. Until then, we're under fire."

"Lansky says he's close. As soon as Prescott is back in the country, I'll put him on tech, too. He's not as fast as Lansky, but he's better at deciphering code."

"Do that. I'll make some calls, light some fires. I'm back in three days. We'll begin preparation for Operation: Enlightenment. It's time we showed these fuckers what happens when they mess with Poseidon."

"Yes, sir," Louden snapped with barely concealed triumph. "We'll be ready."

"Everyone," Nic instructed. "Pull the entire team together. My office, oh-eight-hundred, Sunday morning."

Nic disconnected without waiting for a response. He gave himself a moment to stare out at the ocean, letting the view of the water's dance wash away the disappointment in his gut.

It wasn't that he'd actually considered extending his leave to spend more time with Darby. But by choosing to meet his men the day before he was due to report for duty, he was ending their time together a day early. And damn if that didn't leave a tight ball of regret in his gut.

He should be happy to say goodbye. After all, baring his guts to someone like he had to Darby last night wasn't his usual MO. He didn't like sharing emotions. Hell, he barely liked having them, since more often than not they just got in the way.

But last night was different. Talking with Darby had purged him of a poison he hadn't realized was festering in his heart. It hadn't been necessary to divulge confidential details, or even dance around them. He'd felt just as comfortable talking with Darby as he would any man on his team.

Which meant he trusted her.

So, no. He wasn't ready to say goodbye yet. He passed his cell phone from hand to hand and considered the situation. Perhaps it was time to renegotiate their deal.

Debating the various arguments he could use to convince Darby to continue to see him after vacation was over, Nic turned back toward the hotel.

He hadn't slipped his phone into his pocket before it buzzed again.

"Savino."

"Commander, report for duty."

"Sir?" Subconsciously coming to attention, Nic did an about-face toward the ocean. "Could you repeat that order."

"You were part of the joint operation planning

of Operation: Barracuda. You liaised with Captain Shamon of the Egyptian Navy. You and your men will implement Operation: Barracuda in two days," Admiral Cree barked through the line. "As of this minute, you're back on duty. Report to PMRF base within the hour to meet your flight back to Coronado."

An hour gave him just enough time to grab his gear if he was going to catch that plane. But he wanted to renegotiate with Darby. Or at the very least, tell her goodbye. He needed more time with her. Wanted to see where this could go.

Jaw clenched against the rage of disappointment surging through him, Nic did the only thing possible.

"Yes, sir. I'll be in your office with the operation plans and my team recommendations by eighteen hundred hours."

"Cree, out."

Damn.

Looked like vacation—and everything that went with it—was over.

WELL, HELL. SHE was going to break her vow.

Worse, she was going to be a total girl, and break it for emotional reasons. Was that better or worse than breaking it for unemotional ones?

It didn't matter, she decided as she dabbed perfume on her pulse points. Whatever the reason, she'd spent half the day arguing with herself. When not one of those arguments had panned out, she'd decided to go for it.

She was going to ask Dominic if he'd be interested in a relationship. An actual relationship. She gave a giddy laugh.

Her fingers itched to grab the phone, but she ignored them. A part of her wanted to call Grace, to run her plan past the other woman so she could point out how crazy it was to try to turn a vacation fling into something more. But what if Grace made excellent points? Ones smart enough to derail Darby's crazy intentions? Then she'd have to accept that all she had left were two more nights with Dominic.

Or worse, what if Grace thought it was a great idea?

Knowing herself, Darby figured as soon as the other woman praised the idea, she'd find a million excuses and get her ass on the first plane back to California.

Better to go it alone, she decided.

Alone, but fully loaded.

Darby checked her reflection in the sitting room's full-length mirror.

Step one in her brilliant plan. Blow his mind with a visual reminder of why they should toss that no-last-name vow out the window.

She skimmed her palms up her hips and gave a saucy nod. Yeah. She had the visual down pat. The blue bodycon dress hugged her curves, showing plenty of skin dusted a glimmering gold. Narrow straps plunged in a deep V, the skirt hit midthigh, leaving her legs bare all the way to her sassy four-inch blue satin Manolo lace-up sandals with their tiny black pom-pom trim. Her hair spiked around her face in an edgy fringe that accented the smoky color on her eyes and the slick gloss on her lips.

If a hot-oil body massage, a mani-pedi and her sexy new dress didn't wow the pants off him, she didn't know what would.

Fighting off nerves, she dug into the bags she'd tossed on the chair to search for the bag she'd bought to go with her new sandals. The minuscule black patent-leather envelope purse sported the same pom-pom fringe as her shoes. Darby tossed the few necessities that would fit inside, then flicked one pom-pom with her finger and smiled. She wasn't usually the pom-pom type, but like reneging on her vow, she was willing to give it a try.

She checked the clock to see how much time she had before their six-o'clock reservations and noted the message light blinking on her phone.

She frowned, wondering who'd call her here.

Nic would have come by. Grace would call her cell.

That left her mother.

She cringed, wondering how her mother had found out where she was staying. Nope, not checking, not calling. Tonight was for fun.

Before she could give in to the automatic guilt, she grabbed her bag and hurried out the door.

She knew she'd feel better when she was with Dominic.

She hadn't seen him since the night before.

They'd made love on the beach—and yes, even her own mind faltered at the term *love*, but she knew there was no better description for what'd gone down in that sandy moonlight.

He'd walked her back to her room in silence, a trek she still wasn't sure she could have done on her own given that her knees had been the consistency of Jell-O.

Which was probably why he'd had to prop her body between his and the door when they'd done it again. Everything was a little hazy after that, although she had the vague memory of sighing when he'd carried her to bed.

But as hot as the memories of their night was, she'd woken up alone.

She'd spent the day the same way.

On purpose, she admitted as she wandered down the wide marble stairs toward the lobby. She'd decided that they needed some distance. Or rather, that she needed a break.

A little time away from him to gauge her feelings, to step away from the crazy and figure out if she'd fallen into a sexual haze, or if all of the unfamiliar emotions surging through her system meant that she was truly starting to care about the man.

After six hours of shopping, she was seven hundred dollars poorer and no more sure of her feelings than she'd been when she'd woken.

Darby took a deep breath and stepped into the foyer of the restaurant. She breathed in the heady scent of a floral arrangement almost as tall as her and pressed one hand to her jumping stomach.

So here she was, not only unsure of Dominic's feelings, but also clueless about her own. And she was going to go for it anyway.

With that in mind, she lifted her chin and let her smile widen as she sauntered toward the podium.

"Ms. Raye." The maître d' greeted her with a

warm smile. "Please, let me get you a seat at our finest table."

"It does pay to have connections," Darby said with a laugh, placing her hand in his beefier one and letting the older man lead her through the diners to a secluded corner of the balcony.

The table for two was set with a fat white flickering candle under a hurricane glass and a squat vase overflowing with rich purple flowers. Instead of chairs sitting opposite each other, there was a cozy love seat nestled behind the table, facing the view of the water. Twinkling lights wove in and out of vines dripping from overhead, the greenery heavy with lush white blossoms.

Romance.

The setting was screaming it just as loud as the voice in Darby's head.

"What a beautiful spot," she said instead.

"Indeed. Only the best for you." He kept up a stream of light, friendly chatter as Darby took her seat. "Is this your last night with us?"

"Day after tomorrow," Darby confirmed, trying to ignore the pang in her chest at the reminder that this might be the end of things with Dominic. She draped the linen napkin over her lap and looked toward the string trio, their elegant pewter suits accented with white leis.

Oh, yeah. Romance.

She exchanged a few more pleasantries with the older man and after he promised to return quickly with her wine, settled back to enjoy the ambiance. And glance at her watch.

She was early. She'd deliberately come down early

so she'd have to sit quietly instead of pacing her hotel room while she obsessed over various ways to convince Dominic that it was a good idea to keep seeing each other.

"Your wine, Ms. Raye."

"Thank—" Her words trailed off when she looked at the man setting her glass on the table. Not the maître d'. Not a waiter. He was a good-looking man, young and oddly familiar. It only took her a second to realize he was Dominic's cousin, the one with the band.

"I'm Luc," he said with a wide smile reminiscent of his cousin's. "You're Darby, right? Mind if I join you?"

"Please." She gestured to the empty chair. "I've heard you play. You're great."

They exchanged chitchat for another minute or so, proving to Darby that, yes, every man in Dominic's family seemed to have the same friendly charm.

"It's easy to see why Nic hasn't been around much on this visit," Luc said, leaning forward to rest his elbows on the table and give her an affable smile. "And why he seems so happy every time I've talked to him."

"You call Dominic 'Nic'?"

Darby smiled into her wineglass at the nickname. She liked it. It had a strength, a power that fit the man. Except when they were naked. Then the more romantic Dominic fit him perfectly.

"Yeah, Nic. Only my father calls him Dominic. Well, my father and Nic's dad's side of the family. The Savinos are almost as stubborn as Pop when it comes to their idea of tradition." Luc laughed. "It's probably more protocol than tradition on the Savino side, though. All that Navy training, you know."

Afraid she'd drop it otherwise, Darby carefully set her glass on the table.

Navy training?

Dominic—Nic—was in the Navy?

Like Danny had been?

Darby's mind raced almost as fast as her stomach spun.

"I didn't realize Nic came from a Navy family," she said through tight lips.

"Oh, yeah. He's something like fourth generation," Luc said with an enthusiastic nod. "He's the first SEAL, though. Pretty amazing one, too. He's like the elite of the elite, you know? And the way he founded that exclusive group within the SEALs, that is so cool. When we were kids he was fascinated with Greek mythology. I suppose that's why he named it Poseidon, huh?"

Somewhere in the back of Darby's stunned mind, that name rang a bell. But her thoughts were racing too fast for her to listen to it.

She could almost hear her mother's screams of betrayal. She could almost see her brother shaking his head in disappointment, hurt in his golden eyes so like her own.

Loyalty.

Her family had never been big on love and they'd rarely shown affection. But loyalty? Loyalty was mandatory in the Raye house. And now Darby had betrayed that.

She gulped down what was left of her wine.

Dominic was Nic.

And Nic was a Navy SEAL.

As much as she might resent her mother's obsessive hatred of all things Navy and more, Navy SEALs, she'd never deny that Laura had good reason for her feelings. As much as she'd buried her own grief, tried to ignore her fury over her brother's death, a part of her shared her mother's feelings.

Now, even as clichéd and overdramatic as it sounded in her own head, Darby felt like she'd slept with the enemy.

Slept with him over and over and over.

Slept with him, fell for him, imagined a future with him.

She wanted to blame Dominic. But she knew better. It was all her fault.

She'd insisted they play this fantasy game, keep their lives and careers secret. And look at that whole sexy mystery angle biting her in the butt. Nausea churned in Darby's belly.

"Excuse me," she said, interrupting whatever Luc was saying. She pushed to her feet, and gave him a blind smile. "I'm not feeling well."

She didn't wait to hear what he said and could only be grateful that he didn't try to stop her as she hurried from the restaurant. Darby wove through the crowd, muttering apologizes when she bumped into people but not slowing. She took the stairs instead of the elevator because she was afraid she'd scream the minute she stood still.

As soon as she reached her room, she did just that.

She threw her purse on the bed, clenched her fists at her sides and, head thrown back, screamed her lungs out.

But it didn't make her feel any better.

Dominic was Nic.

Lieutenant Commander Nic Savino, Navy SEAL.

A goddamn SEAL.

Didn't it just figure.

Struggling not to curse, Darby shoved both hands through her hair. When that didn't help, she gave it a good tug.

She'd slept with a Navy SEAL. Slept... Hell, she'd had all sorts of indescribably wild, intense, mind-blowing sex with the man. Multiple times.

She'd come the closest she'd ever been to falling in... Something. Not love, she assured herself. Infatuation. She'd fallen into infatuation.

With a man who, through no fault of his own, epitomized misery and pain.

What did that make her?

How often had she listed to Danny sing worshipful praise of the almighty Navy SEALs?

But Danny was dead.

Tears burned her eyes, rolled down her cheeks. Darby threw herself on the bed to bury her face in a pillow. Finally, out of breath but no less miserable, she rolled to her back and stared at the ceiling.

As she saw it, she had two choices.

First, and easiest, was to make her excuses, call a cab and head straight for the airport before she had to see him again.

Second, she could face him like the grown woman she was and tell him they were through.

As much as she liked her reputation as a hard-ass, Darby knew she was taking option one.

And she was taking it right now. She shoved herself into a sitting position and grabbed the phone to call for a car. This time she couldn't ignore the blinking light, though. She pressed the message button. Her stomach dropped into her feet as she listened to Dominic's voice on the recording.

"Darby, I'm sorry but I was called back to work. I'm sorry I couldn't wait until you returned, but time was of the essence. This week was amazing. I hate to see it end, especially like this. I know we had a deal, and I won't break it by asking my uncle for your contact information. But I'm offering you a new deal. Let's get to know each other. If you're interested, the front desk has my phone number. I hope you call."

Dominic was gone.

But he wanted to see her again.

Even as the tears ran down her cheeks, her brave, girlie plan from an hour ago mocked her.

It was better this way. Darby wiped her wet cheeks and sighed. He was gone, and that was for the best.

Now she could pretend that this week had never happened.

That she'd never met Dominic…or Nic, either. She hadn't betrayed anyone.

Not even herself.

CHAPTER EIGHT

"Lieutenant Savino, reporting as ordered."

"Welcome back, Lieutenant." The stern blonde tilted her head toward the closed door. "The Admiral is waiting for you."

Nic offered a quick nod and half smile on his way across the small office. The beige walls were bland, the beige linoleum spotless, the beige metal desk clear of everything but a telephone, a monitor and the Admiral's beige-clad admin. The only spot of color was the photo of the United States flag framed on the wall. He'd once wondered if the lack of color was a statement of seriousness on the Admiral's part, or if the guy simply had lousy taste in decorating.

Now, he simply used the bland backdrop as a reminder to take a breath, clear his head and prepare.

For anything.

When he stepped through the door, he noted that the Admiral might have been waiting, but he was using that waiting time on the phone. So Nic stood at parade rest, legs shoulder-distance apart, hands clasped behind his back and eyes staring straight ahead.

And waited for his mentor's orders.

A burly man, his personality as imposing as his size, Cree had seen something in Nic back when he'd been a new recruit, his ensign bar still shiny and fresh. Nic, a cocky and focused twenty-one-year-old, had thought he was quite something. The Admiral had shown him how to be better. He'd pushed, he'd guided, he'd demanded.

Nic figured he'd have made a good officer on his own, but would he have become one of the best? He'd have been a SEAL with or without Cree, but would he be Poseidon's leader? Would Poseidon even exist without Cree?

Doubtful.

Cree had made Nic the officer he was today.

He'd made him the man he was today.

The man was his mentor. His commander. And, although Nic would never admit it aloud, his hero.

But damn if this wasn't the first time he'd ever wished his commanding officer had picked someone else for an important mission while letting Nic finish out his leave.

As the force of the Admiral's voice reverberated off the office walls as he wound up his call, Nic focused on the matter at hand.

Duty.

"Savino," Cree intoned when he hung up the phone. "Take a seat."

"Sir." Nic pulled a wooden chair away from its companions along the wall and sat. As soon as his butt was down, the Admiral tossed a file folder across the desk. Typed in bold black letters were the words *Operation: Barracuda. Confidential.*

"You've called up your team?"

"I contacted them while in the air. They're on base and ready to deploy by oh-five-hundred."

Nic took the file, but left it closed. He didn't need it to refresh his memory as the Admiral updated him on the status of the mission.

"Upon arrival, you'll meet Captain Shamon and his team," Admiral Cree instructed, winding up his briefing. "Remember this is a joint operation. Which means I expect you to take the lead and hold control throughout. Any questions?"

"No, sir." Nic glanced down at the file to hide his grin. "Rest assured, we'll handle it."

"On to the other business, then." Cree leaned back in his chair in his version of "at ease," with his hands folded over his belly. "The continued fallout of Operation: Hammerhead. You've been informed of Lieutenant Ramsey's change of counsel?"

"Captain Jarrett brought me up-to-date."

"Did he update you on Naval Criminal Investigation's renewed interest in your team?"

"It was mentioned."

"Something tipped them off," Cree growled. "On my orders, you led Operation: Fuck Up to catch Ramsey. In doing so, you verified that the man wasn't working alone and, in my considered opinion, cleared Team Poseidon of any wrongdoing. After Powers's death I was informed the investigation would be closed."

"What changed?"

"That's the big question. The only answer I'm getting is that new information has come to light." Cree's face folded into angry lines. "In other words, I'm being stonewalled."

"Perhaps I'd better serve the team here instead of leading a routine mission, sir. It seems that this new information has the potential to be a time bomb. I should look in to it immediately."

Nic was proud of himself. He'd managed to make that suggestion as if he wasn't steaming with fury unlike anything he'd known before. What the hell was going on? They'd thought Ramsey had tried to frame Poseidon out of jealousy because he couldn't join, only to realize it was so much bigger. They kept shutting down this ridiculous witch hunt, and someone, somehow, kept lighting it right back up again.

"No. You're needed to lead Operation: Barracuda. You're the best man for the job, you have the strongest skills in diplomacy and to be honest, you need to get back in the field, Savino." Cree shook his head. "Damn if I don't wish I was your age. Still young enough to ride the thrill. You put together a damn good thing with Poseidon. Maybe not the way I'd have done it if it was mine, but you made it shine."

Nic frowned.

"Is this an indication that you have a problem with my performance, sir?"

"Don't be stupid, boy," Cree said, dropping protocol long enough to roll his eyes. "You're one of the best officers I've trained and a credit to your command. But if Poseidon is on the line, I think it's best that you proactively show the extent of the talents, skills and loyalty of *every* member of the team."

In other words, they were all on trial, and this mission, like any more that came their way between now and wherever this damn mess was cleared up, were tests. Tests of Nic's leadership, yes. And of the team's skills. But also of their moral fortitude, since every mission was likely to be carefully monitored for treasonous acts.

"I'll give Operation: Barracuda my full attention, sir," Nic vowed. "The mission is slated to last four days, in and out. We'll leave in the morning."

"When you get back, it's time to find a legal rep to advise you on this other situation." Cree said *situation* like it was a dirty word. "I'll have a list of names for you to consider."

Nic didn't want names to consider.

The entire concept of Poseidon was that they were self-sufficient. Between the twelve of them they'd covered medical, cryptography, EOD, linguistics and, dammit, legal.

Or they had. Before. Nic clenched his teeth and tried to focus through the stabbing grief.

"Although Powers covered our legal end before he was killed, Louden has training. While he doesn't practice, he has gone through Naval Justice School." Before Cree could point out how useless an unused law degree was to their situation, Nic added, "He has connections. He'll use them to gather advice in a purely hypothetical sense. If nothing else, he has sources to tap for ideas while we try to figure out what NI is looking at."

The hesitation was clear in Cree's face, but finally he nodded.

"Tap away, then. I want you and your team prepared. I'm scheduled to travel to Afghanistan next month to serve on the Special Operations Command. Communication will be difficult for a short time, so I'd prefer this was settled before I go."

As Nic processed that information, there was a knock on the door.

"Enter."

Cree and Nic glanced over as Captain Jarrett walked in. Nic automatically got to his feet, to greet the ranking officer.

"Captain," he said, giving Jarrett a nod as the man took his place at Cree's side. But even sitting, the Admiral dwarfed his second-in-command, both in size, and in the aura of power that he wore as comfortably as his uniform. The Admiral radiated strength like an implacable wall.

Jarrett, on the other hand, radiated calm. Amiable, organized and ambitious, the quiet man plowed through problems with the focus of a stealth missile. He'd worked his way up the ranks with the same steady determination in which he served his commanding officer.

"Savino," the Captain returned with a nod of his own. His expression was friendly enough, but there was enough worry in his eyes to put Nic on edge.

"Captain, I was just explaining to Savino his role in the pending operation. I also brought him up-to-date on the Ramsey situation," the Admiral said. Before he could continue to explain his take on said situation, Jarrett leaned forward to whisper in his ear.

The Admiral's face was like a rising pool of lava, reddening, heating and looking as if it'd be deadly when he exploded.

The older man sucked air through his teeth, then clamped his jaw as tight as the hands fisted on his desk. But that was the only show of emotion. In a blink, it was gone. His expression cleared, his eyes calmed and his hands flattened.

And that, Nic acknowledged, was yet another reason why he considered Cree a role model. The man kept his shit together.

"Very well," Cree said after clearing his throat. "Jarrett informs me that we have a new situation at hand."

Are you fucking kidding? Nic barely managed to keep the words behind his teeth. Instead, he growled, "Sir?"

"As I told you before, I called you back for two reasons. First, because I feel you're the best man to lead Operation: Barracuda," the Admiral said, his tone as sharp and direct as a one-two punch. "And second, to inform you that NCIS was investigating the possibility of bringing charges against yourself and members of your team."

Yeah. The new situation was going to suck. All he had to do was watch the other men's faces to know that for sure. Nic's own expression didn't change, but he did get to his feet and brace himself.

"According to the Captain, here, they've concluded their investigation and intend to bring those charges within the week."

Nic took the news the same way he'd take a fist to the face. With feet planted wide, shoulders back and chin high, he didn't flinch, didn't blink, didn't react.

But inside, fury seethed.

"My team?" he asked to clarify. "Poseidon?"

The Admiral inclined his head, but Jarrett, apparently thinking more intel was needed, hurried to explain.

"Naval Criminal Investigation is looking into the events that lead to the death of Warrant Officer Powers. In light of the circumstances surrounding Operation: Hammerhead, they consider his death in an unsanctioned mission after the fact to be a breach of protocol at best, treason at worst." Apology dripped from the words, but Nic ignored Jarrett's puppy-dog stare because he was looking at his commander.

Unsanctioned? Operation: Fuck Up had been led under the auspices of the Admiral, himself.

Cree hadn't filled in the Captain? Nic knew that most of what they did as SEALs was on a need-to-know basis, but didn't this qualify? His team's effing careers were on the line here.

There had to be a reason Cree hadn't said anything. And while Nic wasn't one to question his commanding officers, he damn well wanted to ask why.

But not in front of Jarrett.

It wasn't a matter of trust. It was a matter of training. Cree had done too good a job at pounding protocol into Nic's head. If he was going to ignore regulations, he'd do it in private.

Until then…

"Permission to withdraw, sir."

"Permission granted," Cree said with a dismissive wave of his hand. "Report to my office upon your return for debriefing and further instructions."

Ignoring Jarrett's protest, Nic gave a sharp nod of his head, turned on one heel and marched the hell out of that office.

The roaring in his head was so loud, it took him

until he was halfway down the hallway to hear his name being called.

"Savino. Nic, hold up," Jarrett called, hurrying down the hallway after him. "I want to talk with you for a minute."

Nic wanted to keep going. He needed to work off some of the aggression pounding through his system before he took a swing at the wrong person.

But a command was a command.

So, slapping one hand impatiently against his thigh, Nic paused.

"You should have waited. There was more to my report," the man said when he caught up. "We have a lot to go over."

"I have a mission to lead in six hours, a team to brief and equipment to check. That's priority. You can send me an updated report, or fill me in when I get back from the Middle East."

"This isn't something I can put in a report," Jarrett protested. Shoving a hand over his bottlebrush cap of hair, he looked up and down the hall, then jerked his head toward the nearest doorway. "Let's talk in here. At least we'll have a semblance of privacy."

He had the urge to give the other man a rundown of everything that had to be done before the launch of the pending mission. But it wouldn't matter. Not when Jarrett had that look in his eyes. Nic checked his impatience and followed the other man into the empty room.

"Look, I did what you asked. I told Ramsey's attorneys no deal. But instead of backing off, they pulled out new intel. Big intel." Despite the fact that they were alone in the small break room, Jarrett lowered his voice to a whisper. "They're not telling me what it is, but I got enough to know it's trouble."

"Look, I don't have time for this. As far as I'm concerned, until they present their new intel, it's still a bullshit conspiracy theory. So unless you have solid facts, I've got a job to do."

"My sources say NCIS has not only confirmed your theory that Ramsey wasn't pushing the buttons himself. That he, and Dane Adams, too, were simply tools. But that whoever is behind it has a strong network of traitors working with him. That whoever it is, is high enough up the military ladder to be able to run a ghost operation with stealth, skill and aplomb. Whoever is behind this, Nic, they're a high-ranking officer with enough clout and influence to dump this on someone else and walk away clean."

Was Jarrett saying what he thought he was? Nic blinked. It didn't sound like the man was trying to claim that someone in command—someone who outranked the both of them—was the mastermind behind this mess. It sounded like he was pointing the finger at Cree.

And if that didn't leave a sick taste in his mouth, nothing would.

"I'm not interested in gossip," Nic said, swallowing back the bile. "Like I said, you get me intel, I'll work with it. Until then, it's all a bunch of bullshit."

"Savino." Jarrett laid one hand on Nic's arm to stop him from leaving. "What are you going to do?"

What was he going to do?

Trying to ignore the sinking feeling of dread in his gut, Nic tried to sort through it all. But there were too many thoughts fighting in his head to make sense of it right now.

He wanted a little time, a little space to weigh this new information against what he already knew. To assess how it fit with what he'd always believed. And to figure out who he could trust.

But in the meantime, he had a job to do.

"I have my orders, Captain. As always, I'm going to follow them."

With that and a ghost of his usual polite nod, Nic strode out the door.

He had to find his men.

They had to figure this out.

Or if Jarrett was right, they were all going down.

Fluff.

As Darby sifted through the case she'd found waiting on her desk this morning, she tried not to sigh. She'd promised herself when she'd got off that flight from Hawaii that she'd put the entire emotional roller coaster of a trip behind her. That once she set foot on California soil, all of it was over. Dominic—or rather, Nic, damn him—the affair, stupid vacation thoughts about opening her world to something more than her career? They were history.

And so far, other than the three or four dozen reminders to remember that vow, she'd done pretty well with it.

She had her career. That's all she had, and all she wanted. Damn if anyone could say she didn't know her priorities. And right now, her priority was this case.

But, dammit, it was fluff.

A slam dunk.

An identity-theft case against a defendant using such clever names as Bugs Rabbit, W.E. Coyote and Sam Yosemite. And sure, there were hints of money laundering that, once she tied them together would bring down the questionably infamous Sylvester's Cat House. But in hard-hitting legal terms?

It was still fluff.

Tapping her pen against her bottom lip, Darby glanced around the small, boxy office she'd called home for the last eight months. The ten-by-ten space boasted bland walls and a stingy window overlooking the parking lot, but she'd made it her own.

She figured that her office said as much about her qualifications for success as the way she dressed. Since it was technically a government office and uniformity was the bylaw, she couldn't change the paint on the walls. But she'd dressed the bland beige surface with care, choosing the art hanging there as she did her jewelry. There was nothing timid or shy about the impressionist splashes of red and purple she'd had matted in deep granite. Like her, she thought it was strong, impactful, with just a hint of sass.

She couldn't afford better furniture yet, but she made sure the plain black canvas club chairs were clean, the oak file cabinet was topped with a sinuous Art Deco sculpture in bronze and her utilitarian desk was a good veneer instead of the deep cherry she'd prefer.

But she'd get there.

As soon as she got a promotion, she'd take her first pay increase and upgrade those chairs to leather, the desk to real wood and the lighting? Oh, God, whatever it was, it'd be flattering.

But first she had to get the promotion. That'd prove that her choice to make her career her entire focus, to put it over anything and everything—including off-limits, mind-blowingly sexy men—was the right choice.

All she needed was a meaty case. Something intense and demanding that'd prove her skills and showcase her savvy.

Which wasn't going to happen until she proved she could handle fluff.

So, sighing, she turned her attention back to the papers on her desk. And managed to work her way through a few of them before the door burst open.

"I thought I locked that," she muttered, glancing up. "How am I supposed to get back into the work groove if people keep showing up?"

Grace stood in the doorway, her usually cheerful gnomelike expression looking a little worn around the edges.

"Nothing can keep me out," the woman said, holding a key aloft between two fingers. "Although I might need a raise now. Or at least a cup of warm tea with honey. I talked to more people in the last three hours than we've had through this office in six months."

"How'd you get rid of them?"

"I'm a people person. I can handle 'em. It's lunchtime. Did you want me to order you something?"

"No. Thanks. I'm not very hungry."

She hadn't been much interested in food since she'd gotten home.

"Just as well. Most of the places nearby are probably full right now," Grace declared. "I'm pretty sure every person who works in this building has been in to see you at least once, and all those questions made them hungry."

"Thank God. At least going to lunch will distract them from coming in here, pretending to need legal advice when what they really want is for me to offer to show them vacation shots of me in a bikini?"

"Are you offering?" Grace grinned, her freckled face lit with good humor. Her red curls bounced almost as much as she did as she crossed the room to drop into the chair opposite Darby. "If you are, I'm sure the crowd will line up again. Bet if we get it out fast enough, a few of them would even bring food back with them. I heard Clark say he was heading to Panera. I'll bet he'd bring back some sticky buns."

Sticky buns in exchange for seeing her buns. What a deal, Darby thought.

"I didn't even realize that many people worked in this office," Darby said, pushing back from her desk with a laugh. "I've been here eight months and I swear, I've never met half of them."

"Most of the guys in the building are scared of you," Grace said with a matter-of-fact shrug.

"Of me?" She fought back a grin. "They are not. Are they?"

"It's your shove-off shield. You wear it more often than you wear high heels."

"I always wear high heels."

"Exactly."

"Shove-off shield, hmm?" She thought about that

for a few seconds, wished she'd known about it before she'd gone to Hawaii, then shrugged. "I like it."

"So now that it's just us, tell me everything."

"There's not much to tell. I simply have no interest in these guys. That probably fuels the shield."

"I didn't mean that. I've spent plenty of time
studying the way you step over drooling bodies to
understand the basics. I meant tell me everything
about your vacation."

"Oh. That." Darby shuffled the papers she'd been
working on, tidying the completed pages so they
lined up with razor-sharp perfection. "Vacation was
good."

She added a smile for good measure, hoping
it went with the perfect vacation scenario she'd
claimed. Better to say she'd had a great time relaxing in the sun and surf than to admit she'd had a
mind-blowing affair with a man she'd discovered was
off-limits, then come home two days early to hide
out in her apartment, where she'd been cleaning out
her closet, updating her laptop files and experiment-
ing with online fitness programs to work off all that
pent-up sexual frustration.

"Yeah. Vacation was really good," she repeated.

The chipper smile dropped away as the redhead
leaned forward, her rounded elbows resting on her
thighs as she gave Darby a searching look.

"What happened? And don't even try to tell me
nothing, because I can tell. I've got an instinct for
these things." When Darby started to shrug, Grace
straightened and wagged her finger. "Nuh-uh. I
thought we were supposed to be friends. Good
enough friends that you wouldn't lie to me."

Darby grimaced as she reshuffled her papers again.

Sure, they were friends. But confessing things like sleeping with a guy she'd just met the first night of vacation was one thing. Admitting that she'd come way too close to falling for him, that she'd started feeling all sorts of stupid, emotionally overwhelming attachments to a guy she'd only known five days, was another. Or worse, that the guy she'd come terrifyingly close to falling for—something she'd have claimed was impossible before Hawaii—was a SEAL, the exact type of man her mother blamed for her brother's death.

Nope. They might be drinks-after-work colleagues, pedicure pals and even the occasional shoe-shopping binge buddies.

But they weren't confession confidantes.

Darby didn't let anyone that close.

But as she looked at Grace's face, she realized that distance wasn't mutual. The upbeat, outgoing woman actually considered her a good friend.

Damn. Darby's stomach did a slow dive into her toes, and a sigh choked in her throat. This was why she preferred to not have friends. They required care and handling and, well, friendship. All things she sucked at.

Just like she apparently sucked at meaningless flings. Because no matter how much she tried to put Dominic out of her mind— No, not Dominic. Nic, she corrected for the millionth time. The man was Nic. The enemy. And no matter how much she told herself that, no matter how many times she told herself to put him out of her mind, she couldn't forget him.

Not the man. Not his smile or the deep, intense way he talked. The things he said that seemed to reach into her heart and heal long-forgotten wounds, to touch emotions she hadn't even realized she could feel.

Not the sex.

God, she couldn't forget the sex.

Nope. Not going there. Pretending her insides weren't tingling, Darby leaned forward to cross her hands on her desk and gave Grace an apologetic look.

"Grace, I'm sorry. I do value our friendship."

Before she could figure out what else to say, the sleek black phone on her desk rang out. She grabbed the receiver like the lifeline it was.

"Darby Raye," she said, her words tighter than she'd intended as she tried her friendliest smile out on Grace.

"Ms. Raye, the Deputy Director would like to see you in his office at your earliest convenience."

Her stomach did a slow loop at the woman's ominous tone. But she just replied, "Of course. I'll be there in five minutes."

"Boss's office?"

"Boss's office," Darby confirmed, trying not to be nervous. She'd interacted with the Deputy Director numerous times since her assignment here. They'd even socialized from time to time. But this was the first summons she'd gotten.

She took a few seconds to gather her thoughts as she settled her now tidy stacks of papers into their respective folders. She then placed the folders in the desk drawer and turned the lock, securing them as per regulations. It might be a fluff case, but in the AUSA office, even fluff was classified.

"Saved by the summons," Grace said, pushing to her feet with a stiff smile. "I'll wait until you're back before I go to lunch."

There it was. Her out.

Being a smart woman with an eye for opportunity, Darby took it. She pushed to her feet, grabbed her cell phone, slipped it into the pocket of her jacket and headed for the door.

She didn't make it across the threshold before the niggling pressure tapping at the back of her neck made her cringe.

Dammit.

Sighing, she turned to give Grace an apologetic look.

"Hey, go have lunch now," she said. Then, noting the sad puppy tilt of the other woman's lips, she added, "I can't do it tonight, but maybe we can go get drinks after work tomorrow and I'll tell you all about my vacation."

She wanted to snatch the words back as soon as they left her lips, but Grace looked so damn happy.

"Drinks tomorrow sounds great."

"Great."

With that, Darby did a neat three-sixty on her five-inch stilettos and headed for the elevator, the Berber carpet muffling the sharp snap of her heels.

Once inside, she punched the button for the top floor and automatically checked her reflection in the mirrored elevator walls. Flicked a finger over the edgy fringe of hair skimming her jawline to separate the pieces into distinct points. Tugged the angled hem of her black serge peplum blazer and smoothed her hand over the dark leather of her pencil skirt.

She gave a narrow look to her face, noting the deep chili lipstick suited her lightly tanned complexion, as did the hint of gleam in her bronzer. Her carefully smudged eyeliner was a rich eggplant, giving her day-time smoky eyes a smart elegance.

Slick, sleek and savvy, she decided.

Just the look she'd been going for this morning. Not because she'd expected to be called into her boss's office. But because she never expected not to. Being prepared was just as important to success as hard work.

Maybe that was paying off, she thought as the ele-vator chimed her arrival. Maybe Carson wanted to discuss a promotion. Everyone knew there was one in the works, so this could be it. Her chance to step into the big shoes. Challenging cases instead of fluff. Leading her own team instead of assisting.

Making a name for herself. A successful name. Oh, yeah, that's what she was talking about.

Resisting the urge to dance her way down the hallway now, she hurried toward her boss's office. She calmed her smile from giddy to professional as she strode past the desk of his missing secretary and into the unguarded office of Deputy Director Carson.

And stopped so fast the heels of her peep-toe pumps—teal to match her blouse—almost caught on the carpet and sent her flying.

What the hell was Paul Thomas doing here?

And why did he look so damn smug?

CHAPTER NINE

WHY WOULD PAUL THOMAS be in her boss's office?

Even as Darby gave her ex a long careful study, his sky blue eyes ran possessively over her while he smiled a greeting. He looked pretty damn pleased with himself.

Nerves danced a quick jig in her stomach, but Darby warned herself not to jump to any conclusions. The US Attorney's office worked with the military all the time. Maybe Paul was simply here to recommend her for a case.

He'd been so angry when she'd finally convinced him that they were through that she couldn't imagine he'd want to work with her. Unless this was a ploy to change her mind.

See, Darby thought, this just proved that she and relationships were a bad fit.

She angled a questioning look toward her boss. As he argued with someone over the phone, the burly bullnecked man stabbed a finger at an empty chair, then jabbed it her way.

Resting her hips carefully on the seat's rim—Bill Carson didn't believe in wasting funds on decent furniture—to prevent the rough plastic from scratching her leather skirt, Darby leaned on the armrest for balance and gave the man sitting next to her an arch look.

Paul smiled back, his perfectly capped teeth gleaming against his perfectly tan face. His dark blond hair, just a hint longer than military regulations, was perfectly styled. The man was so studied in his perfection that she'd often wondered if he'd chosen the Navy because the white service uniform shirt looked better with his complexion than the Army's khaki would have. From the polished gleam of his silver Lieutenant's bars to the glossy shine of his black shoes, the man was obsessed with his image.

An image that didn't take kindly to being dumped, she remembered. Anger had slapped his face with red splotches, narrowed those just-this-side-of-too-small eyes into slits and highlighted the fact that he had no upper lip.

So why was he here, sitting in the plastic chair next to her looking like he was perched on a throne.

Darby glanced at her boss again for a clue, but all she got in return was a blank stare. The man had one hell of a poker face.

"You wanted to see me, sir?" Darby said as soon as he hung up.

"You know Lieutenant Thomas from JAG," Director Carson said in that melodious voice of his that was so at odds with his linebacker physique.

Darby relaxed enough to unclench her fingers. His use of Paul's rank and referencing the Judge Advocate General's office told her this was official business.

And if his expression was anything to go by, it

was official business that the Deputy Director wasn't on board with.

"Yes, sir. I do know Lieutenant Thomas."

"He indicates that you're also aware of the case that he's brought to my attention."

"What case is that?"

"A treason case against a Navy SEAL." Darby's stomach tumbled into her toes as Carson glanced down at the papers on his desk to check for a name. "One Lieutenant Ramsey."

Darby frowned.

"On rare occasions, Lieutenant Thomas and I discussed a variety of hypothetical legal scenarios. But I don't recall ever discussing any case linked with that particular name."

Paul's lips tightened at that denial, but Darby didn't know if it was because he didn't like her words, or the implication that he'd exaggerated.

"Given the nature of the charges, I wouldn't have mentioned the name but we did discuss the case in general terms," Paul insisted. "On a covert mission, a Navy SEAL was said to be killed in an explosion. Later, classified information that he had supposedly accessed was sold to terrorists."

He snatched a file off the desk and handed it to her. At her boss's nod, Darby flipped it open and started reading.

Remembering now, Darby nodded as she read the summary.

Lieutenant Brandon Ramsey, a decorated SEAL, was accused of a variety of treasonous acts. The most recent being the sale of a particularly nasty chemical weapon to a group of terrorists. He'd faked his own death. He had millions stashed in hidden accounts. And he was believed to have killed a fellow SEAL.

Her pulse jumped, but Darby kept her expression clear. No way was she going to let on how badly she'd love to be part of trying this case.

"Didn't he have a son who was kidnapped in an attempt to draw him out? And charges are being brought against another officer for treason, kidnapping and child endangerment, correct?"

"That's correct. The kidnapping and child endangerment of Nathan Maclean, as well as other charges, have already been brought against crewman Dane Adams by the Judge Advocate General's office. Treason charges are pending action by the government."

"And you're here because you want the US Attorney's office to bring treason charges against Lieutenant Ramsey, as well?" Not even the idea of working with Paul again could dim Darby's excitement over the possibility of taking the lead on that case.

"No." Paul wrapped his hands around his knee and smiled in a cat-munching-on-a-canary kind of way. "That isn't my case. But I am instigating procedures to bring charges against a high-ranking Navy SEAL in conjunction with the Ramsey and Adams cases."

"Lieutenant Thomas is requesting that our office consider this a case of treason," Carson interjected. "He'd like us to initiate the charge of treason at the same time he brings his own charges."

"Why is the timing an issue?"

"Because this particular officer has an almost mythic reputation," Paul said. "He's regarded as untouchable by many in command, so the timing will be particularly important as we'll have to move on this case quickly, bringing all charges at once."

"Apparently, this Lieutenant Commander Savino has a lot of people in his corner. Thomas is concerned that those people might use undue influence in regards to the trajectory of the case if charges are brought piecemeal," Carson explained.

Her head was buzzing so loud, Darby could barely hear. But she had to force herself to ask the question. "Nic Savino?"

"What do you know about Nic Savino?" Paul snapped, straightening in his chair to give her a look dripping with suspicion.

"Do you know of, or do you have a relationship with the accused?" Carson asked.

Darby's gut clenched in a vicious knot before taking a painful slide into her toes. Thankfully, years of courtroom training and a lifetime of general bitchiness assured her that none of that turmoil showed on her face when she glanced at her boss.

"I've met him," she admitted carefully.

"Would knowing him be a conflict of interest in this case?" Carson asked, his eyes boring into her.

Would it? Darby's mind raced. She was a professional. A woman who put her career ahead of everything and everyone. She and Nic had agreed that their relationship would only exist for the span of that week in Hawaii. They hadn't shared a single piece of information about their personal lives or their careers. Still, given how she'd felt there toward the end, she was pretty sure she could make an argument either for or against conflict of interest.

So it all came down to what she wanted.

She wasn't about to admit to a vacation affair, and the last person she wanted work with was Paul Thomas. But emotions aside, this case could—would—make her career. And if Nic was guilty of the charges—and she'd make damn well sure she thought he was before she brought them—then he wasn't the man she'd thought he was. And he deserved to pay for his crimes.

"I don't feel there would be a conflict of interest, no," she said, hoping she wasn't lying to all of them.

"Great," Paul said, all but clapping his hands in appreciation. "Then we should get to work."

"Not yet," Carson said, lifting one hand. "Before we go any further, Ms. Raye, I'd like your initial thoughts on the merits of this case."

"Without studying the evidence and charges?" Darby tried not to gulp. Practically, a case of this magnitude should take hours to weigh and consider. And that didn't even take into account the emotional demand of bringing charges against a man she'd thought she was falling for. And Carson wanted her to give her opinion immediately?

"You can glance through the files," he said, pushing another file across the desk with one sausage-size finger.

Darby felt as if she was being asked to get up on stage at Carnegie Hall and play after only one piano lesson. But she knew that was Carson's style. He valued intuition in his attorneys, respected instincts and demanded fast thinking.

Proud that her fingers didn't tremble when she reached for it, Darby opened the file. It only took a glance to confirm her suspicions. Paul was going after Nic Savino. Her heart dropped into her stomach as she read the list of accusations. Then, frowning, she set aside the file and opened the Ramsey file again.

THERE WASN'T ENOUGH evidence in these summaries for her to feel comfortable making a recommendation. Carson knew that, yet he'd asked for her opinion. Which meant he wanted her to look beyond the files.

Darby read through the files again, taking in every word in the skimpy folders twice. She was sure Paul had more. He had to. Given that he was making this request to Carson, he must have solid support up the chain of command. But she knew him well enough to conclude that he was like a dog with a bone, refusing to give it up even when it wasn't right. If he'd had a solid case, why was he showing her so little evidence?

Darby took a deep breath and went with her gut.

"Sir, glancing at the case against both Lieutenant Brandon Ramsey and crewman Dane Adams, I see that neither the prosecution nor, more importantly, the defense, have brought up accomplices. I find it difficult to believe that eleven individuals were overlooked in the building of these cases."

"Twelve," Paul interjected, leaning forward in a way that seemed to block her from Carson's view. As if he could negate her opinion. "There are twelve men in the Poseidon club."

"Eleven," Darby insisted, tapping her finger on the list of names. "Your own report states that Team Poseidon, under the auspices of Admiral Cree, is an eleven-man squad. The twelfth member was killed, presumably by Lieutenant Ramsey, in July."

"Which doesn't negate that they could all be in collusion. My findings are outlined in that presentation." Paul jerked his chin toward the file still on Carson's desk. He then proceeded to outline his findings, throwing out legal terms, military jargon and, in Darby's opinion, bullshit concepts in the way of insecure men everywhere.

As if wrapping big words around his tiny claim could make it impressive. But she'd seen his tiny claim already and she was not impressed. And she definitely wasn't going to risk her career on it.

"Sir," Darby interjected as soon as Paul stopped for a breath, "based on what I've been shown so far, Lieutenant Thomas's allegations aren't strong enough to elicit our involvement. Unless he has more than he's mentioned here, there is no evidence to support treason charges."

"Based on what I've heard so far, and what I read in the file, I'd agree with your summation, Ms. Raye."

Oh, thank God. The nasty knot of tension in Darby's stomach started to unravel. As much as she'd love a big, juicy case, a tiny piece of her heart was relieved. Before her shoulders got the message to loosen up, though, he spoke again.

"But Lieutenant Thomas's superiors believe differently and, with the support of Naval Intelligence, will be proceeding accordingly. With the full cooperation of our office." Carson's pale blue eyes stabbed into hers like ice. Cold and unyielding. Darby had worked under the man for less than a year. But she recognized a threat when she heard it.

"Sir, can I speak with you privately," she asked without having a clue what she'd say if he agreed.

"He already ordered you to cooperate, Darby," Paul snapped, giving Carson a look that said, *Women*.

Before Darby could give in to the urge to reach over and punch him, Carson jerked his chin at Paul. "You, wait outside."

Darby watched the emotions chase each other over Paul's face and wondered—not for the first time— why the guy had chosen a career in the military. Because he truly sucked at taking orders.

But after shooting her a fulminating look, he pushed to his feet and, shoulders stiff and chin high, strode out of the office.

"Asshole," Carson muttered as soon as the door closed.

Darby's lips twitched despite the gravity of the situation.

"Look, I know there's personal issues on the table here."

Oh, God. The room did a slow spin, everything going black, flashing white, then black again. Darby blinked, drew a long breath, then blinked again.

"Sir?"

"Look, you're new here. So you probably don't realize that nothing goes on in my office that I don't eventually hear about," Carson said, leaning forward on beefy elbows to clasp his hands on his desk. "I know you had a thing going with the guy. Word is it ended badly. Office grapevine says you threw him to the curb because he's an egomaniac in love with his own reflection. The secretaries claim he was pushing for a commitment that you weren't interested in.

My assistant says the two of you had about as much spark as a wet match."

Darby blinked at the shock of hearing that so many people were talking smack about her love life—such as it'd been. But, knowing her boss wasn't finished yet, she kept her protest to herself.

"I told you, I hear things," he said. "The question is, can you get past that? Set it aside, forget about it, whatever it takes so you can focus on the job at hand. Can you set aside your personal issues and do your job?"

Darby knew perfectly well that he was talking about Paul, not Nic. But her mind couldn't get past *personal issues*. She'd racked up forty-three orgasms with the defendant. Forty-four if the one she'd had thinking about him in the shower this morning counted—and she had to believe it did.

But this wasn't about sex.

This was about her career. Something she'd be damned if she'd throw away just because she'd had a whole lot of amazing sex.

"Look, Raye, you've got talent. You're a solid attorney. You've closed a healthy number of cases. You're respected in this office, not just by the other attorneys but by the staff, as well."

Not sure how to respond, Darby could only blink.

"You're smart, so you know this office is looking for someone to step into a key position on the terrorism task force. You want that position."

When he paused to give her an expectant stare Darby managed a nod. Because, yes, dammit, she did want that position.

"You want that position, this is your shot. A case

like this, it's a fast pass to the top. It's up to you if you want to use it or not."

Talk about dangling a big tasty carrot in front of her.

"Understood." Darby inclined her head toward the door. "Shall I ask Lieutenant Thomas to come back in?"

But as Darby listened to Carson outline how this would work, she wished she'd taken a little longer to think it over. Especially when he got Paul to agree that the federal prosecutor's office would take lead in trying the case. Which meant that she, as the lead attorney, would be the one prosecuting the accused.

Darby tried to catch her breath, but anxiety was gripping her by the throat. She managed to tamp it down by assuring herself that once she'd dug in to the details, she'd find that Paul's case was full of hot air. Which meant she'd never have to actually see Nic again.

"I'm glad we could work this out. It'll be a pleasure to work with your office on this matter." Not bothering to disguise his triumph, Paul gave Darby a taunting smile. "Let's get to work, then. We have two weeks to build a case proving that Nic Savino is a traitor, unfit to serve this great country."

LEGS BRACED AGAINST the rumbling roar of the helicopter's engine, Nic went over the mission plan one last time with his team.

"Gentlemen, we're ready to rock. Captain Shamon is coordinating his troops on the ground. They'll begin their strike in T minus five." Nic glanced from man to man. "Any questions?"

He saw exactly what he expected as he looked over the faces of his men. Preparedness and pride.

"Excellent. We're ten minutes out. Final equipment check," he ordered.

As one, his men went through the usual system check. Weapons, tech, parachutes, infrared. Maps, intel, routes in and out. They'd coordinate with Captain Shamon, time their jump onto the enemy ship at the same time the Captain led his team on the land assault.

Nic glanced at the radar to confirm the ship's position while monitoring Shamon's communications. He took a few minutes to reconfirm the mission protocols, then did his own equipment check. Chute, weapon, tech.

For the first time in years, he was antsy. He wanted to get this mission moving. He needed the action. The demand.

But antsy all the same.

Louden dropped down next to him, resting his rifle at his side and his helmet propped on his knee. Nic finished checking an encrypted message, deleted it, then shifted his gaze to his second-in-command.

"Problem?" Louden asked.

"Everything's on point."

"I didn't mean a problem with the mission. I meant a personal problem." Louden gave him a narrow-eyed look. "Are you letting that NI crap bother you? Ignore it, man."

"Ignoring problems doesn't make them go away," Nic pointed out. "We have an enemy and the first step toward beating an enemy is acknowledging their power."

"You think whoever is pulling this crap has more power than Poseidon?" Louden gave a sad shake of his head. "Dude, the sea god is almighty."

Before Nic could roll his eyes, his second-in-command leaned closer and, his dark blue eyes flaming with determination, said, "We are Poseidon. We honor the sea because we appreciate the challenges it offers. We're trained to be the best, but we never forget that there are things out there more powerful than any one of us. But nothing, my man, is more powerful than all of us."

Yes. Slowly, the knot of tension in Nic's gut unraveled. Louden was right. They were a team, and, by God, they'd beat this enemy.

"Thanks, Ty," he said quietly, clapping the bigger man on the shoulder. "I needed to hear that."

"Awesome." Before he could say more, a chime dinged. They'd reached their coordinates.

As one, Nic and Louden stood. In less than ten seconds, they stood in the open doorway of the helicopter.

With a bracing "Gentlemen, let's kick some ass," Nic tapped his helmet in a jaunty salute and jumped.

SIX DAYS LATER, they stepped off a plane and onto US soil. The sun sang behind the water in a vivid wash of color, the evening air carrying a hint of chill in a sharp contrast to the desert heat they'd left.

"Home sweet home," Louden said, finishing his usual homecoming ritual by bending down to kiss his hand and press it to the ground. "Hooyah."

"Good mission," Nic said, which was as close to a ritual of his own as he got. "Debriefing in ninety minutes. I need to make my report to Cree. You supervise unloading of equipment and tech."

"You got it." Given that he was six foot four, Louden's slap on the back could have felled a lesser man. But Nic held his ground as his second-in-command slanted him a curious look. "So? First time you've had boots on the ground in a hell of a long while. What'd you think?"

"I think I missed it," Nic confessed with a satisfied smile. "I think I missed it enough that you'd better get used to me commanding a lot more missions from here on out."

"That's what I wanted to hear."

Their stride slowed as they both caught sight of Captain Jarrett walking across the tarmac. Nic subtly came to attention as he adjusted the pack on his shoulder.

"What the fuck does he want?" Louden muttered.

"Stand down."

But even as he issued the order, he wondered the same thing. Whatever it was, he knew it wasn't good.

"Take the team," he murmured, jerking his head toward the low, bunker-style armory. "I'll handle this."

He didn't have to look at Louden's face to know the guy didn't like that. The guy didn't believe that second-in-command meant he stood right next to Nic in the line of fire. He thought it meant he stood in front of him.

"Savino," Jarrett said as Nic was within hearing range, his expression as grave as his tone. "Shouldn't you send your equipment with your men?"

"Standard procedure is to take responsibility for

my own equipment, sir." He knew the other man was waiting for him to ask why he was there, but Nic refrained. In part because it wasn't his job to give the man an opening. But mostly because, dammit, the guy shouldn't be here waiting to greet him like some long-lost lover.

Not when Jarrett was actually here to bust Nic's balls. He might try to call it something else, but they both knew better.

Jaw clenched, Nic simply arched his brow.

And wasn't surprised when Jarrett shuffled his weight from one foot to the other, looked over Nic's shoulder, then cleared his throat.

"As you've probably guessed, something's come up."

"Something that you deemed appropriate to share on a tarmac within five minutes of my return from a classified mission?" His tone was even, his expression cold. But inside, Nic was seething.

This was bullshit. Total bullshit.

Because of this situation, Jarrett here like this? It meant whatever was going down with Operation: Fuck Up was bad. Really bad.

He wanted to put his fist through something. He wanted to take his weapon and empty it on the nearest target, killing it dead until he mitigated the fury surging through his system.

Nic ordered himself to focus. He could be as pissed as he wanted on his own time. Right now, his time belonged to Uncle Sam and the US Navy and he'd damn well behave accordingly.

"I thought it was better to share this in a less formal setting." Jarrett gestured toward a series of low-slung buildings in the direction of Officer Country, as he liked to call the buildings housing the brass's offices. "I knew you'd report directly to the Admiral's office and wanted to bring you up-to-date before you see him."

Nic snapped the cap off his head and slapped it against his thigh twice before replacing it. That was the only gesture of concern he allowed himself.

"Then update me," he said, quick-marching it toward the offices. Jarrett had to double step to catch up.

"Cree wants to focus on the mission debriefing. He considers that priority. But I thought you needed to know that NCIS has assigned a JAG attorney."

So?

Nic waited a beat, then angled a look at the other man. And said aloud, "So?"

"I told you before. They have an informant. Someone must have fed them new information. That suggests they think they have a solid case," Jarrett claimed, his tone one degree below frantic.

"Actually, it suggests that they are investigating the possibility of having a case and needed to bring in counsel to advise as to the veracity of their claims."

He saw Jarrett's frown out of the corner of his eye.

"I didn't realize you were so well versed in military law."

"I'm not. But I'm damn well-connected."

"So well-connected that you were able to research legal protocols while on a joint military operation in the Middle East?"

What?

Nic's steps slowed as Jarrett's words circled. How

opportune was it that the first mission he'd run in two years had him off base when some secret informant just happened to slip the prosecution key information?

If that didn't say "tidy frame job," he didn't know what did.

"Convenient" was all he said, though.

"I warned you of my concerns before you left. Do I need to repeat them?"

Hardly.

Nic had spent every spare minute of the last six days considering those concerns. It hadn't taken more than twenty minutes to acknowledge whom Jarrett was referring to. He would have hit it sooner, but it'd taken nineteen minutes of denial before he'd allow the possibility.

He stopped at the door and faced Jarrett.

"I've served with Cree for over a dozen years. If I can't trust him, I can't trust anyone." Nic took one step, moving into the other man's space. "He's a decorated career officer with thirty years of service to his country. He recruited me. He trained me. He formed Poseidon. There is no way in hell he'd blame my team for insubordination, let alone framing us for treason."

Eyes wide, Jarrett visibly swallowed before slipping on a pacifying smile.

"Who said anything about Cree?"

"Nobody," Nic stated. "Nobody did. Nobody will. Because there is nothing to say."

With that threat hanging in the air, Nic yanked open the door and strode into the building. He didn't look back. He didn't need to see how Jarrett was taking his words.

Because they both knew he'd just uttered his declaration of war. He'd go down in flames before he turned on his commanding officer.

Not even if it meant saving his own ass.

CHAPTER TEN

SOMETIMES GIVING SOMEONE news they didn't like was pure misery of the gut-wrenching kind.

And sometimes it was better than a chocolate frosted cupcake with caramel filling and candy sprinkles.

Leaning back in her aubergine desk chair, Darby tapped her pen on the desk while giving her recommendation report a final read-through.

After brushing off Paul's suggestion that they work together, she'd spent the last few days going through every single piece of evidence available. She'd studied the Ramsey case, the Adams case and the available military records of everyone involved.

Including Nic.

He was Nic to her now.

What she'd found was reasonable cause to try the first two for treason, and oh, how she wished she could be the one to lead those cases. But when it came to Nic, the evidence was thinner than cheap tissue.

Satisfied, she laid the report back on her desk just as her office door opened.

"Darby," Paul greeted, his gaze shifting from a careful study of her face to the stacks of files covering her desk. "I'm glad you called."

"Have a seat," she invited, standing but not coming around to meet him. She preferred to keep the desk between them. No point in him getting any ideas about just where their relationship stood. "I know we're both scheduled to meet with Deputy Director Carson soon, but I thought it best to let you know what my recommendation would be beforehand."

"Excellent." He beamed, pulling his chair closer to the desk so he could reach across and pat her hand. His smile didn't dim when Darby pulled hers away and tucked it safely into her lap. "I wish you hadn't been so stubborn about working with me sooner. We've lost almost a week that should have been put toward coordinating our strategy."

"There's no need to coordinate strategy—" she began, before he interrupted.

"Of course there is. Timing is essential. My orders are to ensure that charges are brought before the end of the month."

Because she hadn't seen anything in the files he'd provided to indicate any need for urgency, Darby narrowed her eyes.

"Who gave that order?"

"Someone with a higher rank than me," he said with a smile she knew he thought was charming.

"I'm not under any such orders," she reminded him sharply. "Besides, you know as well as I do that even though our legal jurisdiction is separate, there wouldn't be concurrent trials on this matter."

"We could find a way to make it work. But you clearly don't want that, I see." His fingers steepled under his chin, Paul leaned back in the chair and gave her a knowing look. "Fine. You want the top spot, I'll let your office bring the treason charges first. We'll defer our charges until your trial is finished."

He was awfully eager to see Nic brought up on treason charges. Darby narrowed her eyes. Why?

Was it personal? Since she was just as eager to avoid seeing Nic face-to-face, she understood the emotion. But she was able to sidestep it and do her job. Was Paul?

"Paul, I've gone through the files up, down and sideways. I've looked at it from every angle of the law. The evidence simply doesn't support moving forward with this case," Darby said slowly, watching his face carefully. Fury flashed just a second faster than frustration.

"Based on the information that you've provided, I'll be recommending that the US Attorney's office pass on prosecuting this case."

"The Deputy Director gave you a specific assignment," Paul said, fuming. He shoved to his feet as if looming over her desk was going to make her change her mind. "You don't have a choice."

"Actually, I do. My specific assignment was to assess this case."

Lips tight, Paul sucked in a sharp gust of air through his nose, then huffed it out impatiently.

"Fine. I wasn't going to show you this until you'd committed to the case, but I'm authorized to use it if necessary. So here."

"What is it?" she asked, taking the thick brown legal envelope he'd all but thrown on her desk.

"It's a little history lesson that Savino and his team prefer to keep secret."

"Then why isn't it in evidence?"

"It's classified."

Darby stopped in the act of opening the file she'd pulled from the envelope.

"Then why are you showing it to me?"

"Because it'll change your mind."

"No, thanks," Darby responded. "I'm not accessing classified data without clearance from my boss."

"I'm clearing it," he insisted. But the ease with which he waved away her concern for legalities made Darby all the more adamant that she wasn't touching it. He rolled his eyes when she shook her head.

"You can at least read part of it," he said, grabbing the file himself and flipping through the pages before tossing one on her desk. "There. A statement from my key witness, name and specifics redacted. The witness is a high-ranking officer with an unimpeachable reputation providing specific details that implicate Savino as the mastermind behind these treasonous acts."

"You'll need to reveal your source," Darby pointed out. "You know you can't spring witnesses or evidence on the defense."

"I'm following orders," he said again. "Much of what the witness provides is classified. Those details, and the witness's identity, are confidential unless a judge orders otherwise."

"You've provided plenty of hearsay already. Why would more of it make any difference?"

"Because the specifics are there. Due to the secure details of this witness's testimony, his statement will only be given to those with proper clearance. Which you, as you pointed out, you don't have." His smile widened. "You will, though, when you take the case.

You'll have access to everything necessary, not only for a conviction, but also to skyrocket your career. This is the kind of case that makes headlines, Darby. The kind that would have made an attorney like your late father proud."

She knew she was being played, but that didn't prevent Darby's buttons from being pushed. Her father was the reason she'd become an attorney. He was why she worked in this office instead of some cushy private practice. Her fingers itched to take the witness statement and read it for herself. But her instincts screamed that there was too much bullshit going on for her to trust Paul. Because as much as she wanted to skyrocket her career, that was only going to happen if the case was solid. And no amount of bullshit was solidifying things here.

"Why the secrecy?" she asked, frowning.

"In part, because some of the information is classified. Added to that, Savino is a particular pet in certain quarters, public testimony would ruin this person's career. I guaranteed I'd protect that if at all possible."

Okay. That made sense. And she could tell that Paul believed it 100 percent. But just because she didn't want to believe didn't mean she could avoid looking.

Feeling as if one wrong move would cause her to explode into a million miserable pieces, Darby slowly lifted the papers from her desk.

Sworn testimony.

A detailed report of specific incidents, clandestine meetings and covert espionage.

Pages and pages of computer surveillance.

Darby had to wait until the ringing in her head faded before she could look up at Paul. If this information was accurate, she'd have to work with a man she disliked—teetering on hated—to prosecute a man she had major intense feelings for…teetering on love.

"I'll take this under advisement" was all she let herself say, though. "I need time to read the files and assess this new information."

"There's more."

Darby had to swallow the bile in her throat before she could ask the question. "What more?"

"I know you, Darby. You're wondering why, given our history, I'm bringing this case to you. Why I'm pushing you so hard to take it." His gave her that boyishly charming smile that'd convinced her to go out with him in the first place and leaned closer. "I'll bet you think I did it because I'm trying to get you back."

Given that he was looking at her as if he'd like to lick his way through her red silk blouse, Darby could only shrug.

"But that's not it. I wanted you on this case because I know you have reasons to hate Poseidon as much as I do. And that as soon as you realize it, you'll stop at nothing to see that they pay."

Confused now, Darby shook her head. "Pay for what?"

"Poseidon. This club of Nic Savino's? They're the reason your brother is dead."

The room did a long, slow swirl before Darby could blink it back into place. She tried to breathe but the knot in her chest was so tight she could barely do it. She could see his lips moving, but couldn't hear a thing Paul said through the roaring in her ears.

"Stop," she finally said, lifting one hand. Because it was shaking, she dropped it right back into her lap. "My brother's death was an accident. One for which he was found to be at fault. What would Nic Savino or Team Poseidon have to do with that?"

"I have it from numerous sources that Daniel Raye, like so many others in the Navy, wanted to become a SEAL in hopes of joining the revered ranks of Team Poseidon."

His words brought back vague memories of Danny's hero worship. Of SEALs, and yeah, she remembered with an aching heart, he'd talked about some elite group that he'd wanted to impress. But Darby didn't see how that made them responsible for Danny's death.

"When Daniel Raye earned his trident, he applied to join. And like so many others that were more than qualified, Poseidon turned him down. Three witnesses claim that your brother told them that he'd had a shot, that they'd reconsider if he could prove that he was good enough. That he could handle danger. Danger beyond what most missions would entail."

"So he was trying to prove something?"

"Not according to my witnesses." Paul tapped the envelope. "According to them, Danny had a detailed list of what he had to do to join. According to witnesses, he was acting under their directive. They might not have killed him with their own hands, but it was their actions that caused his death."

She had to swallow, hard, when her stomach

lurched. She was grateful she was sitting because her knees were quaking.

Nic was responsible for Danny's death?

There was actually someone to blame? She could almost hear her mother's sobbing "I told you so."

"I need to take this to Carson," she said. "I'll need his clearance to go through this information. To weigh it into my decision."

"What's to decide? We don't have time to drag this out, Darby." Paul crossed his arms over his chest and glared down at her. "The preliminary proceedings start in two days. I need to know—"

Needing him gone, knowing her control was on the verge of snapping, Darby lifted the four inches of papers, waving them between them so he had to back up.

"I'm not making decisions based on emotions. Especially not when mine are all churned up, dammit," she snapped. It took three long, slow breaths before she could calm herself down. "I need to go through all of this before I take my recommendation to the Deputy Director. If you want it before you go to trial, I suggest you let me get to work."

Brow furrowed, he looked as if he wanted to argue. But he must have seen the barely banked misery in Darby's eyes, because he slowly straightened.

"I expect to see your list of charges by tomorrow," he said quietly as he did a neat about-face and strode out the door.

He could expect all he wanted. Darby pressed her lips together, her hands fisted on her desk. She glanced at the clock, noting that it was time for her meeting with Carson. Moving like an invalid, she slowly stood and gathered her notes, her files. Then, frowning, she stuffed the redacted witness statement in its classified envelope and added it to her stack.

Her arms full, she slowly made her way to the Deputy Director's office. She'd be damned if she was going to rush through the process of ruining a man's life.

Not even the man who'd ruined hers.

Six hours later, Darby sat at her desk, the sick misery she'd had been working so hard to contain threatening to explode. She wanted to scream, to cry, to rail at the heavens.

Instead, with the Deputy Director's permission, she opened the envelope of classified information and got to work. Carson had listened to her report, then dismissed her while he read through the file and, according to him, made the appropriate phone calls. And in the end, his orders were exactly the same as they'd originally been.

Assess and recommend charges.

So she'd assess and recommend. Even though doing so made her ill. Not because charges would mean that she'd be destroying any chance she might have had with a man she never planned to see again. No. What was killing her inside was the fact that Nic Savino was the first man she'd ever cared about like this. The first man she'd ever wanted to care about her in return.

And the man responsible for her brother's death.

Darby forced herself to set aside the misery. She had a job to do. So she gritted her teeth, took a bolstering breath and got to work.

She read through the entire file.

Then she read through it again, this time making notes.

By her fourth time through, she thought she had a solid handle on the scope of the case.

Solid enough that she had to stop to press her fingertips against her burning eyes, trying to relieve the ache throbbing double-beat in her head.

Oh, God.

What a mess.

Her stomach ached. Not just from hunger, but from the choice in front of her.

The strongest evidence against Savino was filled with redacted details from a classified witness. As damning as it was, much of the rest was, at the bottom of it all, hearsay.

But there was enough there to merit action.

Action that would, if proved, mean that she'd slept with a traitor.

Worse, she'd had feelings for him.

See, she thought, biting her lip to keep from screaming. That's what she got for entertaining crazy thoughts about falling in love.

As much as she wanted to put it off, she knew there was no point. Delaying never did anything but draw out the misery.

So she did the only thing she could do.

She pulled her keyboard close and, fingers flying, typed her letter of recommendation to the Deputy Director. By the time she'd finished and hit Send, she could barely see the screen through her burning eyes.

So what? she thought as she dashed the tears from her cheek. It was after hours. She could cry all she wanted.

Because whether her boss read her letter tonight or whether he read it tomorrow, she'd still be playing a key role in prosecuting the case that could not only convict Nic Savino of treason, but might also put him in prison for the rest of his life.

But even as she told herself that's what he'd deserve, a little piece of her heart crumbled.

NIC HAD ASKED a lot of his team over the years. He'd sent them into war zones, he'd ordered them to face fire, he'd spent a decade expecting them to meet his unquestionably high standard, all while regularly putting their lives on the line.

But a few days later as he strode down the hallway toward the office he'd occupied the last three years, he was sure this was going to top every other request.

He stepped through the door, unsurprised to see his men already gathered. He'd ordered them to be there, yet he had to steel himself to walk through the door.

And ignore the urge to turn right around and walk back out.

He didn't want to go through with this meeting.

Fists clenched at his side, Nic tried to figure out how the hell he was supposed to tell the men he'd served with, trained with, hell, grown up with, that he was facing court-martial charges.

He knew the charges were bullshit. Logically, he knew it was a half-assed frame job. His exemplary service record should stand on its own against the baseless accusations. Logistics alone should prove the impossibility of his involvement.

But employing that same logic, the Navy would be

putting its talents and resources to finding the actual criminals. Instead, after months of stonewalling his team's attempt to find answers, they were throwing those charges his way.

But clearly, logic didn't always play out the way reason dictated. So when conventional warfare didn't win the battle, it was time to turn to the unconventional.

With that in mind, Nic stepped into his office. Conversation stopped and while nobody moved, they all turned their attention to him.

"So what's the deal, boss?" Jared Lansky asked from his position slouched against the door. The man's body language might say he was too damn bored to even stand up straight, but Nic knew better. Lansky didn't like to make a big deal out of it, but the guy was as protective as a mama wolf standing guard over her pack. He'd make like he was just chilling, but with ears like a bat and the ability to move like fire, the guy had perfected his early-warning system years ago. Anyone came within a hundred feet of the office, Lansky would know.

"The deal is that we have a situation on our hands, gentlemen," Nic said. He stepped behind his desk but didn't sit. He didn't call them to attention. He wasn't bringing this to them as their commanding officer. Instead, he spoke to them as brothers. He looked each man in the eyes as he outlined the charges he'd been presented with not an hour before.

"All of us in this room know the truth. Just as all of us in this room know that sometimes, the truth isn't enough." He drew a long breath as he glanced from man to man. "Command would prefer I don't tell you this, but I don't believe in leaving my men open. Given the nature of this tribunal and the falsified data targeting me, if a judge deems the evidence to be worthy, I will be court-martialed."

Fury flashed on some faces, frustration on others. But not one man said a word. They simply waited.

Pride wormed its way through the concern sitting like lead in his chest.

"A preliminary hearing wouldn't be called if NCIS didn't feel there was enough solid, irrefutable evidence to move on. I am to report to the Judge Advocate General's office at fourteen hundred hours, where the decision will be made as to whether to try or dismiss the case," he told them in conclusion.

Torres and Prescott exchanged glances. Lansky shifted from one foot to the other, then settled again. A sharp crack echoed through the air as Danby cracked his knuckles behind his back. Based on their years together, he could easily read each man's reaction. But even as he noted outrage and fury, a small part of him wondered.

Given the recent information, he'd had numerous questions about his superiors. Did his own men have the same doubts about him? Did they wonder if they'd served with a traitor?

He wanted to believe they didn't.

But like his faith in logic, his confidence in loyalty was in serious question.

Nic knew it was respect that kept them silent through his briefing. After a beat, he inclined his head and prepared for the worst. "Thoughts?"

"This trumped-up bunch of bullshit is what you're calling a situation?" Looking like he wanted to hit something, Elijah Prescott shook his head in disgust. "No offense, Savino, but as understatements go, that one is a doozy."

"Situation, my ass." Torres all but kicked the desk as he paced his way across Nic's office. "This is complete crap."

"Call it bullshit, crap or a fairy tale, charges are being filed," Nic pointed out. He took a deep breath before continuing. "Given the circumstances, I think it best if I step down from command of Poseidon until I'm cleared of all charges. Louden will lead the team until further notice."

"Nope. No way. Uh-uh," Louden snapped, shaking his head. "No disrespect intended, but that's just more of the same crap."

"No, it's standard protocol," Nic argued. "For the good of the team—"

"For the good of the team, you're in charge," Torres interrupted.

"Look…" Nic said, grateful but wanting them to be aware of just what was at stake. Before he could point that out, Louden lifted a hand for silence.

"Every step we've taken over the last decade was based on what the majority felt was best for Poseidon," Louden said. "So let's keep it simple. Savino thinks his presence on the team is damaging. Anyone who agrees, raise your hand."

That got a few eye rolls, a couple of head shakes and, in Torres's case a muttered "fuck." But nobody raised their hand.

And just like that, the aircraft carrier of stress Nic had been hefting on his shoulders fell away.

"There's a good chance they'll target Poseidon as

a whole if it appears the team supports my actions," he warned.

"Let them try. Who the hell do these fuck-wits think they are, trying to twist this deal around and point it as us?"

Still pacing the office with a scowl dark enough to scare small children, Torres bit off the words with a growl, his expression making it clear he was ready to spit them out at the first person he saw. Nic didn't have to check the expressions of the other men in the room to know they were equally pissed.

Gratified, but knowing the danger of ten furious men trained to kill, he focused on bringing them down to a simmer.

"Let's discuss strategy, then. What's our plan of attack?"

"We need to determine why Poseidon is being targeted. Is it target specific or is it convenience? Until this point, we've operated under the assumption that we were the scapegoat based on Ramsey's issue with the team," Elijah Prescott stated, his eyes on the sketchbook propped in his lap. Nic watched the man's hand fly over the page for a second, wondering how Rembrandt would memorialize this particular moment. Then Elijah looked up to meet his gaze with a look as serious as death. "But I think it's more than that. They've had an agenda in place since Operation: Hammerhead went bad. Now they're playing it out."

"They're playing it out because someone is feeding the NCIS with falsified information."

"Right before Ramsey is due to go to trial. Damn interesting timing, wouldn't you say?"

"Damn interesting. Based on the pissant's personality, he'll roll before he goes down," Torres pointed out.

And just like that, the theories were racing around the room. Shared, discussed, dismissed or fleshed out, depending.

And that, right there, was the reason they were the best. Because his men saw the nuances, the big picture, the strategy. He let them talk it out. Nic had learned years ago that his team didn't need hand-holding. The only time he ever controlled the dialogue was in a mission briefing. Otherwise, rank aside, he considered them all equals.

Something very few people outside this room would understand.

Suddenly, he remembered Darby's face that night on the beach when they'd talked about loss. She'd understood.

Why the hell was he thinking about her right now? Maybe because those few days on the island had been an idyllic window of time when he'd simply been a man.

If he lost his command, that could be his every day. No responsibilities, no training, no fighting for his life on a regular basis.

But as nice as that sounded in theory and as hot as Darby was in reality, that wasn't what he wanted. Not at the expense of his career.

Nic glanced at his watch, then stood. The room instantly silenced. All eyes turned his way.

"You shouldn't be going in there alone," Louden said, repeating the protest he'd already made three times before. "You are allowed representation in any legal proceeding, even a simple presentation of information. I'm your second-in-command. I should be by your side."

"Given the situation, your being my second-in-command would be a detriment in this court-room," Nic pointed out. "You're needed here. I'm depending on you to carry out the rest of my orders."

Seeing the argument forming in the other man's eyes, Nic waited. It only took a few seconds before Louden gave a jerky nod of agreement.

Nic had expected nothing less. He took a moment to gather his thoughts as he waited for them to settle.

How much had he let his team down, adhering to protocol, taking the correct route? Trying to balance right with truth? He'd followed procedure, he'd toed the line. Even while he circumvented the occasional rule, he'd done so under the orders of his command-ing officer.

These men were more than a group of people with a common goal. They were the elite, the best. They were brothers in all but blood. This team, the one he'd built, was a dedicated force with every element working seamlessly together.

And they were under attack.

He couldn't let that go without warning them.

"Keep in mind that based on the information pre-viously gathered, we know that the person behind this is in a position of command. That means there is a strong possibility that if this starts tipping against them, they'll take steps."

Nic had to clear the anger out of his throat before he could continue.

"You're all in danger. Every one of you is facing

fire, and it's impossible to tell right now who the enemy is. Whatever happens to me, you will continue with your mission. You will keep digging into this issue until you find the answers. You will watch each other's backs and take any necessary steps to ensure the safety of the team."

"This is crap," Lansky muttered.

"Crap, it is," Nic agreed. "Which means that every piece of information, every scrap of intel you gather, has to be kept off the base. As of the minute I walk out that door, Operation: Fuck Up goes dark."

Nic arched his brows, waiting until it was clear that they all understood before nodding.

"What happens if whoever is calling the shots railroads this tribunal?" Prescott asked, his fist pounding a beat against the wall. "If that happens before we complete our mission, the damage you'll incur could be irreparable."

"I hear the food in the brig sucks. Are we going to have to sneak you in field rations?" Danby asked, trying for a smile to go with his lame attempt at a joke.

"I promise you, I'm not landing in the brig." Nic flashed a tight smile. "I'll follow procedure until the situation mandates that I take steps."

As one, the men nodded.

They all knew what that meant. If it came down to it, Nic would fight to clear his name. But if things went FUBAR, he couldn't clear himself from inside a military prison.

"Gentlemen, someone or ones is clearly targeting Poseidon as a scapegoat for their own illegal machinations. As team leader, I'll take every step I can to ensure this attack stops with me." Nic looked from face to face, letting each man see the promise in his eyes. "But if it doesn't, be aware that every one of you will be next in the crosshairs. Take precautions."

A glance at the clock on the wall told Nic that his lecture was finished.

"Operation: Fuck Up is still in effect. Nothing less than victory will be accepted in this mission, gentlemen. Louden has your assignments," Nic told them as he grabbed his white combination cap from the peg on the wall.

Unlike his men, who were all dressed in their working uniforms of camo pants and jackets buttoned over tan T-shirts, he was in service-dress blues. The dark slacks, white dress shirt and navy blue double-breasted jacket spoke of the seriousness of the situation, and the fact that he'd been called to report to his superiors.

A first in his career.

Oh, Nic had been called to speak with superiors plenty of times. He'd been briefed, informed, trained and once even disciplined. But this was the first time he'd been called to stand in front of a tribunal.

Nic clenched his teeth. He'd damn well make sure this was the last time, too.

"Sir?"

Halfway out the door, Nic glanced over his shoulder. Ten men stood shoulder to shoulder, hands raised to their forehead in salute.

"We've got your back," Louden said quietly.

Damn if he didn't love every one of them.

But training kept his expression blank as he turned

on his heel and, shoulders erect and chin high, re-turned their salute.

Then, without another word, he left for his solo fight in the biggest war of his life.

CHAPTER ELEVEN

FOR A BRIEF moment as Nic approached the office of the Judge Advocate General of the US Navy, he realized he'd never actually been in this part of the Coronado base. He'd have been just as happy to live out his career without a visit, he decided, giving a nostalgic nod to the good ol' days, when the worst that happened at sea was walking the plank.

At least in the ocean, all he'd have to contend with were sharks.

"Savino." Captain Jarrett hurried down the hall to meet him. "You came alone?"

"Sir." Nic greeted Captain Jarrett, not bothering to acknowledge the obvious. Since he was standing there by himself, he'd clearly come alone. "Will Admiral Cree be joining us?"

"I'm sorry. He's currently at the Pentagon attending a Joint Chiefs of Staff meeting before deploying to his assignment in Afghanistan," Jarrett said with a nod. Instead of looking Nic in the eye, though, his gaze shifted a little to the left of Nic's shoulder.

Why? Was he hiding something about Cree's absence?

Someone had masterminded the treasonous acts, both during Operation: Hammerhead and the previous others they'd unearthed as a result. Someone, Nic was sure, who ranked higher than he did. Someone with the pull, the connections and the ability to run a ghost team.

After serving under the man for a dozen years, he knew Admiral Cree had all of those abilities and more. Added to that, every man Nic's research had tied to the ghost team was under Cree's command.

"You should have brought representation." Jarrett grimaced, adjusted his cuffs, then adjusted them again. "You could have enlisted a legal representative. Or better, you should have brought Louden. He doesn't practice but he knows the law. More importantly, he's one of your own."

"I've done nothing wrong."

"That doesn't mean you should walk in there without support. Anyone not on duty could have come in here with you. It'd make a strong impression on the judge, don't you think? Seeing that kind of support."

Nic appreciated that the Captain was looking out for him. But his suggestions that he leave the team hadn't been an empty gesture. He'd do whatever it took to protect his men. Which meant giving the impression of as much distance between himself and them as possible.

"The team isn't very happy with this situation," he said quietly, leaving Jarrett to draw his own conclusions as to just exactly what about the situation was the issue. "Since I prefer not to have to order them to attend, it was better that I come alone."

"Oh." The other man's eyes widened with shock before he managed to clear his expression. "I guess I thought things were tighter."

"The accusation of treason carries a wide brushstroke, Captain. I can't blame anyone who'd rather avoid being painted with it."

"I don't know what to say, Savino." His expression sliding somewhere between worry and depression, Jarrett shook his head. "I can't believe it's all going down this way."

"Nothing's gone down yet, Captain." Nic inclined his head toward the heavy oak doors. "Why don't we get started and see if anything will."

"Yeah. Sure." Jarrett sighed, adjusted his cuffs yet again, then nodded. "Let's do this."

With that, the man grabbed the brass handle and led the way into the chamber.

Nic had parachuted into enemy territory under gunfire with less trepidation than he felt walking through that door. But a mission was a mission. So he set aside his doubts, concerns and anger and walked into that room with his head held high, his shoulders straight and the pride of being a US Navy SEAL surging through his veins.

Like pennants that hung at competitions in the days of old, flags flanked the door. Because this was a preliminary hearing to decide if there was enough evidence to warrant a trial, the courtroom was all but empty. A Captain Nic didn't recognize manned the bench. His shock of red hair and milky skin contrasted with his crisp uniform. Maybe it was the sea of freckles dancing across it, but his expression appeared relaxed as he sat on the abbreviated podium in front of the emblem of the United States Navy. With him were three officers working at varying clerical roles.

Nic moved through the short row of chairs to approach the two tables facing the bench. One heavy oak table was empty. It was the other one, occupied by two people, that got his attention.

Or rather, it was the woman he was focused on.

Because she seemed damn familiar.

"Captain Jarrett. Commander Savino. Thank you for attending," the judge said. "We'll begin in just a moment."

It was then that Nic saw the woman's face.

It was like being hit by a tidal wave of emotions, all vying to knock him back on his ass or drown him in shock.

Darby?

The sexy woman of his dreams, the emotional touchstone that'd kept him grounded for the last two weeks, she was here?

Not just here, he realized as his gaze shifted to the man she sat next to.

Here, as part of the prosecution.

It was like taking a shot to the helmet. The bullet might ricochet off the metal instead of going through his brain. But the impact was intense.

Well versed in setting aside emotions in order to focus on the matter at hand, Nic allowed himself a single calming breath. He pulled out the chair, angling it for an obstructed view of the prosecutor's table.

And, of course, so he could see the gorgeous probable prosecutor studiously flipping through her notes as if the answer to world peace was buried in there somewhere.

Jarrett walked over to greet one of the officers, their discussion a quiet murmur in the background.

Nic didn't greet anyone. He simply sat and watched Darby.

What the hell was she doing here?

Feeling a little fragile these days, his ego wanted to think she was there to see him. That she'd somehow ferreted out his name, tracked him to California and followed him into this courtroom.

But not even his ego was delusional enough to believe any of that.

Not when she was sitting with the prosecution. And she wasn't acknowledging his presence. Neither fact boded well for their little meet-up here.

While he tried to decide how he felt about that, on top of everything else hitting him today, he gave her a good long look.

She appeared nothing like the sexy pixie he'd played with on the beach. The soft, flowing fabrics and sexy necklines of Hawaii had been replaced by dark colors, hard lines and cold metal. Instead of sassy spikes, her hair was sleek, sweeping back from that stunning face to accent carefully made-up eyes and razor-sharp cheekbones.

He'd never taken her as less than intense, but she had an even stronger edge today. A powerful vibe that told him she knew what she was doing here, and she was damn good at it.

Her civilian clothes and lack of protocol assured him that she wasn't military.

So what the hell was she?

Ready to explode with fury at the lack of control he had over this downward spiral that was his seemingly doomed career, he wanted to stride across the room, grab her by the shoulders and pull her out from behind that desk. He wanted to know what the hell she was doing and when she'd decided to become the enemy.

But he couldn't do any of that.

He could only stare.

And patiently wait.

Finally, when she apparently couldn't ignore him any longer, Darby took a deep, visible breath, then lifted her gaze to meet his.

He stared right back at her.

Her whiskey-gold gaze was like ice. Hard, cold and distant.

He couldn't read her. That shouldn't be so damn sexy, but it was.

"Gentlemen, we'll come to order," the man on the bench stated. "I'm Captain Trenton. Present are Master at Arms Arnold, Warrant Officer Poe and Ensign Harrington."

He gave his notes a brief glance, then directed his gaze toward Jarrett as the Captain hurried over to take a seat on the hard wooden chair next to Nic.

"Also present is Captain Jarrett, as commanding officer to the accused." His innocuous expression became stern as Captain Trenton looked at Nic. "At this time, Lieutenant Commander Dominic Savino will hear the charges leveled against him."

Jaw tight, it took all of Nic's discipline to keep his fists from clenching in fury at those words. He knew better than to show any sign of concern.

"Charges are being presented by Lieutenant Thomas of the Judge Advocate General's office. Also present is Ms. Raye of the federal prosecutor's office."

Federal prosecutor?

Darby was a US Attorney.

"I would like to inform you that if the tribunal deems the evidence worthy, court-martial proceedings will commence." The Captain shifted his gaze to meet Nic's. "Lieutenant Savino, do you have any questions?"

"No, sir. No questions," Nic responded, his words low and clipped.

His jaw clenched tight. Because he did have questions.

About a million of them.

But every one of them was for Darby to answer. And answer she would.

After.

DARBY HAD FIGURED this day would suck.

She'd been sure it'd suck hugely.

But man, oh, man had she underestimated just how much it'd suck to face Nic in this setting, under these circumstances. Worse, she'd forgotten to factor in the effect he had on her. It was like being shot with a Taser, the shock ricocheting through her system like a lightning bolt.

Pretending to sift through her notes, she wished she'd given in to the 3:00 a.m. urge and called Carson to ask to be taken off the case. But no, she'd been so sure she could handle this. Pride and ambition had squashed that urge like a bug.

Damn them both.

She sat silently, again avoiding Nic's eyes while Paul stood up and, in the most pompous tones she'd ever heard, presented the case on behalf of JAG.

"Commander Savino planned Operation: Hammerhead. A mission focused on rescuing a captured Russian scientist and keeping a particularly virulent chemical weapon out of the reach of terrorists. A chemical formula that was discovered to have been transmitted during said mission by one of the men tasked with retrieving and protecting it," Paul explained, his words rising and falling with the fervor of an evangelist minister. "This formula was sold to the enemy in exchange for a half-million US dollars. While he didn't serve on the mission, he was instrumental in all elements, including damage control after one of his team was injured and another, apparently, killed in action."

As she watched Paul pace, gesture and all but call to the gods, Darby felt Nic's eyes on her. Burning, searching, demanding.

There wasn't a lot that made Darby want to squirm. But sitting in a courtroom, preparing to accuse her temporary lover of crimes against country, was definitely making the list.

"In conclusion," Paul intoned, "we will prove to the tribunal that not only was Commander Savino aware of the treasonous acts listed in exhibit A, that he organized and implemented the plans to carry out said acts. We have ample evidence to prove to the federal prosecutor's office that Savino committed treason, or at the very least engaged in a conspiracy with others to commit treason."

His final words ringing with righteousness, Darby was surprised when Paul simply sat down instead of taking a bow.

"Ms. Raye. You have the floor."

Now she wished Paul had bowed. She'd welcome even a few more seconds to prepare. Her heart knotted so tight in her chest that she could barely breathe. Darby rubbed her lips together to check her lipstick. She rose, smoothing her palms over the cool black linen of her skirt, her toes curling in her favorite T-strap pumps.

She wanted to blame her racing heart and dancing pulse on nerves. But she rarely got nervous arguing a case. Which meant the anxiety was all because of Nic.

Use it, she told herself. *Control it before it takes control.*

So, she kept her chin high and focused on the golden ring—career success—as she stepped around the table and approached the desk of the uniformed man behind the desk.

"Thank you, Captain," she said clearly, keeping her eyes on the acting judge. "At this time, the federal prosecutor's office will defer the charge of treason against Commander Savino until you reach a verdict. Upon which time, using the evidence presented here, the Justice Department will pursue the treason charges as a whole against any and all individuals involved in this matter, whether already accused or yet to be named. This includes the pending cases of the United States versus Ramsey and the United States versus Adams."

Paul jerked so hard his chair screeched against the marble floor. At the same time, out of the corner of her eye she saw the slight nod from Nic as if he approved of the breadth of her statement. She knew

Paul didn't like it, and from the look on the Captain sitting next to Nic, he didn't, either.

But the Deputy Director had agreed with her that given Paul's personal investment in this case, if they were going to commit manpower in this case, they'd do so in a way that would use that power wisely.

"Excuse me." The Captain next to Nic stood, lifting one hand in the air.

"Captain Jarrett?" the judge acknowledged.

"Sir, that's a sweeping intention. I'd like some clarification as to the breadth of the federal prosecutor's intentions."

The judge arched his brows toward Darby, so she clarified.

"As my esteemed colleague pointed out, charges have already been filed in the cases of the US Navy versus Ramsey and Adams."

Citing the case numbers and pertinent details, she tapped her pen on her notepad as if emphasizing a point. As she continued outlining the government's position on the Ramsey and Adams cases, a part of her waited for Nic to jump out of that uncomfortable-looking wooden chair and out her as a fraud. And the longer he didn't, the more nervous she became.

To work it off, she paced in front of the bench as she spoke, using her hands to emphasize key points.

"While Naval Intelligence's investigation hasn't yet released their findings into the actions of Lieutenant Ramsey—including the faking of his own death—that there are accomplices is unquestionable. Given the extensive network of skills involved in these crimes, it's the opinion of my office that these two men could not have been working alone."

It was a sad, painful fact she'd finally been forced to accept. Because while Brandon Ramsey might be the face of this crime, someone else was the brains.

And that someone could very easily be Nic Savino.

"Hence, Lieutenant Thomas's charges," she said in agreement. "If the court finds merit in charges, we call for the arrest of Lieutenant Commander Dominic Savino, unrestricted line officer, decorated Navy SEAL and leader of Team Poseidon."

She went on to recite a dozen of the top missions in Savino's file, still impressed despite herself as she quoted them aloud.

Darby wet her lips.

The country owed this man a great deal. It was going to be a disaster if he'd abused that gratitude.

"Top of his BUD/S class, he's a trained linguist, EOD operative, missile tech, aviation specialist and special warfare operative. He's served four tours under Admiral Leo Cree, multiple deployments to hot zones such as Afghanistan and, after two years at Pearl Harbor, is now stationed at the Naval Amphibious Base, Coronado."

As she wound up her statement, she stopped pacing to face the judge, giving him an intense stare to indicate the seriousness of her words.

"While the charges against Commander Savino are quite clear, it is the opinion of our office that, as yet, the full extent of those involved has not been revealed. At such time that it is, the charge of treason will be levied against all of the accused."

Because there were more. Darby didn't discount the extent of Nic's crimes, but she knew he wasn't in it alone. Carson had agreed that they'd ensure a stronger conviction if they went after everyone at the same time.

"Thank you, counselors, for your recommendations," the judge said, his face drawn in sober lines. "This court will take them under advisement. Naval Intelligence has been petitioned to release their findings to this court. Pending the review of said information, we'll make our recommendations."

"Thank you, sir." With that and a quick nod, Darby strode back to her seat. As much as she wanted to, she couldn't avoid glancing at Nic as she went.

And to think just two weeks ago, she'd imagined the look on his face if he saw her again. In none of her fantasies had she imagined the look of promised retribution gleaming right now in Nic's eyes.

"Good job." Paul had leaned close to murmur in her ear. "You did your brother proud up there."

She shrugged, both to dismiss the comment and to get him away from her face. Instead of replying, she focused on gathering her notes. She carefully tucked them into one part of her messenger bag, her yellow pad into another. Timing it carefully, she waited for Paul to rise and start glad-handing his way around the room before she got to her feet.

Despite her best intentions, she didn't make it out of the room unscathed, though.

Darby tensed when Nic stepped into her path, blocking her exit.

"So. I guess you're an attorney," he said in a conversational tone at odds with the accusation in his eyes. "And what a coincidence. You and me, both of us here."

The sarcasm was thick enough to walk on.

"Excuse me," was all she said, though, as she tried to sidestep him. She had to get out of here.

"We need to talk."

Ignoring his demand, Darby shifted to the left. He countered. She clenched her teeth, but didn't bother trying to shift to the right. Why give their audience any more of a show than they were already enjoying?

She flicked a quick glance toward Paul. He was in conversation with the Captain who'd come in with Nic, and the JAG attorney didn't look happy.

She assumed from the way he kept squinting his eyes and jerking his head that he didn't want her speaking with Nic.

It wasn't as if she wanted to talk with Nic, but dammit, Paul had pulled her into this case. So she'd handle it the way she wanted.

Instead of making a scene by shoving Nic aside and scurrying out of the room, she sent Paul a smile and a hint of a shrug.

"I don't want to talk with you," she said quietly, finally meeting Nic's gaze. "I'm sure you can understand why."

"No. Actually, I can't. We know each other. Pretending we don't is not only stupid, it's a lie." He arched one brow in that sexy challenging way of his. "I don't lie, Darby. Do you?"

All the time, she wanted to say she was lying right now, standing here pretending she didn't want to jump into his arms and wrap herself around him. She'd been lying to herself ever since this case landed on her desk, pretending she could separate her feelings for the man from the crimes he'd purportedly committed. And if anyone asked her how she'd walk away from this case unscathed, she'd flat-out lie and say she'd walk away just fine.

"Please," she murmured, glancing at Nic's face only long enough to note his intense stare. "Get out of my way."

"I will. As soon as you clarify a couple of issues for me," he said in a tone so neutral it was almost friendly.

Pushing past the emotions dueling it out in her belly, Darby gave him a closer look.

Shouldn't he be angry? She studied his face. Really studied it this time. And almost sighed.

Why was he so gorgeous?

Unlike his sexy beach-bum look, with the scruffy goatee and ripped jeans, now he was spit-and-polish perfect.

He was clean-shaven and his glossy black hair was cut close on the sides, just long enough to hint at a curl on the top. His eyes looked even darker without the goatee.

She'd never been one of those women who went gooey over a man in uniform, but just staring at the way Nic looked in his was enough to make her soften.

"I really need to go," she said quietly, wanting to get away from him before she did something stupid.

Like apologize.

As if reading her mind, he took a half a step closer and lowered his voice as he asked, "Did you consider the simple courtesy of notifying me beforehand."

"Why would I?"

"Why wouldn't you?"

Darby was irritated with herself for wanting to

explain how important her career was. She wanted to scream at him for creating the unassailable reputation that her brother had died trying to reach. She wanted to point out that the evidence against him was overwhelming and his culpability clear. She wanted to explain that the stakes were too high, the safety of the country had been jeopardized and lives lost because of the choices he had made.

But she couldn't. Not because it'd jeopardize the case, although it might.

But because standing here, looking into the dark mystery of his eyes, she couldn't believe a word of it. Not the charges, not the supposition, not the evidence.

She'd seen the expression on his face when he talked about losing his friend. She'd heard the conviction in his voice when he talked about doing the right thing, about honor being paramount. She'd seen enough bullshit in her life to recognize it when it stood in front of her. But the only thing Nic Savino reeked of was integrity.

Well, integrity and soap.

Darby had to stop herself from leaning in a little closer to take a good sniff.

She told herself that the man was simply skilled at deception. But she couldn't get her heart to agree. She and her heart were going to have a good, long talk later, she decided.

"Despite the evidence presented today, I assume you're trained to follow orders and do your job." She didn't need to wait for his response to know he saw where she was going. The faint frown in his eyes said it all.

"And you'll do your job to the best of your abilities."

It wasn't a question, but Darby answered anyway. "Wouldn't you?"

"I'd say you have a quite a few more abilities in your arsenal than I realized."

"I could say the same about you."

"Could you? Because of the two of us in this room today, only one of us was surprised. Although I have to say, this is a good look for you."

He didn't move, but Nic seemed to take a step back to give her a long intense inspection. Darby tried not to fidget as his gaze traveled from the toes of her T-strap black pumps up her legs to the ladylike hem of her pencil skirt, where it hit just above her knees. The matching ebony jacket was a modified motorcycle style, waist-length, ribbing at the shoulders and black grommets. Because the jacket had an edgy vibe, she'd kept her jewelry mellow, the fat jet beads a vivid contrast to her mandarin-collared white silk shirt.

Given that she considered herself a woman with a strong sense of style, it'd irritated her to all hell when she'd ended up changing four times this morning. She never worried about the image she presented in court.

But the image she'd present to Nic had sent her mind reeling. From the look on his face, though, she could have worn angel wings and a halo and he'd still believe she was the devil.

"For all the ways I imagined seeing you again, this one was nowhere on my list."

He'd imagined seeing her again?

He'd really wanted her to ask about him at the hotel, to get his information and track him down?

What would have happened if this case hadn't come up? If, a few weeks after they were home, they'd gotten in touch and seen each other again.

Except this case did happen.

Because he was a criminal.

And it was going to break her heart to send him to prison for the rest of his life.

Holy crap, she wanted to yell at herself. *Quit being such a girl and get the hell out of here.*

"I'm sorry if you're disappointed," she responded. "But as I said, we both have a job to do. I'm not going to apologize for being damn good at mine."

From the scowl on Paul's face, he wasn't reveling in his success, though. It was hard to tell if it was because it appeared he was being chewed out, or if he was pissed that she had spoken with Nic. Neither option boded well for a smooth, comfortable working relationship, Darby knew.

He gestured with one finger for her to wait for him.

She shook her head. Nope. She'd had enough. And she didn't care if it pissed him off. She was leaving.

She figured Paul had scored enough points today.

She knew it was stupid, but she blamed him for the way Nic was looking at her right now. She flat-out resented having her once-in-a-lifetime happy bubble burst into ugly bits.

So she hitched the strap of her leather messenger bag over her shoulder and headed for the door.

"Ms. Raye."

Paul's voice stopped her when she reached the door. Darby glanced back to see he and Nic's Captain staring at her.

"Good job today. Damn good job."

Unwilling to trust her voice, Darby merely nodded.

She had done a good job.

A damn good one.

Even Carson would agree.

Darby knew she was well on her way to that pretty gold career star.

She just wished it made her a little happier.

CHAPTER TWELVE

EXHAUSTED, BONE-DEEP and to the soul, Darby let herself into her apartment the following evening. She rubbed one hand over her burning eyes, then tossed her purse on the small bench inside the door and let her messenger bag drop to the floor next to it. The heavy thud of leather was a dull reminder of how much work she'd brought home.

Ignoring it for now, and perfectly content to ignore it as long as possible, she stepped out of her heels, letting them lie in the short hallway as she padded, barefoot, toward the small living room.

She didn't bother with a light. She knew her way, and it wasn't as if there was much furniture in her place. So it wasn't a stub of her toe that stopped her in her tracks.

It was the shiver of warning down her spine.

Her body tensed. Fingers clenched, she sidled closer to the kitchenette, where she kept a few handy things like knives and frying pans. Before she reached it, the lights flashed on.

Darby threw one hand up to shield her gaze, and raised the other in a fist. She didn't lower it when she saw who was standing there. But she did clench her fingers a little tighter.

"How'd you get in?" she asked quietly.

"I'm Special Ops. A SEAL. Do you really think my training doesn't include getting into a locked building?"

Despite his relaxed stance as he leaned against the far wall, Nic's smile was anything but friendly, his demeanor anything but casual.

Darby might have wished seeing him in her apartment didn't make her nervous. But she wished even more that she didn't feel sparks of heat under the nerves. Because both pissed her off, she fell back on her usual defense.

Cocky challenge.

"Glad to see our government dollars being put to good use."

"Are you?"

"Why do you sound surprised?" And more importantly, why did she feel insulted at his surprise?

"You're actively working to defend a criminal guilty of murder and treason. You're part of a concerted witch hunt that at best is focused on shifting blame, at worse has framed a team of good SEALs who work hard to protect this country." He arched one brow and, without shifting an inch, seemed to loom over her. "In my book, that'd qualify as a waste of government money. But I suppose lawyers have their own definitions."

"Lawyer jokes?" Darby tried for a mocking eye roll but wasn't sure she pulled it off. "Isn't that beneath you?"

"Sweetheart, you have no idea how low I'll stoop to protect what's right."

She didn't need his derisive once-over to hammer

home that implication. But she did wish like crazy that she hadn't taken off her shoes.

The man had seen every inch of her nude body. He'd licked chocolate off her belly, sipped whipped cream from her nipples. He'd given her more orgasms in five days than she'd had in the rest of her life combined.

It was stupid to feel so naked standing in front of him barefoot. But she did.

Naked and exposed.

"Why are you here?" she asked, finally lowering her fist.

"We have a few things to discuss," he told her, his shoulder brushing the wall as he shrugged. "I thought you'd prefer the discussion be private."

"And rather than ask me to meet you somewhere, you broke into my place? And here I thought you were all about rules and protocols."

"Oh, I am. I'm also an expert on assessing a situation, at measuring potential threats and opportunities in order to best strategize a targeted mission outcome."

Making as if her stomach wasn't tied in knots and her hands didn't want to tremble, Darby rested one hip on the arm of her easy chair, then casually crossed her arms over her chest and gave him a scornful look.

"I'm a lawyer, Lieutenant. Big words and military jargon don't intimidate me."

"Do you really think I'm worried about intimidating you?" This time his smile was real. And, dammit, just as cocky and charming as she remembered. "I'm simply here to exchange information."

"Do you really think I'd ignore the glaring conflict of interest by discussing a pending case with one of the defendants?"

"So you admit I'm a defendant?"

Darby laughed. "Is that out of your Interrogation 101 handbook? Lead the witness with simple, obvious questions."

"Just thought I'd lay out the facts as we both see them. From my perspective? Fact one—Naval Intelligence has already dismissed this as a bogus case. Fact two—the setup is so obvious all it'd take is a magnifying glass and a deerstalker cap to follow the dots. Fact three—you're too smart to get dragged into someone else's political game." He inclined his head, gesturing for her to show her facts now.

Darby debated. She could hear Paul's voice ringing loud and proud in her head. His accusations. His anger over the idea that a bunch of fatheaded ego-fueled hotshots were getting away with a litany of crimes. And, under it all, his jealousy.

Like Danny.

She bit her lip against the pain of thinking about her brother and marshaled her thoughts. Emotions wouldn't serve her. Emotions never served her well.

"Fact one," she said, uncrossing her arms to lift a finger in the air. "You might have assumptions, but you don't know what NI or NCIS concluded or what evidence has been presented. Fact two—you and your team are well versed and smart enough to know how to create a setup within a setup. And fact three—you've made mistakes. Big mistakes. And mistakes have to be rectified. One way or another."

"Mistakes?" His eyes bored into her, his look so

intent that Darby had to wonder if he wasn't searching her soul and delving into every secret she'd hidden there. "Is that what you call the death of Warrant Officer Powers? He was my man, my friend, my brother. He went down in the line of duty. Duty to the mission that you and your team are trying to dismiss as treason."

"In the line of duty? Or on a vigilante mission?"

"You took the case without that basic information?" Nic gave a scoffing shake of his head. "I thought you were a better attorney than that."

"You thought? When was this? While you were romancing me on the beach? Or maybe when you stripping me naked? I seem to recall a little anonymity agreement. Did you recant and forget to tell me?"

"You know I didn't. But you did. When, exactly, did you figure out who I was, Darby? Was it that first night? Did you lay out that agreement as a ploy to keep me from realizing you were fishing for something to help with this little case of yours?"

"You think I slept with you to gather insights for this case?" Darby swallowed hard to keep the bile in her throat from spewing everywhere. "Obviously, you have no idea at all what kind of attorney I am."

"Well, let's see. Based on the evidence so far, I'd say you are so dedicated to your job that you'll do anything to advance up the ladder. You've got talent, enough that your boss believes you can win, despite the obvious fraud at hand. And you're willing to do anything…absolutely anything to win." His look was pure challenge. "Even if anything includes refusing to recuse yourself because you want the glory of railroading innocent men on trumped-up charges."

"You're creating conspiracies where none exist," she said stiffly, not liking his assessment.

"Hey, we spent a week together. And in between the hot and naked times, we shared our own personal tragedies. Are you honestly telling me that doesn't say 'conflict of interest' to you?"

"Why would it?" she asked, irritated that he seemed to think he could push her into stepping down. That he could intimidate her into doing something so stupid that it'd sideline her career at best, destroy it at worst.

And why?

Simply because they'd had sex. Darby surreptitiously wiped her damp hands on the sleeves of her jacket.

Okay, lots and lots of sex. Lots and lots of great sex.

But that wasn't the point.

"I can think of many reasons for you to step off the case." Looking a lot more comfortable than she felt, Nic leaned against the wall, one ankle over the other. The casual pose did nothing to negate the power emanating from him in huge, angry waves. "We could start with the basics, and debate whether or not Deputy Director Carson would dismiss our little vacation fling as no big deal. There's a little thing called entrapment. It's not a biggie in the military, we're pretty lenient about conning the enemy."

Talk about entrapment. Any way she responded to that, he'd be able to use it against her. So Darby availed herself of her right to remain silent and simply arched one eyebrow.

"Nothing to say? I guess I misjudged you. My impression was that you weren't the kind to back down from a little healthy debate."

"I'm not the kind to be tricked into talking about a pending case, either," she snapped.

Nic gave her a long, assessing look, then nodded. She wasn't sure what to make of that, or of the look he cast around her living room.

"Just an observation, but I've lived in barracks with more personality than this place." He scanned the empty walls, as if noting the lack of dust catchers. She thought of Grace's critique the one time she'd visited. No throw pillows, no colorful blankets, no photos. No nothing.

"You want to talk decorating style?" Giving in to the tangle of confused frustration knotting her up tight, Darby sighed.

"Hey, you said discussing the case was off-limits. So I'm changing the subject. In that new subject, I have to admit that given my impression on the island, I'd have thought you'd live with a little more style." He shrugged when she shot him a questioning look. "You dress well. Strong colors that make a specific impression, those girlie things that accent whatever you want accented. Belts or necklaces or whatever. You make an impression."

Darby blinked. Before she could decide if she was flattered or not—and why even wondering made her feel so weird—he continued.

"Even yesterday in that courtroom, you showed style. Take-charge power. From those skyscraper shoes to the way your skirt fits to that gold chain, you embrace your femininity. The colors, the unapologetic black and in-your-face red? They make it clear that you're a force to be reckoned with."

Okay, she actually was flattered. And a little disturbed that he saw so clearly into the very deliberate choices she made about her image. But he didn't need to know that.

Darby shrugged.

"So?"

"So. Given that you know what style is and you have a firm handle on yours, I'd have thought your space would have some." He glanced around again, shook his head. "Did you rent this furnished or something? Do you rent your space to strangers when you're not around, so you keep it as bland as white bread?"

A little offended, Darby looked around.

The entry, only big enough for a small table she used to hold her purse and keys, opened into the living area. It was flanked on one wall by a sliding glass door, the four-foot patio beyond overlooking a spit of emerald grass and carefully manicured bushes. A short, white counter jutted between the living room and her kitchen. It was spotless but a light coat of dust shadowed everything but the coffee maker and sink.

The walls were beige, the couch and matching chairs tan. The wood coffee and end tables were a few shades darker, completing the monochromatic theme. The only shift in color was the flat-screen TV on the wall over the never-used—it was California for crying out loud—fireplace.

So what? She wasn't a homebody, had the cooking skills of a college freshman and if her mother was to be believed, all the decorating sense of a teenage boy.

Added to that, given Southern California's high cost of living and the fact that she spent very little time here, a bigger space would be a waste of money. As it was, rent was high enough to limit how much she could send her mom each month and, worse, how many pairs of shoes she could afford.

Still, she couldn't deny that she felt a little insulted by his words.

"White-bread bland?" she countered with a frown. "Really?"

"You disagree?"

She wanted to, if for no other reason than on principle.

But all she could offer was a shrug.

"It suits my needs."

"If you say so." He nodded slowly. "I suppose it works pretty well at fighting insomnia."

"Now that's just mean," Darby said, trying not to laugh. Then, upset with herself for letting him put even the smallest hole in her defenses, she reached for irritation. Not anger—she couldn't afford anything that passionate. But she could make irritation work. "Did you add poking through my bedroom to your little B-and-E visit tonight? What's next? Peeking into my underwear drawer?"

Nic gave her a long look, those dark eyes moving from the sassily flipped ends of her hair where they skimmed her jaw and down her throat to rest on her breasts.

She was covered. Her jacket, her blouse, hell, her bra. There was no way he could see through to flesh. But Darby felt as if he was running his fingers over her skin. Her nipples tightened as if he'd rubbed them with his thumbs, circling and swirling and teasing her into higher and higher levels of excitement.

Darby barely resisted crossing her arms over her breasts to stop the sensations. She did manage a scowl, though.

It only made his smile widen.

"You know me better than that, Darby. I don't visit a lady's bedroom without an invitation."

"I don't know you," she countered. She knew the words sounded defensive, she knew they were fueled by guilt as much as her work ethic. But she needed some distance from the intimacy that seemed to arc between them like shimmering beams of light.

"Does it help to tell yourself that?" he mused, his expression showing nothing more than mild curiosity. "I've never had to attack someone I've slept with. I'd imagine it goes down a little easier if you deny there was anything other than random sex."

"You consider the charges against you an attack?"

"Is this where we get into the semantics of lawyer speak? I should warn you, I've attended numerous SOC courses at the Naval Justice School over the years. Senior officers courses come in handy, both in commanding SEALs and in leading Poseidon."

Did he do this on purpose? she wondered. Give her these openings to poke and prod, to dig for details she could use against him? She thought back to that talk on the beach, to the way he bared his heart in the moonlight. Didn't he realize she was using his confession of guilt already? Why would he give her more?

Unless he was up to something.

Darby might not be military, but she knew strategy. And smart strategy, at this moment, was to find out what he was up to, then counter it.

So she made a show of giving a deep sigh, hoping it seemed she was ready to relax as she dropped into the chair. She gave him a smile, keeping it on the edge between agreeable and friendly, but not crossing into invitation.

That was going to be even harder than getting any usable information out of him. The pretending she wasn't affected, that she didn't want to invite him into her bedroom, strip them both naked and relive a little island paradise? It was going to take a lot of work.

But she'd never been one to shy from work. Not even when the outcome seemed impossible.

She made a show of looking around, pulled on a disgruntled expression and shrugged.

"My place has more personality than any barracks," she claimed, pretending the chair cushion wasn't as stiff as a brand-new board.

"And you would know this, how? Spent much time in barracks, have you?"

"It's just a place. Where I sleep, store my stuff. I suppose it has that in common with barracks," she said, sidestepping his question. "Is that where you live now? In the barracks? I'd think an officer would merit something a little fancier."

"Just a place? Because your job, your work, it's your priority?" He stretched one arm out across the back of her couch and gave her that long, deep look of his. "You're a driven workaholic, completely focused on career success at the expense of everything else. Not that you care about much else, right? Friendships are low on your priority scale and easy to ignore or sidestep most of the time."

Talk about sidestepping. Darby clenched her teeth against the urge to snap out a few curses and tell him just exactly what she thought of his clever insights.

A mistake, she realized, since he took her silence as permission to keep spouting those insights.

"My family inspires me to be better, to excel. But I'm guessing your family is, what? A burden? A demand?"

A curse, dragging her down even as it pushed her forward.

Darby pressed her lips together instead of sharing that. Instead she pushed to her feet. To hell with strategy. She wanted him gone.

"You don't know me," she snapped. "A few nights rolling around naked together, a few meals and some water play doesn't give you any special knowledge of who I am."

"You don't think so?"

Nic slowly shifted, rolling to his feet in a gracefully sinuous move. Because she was barefoot, he towered over her, his uniform only adding to the impression of power.

"I'd say I know you pretty well. Not everything," he said with a contemplative tilt of his head. "Not nearly everything. Yet. But enough."

Enough for what?

"Is that why you're here? To intimidate me with what you see as clever insights?" Or did he think he could scare her into recusing herself from the case? No, she realized looking at the calm composure on his face. He wasn't afraid she was a threat.

His mistake.

"Is that what you think? That what we had between us was intimidating?" Nic's smile was somewhere between smug and challenging.

Darby knew she should ignore it. She was too smart to step into such an obvious verbal trap.

But she couldn't resist that smile.

"Please, do you think I'm scared of a little moonlight romance and hot sex?" she said with a wave of her hand, ignoring the flare of heat in her belly reminding her that yes, she was a little scared of romance and hot sex when it was unforgettable.

"I don't think you're scared of much. Truth be told, I don't think it matters if you're scared—you don't back down from anything."

Darby hadn't been raised to expect praise—why bother when she'd never been as good as her brother? But she was damn good at what she did, so praise rarely shocked her.

So why did it now?

"What's your point?" she asked, trying to shake off the discomfort as she shifted from one bare foot to the other.

"My point? I don't know that I have one. What I do have is a curiosity." His lips twitched at her stubborn silence. After a dozen or so seconds, he inclined his head. "We spent a lot of time together that week. Despite your mandate that we keep the details of our actual identities secret, you fished for plenty of intel in those supposedly innocent little chats."

She should have. If she'd known who he was, she would have. But damn if she wouldn't have been smarter about it. She'd have asked better, specific questions that would have gotten her solid, indictable information.

But she'd been too busy with that romance and hot sex.

"What are you accusing me of?"

"Accusing you of? Nothing. Actually, I'm only here to get the answer to a single question."

"Just one?"

"Just one. Did you know who I was on Hanalei? Were you already building your case against me? Was that the why for what happened between us?"

She wanted to say yes.

God, she wanted to pretend that everything had been a clever plot. A carefully orchestrated plan to gather insight and information for the case. She wished she was that good. She wanted him to believe she was that good.

But lawyer jokes aside, she just wasn't that good of a liar.

"No." Darby pressed her lips together, the lie bitter in her throat. So bitter, she had to admit the truth. "Not at first. Not until that last night."

"When I was called away." His eyes still locked on her, he walked closer and gave a stiff nod. "So the rest, that was just us. No client confidentiality at stake, of course. But still, everything I told you, I told in confidence."

He skirted around her. Close enough that she could feel the heat from his body, smell his scent teasing her memories.

Darby turned to watch as he strode to the door. One hand on the knob, he glanced back and arched one brow.

"Something to think about."

For a long time after he left, Darby stood next to that stiff, unbroken-in chair. She stared at the closed front door, her thoughts a tangled mess of confusion and doubt.

He'd broken into her apartment with the casual ease of a cat burglar.

He'd waited. Confronted her. Taunted her decorating style—or lack thereof.

He'd put his defense at risk. And with it, his commission. His team. His reputation. His freedom.

Why?

To find out if she'd known who he was on the island?

To ask if she'd slept with him for information?

To… What? Discern whether the feelings— whatever they might be—between them were real or not?

Darby rubbed her thumb against the pain throbbing between her brows and sighed.

Now just what the hell was she supposed to make of all of that?

NIC HAD FIGURED the unending repercussions of someone trying to torpedo his career had hit total crap when he'd buried one of his best men.

Oh, how wrong he'd been.

And it only took getting kicked in the gut by the reality that one of the attorneys prosecuting him was the woman he'd thought he was falling for to make him realize *just* how wrong he'd been.

So he did exactly what he'd been trained to do as a SEAL.

He embraced the shit.

He learned from it. Measured his weaknesses, shored up his defenses and strategized the best way to win this damn war.

He was done with defense.

It was time to launch his own attack.

With that in mind, he strode through the brig the next morning, focused on clearing his mind. He set aside the fury, shifted the memories into a box, sidelined the knife-in-the-back feeling of betrayal.

He put it all aside. He was here for one reason and one reason only.

To look the enemy in the eye.

He silently made his way through a series of security checkpoints, each requiring a higher clearance than the last. The final set of steel doors required a retinal scan, a thumb scan and one of the two guards calling in a verification while the other stood with one finger on the trigger of his rifle.

"You have the green light, Lieutenant Commander," the first guard said once he disconnected the secured phone line. "Fifteen minutes. Master at Arms Quinn will accompany and observe."

Savino nodded. He'd expected no less.

So he waited for Quinn's scan, then for the heavy doors to slide open. He followed the beefy man through the security point and down the steel hallway, their boots clanging dully in the silence. Nic hadn't spent a lot of time in prisons, civilian or military, so he couldn't be sure if this level of quiet was the norm or if Navy prisoners were simply well-behaved.

"Sir." Quinn gestured to the door at the end of a

short hallway. "The comm link is now open. Please be advised that your conversation will be recorded. Your fifteen minutes begins now."

Nic nodded his thanks. Eyeing the communications system, he made a mental note to request access, then he stepped up to the barred door. A glance through the reinforced glass showed a sparse metal cell. A cot, a sink, a toilet and a chair were the extent of the furnishings, all made of the same cold steel as the walls.

The only things that weren't metal were the thin blanket-covered mattress and the man lying on it. Unlike the last time Nic had seen him, Ramsey's hair was once again military-short, his gray digies a few shades darker than the walls of his cell. Instead of spit-and-polish boots, his bare feet were planted on the mattress.

Since the guy had one arm crossed over his face, Nic could watch unobserved for a moment. And he liked what he saw.

He could have had Ramsey pulled into interrogation. He could have had him pulled into an interview room.

But he'd wanted to see him here.

In prison.

Behind bars.

Locked away.

Not caring that the satisfaction in his gut was unprofessional, Nic took a long moment to look over the man.

Lieutenant Brandon Ramsey had served under him for ten months. A golden boy, in looks and reputation, the guy had built a reputation as one of the

best. His problem was he couldn't settle for "one of."
In Ramsey's mind, there could only be "the one."

And he figured he was it.

But ego was no match for training.

Arrogance couldn't top teamwork.

And nothing could beat Poseidon.

But this motherfucker sure had tried.

In doing so, this man had betrayed his commission. He'd deceived the Navy. He'd sold out his fellow SEALs. He'd committed treason against his country.

And he'd tried to set up Poseidon for all of it.

Nic worked to contain his fury. This man, this conniving asshole, had killed a good man in cold blood.

Nic would be damned if he'd get away with ruining the rest of the team, too.

He punched the button to engage the comm.

"Ramsey."

The other man dropped his arm to his side. Contempt obvious in his stance, Ramsey didn't sit up. He didn't stand, he didn't come to attention. He simply turned his head. And gave Nic a cold stare.

Knowing the guy had taken as much pride in his looks as his skills, Nic made a show of looking him up and down. Then, letting his expression fall somewhere between pity and disdain, he shook his head.

"You're not looking so good," Nic observed, eyeing the puckered scar bisecting the pretty boy's cheek. Bitterness had etched lines on his face and the once tough and toned build was sagging without the intense workout regime that turned SEALs into weapons.

"No worries. I'll be looking fine again when I get

out of here," Ramsey said. His tone was mocking, but Nic could see the fury in his eyes.

"You keep telling yourself that."

"Facts are facts, man. You know them as well as I do. Why else would the revered leader of Poseidon be paying me a visit? I hear your kingdom is crumbling, Savino. And you're going to be crushed in the rubble."

"Is that what you hear?" Nic made a note to find out who the guy had been talking to. Solitary confinement should be keeping his intel limited to the weather. But they already knew Ramsey wasn't working alone.

Beyond the personal satisfaction of seeing this rat caged, that was why Nic was here. To keep digging. To find out who Ramsey worked for, who he worked with. Then bring them down.

"I hear you're facing charges." Grinning now, Ramsey sat up and swung his feet to the floor as he rested his back against the wall. "How's that feel? Knowing your ass is being investigated. That people see you as a criminal? Bet it irks the hell out of your high and mighty ass, doesn't it?"

"What infuriates me is knowing scum like you once wore a uniform. Knowing that you served next to honorable men while betraying everything you'd sworn to protect." Nic gave him a cold stare. "But irked? That's like bothered, isn't it? A mild irritation? That's about all you are, Ramsey. Not even impressive enough to warrant pissed off."

Ramsey's face tightened, his glare hot enough to melt the bars on the door. But he still had a good enough handle on his training to keep his mouth shut.

He was pissed.

But not pissed enough to lose control.

So Nic got to try a little harder.

Good. A small smile played over his lips, because he was really looking forward to this part.

"Bet it sucks to be in locked away like this. Imprisoned. Knowing that no matter what goes down, you're done. Nobody's coming to your rescue. Not one person cares enough to even stand up for you."

"Not yet."

"Not ever. Whoever you think is backing you up, whatever power you think you have in your corner? It won't get you out of here. You're going down for murder, Ramsey. You killed Mason Powers."

"Nope. Didn't happen. And you can't prove otherwise." Ramsey shrugged, stepping closer to the door in case his sneer wasn't clear enough from a distance. "Who's going to say different? Powers? Oh, he can't say shit, can he? Because he's doing time six feet under."

Worthless fucker.

Fury surged, hot and intense. Fists clenched at his sides, Nic took the second he needed to grab the ragged threads of control. He'd built his reputation on ice-cold control and he'd be damned if this murderous traitor was going to see him lose it.

So he took that second. Then he took another one for good measure.

Then he smiled.

A chilly look of condescending amusement.

"You can't take Poseidon down. We're a fucking legend, dude. Of course, you knew that, didn't you? You tried hard enough to weasel your way into Poseidon. Must have been hell to realize that you simply weren't good enough."

"You think I give a damn about being part of your lame-ass club?"

"I think you gave a good damn about it. I think you tried to pull strings, to tap favors and get Cree to send down an order for Poseidon to open their ranks and let you in." Nic gave a half laugh. "Dude, that's like crying to mommy to get daddy to let you have your way."

"Fuck you."

Nic had to laugh.

"You do realize that an NCSI was brought in, of course," Nic pointed out, referring to the Naval Crime Scene Investigator he'd called to Tahoe to re-create and verify the evidence. "And then there is the witness."

"Some dumb woman? She didn't see a damn thing because there was nothing to see. I didn't kill Powers," Ramsey snapped, trying to appear as if he didn't care. But his tone didn't come anywhere near close to the dismissive one Nic had used. "You think anyone's going to care what the ex-wife of one of your dirty team says?"

Oh, yeah, Nic noted. Someone was keeping Ramsey up-to-date.

"Shall we review?" Nic offered with a chilly inclination of his head.

"With permission from command and with the aid of specific civilians, a trap was laid for your capture. You not only took the bait, you confessed to treason. A confession recorded by Lieutenant Elijah Prescott, and transmitted to command in real time. That sort of thing prevents any accusations of tampering with the

recording." Nic took a second to enjoy the fury flashing across the other man's face before continuing.
"You then, with the aid of an as-yet-unknown accom-
plice, attacked two SEALs and rather than making
a run for it, proceeded to the safe house with the intention of kidnapping your biological offspring. In
the process, you killed an officer of the US Navy, attacked a civilian and...how did that end?"

Nic tilted his head to one side, taking the moment
to clear his mind of the image of his man lying on
the ground with a bullet in his head. He had a mission, and he couldn't complete it if he was blinded
by grief-fueled fury. As soon as he had control, he
pointed at Ramsey through the glass.

"Oh, yeah. That ended with the civilian female
kicking your sorry ass. How does that feel, Ramsey?
Knowing the only way you could take on a man your
own size was with an ambush, but that a woman half
your weight took you down with a few well-placed
kicks."

He could actually hear the grinding squeak of
Ramsey's teeth as he gritted them together.

And it felt good.

"I was there to get my son," the other man growled.
"I have the right to get my kid."

"Your biological offspring," Nic amended meticu-
lously.

"My son," Ramsey roared, rushing the door with
fists raised. He beat his rage against the steel, the
sound echoing through the comm but not budging
the metal door. "He is my son. Mine. You won't keep
him from me. Not you. Not that bitch, Harper. Not
that filthy gangbanging Mexican."

Nic didn't try to hold back his smile. He shared it. Hell, he reveled in it.

"You're referring to Lieutenant Torres and his wife, I take it?"

Ramsey's eyes bulged, the growl grinding between his teeth before he remembered his training. He wasn't able to reel it in completely, but he did manage to jerk his chin in dismissal.

"Whatever. He's welcome to my sloppy seconds, but he won't touch my kid. My parents, they're getting custody until I'm out of here."

"Is that a fact?" Nic rocked back on his heels while he considered that interesting piece of information. To their knowledge, Ramsey hadn't bothered to let his parents know he was alive. His mother was still crying over the shrine she'd built to her lost son. And now he thought they were going to get control of a child he'd abandoned before the kid was born? "I'll be sure to let the Torres family know your family's attorney will be in touch."

There it was. The lie was just a flash in those blue eyes as they shifted minutely to one side.

"I'll get out of here," Ramsey insisted. "I'll get out, take my son. And when I do, I'll..."

"You'll what? Get revenge?" Nic laughed. It felt good. It felt even better when it had the desired effect.

"I'll get revenge, you stupid asshole. On you. On Torres. On Prescott and his stupid bitch. On all of you worthless losers."

"Losers? Buddy, you're the one behind bars."

"You're all going to rot in the brig," Ramsey yelled, spittle flying from his lips as his face ran through three shades of red. "Me? No way in hell

I'm staying in here. All I gotta do is keep my mouth shut and wait."

Not bothering to hide his triumphant grin, Nic took a deep breath.

Excellent.

"Is that the best you can offer? Guess you didn't pay attention during interrogation training. This is where you're supposed to assuage my anger, offer up a few false leads. Maybe promise intel in exchange for consideration."

"I'm not giving you anything."

Which meant he had something to give.

Good.

"Sir."

Riding on the wave of triumph, Nic glanced over his shoulder, nodding when the guard tapped his watch. His fifteen minutes were up. He considered it time well spent. Especially when, after shooting Ramsey one last smile, he turned on his heel and strode away without another word.

Still engaged, the comm broadcast Ramsey's furious protests loud and clear. Cursing, kicking, screaming for revenge.

Nic grinned the whole way out.

CHAPTER THIRTEEN

"I REALIZE WE haven't known each other for a long time, Darby. I swear, I've never seen you like this." Eyes so round her lashes almost hit her brows, Grace stared across the table in awe. "Don't take this wrong, but don't you think that maybe you've had enough?"

"Nope." Ignoring her stomach's argument that Grace was right, Darby lifted two fingers to signal the waiter for another round. She'd been so upset after Nic's visit the night before, she'd taken up Grace on her offer of dinner after work. Anything to avoid going back to her apartment in case the man came calling again.

"Oh, no." Grace gave a pitying shake of her head. "You've already had two. How can you manage another one?"

"Hey. It's healthier than booze."

Darby stabbed her fork through the mound of whipped cream into the molten lava cake, specks of shaved chocolate falling to the plate as she scooped up a bite.

"Mmm," she sighed as the decadent richness hit her tongue. "Nothing like a thousand calories of deliciousness to make a girl forget her worries."

"No amount of chocolate is going to fix this," Grace said with a frown, digging her own spoon into the dessert. "Your worries need to be dealt with, Darby. You can't drown them in syrup."

"Maybe not, but I can forget them for a little while." She licked a smear of hazelnut syrup from her spoon, giving herself time to process that. She stared, unseeingly, at the river of chocolate floating across her plate and quietly admitted, "He confuses me so much."

"Of course he does." Giving the dessert a look that fell somewhere between regret and disgust, Grace set down her own spoon and leaned her elbows on the table. "You had a thing *for* the guy when you had a thing *with* him in Hawaii. Despite your presence in the courtroom, I know you have doubts about the man's guilt. But at this point, you're still planning a case of treason against him?"

"It's my job," Darby muttered, scooping up another bite in hopes the bittersweet ambrosia would heal the stabbing pain in her heart.

"You care about this man, don't you?"

Darby wanted to lie almost as much as she wanted to lick the plate. But she couldn't do either.

"I did care. At least, I did before I knew who he was. What he was."

"What changed once you knew his name? This case aside, is he a different man now than you thought he was? You sounded so hot for the vacation guy. Aren't you still hot for him?"

Was she?

Since her plate was empty, she scooped up a forkful of Grace's cake while she considered that question. Nic was still just as sexy. Just as strong. Just as honorable—maybe even more so now that she knew his reputation. She remembered how she'd felt last night in her apartment. Just standing next to the man was a turn-on.

"It doesn't matter," she decided when she could feel her chocolate high starting to fade. "We're on opposite sides of this case. Win or lose, he'll always be the man I tried for treason. I'll always be the person who put him in prison for the rest of his life."

"You haven't ruined his life yet," Grace pointed out. "You said yourself that you don't have enough to file charges."

"By the time Paul is through with his case, I will." Darby blew out a long breath, then gazed around the restaurant searching for distraction. Despite its close location to the US Attorney's office, she rarely had reason to eat here. Gourmet decadence was all well and good, but she usually had a burger at her desk. However, when it came to distraction, sometimes decadent was the only way to go.

And God, she needed the distraction. She felt as if her heart and brain were at war, neither willing to give way while the other lived.

"I need another dessert."

"No." Grace grabbed Darby's hand before she could catch the waiter's attention. "One more lava cake and you'll puke."

"I was going to order cheesecake this time," Darby muttered. Tugging her hand free, she swiped her finger through the tiny puddle of chocolate on her plate.

"Hey, set aside the case and all its implications for a moment and deal with your actual feelings. You need to deal with those, clarify them and face the truth, before you can deal with the rest," Grace suggested quietly. "Just for a minute, pretend the case doesn't exist. Why would't you go for it with him?"

"How about the fact that he's a military officer? A SEAL? A man who risks his life for a living. A man who is probably gone as often as he's not." Darby's voice grew stronger as she warmed to her theme. "He'll never put me ahead of his career. Chances are, he won't even share most of what he's doing. Half of his job would be top secret."

"Probably more than half," Grace said before dismissing that with a shrug. "But so what? A lot of your job requires confidentiality. Should a guy ditch you because you won't serve up government case details over breakfast?"

Darby frowned. Before she could argue that, Grace continued.

"And sure, he'll probably be away from time to time. But he's a Commander. That means he's more into the planning and desk work than boots on the ground, right?"

Why was Grace destroying her resolve? Darby searched for a valid argument to put her back on solid footing.

"What about my mom?" Darby said, sure the sick feeling in her stomach was due to thoughts of her mother instead of the chocolate overdose.

"Oh, no. No, no, no, no, no." Looking about as ferocious as Darby had ever seen her, Grace leaned across the table with a furrowed brow. "No way are you falling back on that lame excuse."

"My mother has always blamed the SEALs for my brother's death. I never really listened, I mean, she blamed everyone in her life for my brother's death.

But it turns out she was right. Team Poseidon did play a part in it." Darby had to swallow before the bitterness of those words ruined the flavor of chocolate. "As it stands, this case might actually earn her approval. She'd completely disown me if I did anything less than put him in prison."

"So?"

"What do you mean, so?"

"Look, don't take this wrong." Her round face creased with worry, Grace chewed her bottom lip for a second as if trying to think of a right way to frame her words. "But from what you've told me, she's not exactly mother of the year."

"So? She's still my mother."

"And you're her daughter. Has she ever made that a factor in any of her important life decisions?"

God, she wanted to say yes.

But she couldn't. She'd lost more than her brother when he'd died, she admitted to herself as she slid her spoon through the chocolate left on her plate, absently doodling designs with the speckled brown puddles.

"No," she finally said. "But not putting me first in her life and completely cutting me out are two different things."

"Is it really? Is your mother that black or white?" Grace asked with an exasperated huff.

Was she? Darby blinked in surprise. Was that where she got the all-or-nothing attitude?

"Why would you keep using her as an excuse? Or are you going to base what you want on your own life? Your own needs? Quit seeing life as black-and-white, Darby."

But black-and-white gave her solid ground. It made life simpler. And as much as she didn't want to be anything like her mother, living in the gray was too much to risk.

"It doesn't matter," she finally said, meeting Grace's eyes. "The case exists. If we bring treason charges, I'm prosecuting. And win or lose—and believe me, I'll win—it will ruin his life. There's no future for us. There is no gray."

KNOWING SHE HAD no choice, Darby focused all she had on her work. On crafting an unassailable case. The following day she worked long past Grace's quitting time, knowing she'd get more done without her secretary peeking in with worried eyes.

"Darby Raye?"

Momentarily startled, Darby looked up from her notes. "That's me."

"We need to talk."

If the fury in that gravelly tone hadn't snagged her attention, the sharp crack of the door would have. As if someone had wrapped her office in ice, then the temperature dropped and even the furniture seemed to tense up.

She blinked.

Well, hello.

Pretending her stomach wasn't clenched as tight as a fist, she leaned back in her chair and gave the men her attention.

She'd wondered when she'd get a visit from Team Poseidon. Paul had pulled her into this mess, but had assured her that they'd be too cowed to draw attention to themselves.

Her gaze swept from one man to the next, noting that each of the half-dozen SEALs looked as if they regularly played catch with jeeps in their spare time. If their military bearing and combative stance weren't evidence enough of their identities, half of them wore their Navy uniforms.

So much for Paul's assurances.

Leaning back in her office chair, Darby silently scanned each man's face, assigning a name based on the photos in her files.

Chief Petty Officer Aaron Ward stood to one side of the door, his hands clasped behind his back and his chin tilted at a stubborn angle. Flanking the other side of the now-closed door was Lieutenant Jared Lansky, his Boy Scout visage rigid with anger. Three more stood in formation in front of them. Parade rest, she supposed it was, with their feet hip-distance apart, hands clasped at the small of their backs and their eyes locked on her as if she was some sort of explosive device they planned on either disposing of or blowing all to hell.

Lieutenants Diego Torres and Elijah Prescott and, if she wasn't mistaken, Chief Warrant Officer Beau Danby. Although she wasn't 100 percent on his identity, since the man's face was covered in still-healing contusions and an explosion of bruises that looked as if he'd been hit by a bus.

All that threatening testosterone might be enough to intimidate a more timid woman.

But intimidation was only a step up from fear, and Darby had years of practice at hiding her fears. So she called on well-honed skills to not only hide her emotions, but also to use them as a weapon of her own.

"Gentlemen. Office hours are eight to five, Monday through Friday. I'd suggest you come back then but we all know better. So I'll simply suggest you leave."

"We'll leave when we've finished."

"Finished what?" she asked the one who'd clearly appointed himself speaker for the group.

"Discussing this situation."

She refused to tilt her head back enough to see his entire face, but if she hadn't gotten a good look on his way in, the dangling dog tags clearly identified him as Lieutenant Ty Louden.

Nic's second-in-command.

"What do we have to discuss?" she asked, shuffling papers into files and closing them.

"Do you even know who Lieutenant Commander Nic Savino is?"

"Do you?" she countered, her words as cold as ice. "By your own admission, you consider Lieutenant Brandon Ramsey a traitor. You served with him for some time and didn't notice his treasonous actions. Given that track record, I'd have to believe that your judgment of who a person is might be questionable."

"Don't. You. Dare," Louden warned, biting each word off with a snap of his teeth. "Ramsey killed one of our team. He left another to die in flames. Don't you dare compare that man to Nic Savino, a decorated leader who has served his country with honor and patriotism. If you had any idea who he was, you wouldn't be taking part in this witch hunt."

Darby barely resisted the urge to flinch at the

fury all but slapping her in the face. Instead, she focused on keeping her expression calm and her fingers still. As soon as she was sure she had a firm
grip on her control, she let her lips shift into a half
smile and crossed one knee over the other. The man's
eyes didn't even shift, despite the amount of leg she
was showing.

Interesting.

Apparently the men on Nic's team were as loyal as
she'd heard. It could be training, maybe the guy was
gay. But she was pretty sure it was loyalty.

"Gentlemen, I admire your willingness to stand
behind your leader. It's a testament to everything
you've been through that you believe so strongly in
his innocence."

And despite the evidence on her desk, if she was
defending this case, she'd call them all to the stand
since she thought their faith weighed heavily in Nic's
favor.

"What we believe is that you have no idea what
you're dealing with," Lansky snapped from his position guarding the door.

"What I think I'm dealing with are the possibilities of bringing charges of four counts of criminal
treason, one count of attempted murder, one count of
murder. Oh, and a lousy attempt at damage control."
Darby gave a challenging tilt of her head, daring
them to deny her summary. Instead, Louden latched
on to one single phrase.

"What the hell do you mean, *damage control*?"

Ignoring the muttered curse from across the room,
Darby kept her gaze on the burly behemoth in front
of her. Not only because he appeared to be the leader

of the pack, but he also looked like he'd be the first to set flame to her desk, while the others hauled out the roasting rack.

"Damage control. As in carefully laying a trail of evidence that pointed to a dead man instead of anyone on his team. That's damage control," she explained, glad her voice wasn't shaking like her stomach. "Further damage control was employed when an unsanctioned mission was carried out to rescue a kidnapped child. And then there's the mission that ended in the death of a fellow SEAL. After which, again, accusations and finger-pointing occurred in an effort to steer attention away from those involved."

She paused, not for effect so much as to gauge the room. Of the six men surrounding her desk, five were glaring, two still had hands fisted at their sides and the one looming over her looked as if he'd like to roast her over a blazing fire, then sprinkle her with bacon bits.

This time her gaze searched deeper as it swept the room, hunting for any hint of guilt, one iota of culpability. What she saw was disgust. Prescott, Lansky and Danby looked like they tasted something so nasty, she hoped they didn't spit it out on her floor. She could hear Ward grinding his teeth from across the room and Torres appeared ready to put his fist through her wall. Louden just stared, those implacable blue eyes boring into her like lasers.

"So who are you planning to take down in this witch hunt of yours? Savino? Or everyone on Team Poseidon?"

Breathing through her teeth to filter out the heavy waves of testosterone filling the room, Darby resisted the urge to jump to her feet. But she'd kicked off her shoes earlier and figured it'd circumvent her authority if she had to feel around under her desk for them with her toes. Just as it would if her five foot one self tried to face the room of giants with bare feet.

Instead, she wrapped attitude around her like a thick wool blanket and leaned forward to give them all her hardest stare.

"You don't really think I'd answer a question like that, do you?" Darby laughed. "First off, I'd never jeopardize a case by discussing it with those associated with the accused. Secondly, at this time, treason charges are being considered but haven't been levied. And thirdly, despite this obvious attempt at intimidation, I'm not afraid of you."

"That might be a mistake."

"Are you perhaps threatening me?" she asked, arching her brows. She was pretty damn proud that her voice didn't shake. Because if there was ever a reason to shake, it was being surrounded by a half-dozen hulking hotties, each one trained to kill and all of them glaring at her.

"Nope." Louden shook his head. "We're not here to threaten, intimidate or coerce. We have intel that we don't believe you've accessed. We're here to bring you up-to-date."

Sure they were.

And she was intimidated anyway, Darby admitted to herself as she glanced from man to man.

Nic was lucky to have them on his team.

She looked at the list of theories, suppositions and probabilities spread over her desk. Paul had provided a lot of damning evidence. But he had yet to produce his key witness responsible for the claims. Which left his unassailable truth, well, assailable.

She knew Paul. His personal issues made his judgment questionable.

What she didn't know was whether it was that questionable judgment that made her want him to be wrong. Or if it was her feelings for the defendant.

Maybe whatever these men had to say could help her figure that out.

"Here's the deal. You want me to listen, it'll be on my terms," she snapped.

"What terms?"

"I'll speak with one—and only one—of you. The rest of you can go do push-ups or swim in the ocean or something."

That got a snicker or two.

Darby put on her best bitch face, complete with arched eyebrows.

That got her a couple more snickers.

She locked her eyes on Louden and waited.

After a few moments, he jerked his head.

The others filed out without a word.

"Would you like to have a seat for this? Or do you want to keep lurking over me like a mountain, blocking the light?"

"You've got moxie," Louden observed with a nod. He pulled the extra chair into the precise center facing her desk and sat. The chair groaned, fake leather creaking protest. Damn, he was a big man.

Like a wrestler, his muscles were pure bulk, whereas Nic's build was more like a swimmer. Just as muscular, but sleek.

Deliciously sleek.

Darby blew out a breath.

"Okay. What's the new information that you feel will affect the case?" She flipped to a clean page in her legal pad and tapped it with her pen.

"Recently we've traced key transmissions back to their source. And it ain't Savino."

"Are your superiors aware of these sources?"

"The transmissions were erased, the evidence buried deep in the servers. But we've been able to piece enough elements together to determine the origin point of three specific transmissions. Three that include orders connected with the specific acts you're trying Savino for."

Her stomach jumped. Darby wanted to pretend that it wasn't joy, but she knew better.

"Again, have you reported this to your superiors?"

"Considering they're the source, no."

Darby was a well-trained professional. She was considered to be a badass in court, unbreakable.

And her jaw still dropped.

"No way."

"Way," Louden countered with a hint of a grin. "The transmissions came from one specific building within the Naval Amphibious Base, Coronado. The building that houses our commanding officers."

Her heart was pounding so loud she could barely sit still, but Darby forced herself to try.

"Commander Savino serves on the Coronado base," she pointed out. "He lives there."

"At the time of these specific transmissions, Commander Savino was elsewhere. With witnesses. Including, in the second case, a sitting Senator of the United States."

Oh, damn. This time Darby didn't bother trying to sit still. She didn't even try to sit. She pushed to her feet, then glanced at the SEAL.

"I'll need specifics."

"You'll have them." With that and a nod, Louden got to his feet, inclined his head and, with a murmured thank-you, left.

Her mind racing, Darby stared at the empty door for the longest time after Ty Louden left.

And wondered why her heart felt lighter.

DARBY USED TO think she was a woman of strong convictions.

She appreciated varying shades of gray in the law. But in her life, things were either black or white. And she preferred to keep it that way.

And speaking of gray, she thought as she stepped into the concrete box that was the prison interview room and glanced around the chilly space, the two chairs and small square table were the same cold shade as the walls.

Proving once again that the line between black and white in this particular case was so thin it was invisible. Especially when it came to the man sitting in front of the small metal table, his wrist manacled to the ring in the wall.

His jumpsuit, like the room, was a dull gray. She knew he'd been a handsome man once. It wasn't the puckered scar bisecting his cheek that marred his looks, though. It was the bitter hatred emanating from him like a nasty stench.

"Fed lawyer," he snarled in greeting as soon as the door closed behind her. "I'm not going down for treason, so I've got nothing to say to you."

Darby had heard the same from Hansen, Ramsey's attorney. Despite assurances to the contrary from the federal prosecutor's office, they were sure he wouldn't be charged with treason. Darby wanted to know why.

Gauging her opponent, she silently took the two steps necessary to cross the room, set her briefcase on the table and sat down. She watched Ramsey's inspection, knowing her youth and looks would relax him. She'd dressed softly, a linen skirt and matching blazer in a feminine shade of salmon. The small gold knots at her ears and simple chain of round links were classic, but she knew to a man from Ramsey's wealthy background, obviously cheap.

When his eyes met hers again, she saw the combination of triumph and dismissal in his gaze and knew he'd reached the exact conclusion that she wanted.

"I appreciate you seeing me, Mr. Ramsey."

"Lieutenant," he snapped. "It's Lieutenant Ramsey."

"No. It isn't," Darby said easily, folding her hands on the table and giving him a decisive look. "You've been convicted of desertion, of conduct unbecoming an officer and assault. You're due to stand trial next month for the murder of a fellow officer. In addition to your court-martial, the federal government will be charging you with treason."

"Check your facts, lady," he snapped, leaning forward as far as he could. "That conviction's gonna be overturned. I didn't kill nobody and no one can't prove different. And I already told you, I'm not going down for treason."

Darby had studied his case files carefully, just as she'd read every piece of information she could get from his military records. The man was ego-driven, entitled and arrogant. Guys like Ramsey? Their egos tended to climb right over their common sense. She just had to give his ego a reason.

"You sound very sure of that. Almost as if you have access to information that others don't." She added a searching look to the observation, wide-eyed enough to make him think she was impressed.

"And you're here to get that information?"

Instead of answering, Darby simply inclined her head.

"How's this for information. I'm gonna be cleared. Guaranteed. As soon as they take down the asshole responsible for all of this, my name will be gold again."

Not guilty of, but responsible for. Darby filed that away.

"The US Attorney's office is looking at multiple charges of treason," she pointed out. "It's not a matter of choosing one or the other. It's a matter of convicting everyone involved."

"Which is why I'm gonna be cleared," he said, leaning back now with a smug grin that gave her a hint at how good-looking he'd once been. "The charges against Nic Savino are gonna stick. As soon as Savino goes down, the rest of those Poseidon pricks will tumble like dominoes."

"You're aware of the charges against Commander Savino?"

"My attorney looks out for me."

That could be it. But Darby didn't think so.

"And was it your attorney who told you those charges would stick? That's a strong promise to make. Especially since no charges are being considered at this time against the rest of the men on the Poseidon team."

"At this time," he repeated in a telling tone. His eyes glinted with malicious satisfaction. "Look, you're a hot one. From what I hear, you're pretty good, too."

Darby knew innuendo when it oozed over her, but she didn't blink. She simply waited.

"You're after a big win, right? The big-ass case? Sure, it looks good to nail one guy to the wall. But one guy? That's easy. You want to do it right, you nail them all. You take them all down."

Darby watched his eyes, saw the fervor lighting them and wondered if he realized his words could easily be taken as a confession.

"You believe they should all be convicted? Based on what?"

"Based on the fact that those arrogant assholes think they're above the law. They think they're gods. The SEALs, they're a brotherhood. They're the best. But these guys? They think they're so fucking special. Better than anyone else. Them with their exclusive club. Not letting anyone in. Well, let me tell you, sweetheart, they turned down the wrong guy."

His words rose until, at the end, he was shouting. Spittle bubbled in the corner of his mouth and his eyes flamed with hate.

"You?" Darby put just a hint of derision into the

word. Enough that, combined with her quick glance at the manacles holding him in place, made it clear that she didn't think he was much of a threat.

"I coulda done it. I woulda done it. I damn near did. But lucky for me, those fuckheads turned down plenty. And now they're gonna pay."

And there it was. Darby's instincts hummed with delight and she was careful to keep it off her face.

"You believe they should pay, that they should be tried for treason, based on their exclusivity?"

"They're going down because they fucked up," he spluttered. "Then they're all going to fry in hell. From Savino on down, they're going to pay."

He believed that. That was easy to read on his damaged face. But Darby hadn't come here to confirm Ramsey's hate. She'd come to find something, anything, that would answer the questions she couldn't get out of her mind. She'd needed to see what in this huge mess—including the emotional turmoil dogging her heart and mind—was right and what was wrong.

And he'd just given it to her.

Because she didn't want him to know that, didn't want him sitting in his cell replaying this conversation and realizing that he'd tipped her off, she took him through a few more questions, let him rant for a while, then thanked him for his time.

"You'll see," he said as she rose to leave. "This case is gonna make your name. And it's gonna set me free."

Those words were still ringing in her ears as Darby strode out of the building, stopping for a brief second to lift her face to the sun. Breathing in a long gulp of fresh air, she let her thoughts settle.

Ramsey was right.

This case would make her name.

It'd put her on the fast track to even better things. It'd even get her an approving maternal pat on the head.

Multiple military experts believed that her case against Nic Savino was strong enough to bring before a judge.

If the credibility of Paul's classified witness was as solid as he claimed, there was an excellent chance that he'd be convicted of those charges.

But that didn't mean he was guilty.

Even with Ramsey confirming her suspicions, she didn't have proof. All she had was her gut. Her instincts.

Her damn emotions.

Darby slid into her car and, for a brief second, let her head rest on the steering wheel.

There it was again.

An irresistible shade of gray.

She realized she was walking a precarious line.

She knew she risked facing major repercussions.

But even right was right, even when colored by gray.

So Darby grabbed her cell phone. She had to take a deep breath before she punched in the last number. And maybe her finger trembled just the tiniest little bit.

But she still dialed.

And embraced the terror of the gray.

CHAPTER FOURTEEN

NIC HAD BUILT his career on facing challenges and taking risks. He knew exactly how to assess any threat.

Except this one, he silently admitted as he walked up the stairs to Darby's apartment.

Unlike the last time he'd been here, lights glowed a welcome through the curtained windows.

The question was, why?

What did Darby want?

It had to be information. Because it damn sure wasn't his body. Nic's fingers tightened. Not at the idea of Darby having no interest in him. He was fine with that. Sure, it sucked to be so hot for a woman whose only interest in him was locking his ass in jail.

Nope, what sucked was that she could think for one single second that he'd give her any type of information. That she was that clueless about what type of man he was. That she was that clueless about what kind of officer he was.

More than ready to tell her just where she was wrong, he bypassed the doorbell, using his clenched fist instead to pound his greeting.

Then Darby opened her front door. She was dressed down. Not soft and flowing, like she'd dressed on vacation. Instead, she wore jeans low on the hips, a thick brown belt and a plain white T-shirt. The thick-heeled, military-style boots echoed the masculine look, while her necklace—varying lengths of fat chains—gave her outfit a biker vibe.

He went from pissed to rock-hard in two seconds flat. Okay, so he was still pissed.

But apparently that didn't stop him from wanting her.

It had to be the dimples.

"You called?" he asked, his words as cold and distant as he wished his body was.

"Thanks for coming over," she returned, her tone as neutral as Switzerland. "Please. Come in."

Nic strode inside with the same confidence and caution that he would employ marching into enemy territory. Something to remember, he reminded himself.

Darby wasn't his sexy vacation playmate. The woman was working for the damn enemy.

"Still haven't done anything with this place?" he commented, grimacing at the bland landscape of her living room. "You ever check out a Pottery Barn? Or, you know, flea markets?"

"I already told you, I'm hardly ever here." Darby wrinkled her nose as she looked at her beige furnishings. "Besides, what do you know about home decor? Don't you live in a cookie-cutter box on a regimented military base?"

"You've been checking up on me?"

"Given that I'm part of the team prosecuting you, yes. Your address did land on my desk."

Fists clenching again, Nic sucked air through his teeth.

"So that's what you wanted to talk with me about?"

Nope. He wasn't upset to find out he'd been right. Not one little bit. "What's the legal term for conflict of interest?"

"Conflict of interest," she said drily, turning away. But not before he saw her lips twitching.

Nic frowned.

What was going on? Where did the friendly attitude come from? What was she up to?

"Why am I here?"

"There's an issue I want to discuss and I'd prefer to have the discussion away from my office."

"Conflict of interest?"

"Actually, no."

Darby gestured toward the rock-hard-looking couch. He figured it was some sort of punishment since he could tell she wasn't going to continue until he did, so he sat.

"This isn't as bad as I thought," he admitted as he leaned back and crossed one ankle over the other knee. "It's at least two steps up from sitting on a metal bench in a fighter while it's taking fire."

"Taking fire?"

"Being shot at by the enemy."

"Ah." Eyes wide, she slowly let out a breath as she dropped onto the arm of the chair opposite him. "Has that happened more than once?"

"Is this you trying to get information out of me for the case?" he asked, not sure when this conversation had become fun. "How is that not a conflict of interest?"

"My assignment is to assess the evidence in this case and, pending my belief that all evidence is true and factual, pursue treason charges on behalf of the Justice Department."

It didn't take Nic long to get her drift. But he needed an extra few seconds to accept it.

"You don't think I'm guilty?"

Darby opened her mouth, then closed it. With a shrug she slid all the way into the seat of the chair. "Let's say that evidence has come to my attention that needs to be factored in to the rest of the case."

"What evidence?"

"Information has come to my attention that gives pause to the belief that you planned and implemented various acts of treason. Acts including but not limited to the selling of classified information to the enemy." As if realizing she was beating around the bush, Darby stopped, pressed her lips together for a moment, then tilted head to one side. "In combination with this new evidence, it is my belief that numerous individuals are involved in this case. Individuals whose names have not yet been brought to light."

Shit.

Fists tight, Nic pushed to his feet and glared.

"Look. I know you're considering a joint trial. I heard you were going to try to bring in every member of Team Poseidon as codefendants. But that's crap." The more he thought about it, the more pissed he got. "I thought you were an ethical attorney."

"How would you know what kind of attorney I am?" she asked with a dismissive laugh.

"You graduated from Columbia with honors. Instead of following the lure of money, you took a government job. You have a reputation for closing cases clean, for not being afraid to get your hands dirty and for never backing down." And damn if that wasn't nearly as sexy as her smokin' hot body.

"You researched me?" she asked, her voice rising. He understood the shock in her tone, but the hint of unease made him frown.

Nic gave Darby a narrow-eyed stare. One of the things he'd been most attracted to in Hawai'i was the way emotions would play over that beautiful face of hers.

Why couldn't he read it now? Was that really worry he'd noted, or something else?

The bottom line was trust.

Could he trust her?

His instincts said he could. Usually, Nic relied on his well-honed instincts without question.

But he couldn't right now. Not with Darby. Not in this situation.

Because it wasn't just him who was being framed here. Because Prescott was still sporting burn scars on half of his body. Because instead of making dumb jokes and massacring the latest dance moves, Powers was buried in Arlington. And because for all his bravado and bullshit, Ramsey had come across as legit when he'd claimed he hadn't killed Powers.

Nic didn't figure it was his job to give her any of that information.

Not until he knew where she was going with this.

"Let's keep this simple. Are you considering bringing other members of my team to trial in this matter?"

She took a deep breath, then bit her bottom lip as if unsure of what she wanted to say. He wanted to tell her to stop. She was too damn distracting. Before he could, though, she seemed to reach a decision.

"Actually, I'm reconsidering the veracity of Lieutenant Thomas's secret witness."

Sure she was.

She'd based her entire case on that witness testimony. If the information he'd dug up was correct, she'd worked her entire career for a case like this. And she was willing to walk away from it? Shaking his head and wondering what the hell she was up to, Nic dropped onto the couch again.

"Sure you are."

Darby silently arched one brow. Then, as if wanting to seriously test his patience, she gave him an impatient look instead of rising to the taunt.

But Nic was made of sterner stuff than that. So he stared right back.

And waited.

He used the time to give her a good, long look. Even her chilling-at-home look was a world away from the relaxed vacation style he'd found so attractive. But as he took in the T-shirt cupping her breasts and the denim hugging her thighs, he had to admit that he was just as turned on now as he'd been that first night.

He drew in a long, slow breath, hoping to ditch the interest.

Damn, she smelled good. Like hot nights and great sex. Not what he should be thinking, he reminded himself. Except now that it was there, he couldn't get it out of his mind.

"Fine," he finally said, not sure if he was irritated or impressed that she could outsilence him. "You have new evidence that's strong enough that you're questioning your JAG buddy. But you're not going to tell me anything about it. So why am I here?"

He didn't stem the sarcasm, instead he let it ride on the wave of anger surging through him.

"Because I don't want to be a party to injustice," she said, shoving her fingers through her hair so the dark ends spiked every which way. "And I've come to think that your court-martial would be just that."

Somewhere inside, a small spark of hope lit. Not hope that he'd walk away from this trial with his career intact. He refused to believe it'd end any other way.

But that Darby believed him. He didn't know why, he wasn't sure how much. But her thinking injustice in connection with his name? That made him feel pretty fucking hopeful.

Still…

"You're so sure you'd win the case?" he asked with a scoffing laugh.

"I'm good. Damn good," she said in a tone that left no doubt she believed exactly that. "But in this particular instance, I could halfway suck and you'd still be convicted."

"I beg your pardon?" He scowled to keep the surprise off his face.

"The case against you is strong. Despite your years of unblemished service, this evidence indicates that for whatever reason, you've given up serving your country with honor and, instead, are selling information, biological weapons and other intelligence that comes into your hands for a huge personal profit."

Nic's stomach turned. Not just at the recital of

crimes—although it infuriated him that someone would do that type of thing—but that they were being ascribed to him.

"Of course, you have over a dozen years in the military with an exemplary service record and enough commendations to fill a filing cabinet." She gave him a curious expression. "Do you actually have medals for all of those? Do you wear them all at the same time? They must cover your entire chest."

"I don't wear them all," he muttered.

"Just the special ones?"

He shrugged, trying to ignore the sudden wave of embarrassment lapping at him. He was proud of every medal he'd earned, but wearing them all? That was like bragging.

"What about the ones you don't wear?" she asked, sounding as if she really wanted to know. "Do you keep them?"

"As opposed to, what? Tossing them in the trash?" He rolled his eyes. "Of course I keep them. My mother bought me a fancy rosewood chest when I finished basic training. I store them all in there."

"Tossed in a closet or something?"

"You're kidding, right?" He shot a disdainful glance around the blahness of her living room and realized she probably wasn't. That there wasn't a single decoration said enough about her aesthetic sense. But she didn't have a single photo, nothing that looked sentimental. "Okay, maybe you're not kidding. So, no. First, it's a huge standing cabinet, so it takes up part of a wall. Second, they're important. You don't shove something important in a closet."

"That's what I thought you'd say." Her smile

flashed as she nodded. "They're important to you. You value that recognition. I'd guess, given the parts of your file I was able to read, that you put a huge amount of effort into earning those commendations."

"The Navy doesn't give out participation awards," he said, his words just short of a sneer.

"Do you have an issue with participation awards? Like, what? Only the best should be recognized?"

"Recognition is earned. If someone wants something, they should work their ass off for it. Do their best. Put the time in, do the work." There were no two ways about that, as far as Nic was concerned.

"Your reputation—at least, what I've found so far in my research—supports that opinion. What that tells me is that you have a lot of pride in the work you've done, and that you put a lot of effort into being the best." Darby tilted her head to one side, giving him an intent study. "From what I've learned, you don't believe in shortcuts and, in your own words, there are no participation awards in your life."

"Okay," he said, partially in agreement but just as much because he had no idea where she was going with this conversation. She'd called him for a specific reason. Was this it? "Thanks?"

"No big deal." She shrugged. "You'd think whoever set you up would know that. They're obviously close enough to have deep access to your life. How could they be completely unaware of who you are when who you are negates what you're being accused of?"

Reeling like he'd just been hit upside the head with a baseball bat, Nic could only stare. First, he processed her words, then he tried to assess her expression to see if she really meant them.

She looked as if she did, but he had to be sure.

It was too damn important not to.

"You believe I'm being set up?" he asked. Not because he didn't believe her, but because he wanted to hear her say it again. "You, personally, believe I'm innocent."

"I just said that, didn't I?" She gave him an impatient look. "Whoever set you up did an excellent job of it. The evidence is compelling. They've found links between payments and your alleged bank accounts. And they have a witness willing to tell a judge facts that will disprove your logical line of defense."

Well, that was anything but encouraging.

"Okay." Nic rubbed his fingers against his temple. "Let me get this straight. You believe I'm innocent, but you figure I'm going down anyway?"

"Unless you get some help."

He didn't need help. He had his team, his men. Nothing else was necessary. Ever.

Still, he wanted to see where she was going with this.

"And are you going to—" he had to swallow before he could force out the next words "—help me?"

"No."

What the fuck?

Nic barely resisted the urge to give her ugly-ass couch a swift kick.

"Would you care to clarify that?"

A look flashed in Darby's eyes as she got to her feet. She was damn good at hiding her emotions. Oh, but that expression he read just fine. The woman was laughing at him. Why the hell did he find that sexy?

"I'm the prosecution. It would be a conflict of interest for me to help you."

"Do you enjoy fucking with me?"

"What a thing to ask." She flashed an impish smile that left as quick as it'd come. "The bottom line is that I will be filing treason charges in this matter, which means that I can't help you. I can, however, offer an opinion."

"An opinion?"

"You've heard the saying, 'the bigger they are, the harder they fall'?" she said, giving each word care and weight. "Human nature likes to see the mighty torn apart. There is comfort in thinking that the elite are no better than the average."

What the hell did that have to do with anything? Nic didn't bother to ask. He just stared and waited.

"From what I understand, you and your friends all started in basically the same place, correct? SEAL training?"

"BUD/S," he amended. "Basic Underwater Demolition/SEAL training."

She didn't blink at the correction. Simply inclined her head in acknowledgment.

"You and eleven others, all top of your BUD/S class, set records that still hold before graduating. Once you became SEALs, you formed what is now called Poseidon. An exclusive, closed-door group consisting of only the twelve of you."

"We didn't close any doors."

"You didn't allow anyone to join. Instead, you continued training, each member focusing on a specific field that would add to the skill set of the whole. You developed operations, you performed missions together and, over time, you developed a reputation as unassailable. You were the elite, called in for the toughest missions, consulted for advice on the deadliest operations."

Sounded about right. So Nic wondered why her recitation was making the back of his neck itch.

"So you're saying, what? That we're being taken out because we're a threat? A threat to who?" His shoulders stiffened and he stepped closer to give Darby a hard look. "If someone is taking us out, it's because they are targeting the United States in some way that they believe we can prevent. You need to give me details. Everything. My team and I will handle it."

Nic pulled out his cell phone, intending to record her words. Before he could, Darby laid one hand on his arm and shook her head. He didn't like it, but couldn't deny that the admiration in her eyes filled him with warmth.

"I don't have information that leads me to believe there is an imminent attack planned by anyone. Although it wouldn't be a stretch to think that such a plan would be easier if you were out of the way."

"What's your point, then?"

"My point is that a reputation like yours inspires awe, but it also incites jealousy. From those who can't reach those heights. But more from anyone who could, but was turned away."

"You think someone framed me because they were jealous?" Nic rolled his eyes.

"I think someone committed treason because they

are traitors. I think they set you up because they had access and opportunity to lay out a false trail. I think they believed it would work because you were an easy target."

For the first time in forever, Nic was stunned. He opened his mouth, but his brain went blank. Finally after closing his mouth again, he said, "You believe that I'm an easy target?"

"I believe that Poseidon was the focus, and in order to take them down, you were targeted."

She must have noted the insult on his face because she smiled just a little, enough to add fury to that insult. But before Nic could give in to the rarely felt emotion, she shook her head.

"Jealousy is the key. Jealousy, envy, resentment." Seeing the skepticism in his eyes, she asked, "Why did Ramsey hate you?"

"Because he thought he was the best and my men proved him wrong."

"Exactly. And because you wouldn't let him into Poseidon."

"He hated us. You said it yourself. So even if it were possible, why would he want to be on our team?"

"Because you were the best. Because you had the proven skills to ensure that everyone on your team was better than anyone else."

"You're trying to say that someone I know, someone I trust, did this." Nic shook his head. "I refuse to consider that."

"You need to consider it," she snapped. "This isn't being done by some unknown enemy, Nic. You're being set up by someone who knows you. Someone you've worked with."

"Bullshit."

But he couldn't ignore the ringing in his ears. The sick feeling in his gut. He wanted it to be bullshit. But he knew it wasn't.

"Talk to your teammates. They've uncovered information that could help." She bit her lip, reluctance clear in those big eyes. "But my advice is to take everything you're told with a grain of salt. Consider every person you know. Every one you've served with. Because whoever is behind this, Nic, it's someone you know. Someone who knows you."

Nic banked the fury this time. There was no room for it. Not when he could see clear as glass that Darby was risking her own career to tell him this. Something she obviously believed based on intel she wasn't sharing.

"You believe that I should toss aside my legal representative's line of defense because the inside information my team found is stronger than the inside information your team found? But at the same time, I should consider that one of the men I've worked with for over a decade, the team I've bled with, the people I rely on to cover my back, might have set me up?"

She blinked, then shrugged.

"Sure."

There was too much data coming at him, too many hypotheses and possibilities. Because they all carried more weight than he could hold alone, he set them aside and let his thoughts shift. The answer would come, he knew. He simply had to step away and distract himself while his gut worked it all out.

With that in mind, he dropped to the couch. He shot her a grimace.

"Do you ever sit on this? I've slept on metal cots that had more give than this couch."

"Will you quit bitching about my damn furniture," she snapped, shoving both hands through her hair this time as she scowled.

For some reason, her irritation erased his.

Which was fine, except now that he wasn't pissed, watching her pace was turning him on.

He sucked in a long breath and tried to ignore the body walking back and forth in front of him.

Nic wouldn't term himself paranoid. But he had spent his entire adult life studying strategy. He knew he was innocent. Which should mean that the opposing counsel was going to lose. If his legal rep was on the right track with his defense, a smart tactic would be to send them off on a wild-goose chase.

Did he trust her?

Or didn't he?

His eyes locked on hers, he slowly got to his feet.

"If you're bullshitting me, Darby—"

"What?" she snapped. "What are you going to do if I am?"

A dozen threats sped through his mind, each one more interesting than the last.

So he went with the last.

He grabbed her arms and yanked her against his body. God, the woman felt amazing. Almost as amazing as she looked. Her full lips were damp with invitation. Those giant doe eyes were filled with challenge, making him even harder.

"You play me, you'll pay," he muttered, his mouth an inch from hers.

"You call this payment?"

"I call this damn good."

To prove his point, he took her mouth. And almost groaned, she tasted so good. Berry-sweet and just as tart, that sexy mouth parted under his.

Yeah. This was damn good.

THIS WAS SO not how she'd thought this evening would go.

But God, she was loving this direction.

She felt as if her senses were filled with Nic.

The scent of him, clean with a hint of mossy spice.

The taste of him, rich and addicting.

And the feel of him. Oh, yeah, he felt amazing.

His hard body molding against hers. His thigh thick between her legs. His chest heating her nipples into peak intensity. Those broad shoulders a rigid anchor for her to hold on tight for a wild ride.

She wanted more. So much more.

Still, her mind screamed at her to stop. She should pull her mouth from his, yank her body away and put a few safe yards between them.

But it felt so good. So, so good.

She'd been dreaming about this since the last time it'd happened. For weeks, all she'd thought about was feeling this way again.

"We shouldn't be doing this," she murmured, her lips sliding down his throat.

"Why not?" he asked as he yanked her shirt from the waistband of her jeans.

His hands delved under the fabric, fingers leaving a blazing trail of desire as they skimmed up her waist to cup her breasts. Her nipples pouted through the lace of her bra, wanting more. Needing more.

Darby tried to remember her argument.

"It's wrong" was all she could come up with, though.

"It feels right to me." His fingers found the front clasp of her bra, letting the fabric loose so her bare breasts fell into his hands.

"The case. Opposite sides. Careers," she breathed between gasps.

"So it's wrong. Hawaii was probably wrong, too. You know what that means?"

"Two wrongs make it right?"

"Exactly." He pulled away long enough to whip her shirt over her head. She didn't bother catching the straps of her bra as they slid down her arms. Instead, she let them drop, leaving her bare from the waist up.

"Damn," he murmured. "You are so damn gorgeous. Seriously. You blow my mind."

"Is that a euphemism?"

His eyes widened a second before he burst into laughter. He was still grinning when he ran his hands down her waist to cup her hips and pull her against him again.

His mouth took hers in a hot, wild kiss. Tongues danced, teeth nipped. Desperate for flesh, Darby made quick work of his shirt buttons. Shoving the fabric out of the way, she ran her palms over his chest.

Heaven.

He felt like heaven.

Clothes flew, damp flesh slid over damp flesh.

He combed through her damp curls, then slid his fingers deeper to tease her nether lips until they throbbed. One finger still circling, he slipped two others inside.

The heat in her belly coiled tighter. Her thighs trembled. Sparks shimmered behind her eyes as a tiny orgasm wrapped her tight.

"Oh, that's good," she moaned.

"Let's make it better."

Always the gentleman, he twisted just before they hit the floor so his body hit first. Darby wasn't sure what stirred her up more—that he'd held her high enough that she didn't even feel the impact, or that he didn't release her mouth the whole way down.

"Wow," she said against his lips. "Impressive."

"You think that's impressive? Babe, you ain't seen nothing yet," he joked.

For a brief second, desire's intense demand loosened, letting Darby breathe freely. She sighed as emotions gripped her heart, need and love tangling in tight knots. He was so gorgeous. So sweet. And so appealing in ways she couldn't even begin to list.

Terrified of what she might say aloud if she let these thoughts go unchecked, Darby pursed her lips and blew him a kiss.

"I'm waiting," she teased. "Show me more."

As if that was the signal, they both dived for their boots at the same time, racing to see who could bare their feet first. They stripped off the rest of their clothes, both turning to each other at the same time.

"I told myself my memories were an exaggeration," she murmured. "That there was no way you were as hot as I remembered."

She reached out to run one hand over the smooth heat of his chest, her fingers curling in the dusting of hair before following it down his rigid belly.

"I was wrong. You're even better." She looked into his eyes and realized that as stupid as this was for them to be together, she just didn't care. She couldn't. Whatever this was, it was too big. Too important.

"I didn't forget. The image of you has tormented me every night since Hawaii," he confessed. "Even when it pissed me off, I still couldn't get you out of my head."

Speaking of…

Darby's gaze did a slow meander down his body, her own tightening at the sight of those hard muscles. Then her eyes latched on to the long, hard length of his erection jutting from ebony curls.

Her breath shuddered.

Her body needed.

So she took.

Bending at the waist, she leaned over to run her tongue over the velvet head of his cock. Before she could do more, Nic grabbed her and flipped their positions so he was on his back, her hips toward his face.

And that delicious erection just waiting for her to taste.

Her tongue swirled.

His tongue stabbed.

She gripped the base of his shaft, her fingers sliding up and down in rhythm with her mouth.

His fingers dipped and swirled, teasing in time with his tongue's wild dance.

Darby's body tightened, need coiling. Intense demand gripped her, even as the first wave of pleasure began its exquisite spiral.

"Now," he ordered.

"Yes," Darby breathed, her tongue sliding over the rock-hard silk of his penis before she gave it a gentle scrape with her teeth. "Do me now."

Before he could shift their positions, Darby wiggled her way around so to face him.

"I want to be on top."

"Babe, anything you want, I'm here to give it to you."

Mmm, yeah. After giving his erection one more whispering caress, she poised over his rigid length and teased.

Moist flesh over velvety hardness.

"Damn, babe. You blow my mind." Nic's breath hissed, his chest heaving as he stared up at her with eyes glazed with pleasure.

"More," she panted, taking his hands in her own and pressing his palms against her breasts. She squeezed, the feel of his fingers digging into her flesh, the heat of his palms teasing her nipples sending her even closer to sweet release.

Once she was sure he had that rhythm, she started a rhythm of her own. Knees digging into the carpet, she took the hard length of him into her body and thrust.

Up and down, each slide sending taking her higher and higher up the pleasure chain.

She rode him hard, hips pistoning in time with his hands on her breasts. Then he shifted, one hand sliding down her body while he spread the fingers of the other. His thumb worked one nipple, his middle finger swirling the other.

At the same time, he slipped his other hand between their bodies, working her already aching bud into a frenzy of desire.

"Oh, God. Oh, God. Oh, oh, oh, God," she panted, her breath raspy and shaking as it heaved from her labored lungs.

"Now," he demanded again, his fingers digging deeper into her hips as he controlled her thrusts.

Harder.

Faster.

Deeper.

"Now," Darby agreed on a long keening breath, her body shuddering as the coiling heat in her belly went off like a bottle rocket. Pleasure exploded, bursting in a million heart-shattering directions.

Deep in the grips of a mind-blowing climax, she felt the shuddering burst of his orgasms, wet heat pounding into her like exploding lava.

The feel of Nic coming sent Darby spiraling into pleasure again.

And again.

The only thought she could manage to grasp was how much she'd missed this.

How much she'd missed Nic.

CHAPTER FIFTEEN

STILL A LITTLE BREATHLESS, his mind blown with pleasure, Nic wrapped his arms around Darby and held her tight against him so she couldn't roll away. He settled comfortably between the delight of her slender body and the floor.

After a few moments, he couldn't resist... "Did you know that your floor is softer than that couch?" he pointed out.

"Enough bitching about my couch," Darby muttered, her words reverberating against his chest.

"Want to talk about how good this felt instead?" Never one to avoid the difficult, Nic was ready to take that conversation to the logical next level. As in, what they were going to do next.

"It doesn't matter how good it felt," Darby said, the mellow ease in her tone stiffening, along with her shoulders. "This isn't why I called you."

"You're telling me you didn't want this?" He was too much a gentleman to call the woman lying naked in his arms a liar. But he knew she'd been just as turned on and fully engaged as he had been.

"No." Lifting her head, Darby crossed her hands over his chest, propped her chin on her fist and shot him a tremulous smile. "I enjoyed this. I enjoyed you."

That's what he liked to hear.

As much in appreciation as because he couldn't resist, Nic wrapped one hand around the back of her neck and pulled her down to meet his lips. The kiss turned hot with just a slip of the tongue. Her flavor filled him with hunger again. A sharp, needy sort of hunger that Nic wondered if he'd ever get enough of.

His body was still reverberating from the power of his orgasm, and all it took was a kiss to get him hard again. He wanted her. He had a feeling he'd always want her.

At any age. In any place.

Something to think about.

Later, he decided as he slowly released her mouth. He'd think about it later.

Her eyes blurred with desire, he watched Darby run her tongue over her bottom lip as if relishing the taste of their kiss. This time her smile was sweet. Sweet enough that it made Nic's heart ache in a way he didn't understand.

"We should talk," he said. He didn't know what he wanted to say, though.

Thankfully, Darby seemed to have a handle on her end of that.

"About what?" she asked, her voice as strained as the worry in her eyes. "And I'm not denying that this felt great, but it's not what I called you for."

"So you said. It was something about knowing what needed to be done but not helping me, right?"

All of the languid pleasure fled from his body. Nic had to force himself not to tense as fury shot through him. He was a Lieutenant Commander in the US Navy. A fucking SEAL. He rescued people for a living.

And here he was, pissed off because a woman who weighed less than he bench-pressed wouldn't help him.

"Look, I gave you information I thought you needed." Even though her shrug was an erotic distraction, the way she bit her lip assured him that she wasn't as comfortable as she pretended. "You should leave."

"Not until we discuss this."

"Discuss what?" She shifted, squirmed, then scowled down at him. "Let me go."

"No. We'll set the sex aside. For this moment. Instead, let's focus on why you told me what you did."

"You think you're calling the shots here?"

Nic slid his hand down from the comfortable curve of her waist to her hip, then slipped it between their bodies. She was wet. Hot and wet. The feel of her silken bud throbbing between his fingers was pure temptation. The kind that made it difficult to focus on the matter at hand.

"Okay, fine," she said in a breathless rush. "I focused on the shadows. That gray area between black and white."

"Clarify," he ordered.

"Fine. I can't talk like this, though," she protested, squirming a little. Since the move had his fingers sliding a little lower, a little deeper, he had to agree. A few more seconds like this and he'd be back inside of her.

Talk about needing to get a handle on his priorities.

"We're not finished here," he promised, slowly

unclamping his hand from her waist. She scrambled away as if his body was on fire, but the look she gave him more than made up for it. Because there was passion in that gaze.

Passion and need.

Both of which he planned to fill later.

As soon as they settled this issue.

With that in mind, Nic grabbed his slacks and yanked them on. He didn't bother with zipping or snapping. Neither would feel good right now.

"Excuse me." Scooping her clothes and holding them like a shield, Darby hurried down the hallway into what he assumed was her bedroom.

He paced while he waited.

Her kitchen wasn't as blandly pristine as the living room, he noted. The dish towel draped over the sink was deep blue, a sharp contrast to the gold-speckled red mug on the drainer. She obviously liked color. Which made the drabness of her living room all the more baffling.

"Okay, let's clear this up," Darby said as she came back into the room, tying the sash of a sweeping floor-length robe.

Oh, yeah, he noted, appreciating the way the deep burgundy silk brought out her golden eyes. The woman definitely knew color. She knew how to wear a robe, too. His gaze traveled down the length of that soft fabric to where it teased her bare feet, then back up again. The wide gold sash emphasized her slender waist, the deep lapels gave a peek at the shadowy temptation of her cleavage.

"Um, Nic?"

"Yeah?" He yanked his gaze from her breasts. Blinked. Frowned and said, "Sorry, yes?"

Her laugh was soft and husky. Pushing one hand through her hair so the short ends spiked even higher, she shook her head. "You can't be ready to go again."

"Ready, willing and able."

"Well, put it on the back burner," she said, side-stepping when he reached for her. "Despite that bout of misguided sex, I did have a good reason for calling you."

"Misguided?"

Shooting him an impatient look, Darby tilted her head to one side and asked, "Given the circumstances do you think that sex between the two of us is wise at this juncture in time?"

"Damn." Nic couldn't help but laugh. "You really do sound like a lawyer."

"Probably because I am a lawyer." She stepped around him and hurried into the tiny kitchen. "I'll make us some coffee."

"Coffee?"

"I need something to do with my hands," she confessed with a shrug. "Making coffee, then drinking coffee, will keep them occupied while we get through this."

"Well, that's honest."

"Don't you think the law and honesty go hand in hand?" she asked, watching him over the bar as she pulled a bag of beans from the freezer.

"That's like asking me if caution and the military go hand in hand." He shook his head. "Given the number of jokes on either topic, I'd say we're both the exception, not the rule."

"Well, I don't mind being exceptional," she said, flashing him a quick smile as she measured water into a kettle. After putting on the stove to heat, she poured beans into a grinder. Nic used the noise as an excuse to just watch her.

He frowned when she poured the grounds into the bottom of a tall glass cylinder, then slipped what looked like a metal sieve in a stick on top of them.

"What are you doing?"

"Making coffee." She turned to open a cabinet door. As she reached up to get two mugs she stood on tiptoe so the silky fabric of her robe cupped her butt in gorgeous definition, making him grateful for her petite stature. "What's wrong?"

Since it probably wasn't a good idea to mention that the only thing holding his slacks up right now was his hard-on, Nic went with his second thought.

"Where's your coffee maker?"

"This is it. It's a French press." She tapped the cylinder. "Don't worry, you'll like it."

"Okay." Given the often questionable nature of the coffee he usually got on base, Nic didn't consider himself a snob. "So now that you've educated me and kept your hands busy, how about filling me in."

"Give me a minute."

She poured the boiling water into the carafe. The mesh kept the grounds from floating as she slowly lowered it as if squishing every iota of caffeine from the beans. Nice.

She poured the rich black liquid into each mug

and, apparently remembering he took his black, handed it to him just the way it was.

Then she met his eyes, hers as serious as he'd ever seen.

"YOU'RE MAKING ME NERVOUS," Darby admitted, wishing he'd stop staring. "Why don't you go in the other room and sit while I get my coffee."

"I'm happy here."

"Are you contrary on purpose?"

"No, but I am honest."

Yeah. He was.

Her eyes met his again for a long moment before she turned away to get her own cup, adding a dollop of raw sugar before facing him again.

"Even though treason charges haven't been filed. Yet. My talking with you could still be considered a conflict of interest. It could put my career in jeopardy," she said quietly. "Just like you, I'm proud of what I do. I've worked hard my entire adult life, trying to be all I can be. To be the best."

"That's the Army."

Darby blinked.

"What?"

"Be all you can be. That's an Army slogan."

"What's your slogan?"

"Win."

She almost asked where the rest of it was, then realized that "win" actually said it all.

"That's a good slogan," she replied, pausing to take a sip of her coffee. "I like to win. I've worked hard to make sure that I win as often as possible."

Nic nodded his agreement.

"When I bring charges, I want to win this case." Intent on making her point, she leaned forward to give him a determined look. "And I'm going to win this case."

"Wait." He lifted one palm. "So you didn't call me to offer your help. You want mine."

Well, yeah. But she didn't admit that aloud. Instead, she waited for his reaction.

He took a deep breath. When that didn't seem to calm him, he set his coffee cup aside to pace the room. Darby tried not to get distracted by his unsnapped, unzipped pants and the internal debate over how long it'd take before they simply slid down those slender hips.

"Darby, I care about you. A lot." He ran his hand over his hair, the glossy black gleaming in the overhead light. She wasn't sure if she should be amused or insulted that he stopped then to zip his pants.

"But we're talking about my freedom, here. My reputation. My life."

And there it went. The last of Darby's tension. The few last concerns she'd had about her decision dissipated in the heat of his stare.

"Do you happen to recall the statement I made that first day in court?"

His frown said he didn't.

"I submitted that the Justice Department would pursue treason charges as a whole against any and all individuals involved, whether already accused or yet to be named." She waited a beat, then arched one brow. "That, my friend, is what they call covering the bases."

She loved the way Nic's smile spread over his face. Slow, sexy and even better, knowledgeable.

"You're going to pull a fast one and nail the real traitor."

"I'm going to pull a fast one and nail the real traitor," she agreed.

He finally relaxed enough to sit on the couch and drink some coffee.

"How?"

"A number of your men came by my office the other night—"

"My team came to see you?" he interrupted before she could explain why. He faced her with serious eyes. "Look, I know it probably seems as if my men were out of line. Maybe you'd think a visit like that meant they were trying to influence the case or bring false evidence. But my men would have been acting out of loyalty to their commander."

Her heart melted a little at the strength of his defense of his men. She'd never seen a stronger sense of loyalty in anyone as Nic carried.

"I know."

"What?"

"I know. Their reasons for being there were very clear. And the evidence, as far as I could tell, was legit. I need to submit it to our forensics department. It has to be verified. But the information is strong enough that I'm reconsidering the charges. Which means I need more information from other sources."

"Don't look at me," Nic said with a hint of bitterness in his laugh. "It's not like I have some inside information tucked away that'll tell you the name of whoever is lying to frame me."

"Your men can help there, can't they? They seem to have skills at ferreting out information."

"I'll go over what they brought you and see what I can suggest," he said. "What did you think of them?"

The curiosity in his eyes was obvious, but she wasn't sure what was beneath it. Whatever it was, this question felt like a test.

"I think they're very loyal," she said. Then she admitted, "At first I thought their visit was simply an intimidation tactic."

"Were you intimidated?" he asked with a laugh that made it clear that he was already sure the answer was a negative.

"Actually I was." She shrugged in response to his shocked stare. "It was after hours, I was alone in the office and a half-dozen behemoths with attitudes trapped me in my office. You don't lead small men, Nic. Those guys are big and, admit it, kinda scary."

"That's what the enemy says," he joked.

"Exactly. So don't look surprised that they intimidated me just a little."

"And when you were through being intimidated?"

God, he had a high opinion of her. Darby tucked her feet under her hips and took a second to revel in the delight of someone thinking so highly of her. She considered her ego pretty damn strong, but even she didn't believe she had as much moxie as he thought she did.

That notion made Darby sit a little straighter, unaware that the move put her nipples into sharp relief against her robe until she noticed his eyes widen.

"Once they were finished looming and hulking, they brought new evidence to my attention," she said, pausing to sip her coffee. "Evidence I'd have thought you were already aware of."

She lifted the file she'd set on the coffee table and handed it to him.

Nic held her eyes for a long moment—long enough to make her stomach flutter—then he flipped it open.

While he read, she drank more coffee. Probably crazy to drink this much caffeine so late at night. But she had reason to hope that she wouldn't be getting sleep anytime soon.

From the expression on Nic's face as he read through the summary, this was all new information. By the time he was finished reading, he wore a scowl etched so deep it probably scarred his skull.

"Your men accessed this information. Why did they bring it to me first?" she asked. "Why didn't they bring this to your attention?"

"They'd want to keep the lines of access clean. By bringing it to you without my knowledge, they ensured it as pristine evidence."

Darby frowned as she thought through that.

"But I'm not the prosecuting attorney. Why didn't they bring it to one of your superiors? One not named in that file? Or to the JAG office?"

"Because they are operating under the assumption that every officer in our unit could be involved. Added to that, they are following a very specific chain of investigation that would mandate leaving Thomas out of the equation."

Oh, please let that be for the reason she wanted it to be. But Darby didn't voice that prayer aloud. Instead, she simply inclined her head and asked, "Why?"

"Why assume the unit's involvement?" He lifted the file. "Because of this. Why leave Thomas out? Because they don't trust him. He's made no secret of his hatred of me or my team."

"I'll bet he wanted to join Poseidon and you turned him down," Darby said. She'd heard Paul mention the team a time or two, always in bitter tones. And now she was sure she knew why.

"You think that because we wouldn't let him on the team, he's holding a grudge?" Nic shook his head. "I get your theory, but I can't believe anyone would do all of this because they couldn't play with us. The inception of the team wasn't a secret."

"Was Poseidon your idea?"

"In a vague way, sure. Cree knew my grandfather. He came around from time to time, so I'd mention ideas. You know, like that if a team of SEALs trained in other areas, became a complete unit in and of themselves. He thought it was a solid concept."

"So he gave you the team?"

"He didn't give me anything. Poseidon's formation was based on scores. Only the top ten percent of BUD/S graduates were offered a spot on the team. If I hadn't made the cut, I wouldn't be on the team. Cree planned to lead the group, but he was reassigned to the war zone. I took his plan and ran with it until he was stateside again."

But Cree never actually led the team at that point, Darby knew. He'd become a figurehead, the administrator who looked after the details while Poseidon fought for glory. What did that do to a man's ego?

"Who handled the requests to join?" Darby asked. She shrugged when Nic frowned. "I know you had requests from men who wanted to join. Men you turned down."

Like Danny. Darby shoved that thought away before it could settle in her heart. This wasn't the time, she reminded herself.

"I don't know. Cree, probably." Nic shrugged. "He's the real head of Poseidon."

"No, Nic. He's not. You're the true leader of the team. Everyone knows it."

It didn't take him long to understand what she was thinking. As soon as he did, Nic shook his head. He all but knocked his coffee cup on the table before he stood.

"No. No way. Admiral Cree isn't behind this. There is no way in hell I'll believe he'd do this to me. To Poseidon. Or to his country."

Darby took a careful breath and watched the emotions chasing their way across his face. And, with a heavy heart, she pointed out, "You don't have to believe it, Nic. But for the good of yourself, your career and your team, you do have to look in to it."

THREE DAYS LATER, Nic still hadn't dodged the headache Darby's words had sparked. Like a wildfire, the destructive idea had spread. Had his commander, the man who'd mentored him, taught him, inspired him, framed him for treason?

Cree was a brilliant man, one who'd not only made the military his career, but his life, his family.

The question was how was Nic was supposed to believe that this man had not only betrayed his country, but had also framed Nic to take the fall for it?

And how was he supposed to ignore the possibility?

He sat with his men in Diego Torres's kitchen, a space that could only be called upscale homey. It wasn't the usual space for a team briefing, but given the nature of the information they were sharing, he'd deemed it smarter to use the cover of a friendly barbecue.

"Okay, gentlemen, let's review." He outlined everything they knew so far, all the intel up to and including Darby's belief that jealous resentment was the motive.

"We need to look closely at everyone involved in the front lines of this battle," he told his men. "We know that this setup has been brewing a lot longer than a year. And it goes a lot higher than Naval Intelligence and some butt-hurt Lieutenant who couldn't earn a trident."

He turned to Louden, and with a slight nod indicated that the Lieutenant Commander take over the briefing.

"The butt-hurt Lieutenant in question is one Paul Thomas, Judge Advocate General's office. After failing to graduate BUD/S, Thomas opted to avail himself of the Navy's LEP. Law education program," Louden explained, going into details of what the program entailed even though every man in the room knew what he meant.

But that's one of the reasons Nic had cued the guy up to handle the briefing. Not only did Louden hold his own law degree, but the guy had also gone through Naval Justice School with Thomas and had a firsthand knowledge of the man.

After Louden had finished the briefing, Nic took the lead.

"That's our pivot point," he said. "Envy, covetousness, resentment. Thomas has it. Ramsey has it. Where do we go from there?"

"We've been operating on the assumption that we were a target of convenience. That we were framed because Ramsey's attempt to steal the chemical formula went bad on one of our missions," Prescott pointed out, his eyes on his sketch pad as he drew a target with caricatures of the men of Poseidon in the bull's-eye. "If you look at the common denominator of everyone involved, what if we were the target all along?"

"That's what we have to consider," Nic agreed, pointing an approving finger at Prescott. "This isn't about convenience. This is target specific and we're the target. Which means this just got damn easy, gentlemen."

"Our rep is known worldwide. We inspire a lot of envy, Nic."

Darby's words echoed in his head, but Nic shook them off.

"Don't look to jealousy. Look to rejection. Thomas wasn't good enough to qualify when Poseidon was formed. Ramsey tried to pull strings to get onto the team. The unsub is going to be someone with a similar story." Comfortable in Diego's kitchen, Nic got up to help himself to more coffee.

"What about Cree?" Lansky asked quietly. "Are we looking at him? According to Jarrett, he's claiming he didn't green-light the Tahoe mission. Even if he can't prove anything else, that's the basis of Thomas's case, that we operated a covert sting without approval."

"We have to consider that the Admiral might be the one behind it. He has the connections and the authority to pull this off." Nic clenched his teeth against the bitter taste those words left in his mouth. "And, as you said, he knew about the mission in Tahoe to trap Ramsey. I sent him the plan for approval, so his claiming he never saw it is definitely suspect."

"But you sent it in an encrypted email. That doesn't mean he actually got it. Especially since he broke tradition by green-lighting the mission without a face-to-face discussion first," Danby pointed out. "He sent it in a coded message, ostensibly because he was out of town. He's not the only one who knows our codes."

"Jarrett knows them, too," Louden said, carefully cutting an apple so the peel swirled to the table in a single, unbroken piece.

"That's a big lie for Jarrett to make," Diego argued. "One that would be easy to uncover once Cree's back on base."

"Not if the initial message was intercepted."

"Have you had any contact with Cree?" Diego asked Nic.

"Nothing. Which isn't unusual in and of itself."

"Is it right to narrow our search of the brains behind all of this to either Jarrett or Cree?" Danby asked, shaking his head. "I don't want to miss the architect of this treason ring because we're focused on the obvious."

Agreeing, Nic began handing out assignments. For the next hour, they debated a few, added a couple more and brainstormed where they'd go from there.

The sound of the front door closing echoed

through the room like a gunshot. In a blink, all papers were away, laptops closed, tablets off. The men instantly shifted to casual positions as if they'd just been chatting as Diego's wife walked into the kitchen.

"I'm sorry," Harper said, biting her lip as she noted the tension still shimmering in the air. "I didn't realize you were here. I picked Nathan up early because he wanted to feed his cat."

Which was why the little boy wasn't already in the room, Nic knew.

"No, we're sorry for taking over your kitchen," he said, pouring her a cup of her own coffee. "But we come bearing gifts. Including steaks for the barbecue."

"Are you sure?" Lousy at hiding her concern, she searched Nic's face. "Nathan and I can take off for a while. You guys should finish."

"We are finished." With that and a grateful brush of his hand over her shoulder, Nic raised his voice and called, "Nathan?"

Tall for a seven-year-old, the tousle-haired boy barreled into the room with his beloved baseball in one hand and a cat toy in the other.

"Wow," the boy said, his big blue eyes widening at the sight of all of his stepdad's teammates. "This is so cool. It's like a party. Are you guys here to play ball?"

"How's your pitching coming along?" Prescott asked, wrapping his arm around the boy's shoulder and leading him out the door. After a quick glance at Nic, the rest of the team followed. All but Diego.

"This prosecutor. You trust her?" Diego asked as the others started playing catch in the yard.

Nic looked out the window, watching his men go into goof-off mode with the little boy they'd made their own. A boy who was, in purely technical terms, the child of the enemy. But technicalities didn't matter when it came to love. If anyone could understand that, Diego would.

"Yeah. I trust her," he said when he returned his gaze to the man who'd become Nathan's father. "I'm in love with her."

"Aw, shit," Diego muttered, his face creasing in disgust.

"You object to my falling for someone? Or is it this particular someone you object to?" Nic heard the cold formality in his voice, but he didn't care. For over a decade, nothing had come before his men. He'd vowed to put them first. Not to even consider a relationship until he'd made Captain. Not because the rank held special meaning, but because hitting that rank meant they'd all be on the other side of dangerous missions.

But now?

He wouldn't put Darby before his men. But he'd be damned if he'd put her behind anyone.

"Object? Dude, we've only met her once. And damned if she didn't face us down. Even Louden, who had his bitch face on." Diego laughed as he gave an impressed shake of his head. "She seemed cool."

Nic had to know.

"So if you guys don't have any specific objections to Darby, why'd you say 'aw, shit'?"

"Because Lansky called it. After she kicked most of us out of her office, we chilled in the hallway waiting for Louden. And what did MacGyver say?" Diego asked, referring to Lansky's call sign. "He straight-up said that she was the type you'd fall for."

Score one for Lansky. But Nic knew there was more. He lifted one palm and gestured with his fingers for Diego to bring the rest.

"He was so sure, he put money on it." Diego pulled a face.

"He took you all?" Nic had to laugh. "Nice."

"All but Prescott. You know what a sap he is for romance."

"And you're not?" Nic shot an arch look around the cozy kitchen, noting Diego's satchel tossed over the chair of the built-in desk, the vase of flowers on the counter. Given the haphazard way they'd been throw in the container, he knew the man had bought and personally arranged them. Gracing the fridge was a drawing of a very cozy-looking Diego, Harper and Nathan drawn by the boy's clever hand.

"Seriously, man, you are so in love it's practically oozing out your pores."

"Good thing I'm lucky in love, then," Diego said with a grin. "Because I lost fifty bucks on your sappy heart."

"How do you do it?" Nic queried.

"Do what?" Elijah asked as he came through the door, heading straight for the fridge.

"I think he's asking how I manage to be a kick-ass SEAL while romancing my woman and earning dad-of-the-year cred," Diego said. His tone was joking but his eyes intense as he studied Nic's face.

"If you're looking to El Gato for romance advice, you're in serious trouble," Elijah stated. He dumped the dozen bottles of water he'd snagged onto the table to give Nic a long look. "What's up? You taking about the sexy lawyer?"

"He wants tips on juggling," Diego said, snagging one of the water bottles before he leaned back in the deeply cushioned banquette, one arm angled across the backrest.

"Priorities, man. You know how to do that," Elijah said, grabbing the notepad and pen they'd used earlier, doodling as he talked. "You just put that same dedication, determination and skill to the relationship and it works."

"Didn't you say something along those lines to Ava?" Diego asked, giving Nic a curious expression. "She told Harper you were all about the relationship advice when she and Rembrandt here were working things out."

"I guess it's easier to give advice when you're not the one putting it all on the line," Nic replied.

"I don't agree. You had plenty on the line when you advised Ava to fight for our relationship," Elijah argued. "You're just afraid."

If the man he'd known for a dozen years, had served with for a decade and who Nic had stood as godfather to his late child had leaped across the table and punched him in the face, Nic couldn't have been more shocked.

"Whoa." Diego laughed. "You're gonna need triage if you throw that kind of accusation around."

"Nope. Because Nic knows I'm right." With that, Elijah tore a page from his notepad and handed it to Diego.

With the skill that'd earned him his call sign, Rembrandt had drawn Darby's face. It was a perfect depiction, right down to the sassy tilt of her chin and the challenge in her big eyes. She was it, he realized.

The woman he wanted forever with.

The one who scared the hell out of him.

"I'm keeping this," he said, folding it carefully so the lines didn't crease Darby's face. He got to his feet, tucking the sketch into his pocket. "I've got things to do. Tell Harper I'm sorry to miss dinner."

"More food for me," Diego said, his words as casual as his gaze was intent. "Where you going?"

"To make a bet of my own."

The last thing he heard as he headed out the door was Elijah's triumphant "Pay up, sucker."

CHAPTER SIXTEEN

"I DON'T WANT to do this," Darby muttered as she hooked the back onto one big silver hoop earring, then the other. "I told him I didn't want to do this. I made myself perfectly clear."

So why was she doing this?

Because Nic Savino was as stubborn as he was loyal, that's why. Stubborn, loyal and almost always right. Which could have been totally annoying if he wasn't such a skilled lover.

All of which Darby had spent the last week learning on a firsthand basis. Her days were spent working on the treason case. Evenings were spent fitting together pieces of the puzzle. Nights were spent having mind-blowingly hot sex.

And most of her time was spent with Nic.

A part of her—the cynical part she kept fed with fizzled hopes and blown dreams—had figured that time together away from the romance of Hanalei would put an end to any silly thoughts about love. She'd even hoped that all this time would show glaring issues between her and Nic that vacation hid. Personality conflicts or clashes in taste or, hell, she'd take snoring and poor posture.

But, no.

The man was freaking perfect, she decided, glaring at her own reflection. She even admired his stubbornness and formidable insight. He had a way of using facts, logic and reasonable good humor to make his points, leaving her unable to think of any reason to refuse him anything.

Which brought her to tonight.

He'd wanted her to meet his friends.

Friends who happened to be his teammates, many of whom had hulked over her at their first meet, oozing intimidation.

Friends, and their significant others.

That meant women.

As hard as it might have been for Darby to face down the men who had looked like they wanted to tear her to shreds and burn the pieces over a low fire, it'd be even harder to meet the women.

Women giggled. They chattered and shared intimate details and formed cliques.

That sort of thing scared the hell out of her.

That wasn't why Darby had refused, though.

She'd refused because she was already in too deep. She'd let Nic get too close. She knew her heart was lost. But she'd be damned if the same would happen to her reputation.

She ran it through her head, the same way she'd run it through dozens of times over the last week.

The federal prosecutor's office hadn't, as yet, filed charges. She was doing her job, digging out every piece of information she could to nail down exactly which subjects charges *should* be brought against. She had, other than that one night she'd offered advice, refused to discuss the case with Nic. She'd tiptoed along the gray line as carefully as a tightrope walker, careful—always careful—not to step into the black.

Then he'd pulled that crap on her about wanting her to meet his friends. Even as her heart had danced and her stomach clenched with nerves that he'd make such a sweet gesture, Darby had refused. She'd side-stepped. And, finally, she'd grabbed onto the lesser of two evils like a lifeline and suggested they have a private romantic dinner, just the two of them.

Darby puffed out a long breath and dabbed a little wax on the tips of her fingers, then rubbed them over the ends of her hair to give it a spiky fringe along her jaw.

"This is crazy," she decided as she rubbed her pin-kie under her bottom lashes to give her liner a little extra smudge. Since she'd gone with smoky eyes, she'd done her lips in a pale rose.

She took a couple steps back from the mirror to get a better look at her outfit. She'd paired a sheer pewter blouse with full bell sleeves over a fuchsia camisole with black leggings and matching knee-high leather boots. She narrowed her eyes, debating whether or not the long black lariat necklace was too much.

Nah.

The leather kept the sheer blouse from being too girlie.

Good enough for a quiet dinner for two in a dimly lit restaurant under the guise of wanting a romantic night out. She'd even made the reservations herself, figuring it'd give weight to her claim. And, of course, it allowed her to choose a restaurant two cities away, where nobody she knew would see them.

The doorbell rang as Darby was checking her phone for messages.

Damn.

He was early.

She frowned, glancing at her watch as she hurried across the room to pull open the door. Her frown deepened.

"Grace?"

"Hey, Darby. You forgot your bag at the office," the redhead said, lifting the leather messenger bag by the strap as proof. "I know you usually work at home, so I figured you probably wanted your files."

"Thanks." Taking the bag, Darby studied the other woman. "I appreciate it, but you really didn't have to come all the way over here."

"I don't mind. I figured it'd be a good chance to check in on some things."

Uh-oh. Darby gave her secretary closer scrutiny, noting the lines of stress radiating from her cornflower blue eyes.

"I have a few minutes. Why don't you come in."

"Hey, you look great," Grace said, giving her a wide-eyed once-over as she followed Darby inside. "Do you have a date?"

"It's not a date," she insisted, her fingers digging into the leather of her bag. "I'm just meeting someone for drinks."

"You should go, then. I can talk to you tomorrow. Or, you know, later."

"You came by for a reason," Darby pointed out. "Come in and tell me."

"I figured you might like to know that Paul Thomas was in the Deputy Director's office late this afternoon," Grace said, following Darby into the living room. "According to Carson's secretary, it was a long meeting and neither man looked pleased when it ended."

Darby's stomach clenched for a brief second while her mind raced.

"Do you know what it was about?"

"From what little Eileen heard, Thomas is frustrated that you haven't moved on the treason charges yet. He's making noises about someone else taking over the case."

She'd figured he'd do that when she kept dodging his request, but it still pinched to hear the news.

"Do you know what Carson's response was?"

"I don't know all the details. But I did hear that he told Thomas to back off. He said he had complete faith in your ability to do the job and that he trusted you'd do it right. Carson said he'd be making sure of it."

The stomach that had just unclenched dived right into Darby's toes at hearing that. Oh, hell. She tried to swallow the sick feeling in her throat, but it wouldn't go down.

"But you don't know much beyond that." Struggling against the sick feeling of betraying trusts, Darby looked down at her hands. She made her living dancing in and out of the nuances of the law, but she personally hated to lie. Not seeing that she had a choice, though, Darby put on her best courtroom face and gave Grace an attempt at a smile.

"So that's what you came by for? To bring me my bag and let me know Thomas is pressuring Carson?"

Darby stood, preparing to see her secretary to the door. "I really appreciate it."

"Um, yeah. That's what I came by for." Worry clear in her face, Grace studied Darby's expression carefully. "Are you okay?"

"Sure. I'm fine."

After a long look, Grace shifted her suspicious gaze to her surroundings.

"Wow, I like these pillows." Sliding her hand over the nubby texture of the red one Darby had positioned in the middle of the couch, Grace wrinkled her nose. "Are they new? I don't remember you having this much color in here before."

Her gaze swept over the pillows, which ranged in color from pale coral to deep mulberry. She narrowed her eyes at the deep purple throw draped over the back of the chair, then tapped her finger on one of the trio of fat black candleholders Darby had centered on the coffee table.

Something about the decor seemed to make up her mind, because she squared her shoulders and gave Darby a long look.

"Um, maybe I came by for more than just letting you know about Thomas." She dropped to the couch and snagged a pillow, pleating the fabric between her fingers. "I didn't want to say anything in the office. But I'm worried about you."

"About me?" Aiming for surprise, Darby rounded her eyes. "What's to worry about?"

"Setting aside the decorating, which anyone who didn't know you might consider normal, you're nervous." Grace followed Darby's pacing path with a wag of her finger. "I've seen you tackle some major cases, take on some serious criminals and face down some nasty bullies. But I've never seen you nervous before."

"This is a major case," Darby reminded her.

"One you have a solid handle on."

"Says who?"

"Says the woman who's watched how you work for nine months. I know when you're struggling with a case, and I know when you're worried about something else."

Darby opened her mouth, but couldn't find another lie. So she shrugged instead.

"Maybe I'm dealing with some personal issues."

"You mean you're dealing with Nic Savino."

Not sure what to say, Darby wet her lips. Before she could figure it out, Grace grimaced and shook her head.

"I feel responsible. I told you go to for it. I encouraged you. I all but pushed you into the man's arms." She shoved her fingers through the red curls and blew out a long breath. "Maybe it'd have been better if you'd, you know, waited until after the trial or something. I wasn't thinking, Darby."

The worry and friendship in her eyes dissolved Darby's determination to play dumb.

"It's not your fault. I've never felt like this about anyone before," Darby admitted, dropping onto the couch. "I can't say that I like it."

"Is it because of the risks you're taking on this case? Or is it because of your feelings for Nic Savino?"

"Either. Both." Darby faltered. "Nic."

"You care about him. And you think he's innocent."

"How do you know what I think?"

"Because you'd have nailed his ass to the wall by now if you thought he was guilty."

"What difference does it make?" Darby pushed to her feet, needing to pace off some of the tension. "Facts are facts, and sure, the facts don't support Nic Savino being guilty. But what if these feelings—feelings I don't even understand—are messing with me so I don't see the facts clearly."

"What do you feel for him?"

"God, I don't know. Nothing. Everything. Too much," she admitted. "It's coloring my judgment. And if I'm wrong, it'll ruin my career."

"Any case could do that," Grace pointed out in a practical tone. She ruined it, though, by biting her lip and looking as if she wanted to cry. "And while the timing of your affair might be questionable, as long as you don't have to bring charges against him, it won't matter."

"Really? Do you think Carson is going to shrug it off when he finds out?" The tension was wound so tight in her body that Darby felt like she was going to burst into a million pieces at any moment. "I'll lose everything. My career. My self-respect. And all for what? Because I'm stupid-in-love with the man?"

"You were willing to risk your career by pivoting on the case because you believe he's innocent. Why is it any different to risk it because you have serious feelings for him?"

Why?

Because one was for justice. She believed in justice.

The other was emotion. And emotion was something Darby had no faith in at all.

But she didn't say a word. Because she couldn't. Not to Grace. Not now. Not when Nic was due here any minute.

"Darby?" Grace prompted, probably concerned at the sick expression Darby knew had settled on her face. "Are you okay?"

"I've got a nasty headache," Darby said. Not a lie but she still felt the weight of guilt. "I appreciate you coming by. I really do."

"But you want me to go," Grace said with an understanding laugh. "I will but I'm checking in tomorrow. Call me if you need anything. To talk, to vent. Even another chocolate overdose. I'm here for you."

With that and a gentle pat on the knee, Grace got to her feet, scurried around the coffee table and walked out of the apartment.

And Darby was left trying to corral the hazy thoughts that were spinning through her mind in a dozen directions. She stared at the door for a long time after Grace left.

She wanted to believe her friend, to have faith that it'd all work out in the end.

But what if it didn't?

Her career.

Her mother.

Her peace of mind.

They were all at risk if she continued this relationship. She was stacking up everything she'd lived her life around for nine years against feelings she didn't understand.

But she couldn't do anything else.

Because as sure as she was in her mind that Nic

was innocent, her heart was just as sure he was the man she loved.

Stupid heart, she thought, gritting her teeth.

HE SHOULDN'T FEEL this good.

His steps light, Nic made his way to Darby's door with a grin on his face. An inappropriate grin, he knew. His team was in an uproar, his career was teetering on the edge of destruction and he was temporarily relieved of duty. Something that incited fury and a gut-wrenching pain he worked extremely hard to ignore.

Having Darby in his life—in his bed—didn't make up for any of that, but it was a damn nice distraction from brooding over it.

Ready to be distracted, he gave her door a quick knock. As soon as it opened, he gave into the need and, tunneling his fingers into the silky spikes of her hair, took her mouth in a hot, wet kiss that sent his body humming.

"Sorry I'm late," he said with a smile when he released her. "Ready for dinner?"

"Come in. Please." Her voice husky, Darby stepped back and gestured. And Nic got a good look at her face.

"What's wrong?"

"Please. Come in."

Nic waited until he was in the living room, then asked again, "What's wrong?"

"There's something we need to discuss. I'll keep it brief," Darby said, gesturing toward the couch. "Please, have a seat."

"From the look on your face, it's not because you

want to make dinner." He ignored the couch, instead studied her expression. He knew that face. He'd memorized her every emotion.

It wasn't business. He could see pain in Darby's eyes and knew it was more. It was personal.

"Something's come up. Something that made me realize that I've made a mistake."

The words were clipped, her tone neutral. But Nic saw where she was going. Instead of letting her meander there, he got straight to the point.

"You're ending things between us?"

"I'm ending personal things between us," she said to clarify.

He ignored the vicious burning in his chest.

"Why?"

"As I said, something came up." When he simply stared, she slammed her fists on her hips and glared. "Hey, I helped you. Isn't that enough?"

"Why?"

She gave him a dismissive look. The kind meant to flick a guy off and make him feel like nothing. Nic didn't let it bother him, because he could see something beneath it. He just had to get to it.

"Because this was supposed to be a fling. Just sex. But you're pushing for more. You want me to meet your friends, you act like we're a couple. Dates. You had me making reservations at a mushy romantic restaurant. I'm not interested in any of that," she snapped. "I'm not interested in anything with you."

Nic took the punch to the gut without blinking.

"Why?"

He saw the frustration flash, quick as lightning

in her eyes—there then gone—before Darby turned away to shrug.

"Isn't that enough?"

"No."

His tactic— using a single, unemotional word to push her buttons—worked. She gave a low growl through clenched teeth and seemed to throw aside all semblance of unconcern.

"Why? How about because a relationship with you could destroy my career. Or maybe because my mother would hate you and what you represent. Because my brother worshipped you." Before he could process that, she was pacing, fast angry steps from one end of the room to the other as she spat words at him at the speed of bullets. "You're military. Once you're cleared, you won't have time for me because your every waking minute will be for your team. Missions, secrets, risks. That's your life."

Yeah. It was. A life he damn well wanted back. But that didn't mean he couldn't have her with it. Darby didn't seem to think so since she was still ranting.

"Relationships between nine-to-fivers are bad enough. There's no way two people with careers like ours could make a relationship work. If it was just sex, that'd be fine. But you want more. That's the kind of guy you are. The kind who gives things one hundred percent. But I don't have ten percent to give, let alone one hundred."

Yeah. She did. Why was she refusing to see that?

"You mentioned your mother. Your brother." The one that'd died, he remembered. He also remembered her reference to Mount Hell Yeah. "What do they have to do with us?"

"There is no us," she said, emotions wrinkling in her eyes now. Pain and hurt and loss. "My brother wanted to join Poseidon. He aimed for the elite. And he died trying. Losing him destroyed my mother. You destroyed my family."

Nic almost cringed at the pain in her eyes. In knowing he'd had some part in putting it there.

"He was a few years behind you, so would never have had a chance anyway. But he got this crazy idea that he could do so well, he'd impress you and you'd make him the exception to your rule."

"What was his name?" Nic felt the blow but forced himself to focus. How had he missed this? How had he missed the many ways that his work, his dream, his choices had hurt people?

"Danny. Ensign Daniel Raye," she said. "He died in a diving accident nine years ago. In an effort to impress his way onto your precious team."

Nic's mind raced. He'd served with hundreds of people over the years, but he didn't remember her brother. But now he realized why she'd tapped into the idea that resentment was fueling his frame job. Because she knew firsthand.

"Is that what we were? A chance to get revenge?" he asked quietly.

"Like I said. There was no us." The words were as flat as the expression in her eyes when they met his. His heart ached. He damn near hated her for that. For making him feel, for making him believe.

"You did your research. You know I'm a good attorney. A damn good one. And an ambitious one. I didn't see your case pushing me where I wanted to go, but I knew you'd get me there." She lifted one brow and gave a pitying shake of her head. "I just had to give you a push in the right direction."

Shut it down, Nic told himself.

"Did you know who I was in Hawaii?"

"I told you, my brother worshipped you. Do you really think I had no idea who you were?"

He couldn't read her eyes. He didn't know if it was the pain or if she was really that good at hiding her feelings. Or telling a lie. But he had no choice. He had to take her words at face value.

Jaw clenched, he executed a tidy about-face and headed for the door. Before he reached it, his cell buzzed twice, then stopped. Purpose filled him now, his steps quickened.

"Wait," Darby snapped, crossing to his side. "What's going on?"

"I have work to do," was all he said.

"You're not on duty. But your team is, aren't they?" She searched his face. "What did they find?"

Nic didn't answer. He was too busy grinding his teeth as he skirted around her and strode through the doorway.

"What the hell are you doing?" he snapped when she caught up with him on the landing.

"I'm going with you."

"No. You're not."

Darby grabbed him. He could have ignored her hand on his arm. He could have easily flicked her off. But he made the mistake—what was one more where she was concerned?—and met her steady gaze.

"I'm going. The sooner I get it, the sooner I bring charges and end this."

"You'll get your info." He'd make sure of it.

"The information will do more good if I get it firsthand."

Instead of getting it filtered through him. Nic heard the unspoken words loud and clear. He drew on years of control to give her a dismissive look.

"Like you trust anything my men have to say?"

"I guess we'll see."

SHE'D USED HIM.

The slap to the ego was nothing compared to the pain that realization was digging in his gut. But like anything that interfered with duty, Nic ignored it. Just as he ignored the woman in the seat next to him.

He gave himself the time it took to drive to the meet to focus, to put aside everything. Emotions were pointless. All that mattered now was the win. And to win, he had to take down his enemy.

With that in mind, he pulled into the parking lot. Nic looked at the dingy excuse for a motel, then glanced at the woman sitting next to him. He didn't want her here. She'd hurt him, dammit. She'd cut him to the bone, and now, what? She was going to sit and watch him drain out?

"I don't want you here," Nic stated baldly, not bothering to turn off the Range Rover's ignition.

"Of course you don't. The only people you trust are your team."

He'd trusted her. Nic's jaw clenched.

"I'm here to do a job," she said quietly. "If you

didn't want me here to do it, you wouldn't have let me come."

She was right. She had one purpose now and one purpose only. To ensure that the federal prosecutor's office would bring charges against the person who'd committed treason. Once she'd done that, her place in his life was over.

"I won't forget this," he promised in a low voice. His eyes locked on hers.

"No." Darby unbuckled her seat belt, opened the door and slid out of the car. "You won't."

Nic got out of the car and, ignoring the woman at his side, strode up the stained concrete stairs toward the second floor motel room. He stopped in front of the same room he'd stashed Torres and Lansky in almost a year ago and lifted one hand to knock.

Before his knuckles connected, he slanted a look at the woman he'd thought he'd fallen for. It was, he knew, a look of goodbye.

"Let's just get this over," Darby suggested quietly. "The sooner you know, the sooner it's all finished."

"Yeah," he agreed. "Let's finish it."

"Why is she here?" Lansky asked when he opened the door. He eyed Darby, his Boy Scout face filled with suspicion.

"She wanted the intel firsthand" was all Nic said.

"You're the boss." With that, Lansky stepped back to let them both in the room.

He felt her hesitation before the door closed. Smart woman. She'd just stabbed him in the gut.

"Gentlemen," he said, nodding to the men in the room.

Lansky's spot on the floor was marked by a bag of

potato chips, a note-covered pad and his still glowing laptop. Torres was doing push-ups on the burnt-orange carpet while Prescott sat on the only chair, his booted feet crossed and resting on the bed while he drew.

"Yo, boss," Louden greeted as he stepped out of the bathroom, the handheld device in his hand glowing green. "Just finished the sweep and tweak of the place. We're good to go."

"Sweep and tweak?" Darby asked.

Nic had to give her credit. He was standing right next to her so he'd have felt if she so much as cringed at the intense stares the four men in the room threw her way.

Instead, Darby flashed a bright smile and gave them all a sarcastic finger wave.

"Sweeping," Louden said, shifting his hard stare to Nic then back to Darby again. "Checking the room for bugs. Tweaking. Installing jammers to ensure nobody can tap in to anything we say, do or think."

"Think?"

"What? You'd don't think it's possible to tap in to someone's thoughts?" Louden peered down at Darby with enough intensity to see all the way into her brain. "You don't think our government has experiments into mind control and psychic phenomenon?"

"You do?" Darby slid a questioning look toward Nic as if trying to gauge whether Louden was serious.

He stared back, wondering why the hell she could still stir him after what she'd done.

They were through.

It was just as well, he told himself.

He'd seen enough military relationships to know that they were damn hard to make work. It was even tougher when both partners were all in, totally committed and completely devoted to each other. Like any battle to be fought, it could only be won if you could count on the people by your side.

And now he knew he couldn't count on her.

"Report," Nic ordered. Before anyone could speak, he shot Darby a look and added, "Level three."

In other words, nothing classified was to be disseminated in front of the civilian.

"Rembrandt broke the code," Diego said, ending his workout to give his report. "Once he did, Mac-Gyver identified the fingerprint."

"Sir," Prescott said, standing to give his report. Even though the man wore jeans and a black T-shirt, he stood militarily erect at parade rest. "I was able to decrypt enough of the messaging to determine the signature."

He went on to describe what he'd done in heavy technical terms. Nic, well versed in cryptology, had no trouble following along. A glance at Darby told him that she had a pretty good handle on it, too.

That, or she faked it really well. And he had reason to know that she was good at faking it.

"With that, I handed the broken code to Mac-Gyver." Prescott waited for Nic's nod before sitting again, while Lansky pushed off from the floor with one hand and, mimicking the other man's stance, gave his report.

"Whoever did this, he's good. We knew that. He had enough skills to rewrite code, to erase the trail. As you know, all data carries a fingerprint. And every fingerprint is unique. With the encryption data, I was able to track down every use of the fingerprint in question. That's when Grumpy stepped in."

Nic simply shifted his gaze to Louden.

He didn't need to study the expression in his second-in-command's eyes to know he wasn't going to like what the man had to say.

Cree, was all he could think before he boarded up his emotions and focused on the job at hand.

Forty-five minutes later, he was grateful for the years of training that kept the vicious churning of betrayal from showing on his face. Twice in one night, he'd been kicked where it hurt.

But there was no way he'd let it show.

"Yo," Louden said with a jerk of his chin. Nic followed his gaze toward the bed.

"What are you doing, Darby?"

Her spike-heeled boots a puddle of leather on the floor, she sat cross-legged at the bottom of the bed, her head bent low as she finished filling the page in her notebook. Her hand barely stopped long enough to flip to the next page before she was writing again.

"Darby," he snapped, his tone demanding attention.

"What? Hang on." She lifted one hand for him to wait while she kept on writing. Finally she looked up to meet Nic's gaze.

"Sorry. I wanted to get that all down while it was in my head."

Nic clenched his teeth.

"Did you get everything you wanted? Enough for that big fat promotion?"

The tension in the air was electric. Darby's eyes

flicked around the room, her expression closed. But she didn't hesitate as she got to her feet.

"I've outlined the points I'll use to inform the Deputy Director that I'm ready to file treason charges. Because of the groundwork I've already laid to ensure the Justice Department is bringing charges against everyone involved in the case rather than targeting you specifically, I'll be able to move quickly and tie them in to the current case." Biting her lip, she tapped her pen on the paper and considered the room again. It wasn't nerves, he realized. She was considering her approach. "Is what you have solid enough to clear your name?"

"It's enough to get you out of my life," Nic promised.

CHAPTER SEVENTEEN

Two Weeks Later

THIS WAS IT.

Darby strode toward the courtroom on the Coronado Naval Base with her dignity wrapped around her like a shield. As her heels snapped against the gleaming oak floor, she ran through it all in her head.

She had her argument down solid, she had a firm grasp on the military procedure and protocols.

Now it was a matter of trust.

Not of whether she believed the information Team Poseidon had given her. Despite what she'd told Nic, she trusted him. Almost as much as she loved him.

Which was why she'd ended it.

How many times over the last few weeks had she wished she'd had more time to think that through. Not because second thoughts would have prevented her from ending things. But because with a little time, she'd have figured out how to do a better job of it. Less emotional, friendlier. She'd have broken it off in a way that left things friendly and easy between her and Nic.

Instead, they were ugly and over.

Darby swallowed back the pain of that and told herself it was for the best. Proof, again, she thought, that the smoky gray wasn't for her. When it came to emotions, it was black, white or nothing.

She reached the end of the hallway and paused before the door of the courtroom to run one hand over the lapel of her jacket, smoothing the navy fabric.

Go, she told herself. *Get in there.*

But she had to take another deep breath to calm the fluttering in her belly first.

It wasn't nerves.

She never got nervous about trying a case.

It was concern.

She'd never tried a case worried about the outcome. Sure, she played to win, but losing had never carried the stakes today did.

One way or another, today was going to be a blow to Nic. She was sure of his innocence, but proving it was going to hurt him. Because proving it would destroy a man he'd spent most of his career honoring. Obeying. Trusting.

But just as the country and SEALs had been betrayed, so had Nic's trust.

Just as she'd betrayed it.

Her fingers trembled as she reached for the door handle.

"Are you ready to win?" Carson asked as he joined her. His expression was fierce as he grabbed the brass handle himself and pulled open the heavy oak door.

"I'm ready, sir," she said with a confident nod. "We're going to nail this one."

But when he yanked the heavy door open and gestured for her to precede him, she hesitated.

"I'll be a moment."

Carson gave her a narrow-eyed look.

"Don't forget what's riding on this, Raye," he said quietly, appearing to be carefully weighing each word. "You nail this, you're on your way to the top spot in the federal prosecutor's office. You blow it, you're done with the Justice Department."

Right. Nerves fluttered through Darby like ants beneath the skin. This was it. Her career-making case.

And Nic's career-saving case.

She just had to make sure he got what he deserved today.

Redemption.

She owed him that.

With that and a deep breath, Darby was ready to take on the world. She walked into the courtroom with her head held high and her heart sure she was on the right track.

"I've been trying to reach you since yesterday," Paul murmured as soon as she took her seat at the prosecutors' table. "What the hell are you doing?"

The friendly smile on his face did nothing to hide his irritation. Good, she decided as she pulled her notepad and pen from her bag and began arranging her side of the table. Water to the left, pad in the center, two pens and her closed notebook to the right, just in case she needed to refresh her memory during the case.

She wouldn't need it.

But she knew the look of the fat leather portfolio, clearly stuffed full of page after page of facts, was intimidating Paul.

Which was part of her carefully crafted strategy. She wanted to keep the opposing counsel off-balance and on edge. And even though he didn't know it, Paul was her opposition.

"I've been unavailable," she said, finally replying to his complaint.

"You shouldn't have been. We're supposed to be working together." Seeing Darby's brows rise, he softened his tone and skimmed his fingers over the back of her hand. "This is it, Darby. Your big break. I want to make sure it's perfect."

She eased her hand away. She didn't want to tip him off, so she smiled and made her tone rueful.

"You know the deal, Paul. We're two separate entities here. You'll make the military splash with your charges for the Navy while I handle the treason charges for the government."

"We're supposed to be working together," he repeated, frustration clear in his voice. "This case will make your career. It's going to make mine, too. I don't want anything to go wrong."

"What could go wrong?" Darby patted his hand this time, proud that hers didn't tremble. "Look, Deputy Director Carson wants a clean case. That means our office works alone. Don't worry, though. I promise I'll be dishing up the treason charges today. My case is unassailable."

"I have every faith you'll do great," he said. His smile flashed, excitement with a touch of malice as he glanced toward the empty desk for the defense. "Afterward, let's go out. We'll get dinner and celebrate our victories. It'll be like old times."

Before she could come up with an excuse, there was a furor at the back of the room. They and everyone else in the courtroom glanced back as Nic and his team entered.

Darby automatically took advantage of Paul's distraction to pull her arm away. But all of her attention was on Nic and his team as they strode into the courtroom like a force of nature.

He was so damn gorgeous it hurt.

He looked delicious in his formal uniform. The gold double-breasted buttons and white shirt stood out in sharp contrast to his suit of navy blue, which was so dark it was almost black. She eyed the row after row of medals affixed to his chest below the gold SEAL trident. If those were just a few of his commendations, that rosewood case of his must be bursting.

She knew his team was dressed similarly, but she only had eyes for Nic. His commanding height, his broad shoulders and slender waist. The chiseled strength of his jaw. And those eyes. She felt them all the way across the room, and while she knew nobody else saw it, she could see the distance in that gaze.

Distance that hurt.

He didn't trust her. She knew he had reason, but damn, it hurt. Darby didn't care.

She wasn't going to let him down.

Her gaze shifted to her boss as he shook hands with the judge, who'd just walked into the room. Instead of wearing the black robes of the judiciary she usually stood before, he wore a Navy uniform. Khaki pants and a crisp shirt with its own share of medals. With him was a large man in a white uniform.

Admiral Cree, Darby realized.

Ignoring Paul's continued bitching as he whispered complaints and hissed instructions, she watched the Admiral, the judge and her boss talk. Their expressions were deadly serious, their postures official.

She knew Carson was putting in face time to impress upon the judge how seriously their office took this case. From the cold expressions he kept shooting Paul, he was establishing territory, as well.

Carson really wanted this win. But as much as he wanted it, she knew he'd walk away and leave her hanging if it looked as if things were going bad. And that would be it. The end of her career. The end of her dreams.

Darby tried to swallow but all the spit had disappeared from her mouth. As the urge to jump to her feet and run from the courtroom gripped her hard, she deliberately looked toward Nic. His eyes met hers.

And just like that, she felt the anxiety drain away.

Whatever happened, she was ready.

Whatever happened, it was worth it.

Darby glanced at her watch as the same judge who'd presided before stepped behind the bench.

"Come to order."

As Captain Trenton opened the case, he cast an assessing look around the courtroom, his expression making it clear that he considered this a very grave undertaking. In addition to citing the crimes for which Nic was accused, he detailed every treasonous act on the table. Each word carried the sound of doom. Darby sneaked a glance at Nic.

He was pure strength. He radiated confidence, assurance and integrity. As if feeling her inspection, he met her eyes once more. In the dark depths of his gaze, she saw everything that could have been. Everything she'd ruined.

She wanted to apologize. She wanted to explain that she'd been scared, that she'd slapped him away because the feelings she had for him terrified her.

"Lieutenant Thomas, please proceed."

"Lieutenant Commander Dominic Savino, you stand accused of conduct unbecoming an officer, disobeying orders and conspiracy to commit treason."

She listened as Paul made his arguments before the judge. She held back a smile at Nic's plea of not guilty.

Good. He was so damn good.

She pulled her gaze away to scan the rest of the room. The galley radiated testosterone. Admiral Cree's face was set, his body language screaming indignation. The men of Team Poseidon sat next to him. Unlike their Commander, their expressions weren't easy to read, but she knew them well enough by now to see the pride on his team's faces. Louden, sitting next to Nic, had his official look on, his jaw set with determination.

Jarrett sat in the galley, too. But a few seats apart from the men of Team Poseidon. Darby wondered if that was his choice or the team's.

As Paul finished his opening statement, the Captain turned his gaze toward Darby.

"Miss Raye? Do you have anything to add on behalf of the federal prosecutor's office?"

"I do."

As Darby got to her feet, she felt the pressure

building in her gut. Pressure to do this right. To clear
Nic and get him his life back.

She took her time rounding the desk and approaching the bench. In part because she enjoyed
making Paul squirm after everything he'd done. But
also because she needed those last few seconds to
give her career a just-in-case goodbye kiss.

She stood tall, shoulders back and chin high, and
looked directly at the judge. She made sure her words
were clear, her tone ringing loud enough to be heard
from the bench to the hallway.

"Sir, evidence has been brought to my attention
that, in the eyes of the federal prosecutor's office,
clears Lieutenant Commander Savino of all crimes.
Charges will be filed in US Court forthwith against
the guilty party."

In any other courtroom, the gallery would have
exploded in whispers. But this was a military courtroom and nobody said a word. Then the tension in
the room exploded like a grenade, shards spiking off
the walls and hitting Darby with their vehemence.

"Would you care to expand on that claim," the
judge invited in a neutral tone that belied the intensity in his eyes.

"Excuse me." Paul got to his feet, his body stiff
with suppressed anger. "I was not apprised of this
change of plans. I'd like to request a recess to assimi-
late this new information."

After a long, considering moment, the Captain
nodded before glancing at the clock on the wall.

"Recess. Thirty minutes."

A bang of his gavel was all it took to loosen the

tension in Paul's body. He turned a vicious glare on Darby.

"We need to have a conversation."

He grabbed her arm and pulled like he thought he could drag her from the room. Darby yanked herself free. Before she could snap at him to keep his hands to himself, she saw a wall of men rise on a smooth wave of intimidation. Every member of Team Poseidon, from the leader on down, looked ready to kill.

Whoa. Darby's heart jumped at the fury on their collective faces. Afraid they'd do something to damage the case, Darby gave a tiny shake of her head.

She cringed at the expression in Nic's eyes. Even as she braced herself for violence, Nic murmured something. Just like that, the wall of testosterone stood down. And Nic inclined his head as if to say, "have it your way."

This man was a skilled military operative. He held multiple degrees, his chest was covered in commendations and he was trained to kill in more ways than she could imagine.

And not only was he willing to put his reputation, his career and his freedom in her hands, but he was also willing to stand aside and let her handle herself against an obnoxious bully. After everything she'd said. After all the ways she'd hurt him. He still trusted her.

And just like that, the last line of defense around her heart fell.

She loved Nic.

She gave the team a two-fingered salute of appreciation as she strode out of the room a few steps ahead of Paul, a sappy smile on her face.

"In here," Paul insisted, grabbing her again to pull her into one of the small side chambers. He stabbed one finger toward the line of chairs flanking the conference table. "Have a seat."

"I'd rather stand."

"Fine. Whatever. Where did you get this so-called information?"

"That's confidential."

"Who's your informant?" he snapped, loosening the knot of his tie as if it was choking him. And maybe it was if the red splotches on his face were anything to go by. "I want everything this person has given you. And more importantly, I demand to know who you plan to accuse."

"You demand?" Darby laughed. "You're not in a position to demand anything, Paul."

"You know I've been trying for years to get something on Savino and his team of assholes. Don't blow this." Paul jabbed a finger at her. "Remember Dan. Your brother is dead because of these guys."

"No." Blinking away the tears suddenly burning in her eyes, Darby shook her head. "Danny's death was his own fault. Nothing he did would have earned him a spot on Team Poseidon. He knew that but convinced himself he could change the rules. He took risks he wasn't qualified to take thinking that if he could do the impossible, they'd let him on the team."

As much as it hurt, Darby put the blame for her brother's death exactly where it belonged. On him.

"His death is a horrible tragedy, but the responsibility and blame doesn't belong to anyone on Team Poseidon."

"That's bullshit."

"No, Paul, it's not. Despite what you claim, despite whatever Danny might have thought, Team Poseidon's inception is clearly documented. You gave me the files yourself," she reminded him.

Darby gasped when, teeth bared, Paul grabbed her arms. He yanked her up on her toes to glare into her face.

"I gave you those files as background information on the men you were supposed to build a case against."

"Let me go," she demanded. Her knee was cocked and ready, but before she could launch it the door opened.

"Thomas, you're needed in the courtroom."

As sure as she was that she could handle herself, Darby couldn't deny her sigh of relief. Nothing screwed up a trial more than kicking your coprosecutor in the balls.

"We're not done here," Paul said through his teeth. His fingers clenched once before he let her go with enough force that Darby almost fell over.

His face still creased with fury, he turned to address the person who'd walked in.

Darby turned, too.

Her relief disappeared when she saw the man in the doorway. *Don't freak out*, she told herself as she faced the man she would soon be accusing of treason.

"Sir, I need to—"

"The courtroom, Thomas," the man interrupted. The authority in his voice was so absolute that Paul didn't even look at her again before he scurried out of the room.

Darby was left standing in an empty chamber with

a man who'd betrayed his country, facilitated the injury of one man under his command and the murder of another, all to cover his own culpability.

He couldn't know for sure that they had him, she reminded herself, trying to slow her racing heart. And even if he did, they were in a courthouse full of people.

But that assurance did nothing to calm the shiver of nerves crawling over her skin. Darby curled her fingers into her suddenly damp palms and, even while calling herself a wimp, decided to get the hell out of there.

"Excuse me," she said, giving him a cordial nod as she moved toward the door. The sound of her heels on the wood floor echoed through the buzzing in her ears.

Then the big man shifted, blocking her path.

And that buzz turned into a roar.

"One minute, Ms. Raye."

"I really do need to get back into the courtroom." She shifted to the left, but he blocked her again. She drew in a deep breath and met his eyes.

"Is there something you need?"

"As a matter of fact, there is."

The man's smile was so nasty that it took her a few moments to notice the gun he was pointing at her belly.

Where had that come from? Panic exploded, spinning through her system, tingling across her nerve endings. Darby allowed herself three long seconds of terrified thoughts, then shut it down.

"I'm afraid I don't understand." Keeping her expression confused, she deliberately looked at the gun, then into his beady brown eyes.

"Oh, you understand just fine. Let's go," he ordered, his eyes scanning the room as he gestured her toward the door with his weapon.

Darby couldn't help it—despite everything the man had done—she had to laugh. "You're kidding? You think you're going to get out of this by taking me hostage? We're on a military base. There is a roomful of SEALs, to say nothing of your commander, a judge and a whole slew of legal types, expecting me back."

"They'll have to be disappointed, then, won't they." With that, he jabbed the gun into her side and jerked his head toward the door.

Irritated now, Darby started to snap her suggestion on just where he should stick that gun. The she saw his eyes. The narrow focus in those brown depths did nothing to hide the madness. It gleamed as ugly as the weapon he was threatening her with.

Her belly clenched tight with fear.

"Let's go." He poked the gun her way. Darby stared at the deadly black weapon. She had no idea what make or model it was. Did it have a safety? Were there bullets in there? She lifted her gaze to meet his eyes and knew that yes, whatever type it was, that gun was loaded.

Her knees trembled so hard that her legs shook from thigh to ankle. She knew if she walked out that door with this man, she'd never walk through another one. He wouldn't hesitate to kill her.

"C'mon, sister. You're my shield. My ticket out of here."

It took all her willpower, everything she had, but

Darby managed to turn her back on the fear. Oh, it was still there, breathing down her neck. But she ignored it and focused on what it'd take to get out of here alive.

Nic.

She needed Nic.

Jarrett chose that moment to prod her with that gun of his.

"Oh, no, you don't," she snapped, welcoming the fury. It rolled in on waves, dousing the tiny licks of fear. "I'm an officer of the court. I'm not going anywhere."

"I'm the one holding the gun and I say you are."

Darby flicked it a glance, only letting her eyes rest on it for a brief moment since the sight of it made her head spin in a woozy circle.

She didn't know much about guns, but she'd seen plenty of movies.

"You're not going to shoot me," she said, her tone as assured as she could make it.

"Ms. Raye, I've killed plenty of others in the course of my career. I won't hesitate to add you to the list."

The lawyer in her wanted to ask for specifics. Her research had shown that he was a paper pusher. A strategist with little real experience. She knew he'd been in the Navy for seventeen years, but little of that had been spent in war zones.

So who had he shot?

And were any of them lawyers?

"Captain, whatever you have in mind, let's be realistic," she tried to reason, grateful that her words didn't tremble. "If you do sneak out of here, people will think that you're guilty. If you take me with you, they're going to know you are."

"Shut up." His breath hissed as he jabbed her again before grabbing her arm and pulling her to the door. He eased it open, looking left, then right, before giving her a hard look.

"Okay, here's what's going to happen. We're walking down that hallway. When we reach the guard, you're going to tell him you're ill and that I'm taking you to the infirmary. You're going to convince him to let us go without any questions."

"And if I don't?"

He gave her a tight-lipped smile.

"I'll shoot the guard, let you watch him die, then shoot you, too."

She wanted to believe he was bluffing. But the manic craziness in his eyes assured her that he wasn't. So, as reluctant as she was terrified, Darby could do nothing but jerk her chin in agreement.

He pulled her from the room, his fingers digging into her arm tight enough to bruise bone. He'd tucked the gun between them, hiding it in the folds of her jacket as he strode confidently down the hall.

She looked toward the courtroom, willing Nic—his team, hell, she'd settle for Paul—to come to her rescue. She wanted to call out. She wanted to scream. She wanted to kick this evil traitor in the balls and make a run for it. But as she measured the distance between them and the courtroom, them and the guard, she hesitated. She had no idea what kind of gun he had, no clue how far it could shoot. She was pretty sure it'd leave a nasty big hole in her, though.

So she wet her lips and hoped like hell the guard would stop them.

As if reading her wish, Jarrett gave the gun a sharp poke into her side as they approached the door and the man guarding it.

"Sir."

Jarrett returned the man's salute, then inclined his head toward Darby.

"A sick civilian. I'm escorting her to the infirmary."

The man—boy, really, since he looked all of twenty—glanced her way. Darby didn't have to pretend she was feeling sick. Her heart was racing so fast, she was surprised she didn't pass out.

"I hope you're okay, ma'am," he said with a respectful nod.

Her throat ached from holding back the pleas, the warnings, the screams. But Darby settled for giving the guard the best smile she could, flirtatiously fluttered her lashes and said, "Ms. Raye. You can call me Darby."

If nothing else, she told herself as Jarrett gave her another poke to get her moving, at least he'd be able to tell Nic he'd seen her when he came looking. And he would.

Even as anxiety spun through her like a whirlwind of fear, she told herself that Nic would save her.

"Move," Jarrett muttered when they were outside and a few yards away from the building.

Darby made as if she were having trouble walking quickly in high heels, making her steps awkward in an attempt to slow him down. This was a Navy base. Before noon in the middle of the week. There had been people everywhere when she'd got here. Surely he wouldn't shoot her in front of others. She just had to get someone's attention. She calculated her options, gauged the distance between them and the three men ahead, and prepared to yank her arm free from Jarrett's grip and run.

Three buildings away. She'd wait until they were two, until she could see their faces and they could see hers.

As they stepped closer, her heart raced so fast it felt like each beat jumped over the last.

Then they turned into the far building. She cried out, took a quick step forward, before she could help it. She wanted to scream. Someone would hear. Someone would get Nic.

Nic would save her.

"ONE SOUND, one move, and I'll shoot you here and leave you dead," Jarrett snapped, his breath coming as fast as his racing thoughts. How had this gone so damned wrong? He'd planned every step, put every strategy in place. He'd stood in that courtroom this morning ready to gloat. To celebrate the culmination of his victory. Years of planning, of scheming, ruined.

Or were they?

He'd heard those words, *evidence clearing Savino of all crimes. Charges to be filed against the guilty party.* And he'd panicked. He tried to wet his lips but had no spit. Now, with a little distance, he wondered if he'd been hasty.

His fingers tightened, digging into flesh as he yanked the woman—the enemy—to a halt. He needed to think. She was right. If he hauled her off the base, his options would narrow. Jarrett swiped at the sweat dripping in his eyes and considered. But his thoughts were running, bouncing, racing in a dozen directions. He needed to clear his head. He needed to assess the situation.

"This way," he snapped, making the lawyer in her ridiculous shoes stumble as he pulled her to the right. He didn't slow, didn't let her go. Not even when one skinny heel snapped off her shoe.

"Wait."

"Keep up or die," he muttered, not bothering to look at her. His teeth bared in a narrow smile when she did just that. Yeah. She knew who was in charge. He just had to make sure she kept right on remembering.

"Stop here," he ordered a few minutes later. He kept his gun aimed at her gut while he shot a key into the lock, shoved open the door. "Get inside."

Damn this mess.

Everything had been going great. Smooth and easy.

Then that idiot, Ramsey, had blown his mission. His mission and the building he'd been in. He'd been smart enough to hide, to fake his death. But with one Poseidon team member injured those assholes wouldn't let it go. They'd dug and dug. They'd tagged Ramsey's finances, they'd found his friend Dane Adams's involvement. They'd blown the lid wide-open on the entire operation.

Damn Savino and his team.

Well, he'd shown them.

Jarrett wiped his hand over his forehead, pull-

ing the loudmouth lawyer along as he calculated his
next step. He was a brilliant strategist. Sure, he'd lost
ground, but he had a backup plan. And, like any good
officer, a backup for his backup.

He'd get out of this. He'd be on his island before
morning. Free. Rich and free, and with all the intel
he'd stashed away, in business for years to come.

He'd have settled for that.

He'd have walked away, let Ramsey and Adams
take the fall while the men of Poseidon tried to re-
pair the damage to their reputation.

But now?

Now he was going to make them all pay.

"SAVINO."

Nic ripped his gaze off the door to glance toward
his commanding officer.

"Sir?"

Thomas came in, but Darby wasn't with him.
The JAG Lieutenant hurried toward the table they'd
shared and grabbed Darby's notebook. Nic moved
to stop him, but Carson got there first. After a quick
exchange, the federal prosecutor nodded and stepped
aside as Thomas hurried out.

What the hell? Nic caught Lansky's eye and jerked
his head, indicating he should follow.

"Quite a situation we have on our hands, isn't it?"
Cree said.

Hearing the concern in the Admiral's voice, Nic
gave the man his attention. Not all of it, since he was
still watching for Darby. But enough.

"Yes, sir. It is."

"Why didn't you contact me?"

"I was told you were unavailable." There was no point in admitting that Nic had wondered if unavailable meant guilty. "Given the chain of command, I assumed that Captain Jarrett would be keeping you apprised of the situation."

"You didn't think I'd want to hear directly from you that this bullshit case was about to explode?" Cree's ruddy face creased into a scowl that made crewmen cry. "You've served under me for twelve years, Savino. You know better than to lie to me like that."

"Not lying, sir." Nic hesitated for a long moment, then admitted, "But not the entire truth, either."

"You thought I was the traitor?"

"I was trained to keep an open mind," Nic said in another sidestep. "I never wanted to believe you were behind this, though."

"And Jarrett?"

"Excuse me."

Annoyed at the interruption, Cree turned his glare on Prescott.

"I'm sorry, sir," Prescott said perfunctorily, his gaze meeting Nic's. "But we have a potential situation."

"Is this situation important enough to interrupt a private conversation between superior officers?" Cree growled.

But Prescott ignored the Admiral. Instead, he leaned closer to Nic and said quietly, "Jarrett followed Thomas and Darby into the antechamber. When I saw Thomas in the hall a minute ago, I checked that room. It's empty."

"And the rest of the courtrooms? Antechambers? Offices?"

"Lansky and I checked them all." Prescott's grimace was infinitesimal, but it sent a bolt of fear into Nic's gut. "When we didn't see them, we checked with the guard. He reported that Jarrett took an ill woman who said her name was Ms. Raye to the infirmary."

Son of a bitch.

Jarrett had Darby.

Adrenaline surged as Nic came to full attention. Fury followed, sharp and wicked, but he tamped it down. He couldn't operate at 100 percent if he wasn't completely focused.

With the flick of his hand, his men rose, each of them on alert. He pulled his cell phone from his back pocket and turned it on. His team immediately did the same, ensuring they'd be in contact when they deployed.

"How long ago?"

"Five minutes."

"Check with the infirmary, confirm that they didn't arrive. Torres, Danby, Ward—each of you call the guard stations and warn them," he ordered, his mind ice-cold and his thoughts as sharp as a blade as he planned it through.

"What is this about?" Cree asked with a frown. "Why are you concerned about Captain Jarrett's movements."

"I'm concerned about the federal prosecutor's safety," Nic said, avoiding the actual question. He wasn't going to screw up Darby's case.

Nic didn't know if his urgency gave it away or if

Cree simply had his own suspicions, but a look of disappointed awareness lit the Admiral's face.

"Gather the team," Nic ordered Prescott. "Send someone to get the building blueprint. I want to know every way in and out of that room. If this goes bad, we need a rescue plan."

"Trenton," the older man barked at the judge. "Get over here."

"Admiral?"

"What's going on?" Darby's boss asked, following the judge.

"Brief him," Cree ordered Nic.

While Nic filled in Captain Trenton and the Deputy Director on the situation, Cree continued issuing orders.

Within two minutes the team was armed and a call was out for surveillance equipment.

Poseidon had a solid plan, Cree had ordered the base closed and Carson was freaking out.

"I can't believe this is happening. Does he have any idea the ramifications of kidnapping a federal prosecutor," the bull of a man grumbled, pacing his way to the bench and back. "You don't think he'll do anything, do you?"

"I didn't think he'd betray his country," Nic snapped as he secured his weapon. "So I'm obviously the wrong person to ask."

"We should call the police. We need someone to rescue her."

"We're SEALs" was all Nic said. He gave a jerk of his head and Trenton stepped over to calm Darby's boss.

"Where's Thomas?" Louden asked, looking up

from the blueprint of the base. "Is that obnoxious loser a part of this?"

"Rengel, contact Lansky," Nic ordered.

"Already on it," Rengel said, his fingers flying over his cell phone. "Got it. Lansky found Thomas in the bathroom. He's holed up in a stall. Lansky said it sounds like he's cribbing Darby's notes in there."

"Probably not dirty, then. Just stupid." Nic didn't bother rolling his eyes. All it took was a jerk of his head and he knew Rengel was ordering Lansky to hand Thomas over to the guard until the MPs arrived. As much as he wanted to face Thomas down himself, they didn't have time to babysit. Nic needed his entire team on hand and he needed them now.

"Why aren't you looking for her?" Carson demanded, looking like panic was overcoming his fury. "You said you're SEALs. So go do whatever it is you're so damned famous for."

"My men are doing recon," Nic said, gesturing to the ten men texting or talking on their phones. "We believe that Jarrett is still on base. It's to our advantage if he doesn't see us searching for him. Word is out and we're checking with every unit, every office, every post. We'll know who saw him and where."

"Then what?"

"Then we'll go do what we're so damned famous for."

OH, GOD.

Jarrett had dragged her in here at least an hour ago. She'd left a trail the best she could, snapping off the heel of her shoe as an excuse to leave them behind. Hadn't someone found it yet?

Shouldn't Nic have rescued her by now?

Her eyes locked on Captain Jarrett as he paced from wall to window and back again, Darby did her best to appear still while her hands twisted behind her back, trying to work free of the plastic zip tie he'd used to anchor her to a large crate.

The fear she'd been carefully ignoring took hold as she looked around the warehouse. From cement floor to low ceiling, crates stacked higher than she was tall. From the labels she could see, every one was filled with ammunition.

One stray bullet would blow this place to hell.

Good thing she was going to be rescued by a smart SEAL.

It was like a mantra. As long as she kept repeating those words, she believed it'd happen. Or, at least she wouldn't go crazy and scream with terror.

Jarrett stopped pacing.

Darby stopped trying to free her wrists.

He pulled out his cell phone, his scowl deepening as he scrolled.

Darby's stomach clenched.

Did he have some way of checking on Nic? He was in charge of several SEAL teams, she wouldn't be surprised if he had some clever app that tracked body heat or the proximity of the good guys from the bad guys.

She had to distract him. To give Nic time.

"Captain?"

"What?"

Darby had no idea. But she was a lawyer. She could talk from sunup to sundown.

"Why did you drag me in here? Isn't this a dangerous place to hide from people who will quite likely be looking for you with guns?"

Hmm. Probably not the best subject to distract him, but her brain seemed to be stuck on the topic.

"We're here because Savino'd have to be an idiot to storm this place." His gave a nasty grimace. "And while he's many things, idiot isn't one of them."

"Wouldn't it have been smarter to have waited in the courtroom to see what the evidence was? If you didn't like what you heard, you'd have had plenty of time to get away afterward."

"Wait? That's bullshit. You think I don't know what you were doing in there? I know damned well you're gonna try and hang treason charges on me, lady."

"I haven't charged anyone with anything."

"You think I don't know what you were going to say in there?" he snapped, waving the gun. "There's only one way you'd clear Savino and that's if you found someone else to point the finger at."

"There are already two men implicated in this case," she said, calling up the calm, assured tone she used when arguing before a jury. "Why do you assume I'd point anything at you?"

"You think I'm stupid?" he snapped, pacing toward the window to stare out, then to the door, then back again. All the while, aiming the guns at Darby's belly. "You think I don't see what's going on between you and Savino? You'd do anything to clear him."

Because he was innocent. She bit her lip to keep from throwing the words in his face.

"I'm a sworn officer of the court, Captain. I work

within the law. If Commander Savino was cleared, it'd be because the law was on his side."

"Savino's charges are solid. They are Gibraltar. Thomas assured me he was going down," he said instead of answering.

"You're implicating Lieutenant Thomas in criminal activity?" she asked, feeling sick inside. Paul was a jerk but she'd never have imagined he'd be dirty.

"I could," Jarrett muttered, wiping the sweat from his upper lip with the back of his gun hand. "Hotshot attorney hates Savino and his men like poison. Hates them enough that he was sloppy, he didn't look past the conviction."

"Overzealousness is unprofessional, but it's not criminal."

"No. He won't back off," Jarrett dismissed with a wave of the gun. "Savino's the one. Everything was set. It was perfect. I'd laid it all out for him. Now you fucked it up."

She hadn't fucked it up alone. But Darby was pretty sure that admitting that everyone knew he was dirty was only going to get her in trouble. So she did the hardest thing possible.

She changed the subject.

"You sound as if you hate him."

"Smart woman."

"Why?"

"Because he's so fucking perfect. Him and the rest of Poseidon. Perfect and arrogant and so damn better than everyone else. They think their mythic reputation makes them untouchable. That they can do anything they want because they are pure gold."

Darby realized that hate was a mild term for what he felt for Nic.

"But isn't that what SEALs are all about? Elite and exclusive."

"Poseidon ain't ordinary SEALs. Every man on that team holds multiple ratings, is qualified for every team role. They win every competition, have every commendation." He gritted his teeth so loud, Darby was surprised a few didn't fall out.

She knew all that. What she didn't know was how it was a motivation for treason. Given that as soon as she was out of this time bomb of a building, she was going to bring every charge she could think of against Jarrett, she wanted as much information as possible.

"So Poseidon being the best is bad?"

"Some people think so. Some people don't see Poseidon as motivation, they see it as an obstruction. It breeds jealous envy, bitter resentment." He nudged her shoulder with the gun, scaring the hell out of her, then grinned.

"Do you know how many kids thought they could prove themselves good enough for that team? How many thought if they pushed harder, went bigger, they'd make such an impression that Savino would invite them to join? Think about it. Savino and his team killed your brother. Maybe they didn't do the actual drowning, but it's on them all the same."

There was no room for fear as Darby reeled. She felt as if he'd just kicked her in the gut. Her breath was gone, her body rigid with pain. She'd told herself she'd put it aside. That she didn't *really* blame Nic for Danny's death. But sitting here on a chest labeled AMMO, held at gunpoint by a madman spouting words she'd heard hundreds of times before, she felt it. A tiny seed of shame.

Because for all that she'd told herself that Nic held no logical blame for Danny's death, emotions weren't logical. Because her feelings for Nic were so strong, she'd told herself she'd set it aside. The blame, the anger. But she hadn't.

Not in her heart.

As Darby listened to Jarrett continue his rant, reciting all the reasons that Nic and his teammates were to blame for everything from a lack of morale among some seamen to Jarrett's own paycheck, she realized she'd been just as unfair.

Nic didn't deserve one iota of blame for being who he was any more than the sun deserved blame for shining.

If she got out of this, she'd tell him that.

No, not if, she corrected when Jarrett stopped whining to go check the window again.

When.

Because Nic would rescue her.

If she trusted nothing else in her life, she trusted that.

"You're going to leave me here while you escape, aren't you?"

"That'd mean I'm leaving a witness. Being such a clever lawyer, I'm sure you realize how stupid that'd be."

Oh. Darby wet her lips. She wanted to ask if that meant he planned to take her with him. But she didn't think either answer would make her feel any better. So she fell silent. "Witness or not, they'll know it's you."

"Yeah, but they won't do jack while I'm holding on to you. That'll give me enough time to go under. You think I'm stupid. I planned this all out. Every damn step of the way. I have an escape plan. All I have to do is get off the base."

"Nic Savino will find you. Taking me won't make a bit of difference. He'll hunt you down and make you pay." Darby tried to look intimidating. "He knows what you did. He knows you framed him. And he's going to want to know why."

"Why? Because it was easy, that's why. Everyone treats him and his gang like gods. Those assholes think they're smarter than everyone. Well, I showed them, didn't I? Who used their missions to steal secrets? Who sold those secrets, made millions and dropped it all on Savino's head?"

"What about Ramsey and Adams?" she asked. "Wasn't any of it their idea?"

"Those two idiots? They didn't have what it takes." Jarrett's laugh was nasty. "All I had to do was use Ramsey's ego and his hard-on for Poseidon. And Adams? That dumb-ass would do anything Ramsey told him. Golden boy said jump off a bridge, Adams would leap without question. Idiots. They were easy. Too damn easy. Until Ramsey landed his pretty-boy ass in the brig. I know how that idiot thinks. All I had to do was promise him I'd pin it all on Poseidon, and he kept his mouth shut."

Was this a confession?

Because that fear was scraping at her back with its poisoned teeth, Darby swallowed hard against the knot in her throat and focused on keeping him talking.

All she needed was time.

Time enough for Nic to find her.

She focused on her breathing, kept feeding Jarrett bits and pieces, enough to keep him bragging.

She recited Nic's name in her mind like a mantra.

She'd get out of this.

And when she did, she'd tell him the truth.

She'd tell him she loved him.

That she'd take the shadows and the gray with him anytime. Because this black-and-white crap?

It sucked.

CHAPTER EIGHTEEN

"THE SONOFABITCH HAS her sitting on enough explosives to blow her to kingdom come."

"And take out half the island in the process," Lansky muttered with disgust. "Leave it to a coward like Jarrett to think thousands of people is acceptable collateral damage."

"Coward or not, he's smart," Louden pointed out. "He knows Poseidon has a zero collateral damage policy."

"He'd do well to remember that we have a kick-ass policy, too."

Nic let the chatter roll around him but didn't participate.

His every thought, his every focus, was on the mission ahead.

He had to think of it that way. As a mission.

He used his knowledge of the enemy to map out his weaknesses. He factored in Jarrett's desperation, weighed it against his familiarity with the team's style and the base layout. In the forty minutes since they'd discovered Darby's kidnapping, he'd planned every step of the operation, detailed every move his men would make, coordinated every contingency with the Admiral. He had a solid backup plan, an alternate and a fail-safe. The base was on alert, every single man briefed and ready.

If he thought of Darby, considered what might happen, gave one second to what she might be going through, he might falter. In faltering, she could be hurt. Or worse.

Nic clenched his fists, his jaw tense as he vowed to never let that happen.

But with the vow came the memory of Darby's face. Her deceptively delicate body. That brilliant mind and clever mouth.

At Jarrett's mercy.

His throat was so dry he could feel every pounding heartbeat reverberate. Black spots bounced in front of his eyes, blurring his vision. *Calm down*, he warned himself. He couldn't do a damn thing if he started worrying about what Jarrett was doing to Darby. Fear tightened his gut, mocking his attempt.

He'd never felt anything like it before, so it took a few seconds before he recognized it as panic.

"Savino."

Nic glanced at Cree. On his commander's face was an understanding and a hint of the same fury Nic felt. Not for the same reason, Nic knew, but still, the Admiral's anger calmed Nic's enough to clear his head.

"We're ready, sir," he assured Cree. The older man gave him a long look before nodding. And that, Nic knew, was the green light to move.

He noted the arrival of four MPs and EOD. They wouldn't be necessary, but protocol was protocol, and the base was, essentially, under attack. They were, however, the signal to go.

Nic stepped away from his spot at the window of

the building two doors down from Jarrett's location and nodded to the Admiral.

"Men, it's time."

As one, his team came to attention.

"Rengel, you're on the east side with Davidson. Danby, you and Prescott take the south. Kendall and Ward, you cover west. Louden and Torres with me while Lansky mans the eyes from here and Brandt coordinates with command. Ears on, eyes sharp."

The orders were automatic, as were the men's actions as each checked their weapons and comm system.

Ignoring the urgency pounding at his skull, Nic took the team through the plan. Quick and easy. They'd get in place. Assess. Move. Recover.

"Here." As soon as they were out the door, he handed Louden his pistol. "Hold this for me."

"You're going in there unarmed?" That Nic would be the first one through the door was unquestioned.

"It's safer for everyone if I'm unarmed when I come face-to-face with Jarrett. I trust the team to have my back."

Before Louden could object, Nic held up one hand, then gestured that everyone follow him. Silent as still air, they moved down along the building, each team separating on his mark and heading for their assigned position.

"The target is in the building, twelve paces from the door, three from the right-hand window. Armed with a Sig Sauer, thirty round magazine. No extra clip visible," Brandt said through Nic's earpiece. "Lovely lawyer is strapped with what appears to be a zip tie to a crate four feet from target's current position. Cut her loose, she looks like she'll take down the target with her bare hands."

He'd bet she would, Nic thought with a hint of a smile as he shot a hook onto the building next to Jarrett's. With rope, hands and feet, he scaled the wall to vault onto the roof. He shimmied over the sun-warmed asphalt, keeping low while Brandt assured him that Jarrett's attention was focused the other way. He glanced over as Louden and Torres joined him, then back toward the span of air between the two buildings. Eighteen feet, give or take an inch.

"Clear to set the line," Brandt murmured.

Instantly, Nic and the other two men lifted onto their elbows, aimed and shot a line across the divide. At the same time the barbs of their hooks dug into the wood edging the roof, Cree's voice called through the silence, amplified by a bullhorn.

"Captain Jarrett, you are ordered to present yourself."

Nic grinned as Jarrett's cussing filled the air. The smile still on his face, he grabbed his line, dropped from the roof and swung his feet up to snag the wire with his ankles. Fast and furious, he quick roped over the divide, silently pulling himself onto the opposite roof three seconds before his men joined him. Hooking a carabiner attached to his belt onto a still taut line, Louden flipped off the roof so his feet steadied him against the wall. One hand on the line, the other reached into his pack.

Within seconds, Louden silently drilled a hole in the wall. He carefully fed a tube through the hole, checked the monitor on his phone, then adjusted the tube. With an infinitesimal nod to indicate it as clear, he replaced his drill with a laser.

Nic checked his watch. Ninety seconds from Cree's challenge, he noted, clenching his teeth to bite back the order to hurry the hell up. They'd played their hand, Jarrett knew they'd found them. It was time to get Darby the hell out. She'd been in with that madman long enough.

"Kahuna," Davidson said, his voice so low it was almost a whisper. "Visual is in."

On schedule, the east team had accessed visual inside the building.

Nic grabbed his phone and hit the video screen. The app pulled the camera image onto his phone.

Fury flashed hot when he saw Jarrett pacing in front of Darby, gun in hand. He wanted to break through that wall and beat the hell out of Jarrett. If the man had been unarmed, he would have. But furious or not, there was no way Nic would risk Darby.

Louden's laser stream cut silently into the concrete, searing a thirty-inch square into the wall. As Cree's next demand came via bullhorn, Louden finished his cut. Before he'd put the laser away, Torres was hanging over the side, inserting screws into the wall. Like pulling a piece of pumpkin out of a jack-o'-lantern, the wall slide free.

Nic and Torres grabbed hold, pulling it onto the roof.

He and his men exchanged one last look before Nic silently flipped off the roof and into the hole and into the building's rafters. He waited the count of five before shifting slowly toward the edge of the platform. One wrong move, one wrong sound, could turn the tide against them.

Brandt's voice reported that the men were at the windows of the building. Concealed, waiting with weapons at the ready. Brandt was watching, and would time it so Jarrett was facing away from the door when Nic made his move.

He gripped the edge of the platform, ready to vault to the floor twelve feet below. He waited for Brandt's signal—two vibrates on his phone—that the Admiral and MPs had taken position in front of the building as distraction, then dropped to the floor.

"What the fuck is Cree doing out there? Idiot old man, thinks he can draw me out like a green recruit," Jarrett barked.

While his back was turned, Nic angled silently behind a crate. He looked at Darby. He wanted her out of the way before he moved on Jarrett. She met his eyes, tilted her head and winked.

Damn. Nic couldn't stop the smile. The woman was amazing.

"That's your boss out there? That can't be good. So tell me, Captain, what's your plan now?" Darby asked, snagging Jarrett's attention. "He's not going to let you waltz out of here. Wouldn't it be smarter to let me go, play as if you're sorry and deal with the consequences?"

"Shut the hell up," he shouted, storming to the window to glare at the troops.

"This all really went south on you, didn't it?" Darby continued as if he hadn't snapped. "Just like all the rest. Was it Ramsey screwing up that blew your little treason scheme? Or was it your mistake in trying to pin your crimes on Nic Savino and his men? Either way, you know you're in trouble."

"I've got a plan. I just have to get out of here." His tone grew more and more frantic with each word. "I've got a plan."

"Uh-huh." Darby nodded. "So does your plan include that money stashed in the Caymans?"

"Belize, you dumb bitch."

Nic almost jumped the man then. Darby must have known because she gave a quick jerk of her chin to keep him in place.

"My info might have been wrong," she said in a tone so full of crap that Nic grinned again. "So you have your plan and your hidden money. What's next? Are you going to haul me out of here by gunpoint? Use me as a shield against all those military types out there? And what good will that do you?"

"It'll do me plenty of good since nobody's going to shoot when I've got a gun to your head." Jarrett continued pacing, each trek across the room bringing him closer. Nic tensed, ready to pounce, but Jarrett turned again.

"Nic Savino won't need a gun to stop you," Darby said, shifting her weight as he drew closer. "And there's no way he's going to let you get away with this."

She was right. Nic straightened, ready to launch himself across the room.

"Savino is an idiot. He was easy to set up," Jarrett screamed, as he stormed over to get in her face. "Stupid fucker believes in honor and brotherhood and all that crap."

Before Nic could pounce, Darby growled. Her face

creased in anger and she kicked high, her foot nailing the Captain between the legs with enough force to send him to his knees.

Nic was halfway across the room when she followed that with a kick in the face. Instead of folding, Jarrett swore, one hand on his bleeding nose as he lifted the gun and aimed.

Nic hit him from behind, sending him flying into the table. Chairs crashed to the floor as Jarrett groaned. He tried to lift the gun again, but a chop to the wrist sent that clattering, too. After a quick glance to ensure that Darby was safe, Nic slammed his fist into the face of his superior officer.

"That's for Darby, motherfucker," he said. He followed it with an uppercut, then threw the man down the length of the table. Jarrett bounced off the far end, hit the floor and crumpled into a whimpering ball. "And that's for Powers."

HOLY CRAP.

Darby's heart took a deep dive into her toes as reaction set in. She shook so hard, it was only the zip tie around her wrists that kept her from falling to the floor.

Nic saved her.

She'd known he would.

She almost screamed when a roar filled the air. Poseidon poured into the building from door and windows, surrounding Darby in a protective wall of furious SEALs. Diego clipped the plastic, freeing her hands as Elijah helped her to her feet. The tension that'd held her in its viciously tight grip drained out of Darby's body, leaving her so weak she had to grab his arm to stay upright. As one, the men tightened the circle.

Darby tried to see around them, through them, to locate Nic. "Is he safe? Is he okay?"

"Nic's fine," Diego assured her. "He and Admiral Cree are dealing with Jarrett."

Darby wanted to see for herself, but nobody would move. So she had to go by sound, listening to the discussion between the Admiral, Carson and what she thought was the judge.

"Here, you might want these," Louden said, holding out a pair of sadly damaged Jimmy Choos.

Darby's heart melted a little, not just to see her favorite shoes again, but that these men would care enough to rescue them, too.

"Thank you," she murmured, petting the damaged leather. While she tried to shake off the realization that she could have been just as damaged, she thought she heard Nic cussing from afar, but before she could ask, Lansky nudged Elijah.

"You think this is it?"

"I don't know. I hope not," Elijah said quietly.

"Is it what?" Darby asked.

"The argument will be made that Poseidon should disband," Louden said, turning so they were face-to-face instead of standing with his back to her. "It's been said time and again over the years. But this just gave it weight."

"Savino will take all this to heart," Danby told her quietly. "For Nic, it's always about the greater good. After all this, he's going to ask himself if the existence of our team is a detriment to our duty. If Cree brings the hammer down and Nic agrees, we'll be saying goodbye to the sea god."

As the men continued to discuss the possibility, Darby felt the weight of their concern. Not fear. These men feared nothing. But a heavy sort of mourning. Her heart ached for all of them, but for Nic most of all.

Finally, as the voices faded, the men loosened the circle. They didn't end it. Darby still couldn't see through to the door or either window. But at least she could breathe.

"I'm really okay," Darby insisted, trying to move around the wall of men surrounding her. "Guys, seriously. You don't have to guard me."

"Savino said to cover you until he returned," Louden said, looking like a giant mountain as he stood with his arms crossed and his eyes locked on her like she might disappear.

"I'm fine. I'm perfectly safe. Those big MPs with their mean guns hauled the bad guys off, remember."

"We'd feel better if we stay with you," Elijah said in such a reasonable tone that she wanted to scream.

"Don't bother arguing. You're our responsibility. Besides, we like you," Diego told her with a wink.

Instead of hulking over her like half his team, he'd sprawled on one of the crates, legs stretched out and his hands crossed over his belly. For all his relaxed appearance, though, he snapped to attention at the sound of the door opening.

"Gentlemen," Nic said quietly. "Thank you."

The last of the tension that'd been rippling through her system faded at the sound of Nic's voice. It wasn't until the sea of manliness parted that Darby could see him, though.

She gave a soft gasp when she saw the purple bruise shadowing his jaw. He'd ditched the jacket and tie and rolled up his white shirtsleeves. Even dressed down and bruised, he still commanded attention.

"So, we'll give you that space you wanted," Diego stated, patting Darby on the shoulder before crossing over to shake Nic's hand.

One by one, each man did the same.

And each gave Darby a pat or nod or, in Elijah's case, a hug. Then gave their Commander a handshake, or in Louden's case, a punch to the shoulder.

And just like that, Darby and Nic were alone together.

Suddenly remembering her panicked declaration, she brushed nervously at the pieces of hair spiked around her face and tried to smile.

"Is Jarrett in custody?"

"Cree, Trenton and your boss took charge there. They took a couple of MPs along with them to escort Jarrett to the brig. I'm not sure if they are concerned he'd get away or if they just wanted to make sure I didn't get near him again."

"I can't believe you kept it to a single fist to the face," Darby said, still a little awed. "I mean, I punched him more than you did."

"You do have a solid right hook," he agreed. But despite his smile, Darby could see the tension radiating from him. The nerves that'd finally subsided jumped up again and started bouncing through her system.

"What did you guys do with Paul?" Seeing the

question in Nic's eyes, she revised her query. "Lieutenant Thomas?"

"Captain Trenton requested his presence on the trip to the brig." Nic's smile was just a little vicious. "My impression is Thomas wasn't a part of the treason ring. But there are questions he should have asked but didn't in his zeal to prosecute."

"Not if Jarrett's bragging-slash-confession is true. According to him, he masterminded the entire plan, bringing Ramsey in because he hated your team. Paul was simply blinded by glory. That, and a chance to get back at you for keeping him out of Poseidon. In my opinion, it was easier for them to blame you than to accept their own shortcomings," Darby said. Confession time, she decided. "That seems to be a theme."

"A theme that's been used to betray the country we're sworn to serve. A far-reaching theme that's caused death and destruction."

His men were right. Darby could see the pain in his eyes, the heavy weight of responsibility.

"Don't take this on," Darby insisted, moving close enough to lay a comforting hand on his biceps. "You're not to blame for any of this."

"Aren't I, though?" Nic strode to the window to scowl out at nothing. "Jarrett was able to lure men like Ramsey in to acts of treason because of their envy of Poseidon. Your brother died because he wanted to join the team. Naval Intelligence was able to prolong an investigation a year after it should have been dismissed, solely on the basis of resentment at Poseidon's reputation."

"So what?" Darby snapped, following him across

the room. She grabbed his arm and tugged, wanting to look him in the eye for this argument. "Sure, there is a crap ton of envy. But that's because there's a reason. Poseidon is the best. You own that reputation because you guys bust your ass to go above and beyond."

Sighing, Darby gave in to the need to pace. She wouldn't let him take the blame that people like Jarrett, like Ramsey, hell, like she herself, had tried to put on him. Arms waving for emphasis, she ranted.

"So what if people get jealous. That's their problem. You're too smart to take on their problem. At least I thought you were."

"I'm smart," Nic finally agreed. "I know a lot of this isn't on our heads. But I can still hear the argument that if our team didn't exist, these issues wouldn't, either. There's no argument that it's a valid point."

"It's bullshit." She snapped the words off in her fury. And she'd been afraid of emotion? Here she was, swimming in it. And damn if she wasn't staying afloat.

"Maybe." For the first time since she'd met him, Nic looked worn-out. She could see the pain beneath the polish as he scraped his hand over his short hair. "If Poseidon didn't exist, we couldn't be blamed for others' crimes. But blame isn't responsibility. Jarrett was already a criminal traitor before Poseidon was involved. He was selling secrets to the highest bidder."

"So you're not going to do anything crazy like disband the team?" Darby asked slowly, watching him carefully.

"Why would you think—" A look of under-standing crossed his face. "I take it the team is con-cerned?"

Unwilling to betray the first confidence those men had shared with her, Darby shrugged.

Nic didn't need confirmation, though.

"I'd disband Poseidon if I thought it was for the best. If I thought we were culpable in any way of the crimes we were accused of."

"But you weren't. You aren't."

"You know, this team is my family. They've had my back on every move I've made in the last decade. From training to missions to little things like work-out changes or fighting this personal war."

He gave her an expectant look. Darby wasn't sure what the message was in his words, but she nodded anyway.

"They're my family," he said again. Something in his tone sent a tickle of panic through Darby's belly. "And whether you realize it or not, their confiding in you like that? That's their nod of approval."

Oh. The last of the knots in her stomach loosened. Darby had never had that sort of family that Nic did, but the idea of them approving of their relationship made her feel pretty special.

"So I guess there's something I need to tell you," he said, his eyes so intense her body shimmered. For all her fear of emotion, Darby was desperate to hear what he was going to say.

"I'm listening." With the knots out of the way, there was plenty of room for the butterflies in her stomach to do their loop-de-loop dance.

He frowned at the room, then shrugged. "I should

probably wait for a better setting. But I suppose this one has special meaning to us given what happened."

"Okay," Darby said hesitantly, not sure where he was heading with this.

"Maybe we should go somewhere else, though," Nic mused, giving the room a scowl this time.

"Oh, my God," she said with an exasperated laugh. "Quit stalling and say whatever you have to say so we can get out of here and celebrate your vindication."

"Are you planning to celebrate with me?"

"I'd like to," she said softly, guilt over dumping him the way she had shining in her eyes. "I'd really like to."

"How?"

Darby could see it clear as day. He wasn't going to let her off the hook. Not because she'd hurt him. But because he was a man who lived in honesty. Because she'd told him they were through and they were unless—until—she said otherwise.

She could offer her hand to shake his in congratulations and they'd part ways without recrimination.

She could reach out and give him a friendly hug and he'd let her be a part of his circle, if not his world.

Or she could show him how she felt.

"This is how I want to celebrate." Stepping into his arms, Darby cupped her hands behind his neck and, shifting to tiptoes, kissed him. By the time she slowly pulled away, he wore a smile that said he knew exactly how they'd be celebrating.

"I love you," he said, his tone almost as intense as the look in his eyes. "I didn't want to. Not because I don't believe in love or didn't want it in my life. But I had a plan. Career first, then family. I told myself that love, a relationship, those were things to have after I made Captain."

"Oh," was all Darby could manage to say. Love? Family?

Her smile dropped. Her knees started trembling even harder than they had when she was being held at gunpoint.

"Oh?" He scowled. "That's it? Nothing else to say?"

"Okay, yes." She wet her lips, then took a deep breath. "I love you. I didn't want to, though. My career has been my whole life. The only thing I wanted. I didn't think it was possible for anyone to matter as much to me as my career."

"Oh."

Darby blinked in surprise, then burst into laughter. "That's it?"

"No," he said, sliding his hand through her hair. The feel of his fingers brushing over her cheek made Darby want to cuddle in and purr. "There's more. A lot more."

Her stomach did a fast tumble as Darby waited for the more.

"I knew I cared. I knew I was fascinated. I knew you've spent a lot more time in my mind than any woman before. The sex is mind-blowing. The conversations are fascinating. And the downtime? Those moments when we just hang out and chill? They relax me."

"Is relaxing good?" Darby asked, even as she heard herself echoing his feelings. She felt the same about him, but it was the relaxation part that scared her. "You live on the edge, Nic. Do you ever worry that if you relax too much, you'll lose that edge?"

"You're kidding, right," he said with a laugh. "Didn't you notice? That edge is ingrained. It's who I am."

"But it's not who I am."

"You don't think so? You put your career on the line to fight for my future. Watching while you were in danger, it made me realize just exactly what I wanted in that future." He shifted his hand to rub his thumb over her bottom lip. Desire shivered through her at the delicate touch. "More to the point, you're what I want in my future."

"You want a future? With me?" Did that mean what she thought it did? Did she want it, too?

As Darby stared into those dark eyes, drowning for a moment in their delicious intensity, she knew that's exactly what she wanted.

A future. With Nic.

But she sucked at relationships. Fear slammed through her, drowning the pleasure in jagged waves of anxiety.

"What about your plan? The whole waiting until you make Captain? Can you juggle your career and a relationship?" Afraid he'd say yes, she pulled away a little. She needed some space between them to breathe.

"Plans change." Nic shrugged. "The question is, do you want mine to?"

"I don't know. I'm afraid," Darby admitted. "I'm afraid that caring about something more than my career means I won't be as good at it. That it won't be a priority. Your edge is ingrained, it's who you are. But I don't know that mine is."

"You're kidding, right?" Nic's frown was ferocious. "You're a kick-ass attorney. Everyone says so. You're one of the best and you're only going to get better. Why would you worry about that?"

"Because I put you before my career," she confessed. "There were options. Even options that would have still cleared you in the end. But I took the riskiest route to clear your name, to win this case. If that risk didn't pay off, my career would be over."

"You took that risk because you're good enough to make it work," he argued. "Darby, every mission I go on requires I take the riskiest route in order to achieve a specific outcome. If the risk doesn't pay off? I'm dead."

"That's not going to happen," she snapped. The very idea made her ill.

"Why not?"

"Because you're too good at what you do. You're the elite, the best."

"So are you. We've worked too hard to be less than that, Darby. Our training is ingrained. Our instincts are instinctual. That's never going to change."

And just like that, Darby's fear faded.

And all that was left was love.

"You love me," she said quietly, letting her body relax against the hard planes of his.

"I do."

"And I love you."

Nic's smile spread, so warm and sexy that Darby almost melted.

"So what are we going to do about it?"

She gave herself a moment, waiting for fear. Looking for nerves. But all she felt was pleasure. Pleasure, and anticipation.

"What do you want to do?"

"I want to try forever."

Oh.

She waited for the fear.

But it never came.

So Darby blinked hard to clear the tears burning her eyes. No way she was doing this in tears. Instead, she gave Nic her best smile, letting all the love she felt show in her eyes.

"Forever sounds like a good start."

* * * * *

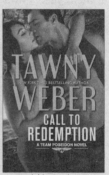

New York Times bestselling author

GENA SHOWALTER

**is back with a sizzling *Original Heartbreakers*
tale about an icy war vet and the only woman
capable of melting him...**

With trust issues a mile long,
Ryanne Wade has sworn off men.
Then Jude Laurent walks into
her bar, and all bets are off. The
former army ranger has suffered
unimaginably, first being maimed
in battle then losing his wife
and daughters to a drunk driver.
Making the brooding widower
smile is priority one. Resisting
him? Impossible.

For Jude, Ryanne is off-limits.
And yet the beautiful bartender
who serves alcohol to potential
motorists tempts him like no
other. When a rival bar threatens
her livelihood—and her life—he can't turn away. She triggers
something in him he thought long buried, and he's determined to
protect her, whatever the cost.

As their already scorching attraction continues to heat, the
damaged soldier knows he must let go of his past to hold on to his
future...or risk losing the second chance he desperately needs.

Available October 31, 2017

Order your copy today!

www.HQNBooks.com

Get 2 Free Books,
<u>Plus</u> 2 Free Gifts -

just for trying the *Reader Service!*

Get 2 Free Books,
Plus 2 Free Gifts—
just for trying the Reader Service!

 HARLEQUIN *Presents*

HP17R2

Get 2 Free Books,
Plus 2 Free Gifts—
just for trying the
Reader Service!

 HARLEQUIN® **SPECIAL EDITION**

Get 2 Free Books,
Plus 2 Free Gifts—
just for trying the Reader Service!